EMPIRE OF SHADOWS

THE HOUSE OF CRIMSON & CLOVER VOLUME VII

SARAH M. CRADIT

Cover Design by Sarah M. Cradit
Editing by Shaner Media Creations

"Shadows"
Written for Empire of Shadows
Lyrics used by permission
Raven Quinn- ASCAP

First Edition
ISBN-10: 1511635967
ISBN-13: 978-1511635967

Publisher Contact:
sarah@sarahmcradit.com
www.sarahmcradit.com

ALSO BY SARAH M. CRADIT

KINGDOM OF THE WHITE SEA

Kingdom of the White Sea Trilogy

The Kingless Crown

The Broken Realm

The Hidden Kingdom

The Book of All Things

The Raven and the Rush

The Sylvan and the Sand

The Altruist and the Assassin

The Melody and the Master

The Claw and the Crowned

THE SAGA OF CRIMSON & CLOVER

The House of Crimson and Clover Series

The Storm and the Darkness

Shattered

The Illusions of Eventide

Bound

Midnight Dynasty

Asunder

Empire of Shadows

Myths of Midwinter

The Hinterland Veil

The Secrets Amongst the Cypress

Within the Garden of Twilight

House of Dusk, House of Dawn

Midnight Dynasty Series

A Tempest of Discovery

A Storm of Revelations

A Torrent of Deceit

The Seven Series

1970

1972

1973

1974

1975

1976

1980

Vampires of the Merovingi Series

The Island

and more

The Dusk Trilogy

St. Charles at Dusk: The Story of Oz and Adrienne

Flourish: The Story of Anne Fontaine

Banshee: The Story of Giselle Deschanel

Crimson & Clover Stories

Surrender: The Story of Oz and Ana

Shame: The Story of Jonathan St. Andrews

Fire & Ice: The Story of Remy & Fleur

Dark Blessing: The Landry Triplets

Pandora's Box: The Story of Jasper & Pandora

The Menagerie: Oriana's Den of Iniquities

A Band of Heather: The Story of Colleen and Noah

The Ephemeral: The Story of Autumn & Gabriel

Bayou's Edge: The Landry Triplets

For more information, and exciting bonus material, visit www.sarahmcradit.com

For:

Shawn Verdin (aka Shawnmuse)
For pushing me when I started to lose sight of the end game. You keep me going in more ways than you'll ever know.

and

The Secret Society of the Crimson & Clover Fleur De Lis
The best group of fans-turned-friends an author could ever ask for.

and

Raven Quinn
For writing the beautiful song, "Shadows," to accompany this book. Your talent and kindness never ceases to amaze.

and

Miss Kitty
The prettiest girl around. Our lives aren't the same without you.

We all have our secrets
We all have our scars
Hiding all our shadows, locked inside our hearts
Face the evolution
Written in the stars
Force a revolution, for us
Awaken at dusk

"Shadows"
On original song written for Empire of Shadows by
Raven Quinn

THE
HEIROPHANT

PROLOGUE

FINNEGAN

Scottish Highlands
May 2006

The further they hurried along, the more challenging it grew to bear Anasofiya's weight.

An hour ago, she'd lost all ability to move herself forward. With a mix of love and fear, Finn and Aidrik now shared the burden of her frail, pregnant frame. Their speed had only slowed nominally, though they needed to be gentle with her. In her delicate state, it would be far worse if she were to give birth in the glen.

"Not much further," Finn assured, but he was frowning. How many years had it been, since he'd seen his grandfather? Ennis St. Andrews was a man who lived today much the same as he'd lived during his childhood. The beastly wilds of the Scottish Highlands were more appealing to him than the bustling activity of nearby Inverness. Hundreds of acres protected him from the outside world, but that same safety net was now a hindrance as the three rebels searched for shelter. *I was a child, last time I hiked this with Dad and Mom. Why didn't I get a damn map?*

When was there time?

"How certain are you of this location?" Aidrik challenged, as Ana whimpered softly against his shoulder. Her belly was now so distended, Finn feared it might erupt like an angry blister. Though Aidrik's intervention had awakened most of the Empyrean within her, enough human remained to deeply concern both men. The few stories which existed of human women bearing Empyrean children had not ended well, for mother or child.

"Sure enough to risk the life of my wife and son. Is that what you're asking?" Finn barked. He had enough pressure on his shoulders, and didn't need this archaic creature reminding him of the risks.

"Emotion will not serve us well, at this hour," Aidrik calmly reminded him.

Finn thought it better not to respond, instead willfully shutting out the heartrending echoes of Ana's cries to focus on the other, helpful sounds around him. The whispers in the trees, and the low hum of creatures inhabiting this stretch of land, might save her. Might save them all.

Help me find my seanair, he pleaded. Abilities, a keener version of the connection with nature he'd always had, were still taking form. Finn understood, though, that he could speak with the trees now. Could converse with the wildlife. Whatever blessing Aidrik had given him, it included the gift to beseech all the natural world to help him find his grandfather.

The wind whipped through tall trees, creating a shimmering blanket of songs above them. The stretch of forest through which they walked remained still, other than the sounds Finn now fixated on.

A tiny fox emerged from behind a tree, halting before the

small party. His beady, black eyes blinked repeatedly as he observed them in silence. Having captured their attention, the creature leapt away in a low sprint, looking back to see if the men were following. Finn's heart surged, as he realized what was happening.

"Come, this way!" Finn cried as a new energy coursed through him.

Aidrik raised an eyebrow, but didn't voice his skepticism. Their pace quickened as the fox wove them down a path Finn did not remember; hopefully, a quicker route, as Ana didn't have much time left. Aleksandr could make his entrance at any moment. While Finn's nearly ninety-year-old grandfather could do little to help, access to a warm hearth, and clean water, was what they needed to save the lives of both Ana and her unborn son. Now at the end of her troubled pregnancy, Aidrik's significant healing abilities were exhausted.

A hospital had always been out of the question. Aleksandr would grow to the size of a child within days, and, in a matter of weeks, resemble a young man. Their path had been limited by this secret, and they were banking their solace on vague memories Finn had of Ennis St. Andrews regaling his grandson with stories of Highland fairies, magic, and lore. Finn hoped if his grandfather could believe in those things, perhaps Finn's new life direction would not be such a stretch.

Finally, the forest grew less dense, and the ground beneath them transitioned from tangled foliage to a deep, emerald moss. A clearing lay ahead, and a small house sat cocooned in the middle, ensconced in a blanket of green. There was no stopping point for the moss, which traveled from the forest floor all the way up the sides of the tiny thatched cottage, broken only by errant strands of persistent ivy. *A lot smaller than I remembered... but it has been over twenty years, I suppose.*

They started their approach just as a door creaked open.

Ana sounded the last of her tortured cries, before her head fell back over Aidrik's arm, surrendering to her pain.

As Finn turned to check on her, a tall shadow appeared in the doorway, revealing a young woman in a billowing dress. She looked familiar. A memory he couldn't immediately place.

"Come w'is," she ushered, her expression kind. "We maun hurry!"

"WHO ARE YOU?" FINN ASKED, AS AIDRIK MOVED FORWARD WITH Ana. "Does my grandfather no longer live here? Ennis St. Andrews?"

The unnamed woman jutted a thumb at the old man dozing peacefully in his rocker, oblivious to the rapidly escalating situation feet away. She never stopped moving, her urgency appearing near as great as theirs. "Yer *seanair* be leukkin mair sleep in his gloamin' years. Aye, I miss th' aul days."

"He... what?" Finn's head throbbed with the surrealistic sequence of events fast unfolding, couched in a burr so heavy he could hardly understand a word. This woman... he knew her. He knew her in the same manner he knew his grandfather, though the mystery of who she could be seemed as far beyond his grasp as everything else in this moment. As he stood at this critical crossroad, the life of his wife and son in the balance, explanations were unimportant.

The young woman's hands rolled through the air as she shepherded them down the hall, her movements possessing the windy grace of someone floating on clouds. Her red hair—a sight to behold on its own, thick as rope and flowing down past her mid-thigh—swayed from side-to-side in equal measure, reminding Finn of the metronome his father used to keep time when playing the old clavichord he'd hauled from Scotland.

She halted, opening the door to a room that featured all the accouterments of a birthing suite. Two ceramic basins, one on each side of the hand-carved bed, stacks of clean linens, a roll of twine, and various metallic instruments Finn recognized from his father's medical office back home.

Mind racing, Finn's thoughts struggled to catch up to what his eyes took in. *They knew. This woman knew we were coming. She'd prepared for it.* Aidrik, quicker to the task, already had Ana moved into the room, depositing her gently atop the bed laden with piles of crocheted blankets.

"Reheat th' water in th' basin and hurry back!" the woman ordered, as Finn shoved in after Aidrik. "Ye were later thae expected, and this cool water willna dae."

This is not happening. The stress has clearly overwhelmed me, and I'm imagining this.

"Finnegan James, gaither yer wits! Time isnae a luxury we hae!"

Finn had frozen in this manner once before, the last time Ana's life slipped away before him. It seemed a lifetime ago, though it was only this past winter. The clarity of that memory snapped Finn back into his current, bizarre reality. He sprang to life, pulling the cool ceramic basin to his side, heedless of the water sloshing down his pants, and fled toward the back of the house. *She can deliver this child.*

When Finn re-entered the room, Aidrik knelt by Ana's side, hand against her brow as he chanted unrecognizable words in a low, deep hum. Ana's head rolled toward Aidrik, her eyes peering through the tiniest of slits. The next words Aidrik muttered were ones Finn understood: "Kjære, you need to push."

"Aye, push, lass," the woman urged. "Juist a wee longer."

"I'm *trying*," Ana cried, face splotched with rosiness of illness and panic, as sweat poured down her brow and temple, matting her copper hair in awkward tangles against her scalp. "God help me, but I can't do this!"

"You can," Aidrik insisted, using the same pleasing tone Finn often found maddening, but was now, somehow, soothing. "Finn and I are right here."

The words returned some life to Finn, and he rushed forward, taking her other hand in his. "You're safe now, Ana. We're at my grandfather's house."

"Your—" Ana started, but a new wave of pain overtook her. She slipped from consciousness.

"What do we do?"

"Th' bairn is comin' on his ain," the woman declared, from under the blanket tented between Ana's knees. "It wilna be lang."

The next moments ticked by slowly. When Aleksandr emerged into the world, he announced his entrance with great bellowing cries before either man could catch a first glimpse.

"Tend to our son, and I shall mind Anasofiya," Aidrik urged. *Our son.* Finn would never get used to the idea that his son had two fathers. But he nodded, and rushed to the bed's end as the woman sterilized a small dirk.

"Ye should do th' honors. I ken he's yer son afore all others," the woman urged with a whisper.

"He *is* my son," Finn voiced aloud in wonder, taking the steel in his shaking hand. He couldn't help losing himself in the image of his first, and probably only, child. *My son. Mine first, before anyone else's.* Even in the infant's soft, formless folds, Finn could see his eyes, reflected back. His own mouth. Only the fine crimson dusting on the crown of his head, far darker than Ana's strawberry hair, revealed Aidrik's involvement.

"Thank you," Finn whispered gratefully, as he accepted the

mewling bundle with great care. He rose slowly, walking to kneel at Ana's side.

Both of Aidrik's hands cupped Ana's face as he continued his healing chants, while Ana stirred beneath him. *Aidrik can heal her enough to bring her back to consciousness, and then she can take it from there. Her ability to heal will never cease to amaze me. Nor will I ever forget, as long as I live, watching her bring Mercy back to life.*

When Ana's eyes at last fluttered open, she turned her hazy, affectionate gaze Finn's direction. His heart flooded with a hopeful reassurance that, despite all that lay ahead of them, everything could be okay. *I'm a father now, and married to the only woman I've ever loved.*

Finn lowered the child against her chest, his eyes blinded with tears of unequivocal joy and relief. "Ana, meet our son. Aleksandr Nicolas St. Andrews Deschanel."

PART ONE
DISCOVERY

"If you can look into the seeds of time,
And say which grain will grow and which will not,
Speak then to me."

William Shakespeare

1

AIDRIK

May 2006 - August 2006

Like a warm embrace from an old, comforting memory, the small cottage welcomed them.

The bread baking in the oven, hearty scents of dark rye and molasses, permeating the small space, reminded Aidrik of Farjhem's scents, and of the purity of youth before beliefs were crushed under reality's heel. The gentleness of Finn's family kindled a keen desire to create an equivalent existence for his own clan. Observing them—Anasofiya, Finnegan, and Aleksandr—thrive under these conditions nourished his thus far secret aspiration.

Aidrik did not relish the duty of being the one to announce the necessity of their departure. Forever restless, remaining in one place for long had never held appeal. Now, as fatherhood took precedence and his small family found their bearings, he found himself longing for a modicum of stability. Roots. *One day, perhaps. But not today.*

For Anasofiya, for Aleksandr, and also for Finn, he'd kept silent these past months as they flourished in comfort and savored this last spark of normalcy before the storm ahead.

Aidrik's adoration of Anasofiya grew as she adroitly assumed yet another irreplaceable role in his heart, that of mother of his child. His uneasy brotherhood with Finn remained largely undefined, but witnessing the man in the realm of his own people gave Aidrik a new insight and appreciation for his evigbond's husband.

Yet none of this likened with the joys of paternity. Four millennia upon this Earth, and this wonder he'd only experienced twice. The first, his Claude, he'd been forced to watch grow, and die, from afar. Aleksandr's presence in Aidrik's life could not be adequately defined. Every word, every gesture, every look from the young being was connected to Aidrik's very soul, the mundane reflected in a warmth which coursed through him.

Yes, it would be facile for Aidrik to embrace this unorthodox family of his, and block out reality. To deny the challenges ahead, and his necessary role in them.

But it was *for* them, that he would not.

Explanations were held until Anasofiya was well enough to emerge from the bedroom without assistance. This matter took three days, and during those hours, Finn and Aidrik sat in silent vigil, taking turns coddling their son.

Aleksandr would not remain an infant for long. Initially, Aidrik feared Anasofiya might rest entirely through this all-too-brief period in her son's development. Had she not risen on her own, he would have roused her.

Ennis St. Andrews, and the curious female acquaintance young enough to be his great-granddaughter, said nothing.

The woman kindly looked after them, ensuring their meals and basic care were tended to, but otherwise waited patiently, offering hospitality in place of explanations.

When Anasofiya finally shuffled from the room, her matted red hair falling down over her borrowed flannel gown, Finn's grandfather roused from his slumber and issued his first formal greeting: "Hou hiv ye been, Finnegan?"

Aidrik, despite having been exposed to a myriad of accents, frowned at the heavy Highlands' burr.

"I'm well, *Seanair,*" Finn replied, and the two men moved to embrace. Hesitance filled the space between them, but their bond was evident. "I'd like you to meet my wife, Ana."

"Aye, indeed," Ennis replied, glancing over at a weary but smiling Anasofiya. "An' a bonny lass she is. Right pleased tae meit ye!"

"The pleasure is mine," Anasofiya replied graciously. She gifted the old man with two kisses, one on each cheek, earning a blush in response. "Thank you for taking us in. I don't know what we would have done, otherwise."

"Dinna fash yersel!" the younger woman spoke up, when it was clear Finn's grandfather was still recovering from the affections of a pretty lady. "Will ye take dennar, lass?"

Anasofiya nodded in thanks, as she accepted the awkwardly swaddled bundle from Finn's arms. Competent in many respects, neither man had been trained in containing an infant. Her entire body came alive as she held her son.

"My name is Aidrik," he began. "And I am—"

"Aye, I ken who ye are," Ennis replied with a mischief-filled grin. Aidrik exchanged a look with Finn, who shrugged. "Ye ken yer the first Farværdig I've seen in all my years?"

"Saecond sight," the young woman explained. "We kenned yer arrival fer some time."

"Aye," Aidrik replied, nonplussed. Unsettling to be caught

so unawares. "I'll not waste time with alternate explanations, then."

"Two da's, eh?" Ennis nodded at Aleksandr. "I kenned tell of it, but ne'er seen it wit ma own eyes."

"Finn is Aleksandr's first father," Anasofiya explained. She passed a tentative glance between her two men. "Aidrik also became his father by way of an ancient process unique to his kind. Well, our kind."

"Sveising," the young woman nodded. Aidrik glanced at her in mild annoyance. He was not keen on being in a room with someone who knew so much about them, when they knew nothing of her.

Before he could amend this, Finn addressed the issue. "I can't thank you enough for how you've helped my wife and son," he began. "I'm sorry. I feel as if we've met before, but I can't place it..."

"Aye, callan. Yer memory ken swash. I a'm yer *seanamhair*."

When Finn's stare went blank, Aidrik helped. "She says your memory is true. She is your grandmother."

For the next couple of hours, while Anasofiya alternately nursed and held their child, they'd listened to the story of Ennis and Fiona.

The woman who sat before them was the same one who had traveled to Maine to help deliver both Jonathan and Finnegan into the world, they claimed. Kept young through the magic coursing through the blood of Ennis St. Andrews, Fiona not only remained youthful, but had, in fact, aged backwards to the days when the two first met. Aidrik sensed the magic in the old man from the moment they passed through the threshold.

Six months ago, Finn might have spent hours refuting their claim. This new man, heavy with experience, simply nodded in wonder.

"Yer granmither will jist las' until a dae," Ennis explained. "Thon, the glammerie will wear oot."

Fiona reached across the table to gently pat her elder husband's knee. "A always loue'd ye. Always weel."

"Your magic keeps her not only young but alive," Anasofiya whispered in wonder, as Aleksandr suckled noisily at her breast. She turned and smiled at Finn, her amazement growing. "And you... you have magic in you as well. I should've known, with your connection to nature."

"An his brither's haeling hawns," Ennis added proudly.

Anasofiya tightened at the mention of Jon, but managed a smile. "I went my whole life without meeting another powerful family."

"Did my father know?" Finn asked his grandparents. He kept sneaking glances at his grandmother, attempting to dissect the magic, as if he might witness evidence of her age beneath the surface.

"Fur why do ye ken he left Scotland?" Fiona replied with a sad headshake. She rose and disappeared into the kitchen.

"Well, he certainly never told Jon or me," Finn mused. "I have so many questions I don't know where to begin."

Fiona returned with a tray of tea and shortbread. When she came to Anasofiya, she traded the infant for a saucer, and Fiona moved to put the babe down for a nap.

"Ye hae time," Ennis soothed. "Maun see th' mither weel afore yer off, aye?"

"Yes, we will stay until Anasofiya is recovered," Aidrik agreed. "And we give thanks for your hospitality."

With her hands now free, Anasofiya set the saucer down

and sipped her tea with one, while the other mindlessly found its way to Finn's, linking them between the chairs. Both seemed unaware of the tender caresses, driven by instinct.

"Wot ye share is *crannchar*," Ennis ventured.

Aidrik's Gaelic was unpracticed, but he recognized the word. "Destiny. A comfortable word for a man of prophecy."

"A Saint Andrews kens his wife aff-han. Athoot doot," Ennis countered. "Na so hoora diffr'nt fro' yer evigbond, aye?"

Finn and Anasofiya shared a confused look before Aidrik translated. "He is of the belief you two were destined to be together. He says a St. Andrews man knows his wife the moment he meets her."

Finn's face erupted into a wide grin. He brought Anasofiya's hand to his lips. "Oh, I knew immediately something was special about Ana. But I would've been blind not to see it."

"Aye," his grandfather agreed, with a smile of his own. "But, daen ye nae ivver ken why ye lou'ed her so quick?"

"I didn't question it," Finn answered. His grip on Anasofiya's hand tightened faintly.

"Isnae a crime to wonder," Ennis replied. "Da ye ken me?"

"My father knew he loved my mother the day he met her. And in the same way, I knew it with Ana. I don't need to dissect the revelation to find joy in it."

"Yer da kenned 'cos *draíochta meallann draíochta*."

"Magic attracts magic," Aidrik translated.

"I love my wife. That's all that matters to me," Finn bristled.

"Aye, 'at is plain as day," Fiona comforted.

Ennis, though, would have the final word. "Yer da kenned whaur he came frae. Ye ha' much tae learn, callan Finnegan. And ah sha' teach ye."

While Finn appeared scandalized by the suggestion his

love for Anasofiya could be "tainted" by the hand of fate, Aidrik heartened at the thought. Fate could be a mistress both cruel and kind. Early indications pointing to the latter could portend well for them.

LATER THAT EVENING, AIDRIK TOOK THE OPPORTUNITY TO EASE FINN'S mind. "Your grandfather means no insult upon your marriage."

Finn nodded. "What I feel for her *is* real."

"With certainty," Aidrik agreed. "The kiss of fate is not a replacement of that love but a complement. It will move to strengthen your bond as times grow darker for us. It may even, at some point, save it."

"Will it come to that?"

"Only Emyr knows."

DURING THEIR STAY IN THE SECLUDED HIGHLANDS GLEN, ANASOFIYA and Finn spent time getting to know Ennis and Fiona. With Finn's life now enmeshed in magic of several arrays, the conversations moved quickly beyond the typical formalities customary between a human grandfather and his grandson. With Finn's father deceased, the lone barrier between Finn and the truth, the need to tiptoe around conversations had vanished. Ennis was a man who spoke in color, but did so with a directness Aidrik appreciated.

Anasofiya helped Fiona tend to the household as she regained strength. Having never met her own mother, Fiona filled the necessary role of guiding Anasofiya in the important specifics of motherhood. Aleksandr's difficult phases would, both sadly and mercifully, pass quickly. Teething and colic did not plague him for long.

But for all Fiona taught Anasofiya, the most important

pieces came to her by instinct. When she was alone with Aleksandr, Aidrik observed the tender and sacred bond with pleasant wonder, bearing witness to a woman who knew nothing about motherhood, yet embraced it more naturally than those surrounded by maternal influences all their lives.

Finn listened to his grandfather tell tales by the evening fire, night after night. It was a relief to Aidrik that Finn questioned very little of what was told to him; this willingness to accept the unbelievable would prove a requirement in the days ahead.

Aleksandr, meanwhile, grew more with every passing day, moving through his toddlerhood to adolescence before the new moon could arrive. As his body developed, his personality blossomed, uncovering a boy with Finn's pure heart, Aidrik's sharp mind, and a passion as deep as Anasofiya's.

Time marched forward, and a simple but powerful joy had ascended in the modest cottage. One which might feel like a costly diversion, with all that lay ahead, but that Aidrik recognized as a needed period of bonding for their clan. Moving toward their future united was not a luxury but an abiding need.

For Aidrik's part, his mind was never far from what destiny might further hold.

Aidrik allowed this peaceful sojourn for nearly three months. His desire to leave waned as he observed his evigbond and child thrive under the kind tutelage of Finn's grandparents.

But he could not deny his pressing need to move forward. It came not only from his own seer's voice, but additionally an instinct that had always steered him true.

On their last day, Aidrik indulged his family's sentiment

with a picnic in the glen, gazing up at the forest canopy as they rested in a patch of clover.

"Too much time has passed since we last contacted my family," Anasofiya whispered to him, as they'd carried the food toward Finn and their son. "They're probably going crazy with worry. Nicolas... and my father, especially. You keep saying we need to wait, but it's been over three months since we gave them any word of us. This is bordering on cruelty, Aidrik."

"Aye," he agreed. "But I would not risk Finn's family with potential exposure of our thoughts. Once we are safely on our way, you may contact Nicolas."

Anasofiya nodded. Her practicality had always been a stronger presence than her sentimentality. "As soon as we leave."

"I wish we could stay forever." Aleksandr sighed, as they eased down next to him. Their son, now a man. It happened before Aidrik could process the way his soft head felt in his hands, or ingrain the sound of baby giggles to memory. He knew this sensation must be worse for Anasofiya, though she said nothing to him on the matter.

"It's peaceful," Anasofiya agreed. "The air is so still. Not even a hint of civilization. Amazing how they've kept it this way, all these years."

"Aye, ye cud stay," Ennis answered, appearing in the glen as his shadow fell over them. He passed a pitcher of ginger wine to Finn. "Ye'd naught be discovered."

Aidrik frowned at both the words, and the way the other three lit up at the promise behind them. It was a dangerous business, planting false hopes. "We thank you for the offer, but we cannot hide forever."

Ennis offered a nod suggesting he knew his words would find no fertile ground. "It's a lang road that's no goat a turnin.'

Lang may yer lum reek." He then slipped away, leaving them to their thoughts.

"Just when I think I've got his words down." Finn laughed. Aleksandr giggled along, twining his fingers through clumps of clover. Anasofiya smiled wistfully.

"He wishes us well on our journey," Aidrik explained. *For, it will be long before the sun shines on us again.*

2
NICOLAS

August 2006

Nicolas watched the sunset, chased by storm clouds over the Mississippi, from the upper veranda of *Ophélie*. The well-kept plantation was no longer a functional farm, instead an ornamental shrine to a dark and colored past that haunted the Deschanel family even today.

Behind him, the double plantation shutters leading back into the upstairs central hall were shut tight, concealing his whereabouts. In one hand, the unopened bottle of Hennessy swung back and forth over the gallery balcony.

The late summer air was thick and suffocating, but still somehow seemed less constricting than what waited inside. Of course, the sensation was entirely in his head. He needn't remind himself he'd chosen these circumstances willingly. The tightening in his chest was not regret at the new life era much as a defiant refusal to accept it. He couldn't will his mind in marriage to his heart.

Though Mercy had lost her powers when resurrected,

Nicolas knew she wasn't blind to the changes in him. Following the overwhelming, intense events that had happened under this roof, their relationship had easily forged ahead on that same excitement. The sex, for sure, the best of his life. But over time the shock of the events began to dissolve, and what remained was the new life he'd chosen. A descent into a domesticity he'd never, not once, desired.

With a patience that should have given him peace, she said nothing when he disappeared for hours on end. Never chastised him when he would go out for "a few minutes," returning instead in the wee hours of the morning, shirt un-tucked, breath foul of liquor. He didn't bother explaining he hadn't been running around on her. Telling her he'd kept his dick firmly in his pants wouldn't change anything. Mercy's views of monogamy were not unlike his: people weren't meant to be with one person, forever. They weren't wired that way.

Deep down, he knew her outlook ran beyond that hollow sentiment, though. On the surface, she may give permission or allow his slips, but her feelings for him had grown and blossomed into something warmer, deeper, far more than just a regular fuck buddy. He knew because it was the same for him. Sex had evolved into lovemaking; passion into tenderness. Tenderness into... well, best not to go there. Nicolas wasn't accustomed to this consuming flurry of emotion, and so had no idea how to feel about it.

He couldn't run away. It would be easier, no doubt, but impossible now. His commitment to Mercy came secondary to the commitment they'd made toward her people—*his* people. Plans had been underway for months getting *Ophélie* ready to house and educate as many Empyrean children as the property could hold. It was only a matter of time before the plans became a reality. Weeks, maybe days. He had no choice but to pull his shit together.

Downstairs, the Deschanels were uniting in a way he'd never seen before. His Aunt Colleen, Magistrate of the Deschanel Magi Collective, took charge without being asked. Probably saw it as her duty, being both unofficial head of the family, and the official head of the organization that held them together. Colleen brought in others, knowing the task ahead required a village to raise the children, so to speak.

Colleen's daughter, Amelia, assumed a position second to her mother, busying herself with the details and plans. She'd left her job as a psychologist and turned her attentions full time to *Ophélie*. Soon, she'd be moving in, with her husband, Jacob. As an empath, she was sensitive to the situation with Mercy and Nicolas, and had more than once delicately resolved a potentially escalating situation. Not so long ago, Amelia had warned Nicolas about Mercy, but somewhere along the way her perspective had changed. His friend, cousin, and supporter, he found her presence comforting.

Anne, Nicolas' younger half-sister, was also involved in the planning now. Nicolas hadn't even known about Anne until a couple years ago, when she showed up out of the blue with a cockamamie story about Nicolas' father having had an affair with her mother. When she spread her arms wide and the plants responded in obeisance, he finally accepted, under no small amount of duress, she was a Deschanel. The only arbor-kinetic the family had ever seen, though likely not Charles Deschanel's only bastard running around South Louisiana. Colleen had all but adopted Anne, folding her into the Magi Collective by giving her important assignments and research.

Others would be arriving soon. Markus, Aunt Evangeline's twenty-one-year-old son, and Tristan, his late Aunt Elizabeth's son of the same age, were being pulled in and given roles. Markus was an illusionist, and Tristan a powerful telepath. Their skills would undoubtedly come into important play here, as they guided young Empyreans through their formative years—or months, as it were.

And Oz. This crazy plan even had a dedicated lawyer attached. Unable to functionally cope since his wife died, Sullivan & Associates assigned Oz to focus solely on the events at *Ophélie*, so he could spend more time at home with his children.

The support enveloped Nicolas, both warming and suffocating him at the same time. Being around more people had the odd effect of making him feel even lonelier than before, because he didn't know how to be a part of them. He wanted to embrace it. Knew he *should* embrace it. But every time he tried, the same old cloud would push through his head and he would end up on the gallery, or in a shady Quarter bar.

Talking about his feelings was out of the question, but he did wish for his one constant, familiar comfort: Ana. Her presence alone soothed him. She was out there, somewhere, though he might never see her again. In a lot of ways, this whole endeavor was for her. And for her son, who was also now Nicolas' heir, Aleksandr.

Ana... if you're waiting for a good time to contact us to say you're okay, now would be fucking fantastic.

Nicolas hid the unopened bottle under a rocking chair cushion, and retreated back inside.

AMELIA SAT AT THE ANCIENT MAHOGANY DINING TABLE SURROUNDED by unfamiliar faces. Contractors. Though Nicolas recognized none, she addressed them all with a cold but familiar ease.

When Nicolas entered, they all rose. Though he assured them they didn't need to stand on ceremony, Amelia insisted they were leaving. "Everything is on schedule," she reassured him with a small smile as the last of the men and women hastily departed.

"How the fuck do you step into this like you've been doing it forever?" Nicolas asked when it was just the two of them again. He flopped down in the tall chair at the head of the table, where his father used to sit.

She shrugged. Her azure eyes were bright and pale, and ice-white hair made her already fair skin look more peaked than usual. "Research, mostly. And Jacob is surprisingly good with this sort of thing."

Nicolas liked Jacob, Amelia's husband. He reminded him of Oz, but without all the emotional baggage. "You look tired. Go home to him. You know, before you two move in here and forsake all privacy and shit."

In response, Amelia yawned, then laughed. "I am. I just can't help thinking we're forgetting things, and I want to make sure we're ready for the onslaught of children."

Nicolas shivered at the thought of *Ophélie* filled with screaming kids. Thankfully, they wouldn't have to find out what that was like. All Empyrean children grew to adult form almost overnight, so the "children" coming their way would appear in their late teens, and yet likely be double the age of Nicolas and the other hosts. Though, that could end up being worse, he thought, remembering his own infamous teenage years.

"This house is huge, and you've already redone some of the outbuildings into apartments. We have plenty of space. They'll be happy for a warm place to sleep, and food to eat. I highly doubt they'll care if the landscaping isn't up to par."

She raised an eyebrow. "Condoleezza is great, but *Ophélie* has clearly suffered over the years without a permanent mistress' touch."

Nicolas met her gaze. "You aren't exactly the angel of domesticity," he accused.

Amelia smirked. "'I've never made that claim." She tucked her light hair behind her ears, looking uncharacteristically self-conscious. "Don't you think it's weird we are coming together to raise children when none of us have any experience with parenting? Does that worry you at all?"

Of course it worried him. Markus and Tristan were basically kids themselves. Mercy had lived three thousand years and did not have a maternal bone in her body. Amelia was a year younger than Nicolas, but, like many others in the family, believed in the fated Deschanel Curse. She decided when she was very young she would never have kids, and married a man who loved her enough that he didn't care. And Anne... well, that girl would have to adjust her standards if she ever wanted to meet a man and settle down to start a family. "Beggars can't be choosers," he said finally.

"At least Condoleezza can cook," she agreed. "Imagine if you and I were left to our own devices in the kitchen?"

"We would need to hire a priest," he joked. "For the inevitable burials."

"That requires a license too, I learned," she returned. "Do you know you can't just bury your dog in your yard?"

"You can't bury shit in South Louisiana, unless you want it floating past your front door after a hurricane," he replied drily.

"Wouldn't that be something."

They sat in silence. That was one thing he liked about his cousin. She didn't need to fill the absence of noise. In a lot of ways, she was like Ana. At the same time, they were nothing alike.

"I know you won't ask for my advice, and I know you don't want it," Amelia announced, as she stood. She straightened her shirt, reaching for her clutch. "I was wrong about Mercy. She's pretty cool. Especially now that she's human. Your anxiety about whatever it is you two have is of your own creation. Which means, you're also the only one who can eliminate it."

With that, Amelia flashed Nicolas a retiring smile and departed, leaving him wishing she had allowed him at least one smart-ass remark in return.

3
ANASOFIYA

Wife and mother. Two experiences Ana never believed would be a part of her future were now the roles that gave her life meaning.

Finn was off talking to Aidrik about a meeting the latter had arranged for them. Ana watched them in the distance, in the grove of trees, as both leaned in close, evidencing how seriously they took the topic at hand. Finn's strong, sturdy frame stood resolved, while Aidrik's long, dark body leaned against a willow. Whereas Finn's hands and face grew animated in discussion, Aidrik's face and gestures were entirely impassive. It was impossible to ruffle the Empyrean's feathers.

Black and white. Oil and water. Her two husbands could not be more dissimilar.

Finn was the love of her soul, and her legal spouse; Aidrik, her evigbond, that instant, chemical bonding that occurred between two individuals of Empyrean blood. Though Ana believed fully in her free will, leaving either of them would never be an option. She was bound to them both, forever, by her own choosing. Moreover, she loved them both too much.

Their willingness to share her, and allow her heart to be whole, was an unselfishness she didn't understand until she gave birth to her son.

As if he sensed his role in her thoughts, Aleksandr ran toward her and squatted low, showing off his kill. "Boar!" he whispered, proud fire burning in his cheeks. She smiled and patted his red hair in approval.

"That's quite the catch, Aleksei," Ana replied, smiling. Her son was only three months old, and already taller than her; as tall as Aidrik. He physically resembled an athletic, sixteen-year-old boy. *Within days of birth, he will begin speaking. In weeks, walking. Months, he will rival you in height,* Aidrik had said, when her son was still growing within her. Though she knew Aleksandr would be born full Empyrean, she hadn't quite prepared herself for the fact her child would literally grow up before her eyes, with no time for her to adjust to being a mother.

"Aye, he chased me, Mora." Mora was the endearment Aidrik taught him, the Empyrean word for mother. Aleksandr continued his story, his bright eyes lighting up with excitement. "When he charged, I did as Aidrik taught me and dodged quickly in a zigzag. He ran ahead but before he could slow and come back for me, I had my bow drawn. I wish Far could have seen!"

Finn and Aidrik were both biological contributors to Aleksandr. Finn his First Father, or father at conception. Aidrik through that ancient, Empyrean bonding process known as Sveising. But only Finn did Aleksandr call Far. This distinction was one he'd come to on his own.

"Did you thank the boar for his offering?" Ana asked.

"Of course!" Aleksandr insisted, offended at the suggestion he might have forgotten this important step.

"Then yes, your far would've been very proud," she finished, kissing his cheek warmly. "As am I."

She glanced over to where her two mates were still engaged in heated discourse. Yes, Finn would have been proud. Finn's connection with nature, an aptitude passed down through his father's side, they now knew, thanks to their Scottish Highlands visit, was amplified since Aidrik gave him the Sveising. He was no longer simply good with animals, he could communicate with them, on their level. A bestiakinetic, Aidrik had labeled him, a term new to Ana in a world where she learned new words every day.

While Finn was an expert fisherman and hunter, now that he had a special rapport with the wildlife, his conscience was heavy, and out of balance. *They understand more than we think,* he told Ana. But Finn was nothing if not practical, and he accepted they needed to hunt to survive. They couldn't simply waltz into the nearest Tesco. If they were seen in civilization, where the Senetat undoubtedly had scouts, they would be putting absolutely everything they cared about at risk.

In pragmatic compromise, Finn had taught his son to be respectful of those animals he needed to kill. This tutelage was dear to Aleksandr's heart, as the boy, like his far, was sensitive to the emotional needs of everyone around him. Hunting had troubled him at first, until Finn and Aidrik helped him see the necessity of it.

Aleksandr went to work skinning and preparing the boar, while Ana set off in search of more kindling and firewood. She wandered in the direction of Aidrik and Finn.

Finn's face broke into a smile as he saw her, instinctively sliding an arm around her waist. "Sorry, I think we're done now," he said, planting a kiss at the corner of her mouth. Across from them, Aidrik bore the disheveled look of someone too distracted to pretend things were all right.

"What's wrong?" Ana asked.

Aidrik's brows knotted together as he looked off, toward the nearby town below. "We may be walking into a trap."

Finn groaned in evident frustration. "For months you've insisted Agripin was on our side. You're not someone who second-guesses themselves, so I can't understand why you're choosing to do it now, when we're so close."

"You think Agripin is aligned with the Senetat?" Ana pressed Aidrik.

"I do not believe so," Aidrik answered, still not meeting her eyes. "But if he means to play us false..."

"Every Runean you've encountered over the years all say Agripin is on our side. That he's been waiting to play his hand," Finn insisted. Ana felt his grip tighten as his frustrations rose up again. "All the intelligence you have assures us we can trust him."

"He is still the son of the grand emperor," Aidrik replied. Ana understood all he didn't say: that Agripin had nothing to gain by aligning with the disorganized Runean rebels, and everything to lose. He would inherit the title of Grand Emperor when his father, Aeron's, time was past. Why would he choose to join forces with a scattered group of rebels who had little shot at beating the Eldre Senetat?

"We can't wander around the Highlands forever," Finn said with a measured sigh. "We're in exile here, in limbo. Nicolas and Mercy are likely chomping at the bit, or have maybe even given up on us. Unless you have a better plan, we need to see this through. We can't overcome the Senetat without a leader, and though you're a badass, I don't think you're the right guy for the job."

"No," Aidrik agreed.

"Aidrik," Ana began, leaving Finn's side. She laced her

fingers through Aidrik's pale ones, as she stepped before him. "You never had these fears before. Why now?"

Aidrik's thoughts betrayed him when his eyes darted quickly to Aleksandr. Then, he squeezed her hands so hard she winced. "Now that the time is upon us, I find it more challenging to take the necessary risks."

"When we agreed to this... *arrangement*... we decided there wasn't just one leader amongst us," Ana said. Their "arrangement," while not defined by any textbook or social standard, had been discussed enough that they knew the basic rules. The three of them were equal partners. No secrets, and no one's opinion was more important than the others.

"My intention isn't to force a belief, Kjære. I aim only to voice a strong concern," Aidrik said, with a touch of rare defensiveness.

"And we hear you. I don't even completely disagree," Finn replied, "but we have no other options. The Senetat has the backing, whether passive or active, from nearly all the Empyreans. From what you've told us, every Runean uprising has completely failed, because no one was brave enough to stand alongside leaders who were perceived as weak. According to you, there is no one else. We *need* Agripin, Aidrik. If he isn't the man for this, then we're screwed whether we meet him now as an ally, or later as our enemy."

Aidrik seemed surprised to be swayed by Finn's logic. "Aye. If he is not with us, it merely delays the inevitable."

Ana studied Aidrik as his eyes again fell on the town below. The Empyrean was nearly four millennia old, and had seen more things in that time than Ana could fathom with her mere thirty years. But for all his age, he had the unlined face of a beautiful, cherubic twenty-five-year-old. His silvery red hair, an Empyrean trait, shone vibrantly in the setting sun. Beautifully curved lips, now pressed firm in determination, showed his distress, where his bright eyes were better at hiding it.

She realized it had been weeks since she'd lain with Aidrik. Once she'd recovered from the delivery, she spent every night with Finn, making up for lost time. For leaving him, twice. And he was her husband now, after all. But so was Aidrik, if not by law, then by agreement of this triad they had formed. It never occurred to her that the stoic part of the equation had emotional needs, too.

"It will be okay," she said. Aidrik turned toward her, and she saw then, in his eyes, more of that need. *He fears losing me. Not just to war. He worries that in sharing me with Finn, he has given me away completely.*

Aidrik nodded, and then gently pulled his hands away. "Assist Aleksandr in supper preparation. I am taking a brief sojourn."

Without another word, Aidrik sprinted down the side of the hill, heading away from the town. Finn's strong arms came around Ana's waist again and she turned, letting his comforting gaze fill her with a sense of ease. *My Fisherman. My Man of the Sea. The Mighty Poseidon.*

"He needs you," Finn said. "You should go to him. I'll help Aleksei."

Ana searched for any signs of resentment in Finn's eyes at this suggestion, and found none. They were still finding their boundaries in this triumvirate, but she knew it must be harder for the men than for her.

She nodded, and kissed him before going off in search of her other mate.

Forbia followed Ana down the hill, her furry bodyguard. She smiled and knelt to gently stroke the white wolf's mane. Finn's familiar nuzzled her nose under Ana's chin in response.

The wolf's felicitous arrival into their little clan was a memory she'd hold close to her always.

The day they'd left the comforts of the St. Andrews cottage, Finn stumbled across a litter of wolf pups, abandoned and seemingly all dead. One resilient pup cried out, appealing to Finn's tender heart in a single instant. All discussion on the matter was pointless.

"I thought wolves were extinct on the British Isles," Ana had wondered aloud.

"Aye," Aidrik agreed, inspecting the tiny ball of fur. "Black market breeders bring them in for sport, but then leave them to nature. Most don't survive alone. This one is a Hudson Bay wolf, from Canada, if my canine senses steer me correct."

"Can we make her like us?" Aleksandr had asked, eyes innocent and searching.

"Like us?" Aidrik repeated.

"Sveising," Ana clarified with a knowing smile, understanding exactly what her son was thinking. "He's wondering if you can give an animal the Sveising and gift her with longer life as you did Finn and me."

Aidrik unexpectedly warmed at the suggestion, but first searched for Finn's permission, as it was plain the wolf was already bonded to him. Finn nodded and handed the squirrelly ball of fur over, as Aidrik worked his rare magic, as much a gift to the wolf as to their small family.

"Forbia," Finn whispered, planting a kiss on the wolf's nose as he welcomed her back. A greeting she promptly returned with a tentative lick. "That will be your name."

And so he'd named her after his beloved ship, left behind in Maine when he'd gone in pursuit of a life with Ana. It was one hole she couldn't fill for him and, with a secret, burgeoning optimism, she hoped Forbia the wolf might both help fill that hole as well as marking a solid line between past and future.

The bond between Finn and Forbia was almost enough to make Ana jealous. Finn could communicate with the wolf, silently, in a language none of the others understood, and Forbia quickly moved from being merely a pet to also a useful guard and scout. As the days wore on, Ana recognized Forbia gave Finn a unique purpose and role in the group that nothing else could. Perhaps Forbia's addition to their family was more than chance.

"You did not need to follow me," Aidrik spoke up, appearing from behind an alder tree. His feet crunched in the leaves, which had died and fallen early in this part of the world. Forbia trotted forward and nudged the side of Aidrik's leg. He snaked his hand down to stroke her pale mane, offering a half-smile as he added, "Either of you."

Ana resisted the urge to accuse him of pouting, remembering he'd lived solitary for most of his wandering. "If you'd like me to leave, I will."

Aidrik shook his head and extended one arm, inviting her in. As she accepted, she looked down at Forbia and instructed, "Tell your master I'm fine." Forbia uttered a small yip of affection and bounded off in the direction of their abandoned estate.

"It's not only us I fear for," Aidrik ventured. "Nicolas and your family live under my protection. In sending more Empyreans their way, the risk of exposure increases. If Agripin's word is not true—"

Ana silenced him with a kiss, something so rare these days that it stole both their breaths in unison. "You can't take all of this on your shoulders alone," she whispered. His hands traveled the length of her back as his heartbeat ran faster. "Please don't feel as though you have to."

"I would not tarnish the purity in any of you. I do this so that you can exist in a better world, and in safety," he countered, holding her tighter.

"I know," she answered. "But we have to accept there aren't many outcomes which will have us all happy and smiling at the end. I don't think we will come out of this unscathed, Aidrik. It terrifies me to say those words aloud... but if we don't say it, we can't prepare. And if we can't prepare, we can't protect Aleksei."

"I would seek to protect all of you."

"And if you can't, it won't be a failure of yours," she sighed against his mouth. "You give me strength. I don't mean that you are my strength, exactly, only that you've shown me how to use what I already have. I'm not the scared girl you found at *Ophélie* seeking an escape from herself."

"Aye. And that is what scares me, Kjære. Fearlessness, even with solid foundation, is a dangerous thing."

"Do you see me as dangerous?"

Aidrik hesitated, then nodded. "The darkness within you..." He left the thought unfinished.

She had no response. The darkness she'd lived with her whole life was a daemon, haunting her. But it had evolved and now it was... something indescribable. Indefinable. A whisper against her heart, a tangible traveler on their journey. Perhaps not a weakness as she had always perceived. Though Aidrik had labeled her fearless, when it came to the solving of this mystery, she was very much afraid.

"Whatever comes, we'll all face it together, as we've promised," she said instead. "Now, let's go enjoy the boar our son took down, and get you and Finn prepped for this meeting with Agripin."

4
AMELIA

Cianán pulled Cerridwen atop him and entered her, the joining bringing forth inception of the sacred Quinlan ceremony.

Around them, Fires of Bel burned bright as the cycle of fertility began, blessed by the consummation of Cianán and Cerridwen in their fortieth turn upon the Earth.

It would end when Cianán granted her his seed, promising a benediction of fertility upon the Quinlan druids and their land until autumn's harvest.

Amid the rhythm of their lovemaking, Cerridwen felt a rebellious streak. She did not want this to end so soon. Defiant of their audience, caught in peaceful chant, she drew his pleasure out until she reached her own, his eyes beseeching her for mercy. She pressed his strong hands down between her legs, showing him his way to release.

Cianán bit down on her lower lip as his warm fingers brought forth her desire, sharing her mischief in drawing the moment out. At last she erupted, her icy hair falling back as she came over him, clenching tight, the songs of the goddess raining down around her.

With a flush in her cheeks, and a hitch in her breath, she finally granted Cianán mercy.

AMELIA AWOKE AS A FLASH OF BRIGHT LIGHTNING FILLED THE ROOM, cutting a jagged swash over the quilt which now dangled precipitously over the bed's edge, hanging on only by one of Jacob's feet.

Outside, the late summer storm raged, pouring heavy rains from the heavens onto the Garden District, on this, their last night in the house on Seventh. She stood to crack the window, to listen. Overhead, the fan ushered soothing air into the muggy house, cooling the sweat beading at her brow, and across her chest and legs.

This summer had been untenable. But another heat now throbbed between her legs, brought on by the seer's dream.

Sneaking back into bed, Amelia slipped a hand under Jacob's sleeping chin. He stirred and then woke, his eyes widening at once at her rasping breaths.

He didn't protest as she first kissed him, and then gently but firmly coaxed his head down, down between her legs where there was only one cure for the throbbing causing her breaths to falter.

Jacob nestled between her thighs, his tongue finding what she sent him after. The connection traveled through her, a spark that brought her to life under him. She arched her back as his hands slid underneath her, cupping both cheeks in his palms as he pressed her further into his waiting mouth. His thumbs moved to spread her wider, tongue traveling back and forth between her two pleasures.

Amelia speared her hands through his dark hair as the storm flashed outside, the smell of her husband's musk mingled with dusty rain and memories of the old glen drawing her closer to conclusion. She pressed down on his face, and they moaned in unison, her cries growing higher and higher until at last she unfolded beneath him, the orgasm rocking through her in violent, delicious waves.

Before she could catch her breath he slid up beside her, then flipped her atop him, guiding himself inside her with one hand. This was his favorite; her on top, where she could control his pleasure, and he could see her, all of her, in full view.

Jacob's protective hands settled firmly on her hips, directing her through their favorite rhythms. She very nearly came again as she observed Jacob's half-parted mouth crying out for her, his eyes heavy with sleep and sensuality.

In the next moment, he rose to a sitting position, wrapping one hand around her damp back, and the other through her hair. When he kissed her, she tasted herself on his lips. "You're so wet already," he panted in time to the movements, his hot breath against her ear driving her mad beyond words. "I don't know if I can last."

"Don't torture yourself," she purred, squeezing her thighs together, enjoying his eyes rolling toward the ceiling. Taking his bottom lip in her teeth this time, she added, "We can always do it again."

This was all the permission Jacob needed. His groan filled the room, mixing with the rainstorm and her own desperate cries, as he spilled deep inside her, slowing his movements as the orgasm left him.

When she was sure he was finished, she slipped out of his arms and curled up beside where he lay, winded. Another flash of lightning filled the room, briefly illuminating his beautiful face, painted with love, desire, and inevitably, exhaustion.

"Every time you say we can do it again, it sends me over the bloody edge," Jacob murmured. "And then I remember I'm not twenty-one anymore."

"I never said we had to do it now," Amelia teased, brushing his sweaty hair from his brow. She adjusted so her head rested against his chest, listening to his skipping heart rate, and the ragged rise and fall of his slowly steadying breaths. "After breakfast will be fine."

"Will it, now?"

"I might let you sleep until then. Maybe."

Jacob yawned into her hair, nuzzling her into him as his sleepy voice cooed, "I love you more than I did five minutes ago."

"And five minutes from now, you'll love me even more than you do in this moment," she whispered back, but he was already drifting into peaceful rest.

A NEW LIGHT WASHED THROUGH THE ROOM, THIS ONE A STEADY WARM glow from the morning sun. Amelia stretched, turning to face her husband and wake him again with something exciting, when she discovered he was no longer lying next to her.

Jacob slept as long as life would allow. With burgeoning curiosity, Amelia slipped a t-shirt over her head, pulled on a fresh pair of panties from the mostly-packed suitcase, and ventured downstairs.

She found him on the back porch, enjoying his coffee and the newspaper. Miss Kitty perched like royalty on his lap, as his hand mindlessly stroked her white fur, eliciting deep rumbling purrs.

"Good morning," Amelia greeted, slipping into the rocking chair across from him.

"*Blanca*," he responded groggily, as Miss Kitty leapt down

and sauntered into the garden, the tip of her tail dancing in a happy twitch. "I didn't wake you, did I?"

"No, but I can't fathom why you're up so damn early," she teased. She reached across the table and stole a sip from his mug, feeling altogether too lazy to pour her own. "Two-for-one cheese grits at the Waffle House?"

"Hysterical," he grinned. "Maybe I was looking forward to what you promised after breakfast."

He'd not met her eyes once. Amelia observed his fidgeting foot, and the ongoing twisting of his lips, as his mind clearly moved between a myriad of thoughts. "You said no secrets between us," she started.

Jacob chewed his lip and then meticulously folded the paper, setting it next to his coffee. His eyes slowly traveled to hers. His expression was dark, and nearly ominous. "I can't stop thinking about Father O'Connor's words to us after the wedding."

Her heart skipped; this was a conversation she'd been dying to have but respected Jacob's hesitance. "I can't either."

"But I want to," Jacob continued. "Forget them. I want to pretend he never said them, and enjoy that my life is finally, exactly the way I wanted it."

She considered her next words carefully. "You can and should enjoy that we are finally where we wanted to be, while still gaining a better understanding of the truth. Don't you want to know who you really are?"

He set his jaw tight. "I know who I am."

"Where we come from matters," she offered gently. "My past, and my family's history, is a significant part of who I am."

Jacob released a measured breath. "Amelia, I know all I need to know. I'm married to the only woman I've ever loved, and I'm at peace. That's all I need. Nothing else."

Evidently, this wasn't the time to press the matter. Instead, she stood and cast her shadow over him, climbing into his lap. Finally, the Jacob she loved best emerged. "Well, then, why don't we make the most of our last hours in the house?"

AMELIA WASN'T SELLING THE HOUSE, BUT THEY'D PREPARED IT FOR their long absence. Covers were placed on all furniture, food disposed of or sent to her mother's, and the overseer hired by the Sullivans left with care instructions. Ashley, who had been staying with her following the defection of his wife, had moved in with their mother until he could get things sorted. She'd left no loose ends.

Nevertheless, it felt like goodbye. She'd bought this house with part of her portion of the Deschanel Trust while still an undergrad. Around the time she fell in love with Jacob, in fact. Every important moment in their relationship, both the good and the bad, happened while living under this roof.

They were trading one home for another, perhaps temporarily, but at least together. Her darkest moments were those when she'd been sure Jacob's life would be better without her. No matter what was ahead, she swore to him she'd never make that decision again.

"Phase Two: Engage," Jacob wisecracked, followed by a series of sounds he likely thought belonged on a starship. When he didn't draw the expected smile, he looped his arm around her waist, dropping his head on her shoulder. "Please cheer up, *Blanca*. I only know of one way to help when you're like this, and you've worn me out this morning. The well is dry."

At this, she did laugh. "I let you off easy."

"Five times before noon is honest work, Mrs. Donnelly."

"I only hope Giselle's suite at *Ophélie* is soundproof."

"Maybe we'll find we work better with an audience."

Amelia rewarded him with a kiss, as his playful expression dissolved her foul mood.

5
AIDRIK

Aidrik monitored Anasofiya sleeping beside him. Her breathing was shallow, her pulse slow. No risk of her sleepwalking this eve. If his mind would allow it, he could also rest without worry.

He carved a now-cold piece of boar with his knife, slipping the meat between his teeth and tearing it with his incisors.

Across the crumbling manor, in another wing, Aleksandr and Finn slept. In this new arrangement, whoever stayed with Anasofiya was afforded privacy. Mostly that had been Finn. Tonight, she had come to Aidrik instead. Out of pity, he deduced, though the conclusion was puerile, insecurity a waste of precious thought.

Her passion seemed sincere enough. Yet her thoughts were far from him during the act. Aidrik guessed they were far from Finn, as well. Anasofiya rarely voiced her fears, but Aidrik sensed them with great clarity. Her confidence wavered at the awareness Aidrik's own resolve was waning. Knowing he caused her such duress filled him with guilt, but he refused to deceive. He was no longer certain Agripin was interested in aligning with the Runean cause. His instincts bade caution.

Seer's visions taunted him, whispering of things he knew could not be wholly accurate. Anasofiya covered in blood. Aleksandr in chains. Aidrik greeting his own executioner. He knew better than to entertain these ghastly images, but that did not stop their plaguing.

Aidrik was startled as he looked up to see Finn standing before him, his figure an outline against the moonlight behind the glassless window. Annoyed he had allowed his guard down, Aidrik frowned, then stood to join him.

"Something amiss?" Aidrik asked, his sword hand pressed tight against Ulfberht.

Finn shook his head. The man's eyes then darted down toward his sleeping wife. *He fights with himself over his innate jealousy. He knows this is what he agreed to.* "Can't sleep."

Aidrik nodded, relaxing. He settled back down near the fire, and motioned for Finn to join him. "Aye, nor can I."

"I've been thinking..." Finn settled his arms around his knees, resting his head as he gazed through the fire, at Anasofiya. "We need to do this, but if you're right... if your concerns end up being valid... well, I worry about having us all in one place. Aleksei and Ana would be put to death, without so much as even a trial."

Aidrik drew in a breath of night air, nodding again. "Not only them. I gave you the Sveising also."

"And you, for certain. As far as they know, you've been dead for a thousand years. They'll want to correct that misunderstanding." Finn looked at Aidrik, gazing thoughtfully. "I suppose that's where your last minute concerns might be coming from? It's a risk, playing this hand. You can only do it once."

Aidrik gave a slight laugh, shrugging his shoulders. "Once,

aye. But I am in accord. We can't all risk walking into a trap." Aidrik sliced off another hunk of boar, offering it to Finn, who shook his head. "Take Anasofiya and our son into hiding until I return."

"No," Finn said, firmly but without bravado. "You shouldn't go alone, and Ana would never allow me to send her and Aleksei away. We agreed we wouldn't keep things from her."

Aidrik's jaw tensed, as an image of his evigbond struggling in chains flashed through his brain. Yes, he had promised, a vow he'd already come to regret.

"I don't like it any more than you do," Finn continued, "but I'm not gonna leave her in the dark. She deserves better, and she won't put up with us acting like cavemen for long."

Aidrik considered Finn's words, deciding he didn't have to like them for them to be true. "Aleksandr, then. Perhaps it is time to send him to Nicolas and Mercy. We've delayed long enough."

Finn's eyes widened. It was apparent he had never considered that Aleksandr could not remain with them forever. Not with the unfinished business at hand.

"He is in more danger than anyone on this Earth," Aidrik said, attempting a gentle tone. "We can't shield him here. *Ophélie* remains under my protection, and is the only place where an Empyrean can stay out of the Senetat's purview."

"He isn't ready," Finn insisted. "We still have so much to teach him."

"Do we? You've done a fine job instructing him on basic survival, and guiding him on how to interact with the natural world. His mother has taught him about his people, and compassion. A challenge, undoubtedly, to process his rate of growth, but Aleksandr is a man now. And the Deschanel heir."

"I don't know..."

"You do," Aidrik insisted. "Humans are overly sentimental. In you, that weakness is balanced by the Sveising now. A halfling, you've ceased aging. You will live far longer than expected. Hundreds, if not thousands, of years. Aleksandr, if protected, could live forever. Think for the future, not the present."

A flash of defiance in his expression, Finn gazed at Anasofiya and said nothing.

"Palaver with Anasofiya tomorrow. Bring her around to the idea. From me, she will balk. From you, she will see reason," Aidrik said. He pushed ember coals from the dying fire with a long branch. "And you, Finn, hearten at the realization the sooner you send him, the sooner we can attend to what must be done. Then you can be with him again."

Aidrik stood, then, handing the stick to Finn. "I'll look over Aleksandr. You stay with her."

Finn made no attempt to hide the relief and happiness in his face, as he slid in the makeshift pile of cloak and blanket, next to his wife.

6

NICOLAS

Nicolas stood with his arms crossed on the upper gallery facing the rear of the house, Brigitte's Garden, and all of *Ophélie's* many outbuildings: the old blacksmith shop, *pigeonnier's*, kitchens, overseer's cottage, and countless other relics he couldn't be bothered to name. Living monuments and witness to all deeds, glorious and terrible, on the plantation, which dated back to thirty years before the start of the Civil War.

Dozens of contractors bustled to and fro. A horde of worker ants, doing he-had-no-clue-what to get the buildings into a condition suitable for housing, without compromising their original design and historical integrity. They had all, of course, signed a disturbingly worded non-disclosure agreement before they could be contracted. If they spoke to anyone about the work they were doing here, they would lose a lot more than their jobs. Security for this project was paramount. Nicolas wondered how the Deschanels hadn't unearthed the power of construction somewhere in their ranks yet.

Tucked sporadically between the ancient wooden structures were newer ones, gleaming white double-wide trailers. If anyone had told Nicolas Deschanel he'd one day host a trailer park in his backyard, he'd have laughed and told them to go to hell.

The long list of efforts might all be too much. Then again, they could be too little. No one knew how many children were coming, and what the hell they were supposed to do with them when they arrived. Mercy insisted Aidrik would send them a messenger, someone, to give them better instructions. To guide them through these unknown waters. But so far no one had arrived, and without word from Aidrik or Ana in months, Nicolas' already deficient patience levels were dwindling into the humid breeze.

A rush of chivalry and idealism were the culprits for Nicolas' easy acceptance of Mercy's plea, but regret and resentment had crept in. Knowing it didn't mean he had the power to stop the conflicting emotions. Or the desire.

The object of his frustrated affection appeared at his side, leaning against the columned gallery as she also surveyed the construction. "This must all feel very invasive to you," she observed.

Nicolas flashed her a quick peripheral glance, keeping his expression pointed safely ahead. "Aunt Colleen is overseeing the process to make sure they protect the structural design and antiquity of any buildings listed on the historical register," he recited.

She smiled. A breeze caught her silver hair, exposing an anxious expression behind her long bangs. "You know what I mean."

Nicolas shrugged. He wasn't equipped for the discussion she seemed ready to drop on him. Blah, blah, blah... he'd agreed to do it, hadn't he? "It's fine. I've never been overly sentimental. Change doesn't bother me."

Mercy said nothing further, a blessing and a curse. The unspoken words had hovered between them for weeks, haunting their discussions, and even their bedroom, which had until lately been the one place nothing could touch them.

She backed away from the edge to leave. Nicolas was jolted back with a light tug as she slipped her hand under the back of his jeans, guiding him through the double doors. With a gentle click they closed, and then Mercy, that beautiful creature living under his roof, sharing his bed and heart, sunk to her knees before him.

"Thank you," she whispered, as her long fingers popped the top button of his pants. They dropped in a rustle, scrunching unevenly at his ankles. Nicolas looked down with a sudden urge to gaze into her eyes and say something... *tender*... but her lips were already around his cock, and his mind dismissed everything but the immediate pleasure washing over him.

As she conveyed her wordless appreciation, Nicolas' stress fell away.

AUNT COLLEEN BRIEFED NICOLAS ON THE PROGRESS AND PROJECT completion dates, while he daydreamed about the nap he'd take once she finished. She said a lot of words, but all he retained was: workers would be done by week's end.

"Swell," Nicolas offered, eyeing the silver tray that used to hold crystal decanters of cognac. His mouth watered, and he quickly snapped his gaze away. Never would he have promised another to put away the drink, but the promise to himself meant something. His self-control was the one thing he possessed that kept him cohesive. His last shred of sanity in a world gone completely fucking upside-down. Without it, everything would slip into chaos.

His aunt towered over him, her disapproval reflected in the study window. "Since you haven't asked about the mobilization of family resources," she went on, drawing in a subtle but noticeable deep breath, "I'll relay what I know. Amelia and Jacob are on their way today. They've left the keys to their house with the overseer and plan to stay here, in Giselle's suite, for as long as they are needed. Our dear Anne will stay in Adrienne's rooms. Markus, Tristan, and Harriett—"

"Harriett who?"

"Broussard, dear. Jasper's youngest. Please keep up. They will all arrive today, and Markus has offered to stay in the blacksmith shop, to help oversee any of the children who may stay either in outbuildings or the pre-fab dormitories. Anne has also offered to move out there, should enough children show up to warrant additional supervision. Harriett and Tristan can take Lucienne's suite, and—"

"What, together? Are they fucking?" he interjected, recalling the Broussards were distant cousins.

Aunt Colleen's heels clicked against the old cypress floor. "This is your home, so I'll not chastise your choice of shocking vulgarities and unfortunate vernacular. But I'll thank you not to give poor Tristan a hard time about his relationship with dear Harriett. They've both been through enough."

Nicolas looked out the window in response. What did it matter, really? He'd once been in love with Ana.

She continued to pace before the hearth. When she spoke again, her tone was heavy, and Nicolas imagined what a disappointment he must be to her. He'd embraced this idea with all the transitory excitement of a toddler.

Well, she could stand in line behind Mercy. Nicolas

frowned. Where was Mercy anyway? Shouldn't she be the one receiving this direction?

"There are others we can call upon, should we need them. The Collective Council met several days ago to discuss back-ups, and we've had plenty of volunteers, whom we've ranked in order of appropriateness. I can show you the list, if you'd like."

Nicolas waved her away.

"Fine, then. The last member of the team is likely going to come as a surprise. Oz has resumed the care of his children and returned to the firm."

"I already know. He's ours."

Aunt Colleen wrinkled her mouth into a skeptical grin. "Given your other apparent lapses in memory, I'll summarize anyway. His return to the firm is on a limited basis. I approached his father, Colin, about our Deschanel attorney resource moving from shared to dedicated. What this means is, Oz will cease to handle any other clients, and will work solely for us. The legal effort is unlikely to be full-time, which is a win-win for the firm, as they will receive full compensation regardless of the hours he commits. Oz, then, will get his time to heal, with his children, and we will have a dedicated legal resource to assist where needed." She paused, deep in thought, then added, "Of course, our concession to pay full price for a part-time lawyer was not purely philanthropic. His children are Deschanels, and I would see they get proper care."

Nicolas couldn't imagine what good a legal resource would do when up against a race of supernatural beings set on killing everyone under his roof, but he once again nodded. "Sounds like you've got it all covered."

She stopped, facing him again. In her crisp black suit, she appeared an imposing monolith, despite her slight frame. "If I were your mother, I would be reminding you that you need to be searching out healthy coping mechanisms for your unease."

"My mother was a textbook sociopath."

"I realize you may be, rightfully, feeling in over your head right now," Aunt Colleen responded, unruffled. He'd never been able to get under her skin. "But you are not alone. You have an entire family backing you."

Nicolas wished she would go away. Stop filling his head with nuggets of wisdom he knew to be true but didn't care to incorporate. No one had ever succeeded in forcing Nicolas to accept something if he wasn't ready.

"Nicolas," she ventured, softening her inflection, "this is the purpose you've waited for all your life. The direction. Some meaning to all you've endured. I know this notion terrifies you, but it needn't be so awful."

Direction. Purpose. Nicolas had not ever desired, or needed, either. This was hard for someone like Colleen Deschanel to understand when she lived her life steeped in reason and questing for the ultimate truth in all things. But Nicolas Deschanel had always been content to move through life with an easy finesse, never wondering what might come next, and more, never caring.

And if he said this to her? What then?

He stood, moving toward the long foyer and the massive oaken entrance, in a move he hoped would bring end to the uncomfortable conversation. "Thanks for coming out today. And for all your help," he managed, as he swung the door inward. His mind was fixed on the need for a long nap to clear his head. "I'm sure we'll have some direction from the Empyrean side soon."

"I have faith Aidrik would not lead us into this without proper reinforcement. After all, he's protected our family for centuries," she agreed, heels clicking as she stepped on to the front veranda. "Ahh, and look at the timing!"

Nicolas didn't need to follow her gaze. He heard the sound of tires crunching on gravel as a car eased down the long, private drive. One, or more, of his cousins had arrived.

"Markus, Harriett, Anne, and Tristan," Aunt Colleen confirmed, smiling. "Amelia and Jacob will be not far behind."

Nicolas' shoulders rose and fell in a heavy sigh. The nap would have to wait.

7
ANASOFIYA

Ana rose before the sun. Beside her, Finn snored softly, one arm draped over her belly. She frowned, realizing Aidrik had switched places with Finn during the night.

Don't concern yourself, he'd said, a few days ago, when she apologized for the imbalance in time spent with Finn in comparison to him. *Needs ebb and wane. At present, you need him more.*

Finn's physical presence gave her a unique, raw strength she required right now, as they faced the unknown. Finn seemed to need her equally, as he swallowed back the fear she might walk away again. Reassuring him with words would mean little. She needed to prove it with time.

Ana wrapped Aidrik's cloak around her, breathing in the crisp fall air wafting through the jagged wooden beams barely offering shelter in this aging manor house. But it was enough, and for that she was thankful.

The town below them lay quiet, its inhabitants still resting. Even the wildlife was still. But Ana knew Aidrik would be awake. He rarely slept, and when he did, it was never heavy enough to slumber through the waking of another.

As she made her way down the stone steps, and into the adjoining grove, she confirmed her guess. Aidrik perched, stoking a fresh fire, with the remains of Aleksandr's boar to his left.

"Morning," she said, taking a seat on a log across from him. Glancing at her, he offered a small smile, then returned to the task at hand.

"You rose early," Aidrik replied, eyes focused on the sparks dancing from the fire pit.

"There's a lot on my mind. All our minds," Ana said, dully tranced by the way his branch moved through the coals. There was a rhythmic quality to it, as if the pattern were deliberate.

"Aye," he agreed. "There is."

"Our meeting with Agripin is soon?" Ana asked hesitantly, wondering how far she would need to push for answers. Aidrik was never overly effusive, but he seemed especially judicious with his words now.

Aidrik nodded.

"Should I wake Finn?"

Aidrik set his stick aside, then sat up straight on the log, watching her. "I deem it wise you stay here with Aleksandr, while Finn and I go on ahead for the meeting." He continued to study her after he finished speaking, watching for a reaction.

"Of course you deem it wise. You never have seen me as an equal," Ana snapped, with unhidden disdain. "I told you the day I left with you, I was coming of my own agreement, and that you should see me as a partner. You said you would, but you don't."

"You take offense, but you should not. You understand it is affection guiding my caution, not a desire to be your gaoler."

"The result is the same," Ana argued. "I was raised to see myself as equal to any man."

"Kjære. You know I don't see you as less. I worry for your safety," Aidrik said reasonably.

"I'm no more of a target than you, or Finn," she retorted. "Any of us would be executed simply for existing. And if you think it's okay for you to leave me behind for fear of losing me, only to put yourself in mortal danger so that *I* am the one forced to feel loss—"

A man of action, if not words, Aidrik was at her side before she could finish speaking, and pressed his lips to hers in a gesture of comfort rather than tenderness. He wrapped his arms around her and pulled her against his chest. "The meeting must occur. Finn was right about that. And I must be there. Agripin knows me. Once, he trusted me, but my demise is a possibility. I can't protect you from that, but I can safeguard you from harm."

Ana grudgingly allowed Aidrik's words and arms to ease her, knowing he was right but hating it just the same. It did need to be Aidrik. And knowing he might not walk away, they needed to minimize the losses of their party.

She steadied herself for the words that must be said next. "If things don't go well in this meeting, we'll need to send Aleksei away... won't we?"

Aidrik's nod was slow and resolute. "I know how that will pain you, but aye."

"Why is this all happening now?" Ana ventured. They'd held this conversation before, but his answers had been evasive. "Why, after thousands of years, are you only now pursuing this?"

"I've explained it to you before," Aidrik replied, stepping away to renew his focus on tending the coals. "Our kind was not ready."

"Nothing has changed with the Empyreans, though. The Runeans are still spread across the world, disjointed and lacking leadership. According to you, that's been the state of things for thousands of years. The chance for success is no better now than it ever was, if we can't organize the rebels effectively. So... I ask you again, Aidrik. Why now?"

His hand stopped, the stick settling into a crevice in the perimeter of skull-sized rocks encircling the fire pit. When he looked up, his eyes were heavy with a fear she was not accustomed to witnessing in their intrepid leader. "Aye, nothing has changed with our people. But everything has changed for me."

Ana's breath caught as she waited for him to finish.

"Until now, I had nothing worth fighting for. Nothing I feared losing."

"I'll stay," she said finally. In this way, she could protect him as well. Sometimes doing the right thing was better than being right.

"Thank you, Kjære," he whispered, with a light sigh.

The following day, when Anasofiya awoke, rising before dawn, Aidrik and Finn were already gone. *Without even a goodbye,* she thought, and then quickly shook away the sentimentality. Goodbyes were too final. Had they stopped to do so, her fears would have been insurmountable.

Forbia had apparently gone with the men. That was some consolation, at least. They were not alone.

Positive thoughts. No turning back now.

"Mora, tell me again about the Eldre Senetat," Aleksandr requested. His long legs swung over the short cliff, dangling inches above the crystal-clear lake. Every now and then his heel made contact, creating a ripple that resonated across the glassy surface. Ana, lost to her fears and thoughts, focused on this motion, allowing it to occupy her and keep her fears safely at bay.

"What would you like to know?" Anasofiya asked. Both of their reflections gazed back from the water, Aleksandr's towering several inches above hers. *My son.* His red hair reminded her of Aidrik. The softness in his unlined face, and his large, strong hands were Finn's.

Aleksandr gazed at the water thoughtfully. Ana was always awed by how kind and sensitive her son was. She tried to be these things, but her efforts materialized in more subtle ways. Aleksei had inherited this sweetness from Finn.

"I know they want us all dead, but I still don't understand why," he hesitantly prompted. Though he was the image of a boy becoming a man, he sounded every bit a child. The youth in him showed strongest when faced with the awful realities the world promised but had not yet shown him.

"Well," she began, not wanting to speak of a topic so close to the fate that might await Finn and Aidrik, but understanding talking might help keep her mind busy. If she focused too long on what could be happening at their meeting with Agripin, she'd quickly lose her wits and go after them. "It isn't entirely true they want us dead. The truth is, they don't know any of us exist."

"Then why are we in danger?"

"Because if they *did* know, they *would* want us dead," she explained. Guessing he wouldn't be satisfied with that, and his questions would only continue, she went on, "The Senetat was formed many, many thousands of years ago. Long before Aidrik was born."

"How long?"

"I don't know, exactly. Aidrik would know. We can ask him

when he returns." She swallowed back the fear he might not return. "But longer than almost any living Empyrean has been alive. Do you know much about the Roman Senate of the old Roman Empire?" Aleksandr had been devouring books Finn snuck to him from nearby towns, as they traveled.

"They rejected the idea of a king, and represented the people's interests," Aleksandr said wisely. "Well, in the beginning, at least."

"Yes, precisely," Ana praised, patting his leg. Her heart swelled with love and awe. Each day this being she created surprised her. "The Senetat formed for very similar reasons, as I understand it. And equally good intentions. But good intentions don't always lead to good results."

"Did they kill their emperor? Like the Roman Senate killed Caesar?" Aleksandr asked, wide-eyed.

"No. The emperor was content to benignly sit back and let the Senetat do as they wished. Maybe if he *had* stood up, things would be different," Ana went on. "No one knows exactly why the Senetat grew corrupt. I suspect once they got a taste of power, they wanted it to be absolute. Some decided they wanted more power than the role originally intended. They grew greedy."

"I don't understand why everyone can't share," Aleksandr replied. His freckled reflection looked troubled. "There's plenty in this world."

"You're a wise boy," Ana answered with a sad smile, "and I wish everyone thought like you. But Empyrean nature is not unlike human nature, and eventually there are those who want more than they need. The Senetat began establishing rules and laws that severely limited the rights of the Empyrean race."

"Why did the people let them do this?"

"In the beginning, Empyreans still believed the Senetat's motivations were pure. Many of the laws were formed under the guise of protecting the race and sustaining it. A lot of Empyreans were in support of those laws, and some of them made sense. For example, when Empyreans mated with humans, it often diluted the specialness of Empyreans. Many started to lose their extraordinary traits, like your handsome red hair for example, or their psychic connections. Healers, over generations, became less effective, and so on. Empyreans outlawed mating with men to preserve the purity of their race. The source of what made them strong."

"I guess I can understand that..." Aleksandr hedged, pondering the circumstances. "That doesn't sound so terrible."

"Maybe not, if it had stopped there. But more rules were put in place. And soon, the Senetat realized they had no way of holding offenders accountable. So they invented the Mark of Emyr, a magical infusion placed on every single Empyrean when they came to maturity. They told the Empyreans it was a symbol of Emyr himself, and that, when Emyr determined them worthy, they would ascend to him and start their true existence, one far more glorious than anything they could ever find on Earth. It was pitched as the ultimate reward for their piety."

"Aidrik told me about that. He said the mark was evil, so he removed it."

Ana suppressed a smile. She pictured Aidrik telling his son, in stark words, about the crude way he sliced the phoenix-shaped infusion from his beautiful face. "He did. Not long after he was, himself, inducted into the Senetat."

"But why was the phoenix evil? He wouldn't tell me."

Aidrik was notoriously transparent with facts, so this surprised Ana. But she saw no reason her son shouldn't know the truth of where he came from, and what they were up against. Deception had no place in their small clan. "He discovered the truth. That the mark was not a symbol of Emyr, but a method of control by the Senetat. Ascension was nothing more than the Senetat 'activating' a mark using dark magic, killing the Empyrean. There was nothing spiritual about it."

Aleksandr frowned. "What happened when Aidrik removed his?"

"Nothing, if you mean physically. But it removed him from the control of the Senetat, and they believed him to be dead. In fact, they still do. If they knew he removed the mark, and lived, he would be declared a traitor and executed."

Aleksandr said nothing for a long period. He watched his feet skate across the otherwise still lake, and took several deep breaths, carefully measuring and arranging his thoughts. "Aidrik is a traitor for removing his mark. He's a traitor for illegally giving the Sveising to you, and to father. You're a traitor for being born halfling and now being more Empyrean because of the Sveising, and Far for being given the Sveising as well. And I'm the biggest traitor of all, for being born of these combined acts."

How could I have thought he sounded like a child? "Yes, sweetheart. That sums it up nicely."

"Aidrik and Father are appealing to Agripin, because, as the son of Emperor Aeron, he might be the only Empyrean who can get the military power and backing to overthrow the Senetat. Like Emperor Augustus. But Aidrik is worried his assumptions about Agripin are wrong, and that he and Far are walking into a trap. Right?"

Ana, speechless, nodded. She wished in her heart of hearts she didn't need to be having this discussion with her son. It was so unfair he could not mature as human children did, at a slower pace, with the benefit of enjoying his childhood. She had never wanted to be a mother, but now that she was, she wished for more than the few hours she'd been able to hold her child at her breast, as a babe.

"They're okay, Mora," Aleksandr assured, leaning his head on Ana's shoulder. "I can always sense them both. And they're fine."

"You can?"

Aleksandr nodded. "I only wish I could hear what they're saying!"

8
AMELIA

The long dining table at *Ophélie* was full of Deschanels. It was unusual to see so many in one place these days, outside of a Magi Collective meeting, and the rarity of this occurrence was acutely reflected in the eyes of all present.

The mahogany table had been stripped of the formal antiques usually adorning the polished surface, replaced by several pitchers of sweet tea. The overhead fans, usually enough to cool the room with the river's breeze through the windows, were switched off in favor of the rarely-used central air conditioning.

The family's core leadership, Colleen, Evangeline, Luther, and Jasper, all had varying ideas, but commonly agreed on one thing: they'd gone too long without solid direction. Others, those volunteering to stay on the property during the endeavor, felt they'd earned the right to demand answers by giving up their time, and vied for the privilege to speak first.

In the beginning, it was chaos.

Tristan made his discomfort over the lack of direction well-known, asserting that a family with this many resources should never be wondering what comes next. Markus didn't care *what* they did, so long as he had direct contact with Empyrean visitors and license to ask his cache of carefully prepared, scientific questions. Anne worried immensely about the absence of communication from Aidrik, having a "terrible feeling" they might receive well over a hundred children.

Amelia and Jacob kept their counsel, taking it all in. Nicolas, equally, said nothing but appeared either painfully bored or distracted with something unrelated.

Even Condoleezza had a spot at the table, the old and venerable chief of staff who had seen so much over the years and faithfully kept their confidences. When she expressed a strong opinion, she would meet Nicolas' eyes and his silent response back seemed to say, *Noted.*

Harriett, of all the guests, said the least, though it was clear she had something relevant to say and was actively choosing her silence. Biding her time.

"We can all agree on one thing, at least," Jasper said with an air of embellished exasperation. His embroidered handkerchief dangled from one hand, at the ready. "We are fully prepared from a facilities standpoint but entirely clueless on anything to do with the actual mission: tending to these rebel children."

"I hate that word, rebel. It sounds so crass." Colleen shook her head. "Can we all agree to instead simply call them children?"

"Fledglings, perhaps," Evangeline added thoughtfully.

"Until they win, they're still rebels," Markus retorted. "But we can call them prize game hens if it pleases you, Aunt C."

Jasper dropped his hanky on the table in an emphatic flourish. "What does winning even mean? The extermination of the Eldre Senetat? Some new-fangled Empyrean constitution giving them back their freedoms? No one's told us anything. We don't even know what we're doing here! Why are we sure this is our battle to fight?"

"Unless we want to be wiped out by a bunch of power-hungry preternatural politicians in the North Sea, then yes, it's our battle," Evangeline snapped. Amelia wondered why she was here, and not tending to Katja and the twins. Then she remembered Katja was sequestered away with Olivia, neither woman talking to anyone.

"Based on the word of a man we've had no communication from in months," Luther added, but his expression was less combative than exhausted. They'd all lost so much in this last wave of the Deschanel Curse. With the dust settling, reality painted a bleak picture for the survivors.

"Aidrik will send us guidance," Mercy asserted quietly. She was the one person present who had any working knowledge of what they might be up against, but something had caused her to retreat from them all. Amelia couldn't get a strong sense of why and that further unnerved her. "He's protected your family since the day you purchased this land. He wouldn't abandon you now, when you most needed him."

Colleen nodded. "Yes, he must send guidance, and he will."

"How do we know Aidrik is even still alive?" Tristan asked, looking away from Mercy as he spoke the question in a low tone.

"Who let you sit at the adult table, Tristan? If Aidrik were dead, Ana would be too. And I'd know if Ana was in danger," Nicolas retorted sharply. He threw both hands up in mock surrender. "Why are we debating ambiguous bullshit? Was the purpose of this meeting to sit and discuss all the shit we don't know? I hope someone is taking notes so we can revisit this clusterfuck over and over and over again, and engage in endless pointless discussion."

Amelia's mother sighed. Jasper slow-nodded in appreciation, then dropped his gaze when Colleen sent him a scathing look.

"Shall we start with what we do know?" Luther offered. His presence in the room was, as always, equally seen and felt, his tall stature and commanding voice holding the audience with every measured word.

"A startlingly long list," Nicolas quipped. "Might be here a while."

"You're kind of an asshole since you stopped drinking," Tristan accused. "If you don't want our help, say so."

"Nicolas is just overwhelmed, darling," Evangeline soothed, patting Tristan on the shoulder as though he was a confused child, which certainly wasn't going to help his cause. "Don't take anything he says personally."

"I don't know where you've been, Mother, but he's always been like this," Markus chimed in with a smirk.

"Start from the beginning. Please," Harriett whispered, bringing the attention back to the last discussion point. "Not all of us know all that's happened to date."

Amelia took this opportunity to speak up. Not only to contribute, but also to show they didn't necessarily need the elders to run the show. If they were to succeed here, in whatever it was they were doing, they would need to prove the ability to manage themselves.

She summarized all they knew, of their Empyrean heritage through Aidrik, as well as the limited knowledge they had of the Senetat, an adversary who, as yet, did not know of their existence, thanks to Aidrik's protection. "The Deschanels are all halflings, by their definition, and not allowed to exist. If they ever were to find out about us, it would be the end for our family."

"Finn is also halfling now," Aunt Colleen added. "Aidrik

offered him the Sveising at his wedding to Ana, same as he employed it when he saved Ana's life, so that they could both enjoy longer lives. Through his marriage to Ana, and his now-gifted life, Finn is one of us."

Amelia smiled at her mother. "Harriett, unfortunately we don't know much more than that. But all this background leads us to where we are now. All past uprisings against the Senetat have failed, yet Aidrik believes he may have an ally who can rouse all the rebels and possibly unite them in a successful push to overthrow the leadership. How they plan to do this, and what that victory looks like to them, I have no idea.

"However, what we *do* know is once these rebel leaders start assembling, they will need a safe house for their young ones. Children they call them, though they will be young adults to us due to their rapid growth. Nicolas has graciously offered *Ophélie*.

"Unfortunately, we haven't heard from Ana, Aidrik, or Finn in months, and so we're in the dark as to when the children might arrive, and how many. We've proceeded forward with the most elaborate planning we could, to prepare for the worst. Does that cover it, Mercy?" Amelia threw a polite glance at the other woman, hoping to engage her in the discussion, or at least get a better glimpse into what drove her unusual silence.

Mercy nodded. "What they are preparing to do is dangerous. Once they engage Agripin, the emperor's son, to discover if he is truly a rebel sympathizer, they will no longer have the veil of secrecy to hide under. They will be exposed, for better or worse. I believe this is why they haven't contacted us. Their thoughts could be intercepted, which would put all of us at grave risk. I know Aidrik, and he will contact us as soon as he is safely able to."

"Thank you Amelia, and Mercy," Colleen acknowledged.

"With our groundwork established, what remains to be discussed is what we will do when they arrive. We're all assembled here, with the intention to assist where necessary. We've put considerable money and time into preparing the proper accommodations. And while simply housing the children may be enough, when Aidrik last contacted us, he mentioned training. Unfortunately, he was vague, and so we are left without context or meaning. Mercy, can you give us any hints?"

"I was instructed under the rule of the Scholars, who were employed and hand-selected by the Senetat. The coursework lasted a century, and covered all areas of learning, from scholastic endeavors to mastering our individual abilities. Mostly propaganda. I cannot fathom how the rebels might train their young, though I'd hope the instruction comes with more truth."

"Super. I suppose we could sit here and practice reading each other's minds all day," Nicolas muttered.

"If you're not equipped to contribute, then at least remove yourself as an obstacle," Luther commanded. Amelia suppressed her look of horror. "You're one of the seven Magi Council now. Making snide comments in the back of the classroom is no longer an acceptable pastime."

Nicolas pretended to draw swirls in the dark wood.

"How do young Empyreans learn to use their abilities, Mercy?" Jacob ventured.

"Same way anyone learns anything," she replied with a light shrug. "Practice. Usually with those who are older, and more skilled. There's no trick to it, really, other than that."

Anne poured herself some tea from the pitcher. "Then maybe our role is as simple as that, to help them practice. We're not in a position to do much more, right? Mercy could teach them about their history, perhaps."

Mercy snickered. A dark look passed across her face. "The version of history I learned is not one I would teach them."

"You're in a perfect position to separate fact from fiction, actually. You know the truth," Amelia said.

Mercy shrugged, but didn't argue further.

"In theory, your idea makes sense," Jasper interjected. The handkerchief had been relegated to finger twirling. "But is it not also fair and right to say that most of us could benefit from training ourselves? Why, we learned our own abilities without any formal direction. It's possible, perhaps even likely, we aren't aware of all we can do."

"I'm sure you're correct," Colleen replied. "But without better direction, or ideas, it's all we have."

"And hopefully the war, or whatever they're doing, won't last long... right?" Tristan asked.

No one answered. No one knew.

"For now, that's the direction, then," Amelia asserted. The resumption of control was deliberate, and careful. *We need you, but we are not children.* "We will pair up with the children whose abilities match ours, and do our best to help them cultivate whatever they have. Mercy will give them the correct version of their history, assuming their parents have not already done so, and we'll attempt to fill in whatever gaps we find when they arrive.

"Primarily, we're here to protect them. If things get bad, and if need be, this property can house almost every Deschanel, Broussard, Guidry, and Fontenot in Louisiana, as well as whoever the rebels send us. As long as Aidrik lives, we're all safe here."

Condoleezza spoke up, as she signaled for one of the maids to collect the near-untouched tea pitchers. "And what if he dies? What then, child?"

Amelia opened her mouth, then snapped it shut. Her

mother would know what to say, but she was looking at Amelia, respecting her desire to lead this initiative. The fact was, they were not entirely sure how Aidrik's protection worked, nor how the ward was sustained, as it seemed other family homes also had some modicum of protection.

"We may need to be prepared to fight," she decided finally. "All the more reason for us to understand what we're capable of. Individually, and collaboratively." She directed her last words at Nicolas.

"Soon," Harriett piped up. Her expression was shy, uneasy as every person at the table looked her direction. "I can see it. The children are coming."

"Are you sure?" Markus pressed. "How sure?"

"My daughter is the most powerful seer at the table. Perhaps in this entire family," Jasper defended, smiling proudly at Harriett. "If she says the children are coming, then it's time to prepare."

JACOB HAD BEEN SHOWERING FOR THE PAST HALF-HOUR IN THE bathroom adjoining their suite. Amelia was tempted to join him, but even with her skills in protecting her emotions, she couldn't turn her thoughts off. The words on her tongue were ones he wasn't ready to hear.

Everything changed for them three days after their wedding, on their last night in Ireland. The rest of the family had already returned home to New Orleans, but Jacob and Amelia indulged themselves in a couple of nights respite from all the madness awaiting them.

In hindsight, it was no wonder Father O'Connor waited until their last evening to speak his piece. He must have foreseen Jacob's reaction, and his unwillingness to hear the words.

Jacob's large heart and open mind only extended as far as her own family and their eccentricities.

"Yer ma woulda been proud on t'is day," the old priest said, as a young woman served their meal in the old cathedral dining hall. "She loved ye so. As did yer pa, though it may seem the opposite."

"I miss her," Jacob replied with a wistful smile. "She had peculiar ideas, but she was a good mother." He said nothing about his father. Some wounds ran too deep.

"Not so peculiar as all tha', lad," Father O'Connor replied. His eyes twinkled. "Yer ah th' age now where I'm permitted to share some stories wit ye. Stories yer ma held close to her heart, God rest her soul."

"I would love to hear her stories," Amelia said. Jacob spoke so little of his mother, or siblings. Their father's crime had never healed in Jacob's heart. "I wish I could've known her."

"A charming and brilliant lassie, aye," the priest responded. Jacob tensed beside her, but she slipped her hand through his, showing him he was safe, here, now. "And a Quinlan. Tha' word mean anything to ye, lad?"

Jacob shook his head. Amelia sensed his growing discomfort. She wanted to be his champion and end this conversation politely, but detected they were on the verge of something terribly important.

"Ye are a Quinlan too, son. A draoi, as we sometimes refer to th' males, something of a rare occurrence. There's a prophecy—ach, now I get ahead of myself. All this, ye must wish to learn on yer own accord. With an open mind and heart."

Jacob stood abruptly, spilling the red wine all over the old, porous wood. The young girl rushed forward in a frenzy to clean the spill. "We've all had too much to drink," he muttered, searching for his sport coat and tweed flat cap. Amelia quietly handed him both, her head circling over everything brought forth to them in only a few words... Quinlan... draoi... prophecy. She had so many questions!

"Aye, though nothing rare about tha'!" Father O'Connor

exclaimed, followed by a slap to the table and a guffaw of laughter. "My judgment is no' impaired, if tha's what yer suggestin', lad. There are words ye need to hear. Words yer ma insisted ye hear, and tha' I be a part of telling ye. Your being sent to New Orleans was no matter of chance, Jacob. Nor was yer meetin' this fine lass." He smiled and tipped his head in Amelia's direction. "Does not need to be tonight, if I've caught ye in a bad way. But soon."

Jacob's face went entirely pale and he was scoping out the nearest escape. After quick goodbyes, Amelia ran after him into the small courtyard facing the church.

"I know that must have been a lot all at once," she offered, heart racing.

"He's drunk," Jacob snapped, directing his quick anger at the night. "He loved my mother. And not in the way a priest loves his flock, I assure you."

Amelia had an entire accumulation of words loaded on her tongue, ready to toss his way in an attempt to both assuage and encourage. But all she could bring herself to say was, "Why don't we get some sleep? We have a long flight tomorrow."

And then Jacob had offered her a real smile—his smile, the very one he'd given her that day over ten years ago, when he greeted her in the campus pub—and she temporarily forgot her pressing need to unravel Father O'Connor's mysteries.

They'd been back not even two weeks, and her visions escalated to the point she could no longer escape them when she closed her eyes. In each, Cianán and Cerridwen moved through the centuries arm-in-arm, sometimes greeting one another for the first time in that lifetime, other times saying goodbye. But the increase in frequency was no coincidence, she was sure of it. Neither were Cianán's beautiful green eyes, so like Jacob's, or Cerridwen's white locks.

If only she could talk to Jacob about it... she never kept such things from him anymore. That had been one of many vows they made before they pledged their hands in marriage. But neither could she take the conversation to the level she needed. She couldn't just say, *Whatever Father O'Connor has to tell you, it's related to these visions I'm having. I'm* sure *of it!*

The shower switched off, and the glass door slid open. Her conversations, her fears, would have to wait. At present, her only desire was the comfort of her husband's arms and the promise of sleep.

Jacob's soft embrace swiftly faded to the comforting arms of Cianán, encircling her waist.

Nearby, a baby snored softly in a hand-made cradle, feet away from the crackling fire. Across the glen, the songs and chants of the Quinlans filled the air, as the melodies of Midsummer danced through space.

"What has you so upset?" Doran asked. He was Doran in this lifetime, and she was Nighean, though their memories of the origin days, of Cianán and Cerridwen, and their legend, were still present. For now.

"The goddess' words trouble me," Nighean admitted. When a small cry emerged from the cradle, she moved forward to hold her daughter, Eara. The babe's eyes dazzled her, a living reminder of the man who had given her half her life. But why now, after many dozens of lifetimes, were they permitted to have a child? Why only now, when their memories were fading and the next lifetime... the next...

"I am concerned as well," Doran agreed. He rose and joined her, smiling down at their child. "But she promises us that, though our next lifetime will see us with no memory of our past, we will find one another. I trust in the goddess."

"I trust as well!" Nighean exclaimed, settling Eara at her breast. "But Doran, how am I to wake in the next life not knowing I love

you? What if it is not the same? We awake each life with the memory of a hundred shared lifetimes, and this binds us. How shall that be when we have only the memory of the one we are in?"

It troubled Doran, not having the answers. She loathed putting him in such a position, but there was none else she could speak of these things with. "I know not," he admitted. "But we are still many lifetimes away from the one she talked about. That which will be our last, granting us eternal life, and a peace between our peoples."

"Ah, yes, opportune of her to gift us this news knowing we will forget it in the next life," Nighean laughed bitterly. Inside, she was angry at herself, for these feelings against the beloved goddess. She did not want to lash out. But the loss... oh, the loss of Doran! How could she bear knowing the next many lifetimes would be fraught with obstacles, worry, and pain?

Doran did not chide her for her outburst. Instead, he smiled, and brushed his hand over Eara's swash of black hair. "It will be worth it, in the end days," he sighed happily. "When we may live, you and I, with our daughter. To never age. And to do so knowing our sacrifice has brought forth peace." His kiss against her brow wrenched free the sobs in her chest. "I would wait a thousand lifetimes for this gift. A million."

"Síoraíocht, Mo mhíle stór," *Nighean whispered the words, his words, back to him. Eternity, my dearest.*

"Warms my chest to hear it from you," he replied. A small breeze moved through the glen, as the songs and chants grew to a low din. "We should rejoin the tribe."

A midwife appeared from the thicket of trees as if commanded, taking the infant from Nighean's arms. Nighean nodded, and took Doran's hand in hers.

"Remember," he whispered, as they returned to the celebrations, "the goddess said one of us would turn our back on the truth, when the time becomes right. Whoever this is, the other must take up the yoke for both, and see us forward to the path she has set for us."

Nighean nodded silently, hoping beyond hope that it would be Doran, her Cianán, who would be the strength when the time came.

JACOB SHOOK HER, AS THE VISION SLIPPED AWAY. "*BLANCA*, WAKE UP."

"I'm up," she grumbled. She hadn't wanted to wake, not this time. The visions were not only more frequent, but she felt more firmly rooted in them, as if she could not only see but hear and feel Cerridwen's thoughts and emotions. She, Amelia, ached with agony when thinking about leaving Cianán behind; of not remembering him.

"Another vision?"

Amelia nodded. She took a sip from the water glass on the gilt nightstand. "I can't sleep anymore without one."

Jacob's hand moved in a tender path up and down her back, as her heart rate slowed to normal and the rest of her surroundings grew solid. At times, the space between her visions and reality rode a blurry line. She feared looking at Jacob and seeing Cianán.

"I'm worried about you. You've never had visions like this before."

"They aren't harming me," she assured him. Outside, the steady rattle and hum of the cicadas in the live oaks continued to calm her. The evening breeze carried through the wispy curtains, filling her lungs. "But I don't think they'll stop until I address them."

Jacob's hand slowed its movement, but it remained fixed on her. "Father O'Connor. Right? That's what you're going to say? We need to talk to him?"

"Jacob, I have no idea what he is going to tell us," she hedged, "but wouldn't you at least like to—"

"No," he interrupted, firmly. In a swift move, he pulled her against his chest, sinking back down into the sheets. "He saved my life, and has been good to me. But the man is full of superstition, and stories of fairies and goddesses and all sorts of nonsense."

"But—"

"*Blanca*, you know I believe. I believe in your family. In you. I've seen things most would convince themselves were illusions. Honestly, I think most people would go insane!"

They both laughed, and she closed her eyes, riding the rise and fall of his chest.

"You wonder why it took me so long to consent to marrying you," she teased.

"Stubborn," he charged, planting a kiss atop her head. "I'm telling you, though, that I love you, and I have never, nor will I ever, deny the things I've witnessed as part of your life. You've made a believer out of me, *mi bruja blanca*. But I've only got room for one world of magic in this messed-up head of mine."

She wanted to play, to tease back. To respond with some lighthearted quip. To do so would be dishonest, though. "Jacob, I think the visions are related to whatever he has to say. They started after we broke up and they've grown increasingly intense since we got back together. I can't tell you what they mean. I have theories, but I'm trying not to entertain them too much, because I don't want to fall down the wrong rabbit holes. But when Father O'Connor was talking... it felt like... well, it felt familiar."

Jacob seemed to know better than to try to pacify her, or diminish the need behind her words. "Maybe there *is* something to it," he acknowledged with a ragged sigh. "I trust your instincts. I know I'm being difficult, and I can see it frustrates you, but this is one thing too many on the list right now. To know your family's dark secrets is enough. I'm not sure I can handle more darkness from mine."

"I understand." And she did. "But it doesn't have to be

darkness. For all the bumps in the road my family has seen, it's all been worth it. To be who we are."

"I certainly wouldn't change a thing about you." He winked, and nibbled her lower lip until she squirmed away giggling. "Let's face one thing at a time, *Blanca*. Okay? Let's get these rebel babies squared away and then see where things stand."

Amelia slowly nodded, grasping at once this was both progress and a stalemate. As long as the promise hung out there, unfulfilled, there would exist a space between the two of them.

She prayed it wouldn't grow.

9
AIDRIK

The town was small, and finding the old inn not challenging. But Aidrik was struck with the sense this was not a town at all, or, at least, not anymore. It reminded him of America's ghost towns: shells of their former self, no longer inhabited by anything other than dusty cobwebs and spirits of the past. The streets were empty of souls, yet littered with debris. Most of the buildings were missing windows and doors, and rogue weeds peeked around weathered sills, offering a glimpse of what now inhabited the structures. One street lamp lay bent, and crooked, against the roof of a pub. The others, it could be presumed, had long since fallen and become part of the foliage.

"This isn't right," Finn said quietly, as his eyes nervously scanned the village.

"It may not be wrong, though," Aidrik replied. The abandoned town could lend itself to an ambush. No witnesses. But it equally could indicate forethought to privacy for their meeting.

"Is that it?" Finn asked, pointing to Pub Bothwell. It was

the only building which appeared remotely habitable. At three stories, taller than the surrounding businesses, regular windows suggested the pub also served as traveler accommodations.

Aidrik nodded. "What are your senses telling you?" Earlier, he had explained to Finn the Senetat employed hawks for their bounty hunting. Their presence would signal an immediate retreat.

"Nothing," Finn replied, after a moment to consider. "At least, nowhere nearby. Forbia is calm."

A small consolation, but Aidrik suspected the Senetat would be more careful than to show their hand so easily to one who knew all their secrets.

As they approached the structure, Aidrik put his hand out, stopping Finn. "Let me go first," he commanded. "Keep Forbia at the perimeter. Have her keep watch, and if things do not go as intended, engage our backup plan."

Finn frowned, obviously concerned. Forbia had marginal success appealing to bears, or mountain lions. Especially after Aleksandr's takedown of the boar. However, Finn's loyal wolf pup might be the only thing that brought either of them out alive, and Aidrik would not discount her usefulness as an option.

"I need your confirmation," Aidrik urged. "I must know your judgment isn't compromised."

"I'm fine," Finn assured. Aidrik studied him closely, attempting to gauge the truth of his words. He realized they were as true as they could be, under the circumstances. "I've already sent the message to Forbia."

"Good."

Before Aidrik could plan his approach, a tall, lanky redheaded male exited the inn, followed by an even taller redheaded female. Both clearly Farværdig.

Without ceremony, they were ushered inside. Sitting in what would have been the main pub area were a dozen or so other Empyreans, all of whom looked up as Aidrik and Finn followed the two attendants. They wound back behind the empty bar, into a long hallway, and then were led up a narrow flight of stone stairs.

At the top, they moved to the end of another long, dark hallway. Doors on either side of the hall were closed, but there was a stark emptiness. No guests had stayed behind those thresholds for many years. Toward the end of a passageway, a small light spilled from under a door on the right, and it was through this door they were directed.

Aidrik turned back to acknowledge the two ushers, but they were already moving down the hallway toward the stairs. Finn's wide eyes darted around the dark hall, but Aidrik used his deeper senses to assess the situation. *One Empyrean inside. The rest downstairs.*

Aidrik entered first, but Finn was so close on his heels he worried the man might run into him. Once inside, they turned a quick corner, and the room became awash with the light they had glimpsed from the hall. Before them stood a stocky redhead, shorter than most of his race. He wore what looked like an old Roman centurion uniform, one that had seen its share of battle. An image of the current wearer ripping it off a dead soldier flashed across Aidrik's mind.

"Aidrik the Wise," the swaggering Empyrean declared, hands on hips. His face stretched into a large, but unreadable smile. Then, he shook his head slowly. "As I live and breathe."

"Agripin," Aidrik replied tersely.

"*Grand Duke* Agripin," he corrected, in a manner that was both courteous and condescending at once. "By the Grace of Emyr."

"Grand Duke," Aidrik conceded, through gritted teeth. "Allow me to introduce you to—"

"Finnegan, of the St. Andrews clan. Already got it covered," Agripin replied, that same, artificial grin lighting up his face. "I understand you're a real charmer with wildlife, Finn, is that right?"

Finn's expression went blank. Appropriately stifling his anger, rather than employing it. "Something like that," he muttered.

"Outstanding," Agripin said, the smile still plastered across his youthful, haughty face. "I'd suppose you've got some animal associates out checking the scenery, eh? Well, no need for that, halfling. I haven't brought any rogue beasts. I'm not after a bounty."

Aidrik winced at the word *halfling.* He had not counted on Agripin having information on them when they arrived. It meant Finn was already marked for death.

And they hadn't even started with the business of their visit.

"Then let's talk about what it is you do want," Finn said, stepping forward. Aidrik started to quell Finn's assertive manner, which was not part of the plan, but Finn didn't notice the gesture. "Because I'm tired of wondering whether this is an ambush, or if you share our beliefs and might actually help us."

Agripin tilted his head to the side. His ruddy hair resembled rogue sparks in the light. "I may like you yet. Not so shrewd with your words like Mr. Wise here. I loathe trying to guess what others are thinking, don't you?"

Finn glared in response.

Aidrik eyed them both, realizing Finn's approach might be better-suited for the occasion.

"Allow me to conquer the suspense then," Agripin said, gesturing for them to both take a seat. He relaxed in an old, rotting green recliner before the two chairs Finn and Aidrik sunk into. "Yes, I identify with the Runean cause, though that word is a slur invented by the Senetat. I prefer another title, though let's not get ahead of ourselves. The Senetat outlived its usefulness many, many years ago, and if my father was not such an insipid imbecile, we might be a better race than we are today."

The duke reached for a bottle of whiskey, and drained it in one noisy gulp. It reminded Aidrik of Nicolas. "Like you, Aidrik the Wise, I removed my mark. Unlike you, the Senetat knows exactly what I've done. They're far from pleased about it, but they know better than to attempt to dispose of me. The royal family's existence provides the illusion of a balance in power, and we represent a time when the Senetat wasn't needed. They can't touch me, and they know it."

"This explains the lack of silver in your hair," Aidrik mused. "What of your father, the emperor? And your siblings?"

"My father nears the end of his reign," Agripin explained. He lifted one leg over the arm of the chair, flaunting a rather large codpiece. Finn's eyebrows rose in Aidrik's peripheral. "I expect them to activate him soon, but the reason they haven't is me. The crown will come my direction, as his eldest offspring, and the Empyreans would frenzy if they tried to pass me over in favor of Oriana or Nerys. You know how we love tradition. Nearly as much as Children of Men do."

"So, what, they think you might change your mind? Come back to the dark side?" Finn pressed.

Agripin shrugged, spinning the narrow glass bottle around in his hand. "Who knows? For now, I'm only a quiet threat. No one outside the Senetat and my father knows I've severed the mark from my being—well no one except you two now, and, of course, if you ever tell a soul I'll murder you both in your sleep. They believe I'm merely selfish, trying to save my life. If they thought I was mad enough to start a revolution, I'm quite sure we wouldn't be having this meeting."

"Indeed," Aidrik agreed. He relaxed slightly. The danger hadn't entirely departed, but he did not sense anything other than defiant arrogance in Agripin. "How long ago did you sunder your mark?"

"The day the first silver strand appeared on my head," Agripin said boldly. "I ripped it from my scalp, then took my father's sword and sliced the mark off."

"I'd like to see the scar," Finn said, once again surprising Aidrik. "Assurance your story is true."

Agripin winked at Finn, then said, "You want to see my arse, then?"

A blush spread across Finn's face. Aidrik leaned in. "That won't be necessary. But if you are, as you say, considering a revolution, why haven't you begun already?"

Agripin gestured to the austere, rotting room around him. "A rebel can't just traipse around in the open, living as he pleases. They meet in dusty, rundown pubs in towns long abandoned, such as the one we sit in now. This may suit you fine, old friend, but I'm rather put out by the accommodations."

"It's not the palace," Aidrik agreed. "But I daresay if a leader from the royal family took charge of this revolution, you wouldn't be living in abysmal conditions for long."

"Perhaps. Perhaps not," Agripin replied. He dropped his leg, and his foot hit the wooden floor with a heavy thud. A cloud of dust spiraled in the musty air. "But have you ever *tried* managing a band of disorganized rebels? No? Well, I don't recommend it."

"That's why they need a leader!" Finn protested. "That's been their problem all along."

Agripin chuckled good-naturedly. He then pulled out

another bottle of liquor, from inside the seat cushion. “And what do you know about it, with your twenty-seven years behind you? I do love your idealism, halfling. I really would like to see the world through your eyes someday.” He uncapped the bottle, tossing the metal lid aside, then stuck out his tongue, receiving a waterfall of booze. “Now that I no longer have the mark, what really do I have motivating me to give up everything I have?”

“What about your wife and children?” Finn asked.

Agripin scoffed. “What of them? They don’t exist.”

“You care nothing for our race, then? Our people?” Aidrik queried.

“I care enough that I’m not collecting a bounty on your head,” Agripin retorted. “Or his,” he thumbed at Finn. “Or his pretty wife, and your beautiful vagabond son.”

Finn gasped. Aidrik pressed a firm hand against his leg. *Careful.*

“Yes, of course I know about these things. Do you really think I’d have agreed to meet you blindly?” Agripin challenged. He stood, moving toward a window. As he leaned against the frame, he looked out toward the empty street. “There are some who live without knowledge of the Senetat. But even if we convinced them to rise in our cause, it would do us no good without pulling resources from those controlled by the mark. Unless you’re a master at large-scale diversions, I cannot see how to accomplish that without raising suspicions.”

Aidrik conceded his point. If large numbers of Empyreans began to vanish from the Senetat’s purview, it certainly would be a cause for alarm. “Could we not do it while they are still under control?”

Finn spoke up. “But... what if they were caught? The Senetat would activate them. They would all die.”

“Your halfling conscience is touching. You might be scarred

for life to know your companion here could care less about the collateral damage," Agripin accused. "All for the greater good, right Mr. Wise?"

"Stop calling me that," Aidrik griped. "And caring is irrelevant. If we do not move fast, they could annihilate the entire race, not only the rebels."

Agripin laughed with a flippant head toss. "Their power means nothing without a race to lord it over. They wouldn't go that far. They might make some examples, however."

Aidrik tensed his jaw; this wordplay was going nowhere productive. "What do you suggest, then?"

Agripin shifted his focus back to the two men. "I agreed to meet you because, once, we were friends. And a sliver of me would genuinely grieve if they discovered your ruse and disposed of you. You should back off these ridiculous plans, and focus instead on self-preservation. As bizarre as the notion is to me, you're a father now."

"That's why we're here," Finn interjected. "We don't want our son to grow up living in fear."

"He can either grow in fear, or die in it," Agripin said simply. "The choice is yours."

"This plan will not work without your involvement," Aidrik replied.

"It likely won't work with it, either," Agripin countered. "We have no connections on the inside, and—"

"Your father is the emperor!" Finn declared.

"My *father* would be the first to put me against the wall if I threatened his power or authority in any way!" Agripin nearly yelled. Aidrik saw his old friend begin to lose his sacred control. "My *father* very nearly had me executed when I removed the mark. Would you like to know why he didn't? Not out of love, I assure you. He worried his admiration would suffer."

Aidrik could not find it in himself to feel sorry for this spoiled, entitled being. "You said your father is near Ascension. Activation. Why not use him as the diversion?"

Both Finn and Agripin whipped their heads toward him. "What?" they asked, in unison.

Aidrik's mind had been working on this solution. Convincing Agripin would be no simple matter. "Put out the intelligence that it is your father, not you, stirring the rebels. Outwardly portray the guise of dutiful son, and heir apparent. Be ready when they activate your father, to step into his role. Beginning a new regime."

Agripin blinked, mouth agape. "You would have me send my father to his death?"

"Didn't you say he nearly did the same to you?" Finn pressed, mildly. Aidrik recognized Finn had the sympathy for Agripin that he himself could not find.

"I'm proud of not being like him," Agripin replied, once again diverting his gaze outside. "I can sleep at night, knowing I'm better."

"And you can sleep at night with the knowledge you're turning your back on your people," Finn challenged. "Sounds completely illogical."

"Leave," Agripin said. His tone and demeanor conveyed the finality in his words. "The conversation is over."

Finn looked at Aidrik for guidance. Aidrik nodded, then motioned for Finn to depart.

NEITHER FELT COMFORTABLE SPEAKING AS THEY WALKED DOWN THE abandoned streets. Far from the haunted village, they found words again.

"It wasn't a trap, I guess, but it wasn't useful, either," Finn said. Forbia trailed behind, keeping guard.

"I disagree," Aidrik replied. His hand moved instinctively to Ulfberht as he sensed an animal nearby. Supper. Finn perked up as well, and pointed to the left.

"How do you figure? He's a spoiled brat who would rather live off the fat of the land than lift a finger to improve things," Finn whispered, as Aidrik motioned for the man to draw his bow.

"Agripin is all of those things, yes. But he is also honorable. His outward objections are a mirror of what he weighs within. He heard our arguments."

Finn slowly drew back the bow, brows tensed. As he sighted on the deer, he whispered, "Forgive me. This is to sustain my wife and son," and then released. The arrow hit the deer square in the heart, ending the pain immediately.

As they moved toward their kill, Aidrik added, "I cannot predict the final outcome, but I don't believe all is lost."

"Were the two of you really old friends? You never mentioned that."

Aidrik nodded. "Aye. We fought in the Second Runean War together. Both of us with enough youthful naiveté to believe what we did was right. We both walked away jaded and determined never to fight for this cause again."

Finn hoisted the deer to his shoulders, and they turned back toward the grove. "There's a storm coming. We may need to find a better place to stay. One with an intact roof."

"Aye," Aidrik agreed. "I scouted another abandoned estate several miles from us. Little to no damage. We will retreat there this eve."

"What about Agripin? How will he know where to find us?"

Aidrik smiled wryly. "After meeting Agripin, do you really doubt his ability to find us?"

10

NICOLAS

Nicolas was having the most amazing dream!

Anasofiya stood against the glowing bark of an alder tree, amongst a grove of similarly vibrant hues. She wore a brilliant green cloak, hood pulled up to frame her intense gaze nestled between waves of dazzling crimson hair. In all their years together, from climbing trees to sharing secrets, he'd never seen her look so radiant.

When she spotted him, her sapphire eyes widened and she smiled. "Took you long enough," she purred.

"I'm not exactly steering this ship, sweetheart," he retorted, but took her into his arms, pressing her face to his chest with one firm hand. "Dammit, Ana, it's been months."

"I know," she acknowledged, breaking the embrace. Her face was ethereal… nearly preternatural. The same effect Mercy once had on him, when she stood before him on Deschanel Island's shore. "It wasn't safe to contact you sooner. And it wasn't safe for Finn's family. Aidrik got all bent out of shape about me contacting you now, even, but I don't have much of a choice. No, don't ask. One day I'll tell you all of it, I promise, but I have so little time now and there's something very important I need to ask of you."

The air shimmered around them in this reverse nested vision. He wondered, briefly, at Ana's powers. All at once, Nicolas realized the shimmering was coming from *her*.

"Anything, you know that," he replied, unable to take his eyes off her.

"My son, Aleksandr." Her son. Acknowledgement, finally, of the birth. "Aleksandr Nicolas St. Andrews Deschanel," she continued with a smile.

"Nicolas!" he exclaimed. "Well, shit." She could have given him her father's name, or Finn's father. Or even Aidrik's. But she'd chosen him.

"Yes," she said, smiling.

"Tell me about him," Nicolas insisted. "Jesus, Ana, you're a fucking *mom* now. Even a year ago, we would have laughed our asses off at the thought of it."

Ana smiled as she drew in a light sigh. The leaves around her swirled into a pattern before her, and the air, again, twinkled. "Seriously!" she laughed. He joined her. "Being a mother has added a layer of meaning to my life that.... ahh, you don't want to hear about my maternal sentiments. When you meet him, you'll understand."

"Well, then you need to kick those assholes out of Farjhem, and get your shit straight, so I can."

"Aidrik is meeting with Agripin today, and hopefully they'll come back with a plan." She pulled her hood down, and now Nicolas could see beyond the shimmer, to the darkness, a halo of it, which surrounded her. Around her, but there was also a distinct sense of it being *separate*. "Aleksandr isn't safe with us."

The tears glistening at her lash line were enough to gut him. He wanted desperately to reach out and hold her, reassure her, the only woman he'd ever been able to do so with. But something about her inexplicably terrified him. As if to touch her would scorch him, from the inside out.

"He's welcome at *Ophélie*, of course," Nicolas assured her. "You know that. He's my heir, after all. I'll protect him beyond whatever Aidrik's ward already offers."

"More than protection, I want you to *guide* him, Nic. Teach him about who we are, so he doesn't lose what little human influence he possesses. I'm afraid the world we've brought him into will take that from him."

"I'd make a terrible teacher!" Nicolas returned, but the look on her face sobered him. "Okay. Of course, I'll guide him. Shit, Ana, what the hell is going on with you?"

"I can't bear to part with him. I can't, but I have to, for his sake. And if something happens to me—"

"Don't even say that. I will destroy this world and rip it from its axis before I let anything happen to you."

"You and words. You never have a shortage of them," she teased, leaning back against the bark. "I can't stay. The longer I'm here, the more vulnerable all of us are. And you, there. I only wanted you to know Aleksandr will be on his way to you soon, and he'll need you."

"I'll never have my own children, Muffins, you know that. Aleksandr is the closest I'll ever have to a son, and I'll treat him as if he was mine. You have my word."

The tears that pooled under her lids spilled forth. "I love you."

Three decades of love, lust, and frustration boiled up within him at those words, but when he went to return them, she was gone.

• • •

He should wake Mercy to share the news. Instead, he descended to the second floor of the mansion and entered the gallery, where he could see the muddy river beyond the high rise of the levee.

The sky was alive with crackles of light. A storm was coming, but he'd tolerate the entire heavens pouring down upon him, so great was his distraction.

Nicolas wasn't alone. Amelia leaned forth over the columned railing, her ghostly hair spilling down into the night.

"This is my spot," Nicolas grumbled, but he sidled in next to her.

"It's a good spot," she agreed, slipping her arm through his. Her head fell lightly on his shoulder and he allowed it, his mind full of visions on how his Ana had changed.

"Ana came to me tonight," he confessed in a rush. He wasn't sure why he said it. "She's sending her son to me. Aleksandr."

Amelia backed away, leaning against the white rail. "Her son... wow, so everything went okay. I was worried."

Nicolas nodded. "We all were."

"And coming here? At least that answers some questions about what comes next. What about the other children?"

Nicolas mentally smacked himself. Until the words were out of Amelia's mouth, he'd entirely forgotten, in his excitement at seeing Ana again, to ask about Aidrik's plans. "She didn't say." *Because I didn't fucking ask. Dumbass.* "She didn't have much time."

"Things are starting, Nic. All of our efforts are finally going to be realized."

He turned back toward the river, watching a long, flat oil barge navigate slowly toward the port a mile downriver. "Yeah."

"This is what you wanted, right? Most of this was your idea."

"Amelia, I came out here for some quiet, not to dissect the bullshit."

She stepped in front of him. "I'm not Mercy. I'm not my mother. I'm not gonna force you into uncomfortable intimacy."

Her words made Nicolas miss Ana all the more. Their long talks about nothing, railing against the family establishment and the expectations they were born into. But she was not Ana, and the ease of his youth was quickly fading to memory.

"You're right, I'm not Ana either," Amelia said quietly. "Sorry, your guard was down. I didn't mean to pry."

Nicolas laughed. The sound was ugly and foreign at this early hour, when all but they and the river slept. "You really wanna know? Yeah, this was my idea, for the most part. I got a wild hair up my ass, decided it would be fun to play the good guy, the hero for once, and then by the time my head was clear I realized I'd acted impulsively. But even if I could back down from this, I won't, because this isn't about Mercy, or Aidrik. It's about all of us. Motherfucking fate and shit."

"Motherfucking fate and shit," Amelia repeated, musing. "Poignant. And you're right. Hell, maybe I should have dragged Jacob out here. He could have used your speech more than me."

"He's having second thoughts about being here with us lunatics?"

"Not about that." She wrapped her shawl tighter as a light breeze passed through the muggy air. "When we were in Ireland, an old family acquaintance dropped some news on him, about his heritage. He basically dismissed the revelation, and won't talk about it."

"Let the man have his peace," Nicolas replied. "It probably gives him some sort of fucked up comfort to know you're the only weirdo in the relationship."

"Hey!"

Nicolas shrugged. "You think you're helping by pushing him to figure shit out, but you're not. Trust me. You're only going to push him away." His mind traveled to Mercy, lying alone in the bedroom. Giving him all the space he needed, but wouldn't formally ask for.

Amelia smiled from her peripheral, shaking her head. "Look at you giving relationship advice."

"Eh, it's not rocket science. Men are easy to figure out. Feed us, fuck us, and pretend to enjoy a Saints game from time-to-time. The rest is noise."

"Everything will work out," Amelia said after a comfortable pause. "This is a new era for the Deschanels. Now that we know who we are, where we come from… there's no going back. We either embrace it or drown in it."

"I hate swimming," he said drily.

"Well, no wonder after your dad threw you in the Mississippi and told you to find your way to shore," she teased. "Anyway, look. What I was trying to suggest earlier is that I'm not the people you're trying to avoid. I'm happy to be your ally and, well, your friend. If you want me to listen, I can listen. If you want to share a bottle of that Hennessy tucked into the chair over there with me, I'll do that as well, and I won't even piss on your parade with talk about how you don't need alcohol to get through this."

Amelia planted a kiss against his cheek before she walked back toward the double doors. "We'll get through this. 'The strong shall rise again,' is our family motto. Probably for good reason. This isn't about our parents anymore; it's about us, and what we can do. Maybe this is our hour to shine."

"I guess we'll find out," he murmured through a smile as she disappeared.

11
AGRIPIN

"How many different ways can I hint that we're out of whiskey?" Agripin thundered down the dark hallway. The sound of Empyreans scrambling behind the bar, fighting for who would take the bottles to their master, made him smile, pleased their oversight was being handled. His satisfaction was tempered only by the fact that no one had the balls to stand up to him. To tell him to get his own damn whiskey.

It had been like this his whole life. The oldest child and only son of Emperor Aeron was groomed to be a ruler since the precipitous day of his birth. Had he a need, it was always met. Promptly. While Agripin occasionally lamented never knowing the gratification of a day's labor, he wouldn't have changed his circumstances, either.

His sister, Oriana, reveled in the lifestyle. She never left the palace, instead choosing to have any amusement she could imagine delivered to her. Mostly, this consisted of men and women, humans who were not exactly slaves but weren't allowed to leave, either. Her illusions had grown to such heights that Agripin was no longer sure Oriana understood fabrication from reality.

Agripin's other, younger sister, Nerys, longed to be a warrior. As a fledgling, she brandished anything she could find as a weapon, and studied all the great battles at length, both Empyrean and man. Nerys alone might be moved to his cause, though he'd never known her well enough to understand the truth of her heart. Siblings meant little to Empyreans. Men placed greater stock in family.

Several younger Empyreans rushed in, arms full of Jameson. The halfling, Finn, thought Agripin was a lush. Lacking knowledge of the Empyrean metabolism, he'd no clue Agripin processed his liquor significantly faster than he would have liked. Even his long, greedy gulps didn't make him near as drunk as he wished.

His mind wandered to Aanya. Beautiful, kind Aanya, with the maternal face and bashful gazes. *Bloodlines are not strong enough,* his father had decreed, ending any conversation on the matter. Underscoring her lack of suitability further, she was sent away from Farjhem, before Aeron's son could do anything foolish.

With practiced theater, Agripin opened two bottles at once, letting the hot, burning liquid pour down his throat in tandem waterfalls. Drunk, if only for a moment.

Had he loved Aanya? Agripin didn't understand the nature of romantic love. It seemed risky, foolish, and altogether unpleasant. But he had wanted her, and as with everything else meaningful he wanted, his father found a way to keep her from him.

His buzz passed quickly, as usual. Disappointed, he smashed one bottle errantly against the stone hearth, then sunk into his chair with a disgusted sigh. The conversation with Aidrik and his halfling tormented him.

They would dare accuse him of not caring! Agripin chuckled, finally admitting it was not far from the truth. He cared about a great deal, but lacked the desire to put his neck on the line. He was not so blind to himself that he couldn't admit this. He didn't see it as a fault, but rather the backbone of his survival.

He enjoyed the look of shock on both their faces as he revealed how much he knew of them. Even from his old friend, Agripin had kept the secret that he could breach the barriers of a telepathic block. No matter what defenses a person put up, Agripin could break them down. He could read any thought, as long as the target was in the vicinity. It was how he knew Aidrik and Finn's intentions were pure. And why he didn't kill them.

Was it time to call the Brotherhood? They'd be shocked to hear Aidrik lived. Even more, that the pacifist nomad was trying to stir a war with a couple of halflings.

No, he decided. Not just yet.

Closing his eyes, Agripin conjured up all he had seen in his mind's eye. Beyond Aidrik and Finn, there was the boy, Aleksandr. A very strong Farværdig, whose full strengths would not be realized until he hit maturity. And the once halfling, now something more, Anasofiya. Locked into some sort of arrangement with both Aidrik and Finn. Very progressive for a Child of Man, he had to admit.

It was Anasofiya who gave him pause. Her intense, thoughtful face. Searching eyes.

How much did these men love her? Would they be willing to bargain with her, as the price of his soldiering?

12
AMELIA

Two days came and went. Never had time weighed so heavy, so anxious-ridden, than the days since they'd been given news Aleksandr was on his way. The house buzzed with activity and conversation, as if preparing to host the parish cotillion.

Amelia couldn't fault Nicolas for how little information he'd obtained during Ana's nested vision with him, but it sure would have been nice to know if they had days, weeks, or months. The energy at *Ophélie* held the undercurrent belief he could, and would, arrive any minute.

Harriett, their strongest seer, ceased speaking again. Something in her visions deeply troubled her, enough to steal her voice. Tristan was beside himself with this unfortunate return to her old comfort.

Amelia stood at the center of whirring activity, observing her cousins. Anne directed one of the kitchen maids on which fine china should be stored and which brought down for daily use. Jasper suggested practically that all the fine oriental carpets and the true heirlooms—those artifacts which had traveled with Charles Deschanel I from France in the early 19th century—also be stored in the attic, because one could never be too careful when strange children were afoot. In the study, Mercy clickety-clacked away on Nicolas' laptop, documenting all she knew of Empyrean history, both what the Scholars had taught, and what she'd learned once free of them. Oz was here today, too, out back with the assessors. Colleen advised Condoleezza on the appropriate menus for youth who had lived across the world, discussing regional dishes that might be savored by all.

This last should have been Amelia's job. She was now the self-nominated woman of the household, and this meant directing such activities.

But this letter. This damnable letter.

She hadn't shared it with Jacob. Not for any intentional deception, but thankfully he'd run into town to pick up some paperwork from the Loyola laboratory, his old place of employment, and so she was left to process the contents alone.

It was addressed to Amelia at *Ophélie*, from a woman named Nora Quinlan. There was that name again, Quinlan, and it was written to Amelia's attention, not Jacob's. That exclusion was curious to her, before she even read the handwritten missive.

Dearest Amelia,

You may not remember me. I last saw you when you were but four, and climbing the knobby trees in your parents' garden. It's equally unlikely your father, my brother, mentioned me, but he was raised in our father, Kellan's, shadow, whereas my sisters and I blossomed under the knowledge of who we really were. Deirdre, our mother and your grandmother, is a woman I hope you'll meet soon enough.

So many stories to tell you! But they are not for this letter.

Your great-great uncle Flynn, whom Jacob knows as Father O'Connor, is deeply concerned Jacob has not come around yet. We understand his hesitation, as well as his history. We all played a part in it. But we had hoped, given his exposure to your abilities and family, he would come to us with a more open mind. From here in Ireland, we can only pray he is slowly warming to the knowledge, as we cannot see the thoughts of a draoi.

Amelia, for many years we have sat dormant, content to give blessings to the goddess and meditate on the future coming together. Now, the future is upon us, and time is no longer something we can ignore. Jacob must find it within himself to learn his truth. You, also, must do the same. Your history is far richer than the one you've been raised to believe.

Please understand, reaching out was never in the plan. The prophecy is clear on the two of you coming together on your own accord. And you have come together, thank Morrigan! But you have not come to us, and that deeply concerns me.

Apologies for the vagueness of this letter. There is only so much I can safely say on paper. The rest, so much more, I save for the day you and Jacob come to us with open hearts and minds, to learn your truths. On a more personal, selfish note, I also long to know my beautiful niece.

Yours in the goddess' peace,

Aunt Nora

Safely in their suite, Amelia read the words again. *Your great-great uncle Flynn.* Her uncle... Father O'Connor, Jacob's old friend and savior, was *her* uncle? She couldn't wrap her mind around the possibility.

Or this Aunt Nora, a name she'd heard in brief passing as if she belonged to another life. The only thing Amelia knew about her father's people was the small nuggets he'd shared: Noah had three older sisters, but his memory of them was scarce because when he was very little, his father left their mother in Ireland and took Noah with him to New Orleans. Noah was told almost nothing about his mother, Deirdre, or his sisters. As adults, they'd exchanged a handful of letters. They existed in two different worlds... no regret or sadness about it, just the reality given them.

Amelia didn't remember Aunt Nora visiting them at The Gardens. Truly, she couldn't have called any of her aunts by name before this strange reminder, as she'd come to think of them as "Dad's three sisters."

As Amelia's visions began to take greater form, they were beginning to intersect with the real, contemporary world around them. Her story, Jacob's story, they were intertwined beyond the chance of their decade-long love affair. There was more, so much more, and the answers were out there. The loom had begun to weave, and soon a clear tapestry would form.

But not if Jacob continued to hide from an uncomfortable truth.

If Colleen Deschanel had taught her daughter anything, it was that hiding from the truth would do nothing but make it harder to accept. They must face these facts head-on, come what may. And Jacob had proven, time and time again over his troubled life, that he was better at this than anyone, when he needed to be.

I really ought to go downstairs, and participate. Lead and guide them, as I insisted I wanted to do. We have so much to do, things more urgent, maybe, than anything going on in my own world.

But are they? More urgent?

Amelia understood she couldn't address either concern with her mind so heavy. She closed her eyes, and prayed for at least thirty minutes of peace.

• • •

She awoke to the wide eyes and grinning face of her cousin Markus. When her own lids opened, he batted his eyelashes and pushed his face to hers, causing her to jump and smack her head against the rosewood half-tester bedframe.

"Markus, what the hell?"

"Sleeping on the job," he accused lightly. "Is this what businessmen call working smarter, not harder?"

"Only closing my eyes for a moment," she defended, pulling herself to a sitting position. "Did you need something?"

"The workers finished carrying the antiques to the attic. Jasper asked me to come see if you had anything else you felt merited storing. I could come back after your beauty sleep has time to fully bake. There are still some lines around your eyes."

"Hush." Glancing at the clock, only twenty minutes had passed, but she felt better already. "You two are ridiculous, you know, hiding all the fine furnishings from the children."

Markus set his mouth in a firm line. "You can never be too careful."

"Mark, they're here for our protection, not our gold."

"Spoken like a true Uptown girl with no fear of the world around her," he teased. "Spend a couple decades in D.C. and you'll have a healthy skepticism, too."

"My skepticism is finely intact, thank you. To answer your question, no. You've sent plenty to the attic. We still need chairs to sit on and table to eat at."

"Fine. That's not really why I came up, anyway."

"What's going on?"

His eyes lit up as he leaned toward her. "Aleksandr."

"I can't wait to meet him either." She smiled, but it quickly faded. "Oh, *I* know where your head is at. Your research, right? Aleksandr is our blood, and these other children may share our blood, too. But even if they don't, we are not experimenting on them!"

Markus smirked. "You have such a high opinion of me. I don't want to cut into them, Amelia, shit. Actually, I do, but it's beside the point because I won't. I'm not entirely without ethics."

"Not entirely?"

"You can learn a lot without slicing into someone."

"I agree. Much more can be gleaned from understanding a person's unique experiences. You can't get that from looking at brain tissue under a microscope."

"Said the therapist."

"You can call me doctor, now. The paperwork came in a few weeks ago."

"Dr. Donnelly," Markus grinned. "Or is it Dr. Jameson?"

"I haven't formally taken Jacob's name yet. There hasn't been time."

Markus slid off the bed and moved toward the teak refreshment table across the room. He poured a glass of water from the warm pitcher. "You're testy. Everything okay?" He put his hand up. "That wasn't an invitation for you to pour your heart out for the next four hours. The basics are fine."

Amelia shot him the expected glare, and then said, "Jacob and I have our own stuff going on, separate of all this." She gestured toward the door, and the activities beyond. "Not problems between us or anything like that. But issues that might be important."

"Heavy," Markus replied. His eyebrow lifted. "Is that why you're still clutching that piece of paper?"

Amelia glanced down at the crumpled letter clenched in her fist. She hadn't realized. "Yes... and I guess what I'm saying is, I might not be able to help you with this research, Mark. Jacob and I might be going on a trip." She braced herself for the inevitable judgment.

Instead, he looked disappointed. "You gotta do what you

gotta do," he said. "And you're clearly too distracted to do what needs to be done here. Maybe we have time. The Curse seems quiet for now. So, go. Take Jacob on this trip, figure your shit out. Find your zen or whatever. Obviously this needs to happen before you can move on, so do it."

Move on... if only Markus knew. Whatever they learned in Ireland, assuming she could convince Jacob to go, she was skeptical that there would be any *moving on.* Only moving forward, to whatever fate held for them.

"Yeah," she agreed. "The trick is convincing Jacob."

"Amelia, the man nearly signed his own death warrant out of love for you. You honestly think it's going to be hard to convince him to take a simple trip?"

If only things *were* simple.

But she wouldn't deceive Jacob. Not now or ever.

13
ANASOFIYA

"This is happening too quickly!" Ana exclaimed, pacing the stone floors as Aidrik stood before her to deliver the news. "And how the hell did you know they were coming? What else aren't you telling us?"

"I did not send for them," Aidrik replied evenly. His palms went up, in mild surrender. "We will inquire on their presence, but to do so necessitates returning to them."

"I can't just leave my son with this couple! I know nothing about them, Aidrik, nothing! You've never mentioned them, and there are far too many unknowns right now. No, I'll take Aleksandr myself."

"Out of the question. And I've known hundreds of Empyreans over my years, including Astrid and Birger. It would not be practical to regale you with tales on all of them."

Ana stopped. She tilted on the verge of hyperventilation. "Sometimes I hate your need to stay calm. You're suggesting we turn our son over to two beings I've never met, on the brink of a war where we don't know who are allies and who are enemies. Is nothing sacred to you?"

"You know the answer to your hypothetical question." Aidrik's demeanor did not budge, though a flash passed across his eyes. Fear. Of her? "Aleksandr is not safe here. We are in agreement on this, are we not? I cannot risk you or Finn being exposed in taking him to *Ophélie*. Astrid and Birger have been long respected amongst Runean leaders. It was a relief and a joy when they crossed our threshold."

"I'm so thrilled one of us can be filled with joy on the eve of saying goodbye to our child," she spat. Tears threatened, but they were not from sadness. The rage, the pure wrath building within her, began to escape. Aidrik's faint flinch showed he witnessed it, too.

"Twisting my words is beneath you," Aidrik replied. His calm resignation was maddening! "And your lack of confidence in my experience is beginning to wear thin. Have we really come this far, only for you to continue your assault on my intention?"

"Fuck you." Ana snatched her cloak from the broken table. "You've kept your secrets, Aidrik, and I've said little about it. I can see your thoughts spinning, and your conscious decision to keep your counsel, leaving us in the dark. Fine. You say we can trust these two? Fine again. Pissed off as I am at your heavy-handed methods, I still know you wouldn't send Aleksandr into the hands of the enemy."

Aidrik relaxed slightly. "Thank you."

"But it ends here. This very moment, Aidrik. You are *not* going to continue to treat us like children who must be tiptoed around. This isn't what either Finn or I signed up for."

He nodded in visible relief.

"And if anything happens to Aleksandr as a result of this decision," Ana finished, pulling her hood up, "you'll have a lot more to fear than my hatred."

. . .

Ana's foul mood partially slipped away as she stepped into the awkwardness of Finn attempting to entertain the venerable guests. She imagined him telling silly jokes, and them smiling politely in return, hiding their confusion.

Wary, Forbia walked cautious circles around the crew, waiting for direction.

Astrid and Birger really were a sight to behold. Ana didn't know if Empyreans had any visible age markers—especially Runeans, since they were not under the thumb of the Senetat—but it was readily evident they were older than Aidrik, and he'd walked the Earth for over four thousand years. How many times around the sun had these two seen?

Both had shocks of flaming red hair. Astrid's cascaded down her back in long, thick waves, broken up by woven braids. Birger's was cut close to his scalp, like a modern military man. Their clothes were practical. Both dressed in close-fitting leather pants and jerkin, covered by a serviceable traveling cloak. Astrid's longbow nearly stretched the length of her tall body, while Birger's sword—as majestic as Aidrik's Ulfberht—hung close to his side. They reminded Ana of the Silvan elves in Finn's beloved *Silmarillion.*

Their evigbond was apparent without explanation. It was also markedly ancient.

In the distance, Aleksandr sat on a fallen tree with a much younger Empyrean, in the animated discussions of youth. Astrid and Birger's daughter. Eydis, was it? Ana had been too worked up to retain much of the original introductions.

"I'm sorry for my coldness earlier," Ana apologized, extending a hand toward Birger. Instead, he moved to embrace her, and Astrid joined in.

"No remorse is required," Astrid said warmly, smiling down at her. She was a good head taller than Ana. "Aleksandr is your son, and you are rightfully protective of his well-being. As a mother, I understand."

Ana returned the smile. "I might feel more at ease if I knew a bit about you and your mate. Birger, right?"

Birger nodded, followed by a half-bow. "I assume Aidrik has told you that those of us living away from the Senetat are spread across the Earth? Some of us have assumed the yoke of leadership. Runeans, the Senetat calls us, but we go by another name."

"What is that?" Finn asked, as he sidled in beside Ana.

"Soon, we will share more," Astrid explained. "Such discussion will be better suited, once Aleksandr and Eydis are delivered safely."

"Aidrik's told us nothing," Ana answered the earlier question. She tried to keep the bitterness out of her words, as she didn't want to reveal the rift growing in their small circle. "You're welcome to start at the beginning."

Aidrik cut in. "I've said nothing because I know nothing. I'm aware of no secret organization among the Runeans. Is Agripin involved?"

"Now is not the time to teach you, nor am I the appropriate instructor for that lesson," Birger said amenably, gracefully dodging the question. "But I will tell you briefly about the life Astrid and I have built."

The gazes of all five adults traveled to where their children talked. On this, they were all united. A command from Finn, no doubt, finally settled Forbia at Aleksandr's feet.

"We have resided peacefully in Ireland since the early days, when it was known as Hibernia. The protection we offer to other like-minded Empyreans is as old as we are, and we built a tribe we've come to love. We've learned, over the years, to live in a symbiosis with select Children of Men, who understand we are more than human, but less than gods. They protect us, as much as we do them."

"Astounding," Aidrik mused. "Is this common?"

"No," Birger shook his head. "Not at all. Our setup is distinctive. We are also the only tribe who still maintains relations with the Quinlans."

"Who are the Quinlans?" Finn asked.

"And how is it that *you* do not know of the Quinlans, Finnegan?" Astrid challenged with a raised brow.

Birger's glance traveled between Aidrik and Finn, and then he shot his mate a warning look. Anasofiya noted it. "We live in peace and partnership. Not all of us live as thus, and not all of us are united, but we are happy in the society we've created."

"Happy enough we'd defend it to the death." Astrid's green eyes sparkled.

"We can say no more, though. He will come to you, I am sure, and he'll explain it all," Birger concluded.

"He?" Finn tried, but this was another inquiry that would go unanswered.

"May I ask a more personal question?" Ana ventured, as her eyes again settled on the young beauty visiting with her son.

"Of course," they replied in unison.

"I don't know your exact age, but obviously you've been around many, many years. Your daughter is only a babe by your standards. How is it you waited so long to have your only child?"

A look passed between the mates. "At first, our instability bred fear. Then we found solid footing, but Emyr didn't deem it our course to be parents." Astrid passed a quick thought to Ana. *Miscarriages. Many.* Ana nodded in empathy. "And then Eydis came along. A true blessing of Our Father."

"Her birth is what has stirred you to action," Aidrik deduced. "Why you've not done so before now."

"Aye," Birger confirmed. "Around the world, others of our ilk are experiencing similar miracles. It cannot be coincidence. Our Father is prompting us out of apathy, and into action."

Ana remembered Aidrik's words; that he had not sent for these two, nor known they were coming. "Who sent you to us?"

Astrid sighed. "Birger intercepted your thoughts to the halfling across the ocean. Not many have this skill, but with certainty, the Senetat has someone equally able. You really must be more careful, Ana."

Ana's heart dropped. On either side, her men experienced their own sagging regret. "So Nicolas is exposed? Is *Ophélie* no longer safe?"

"Once I detected the nested connection, I inserted interference to prevent others from doing the same. In your modern terms, you might call it message scrambling," Birger assured. "But this was a fortuitous catch. You can't risk it again."

"We have to tell Nicolas that Aleksandr and Eydis are on their way! I can't keep leaving him in the dark."

"Nicolas is safer this way," Aidrik replied. "He will gain no advantage with a timetable. You've already assured him things are happening."

"And we will tell him all he needs to know, when we arrive," Astrid promised. "He is doing us all a great favor, and we won't let him suffer in the dark, as you say."

"All?" Finn asked. "Are others sending their children then?"

"Soon," Birger replied, with a shrug suggesting his ambiguity was intentional.

"Aidrik," Astrid turned toward him, "who are you sending to assist with their training?"

"I'd hoped our meeting with Agripin would have borne more fruit. I expected him to have a resource for us."

"Oh dear." The mates exchanged looks once again. "You

cannot expect your Children of Men, halflings or no, to understand how to guide our youth," Astrid chided, then waved a hand toward the sky. "No matter. We will see to this as well."

"I thought they were being sent for protection," Finn pushed. Over the course of the discussion he'd grown increasingly tense, and Ana realized he was barely holding it together. Trying to be strong for her, too. "What training is needed?"

"A battle is looming," Birger said, looking to each of them individually before adding, "finally. We would seek to keep our offspring safe, but should it become necessary, we would not leave them vulnerable. They must learn to defend themselves."

"We have so much to tell you." Astrid shook her head. "So much! But first, the children to safety. The time has come to say your goodbyes."

AIDRIK WENT FIRST. INEXPLICABLY, HE ASKED TO SAY HIS FAREWELL TO Aleksei alone, and Ana could do nothing but agree. She needed the time to steel herself, so she could be strong for her son.

"This is right. He will be safe," Finn kept repeating, but the hollow sadness of his words muted the meaning, and in the end, his strength was nothing in the face of this loss.

What if this was the last time they ever saw their son? The last time they would observe his kind eyes and beautiful, boyish smile? To hear his slowly deepening voice share his thoughts on the world around him? *No, don't think it. Don't ever think it!*

When Aidrik was done, Aleksei wandered over to his parents in a daze, eyes rimmed with a red he tried to hide.

"Mora," he cried, and fell against Ana's chest, dissolving. The last of Finn's strength went with this gesture as he wrapped his strong arms around them, buckling with sobs.

"Aleksei." Ana's voice cracked, and her heart caved. "You are the greatest thing I've ever done."

"Mora, I can't go. Please don't make me. I'll learn anything, do anything. I won't get in the way!"

"Son, you're never in the way," Finn cried. "You could never be a burden. But you're not safe with us. You understand that, don't you?"

Aleksei nodded, sniffling. He refused to look at either of them, and this crushed Ana further. "If we had more time, I could show you what I'm capable of!"

Ana's breath caught at the tragic innocence, the utter sadness in these words. "Aleksei, you have so much more than any of us. In you is the best of us. This is what we're trying to protect. We'll never, ever leave you alone. I'm sending you to the only person in all the world, other than your fathers, who I trust without question. Nicolas is your godfather. His protection, and the ward Aidrik placed over his property, will keep you safe until we can come to you."

"Aidrik says we can't communicate with our thoughts." Aleksandr sniffled. Finn kissed his forehead as his own tears spilled. "How can I live without knowing you're okay? I can't do it!"

Ana pressed a trembling hand to her son's chest, drawing in a slow breath. "You know in your heart. You told me yourself, you can sense all three of us. You'll always know, Aleksei. Our love for you is too great to be contained and separated from you."

Finn stepped back, reaching behind his neck for something. *The crosses. My mother's and his mother's.* Finn re-linked the chains around Aleksandr as the young boy bowed his head.

"When I was forced away from your mora, I wore these close to my heart and kept her always with me. Keep them close to your heart, Aleksei, and know we're always with you."

Ana bit down on her tongue and pressed her toes deep in her boots, begging for courage. She couldn't lose it, not yet. Aleksei needed to see her strength and to draw power from it, before he faced his own unknown.

"Thank you, Far," Aleksei wept. He threw his arms around Finn's neck, and the two embraced each other in a mess of vigor and tears.

Astrid and Birger nodded in the distance. Ana wiped at her eyes and took her own turn embracing Aleksandr. *Strength. Your darkness. Draw upon it now, as you have so many times in the past months.* "Be strong, my darling boy. I love you."

"We will see you before you know it," Finn added, joining them in their final embrace.

As evening fell on their first night without their son, Ana curled up near the fire, lost to her thoughts. Aidrik was dozing—which she knew to actually be meditation, and reflection—while Finn huddled around a book Aleksandr had left behind, Forbia pressed tightly against his back. For all the hopelessness of their situation, she couldn't help feeling heartened knowing her son was on the way to safety. *Safe for how long, though?*

Ana began to doze herself, hypnotized by shadows of flames dancing against the old stone. There was a brief moment where she realized she'd passed from being awake to that of sleeping dreams, and then she was overcome with the sensation she was no longer in the castle at all. But she wasn't alone.

She stood in a meadow. Despite having fallen asleep in the darkness, everything around her was vibrant, full of color, and light. The grass a brilliant emerald, clothed in thick blankets of stark white daisies. The colors were unreal.

Standing before her was a man who reminded her somehow of several men, all at once. His smug stance had all the haughtiness of Nicolas, while his red hair, sticking up and sideways as if he recently exerted himself, reminded her of Aidrik. His smile was youthful, and welcoming, like Finn. The thick, defined muscles in his chest glistened, as if affected by whatever enhanced the colors around him. He was beautiful, and brash.

"This isn't a dream," she said quietly.

"Not the way you'd define it," he agreed. "You've spent enough time with Aidrik, you should know a mystic when you see one."

Ana studied the man; no, not man, an Empyrean. And a mystic, which was rare, even for their race. Aidrik told her mystics all manifested their powers differently. *Some can invoke dream suggestion,* he had said.

"Dream suggestion," she repeated, aloud. He nodded, smiling at her quick resolution to what her eyes were seeing.

"Aye! Very good. Especially since I doubt you've seen it before. Aidrik doesn't have that power. Or if he did, he was never imaginative enough to employ it. A dry fellow, that one."

Realization washed over her. This was precisely the man Finn had animatedly described upon his return. "Agripin," she guessed. "Why are you here?"

"I have to say, you're taking all the fun out of this surprise," Agripin said, with an intentionally dramatic frown. "You've denied me the rare opportunity to speak in riddles as a means of getting my point across."

"I was never very good at riddles."

"A shame," he replied. Stepping toward her, he held out one hand, nodding at her to take it. "Let's walk, shall we?"

Ana eyed his hand, with a rising dread and suspicion, but quickly reminded herself that what was happening right now might matter. Aidrik and Finn had returned without success. Yet, Agripin was here now. Appealing to *her*. Whatever passed here, in this dream suggestion, might dictate their entire future, for better or worse.

With this in mind, she took his hand.

"You didn't answer my question," she reminded him. His large, warm hand enveloped hers, squeezing enough to cause mild discomfort. "Why are you here?"

"I was hoping to get to know you first, before discussing business," Agripin replied, smiling at her from the side. "Tell me about yourself."

Ana stopped walking, jolting him to a stop with her. "Aidrik told me you know everything about us, so you should already know I'm not fond of small talk."

"My dear," Agripin said with an exasperated sigh, turning toward her. He laced his other hand through her untethered one. "It's no great matter for me to dive into your head and spend the day sifting through any memory I want. But I would rather hear it from you. Tell me what you love. What you hate. What you long for, but can't have."

"There's nothing complex about my answers. They won't surprise you," she argued. "I love my husband, and son, and Aidrik. I long to be able to enjoy my family, without the constant fear of losing them. I hate when people toy with me." With this last, she narrowed her eyes.

"You hate me as well. And you don't even know me," he challenged.

"Hate requires a lot of energy. I don't know you," she countered. "Annoyance would be more accurate. Tell me what you want, and we can both get back to what we were doing."

His eyes twinkled as his face spread into a large, brilliant smile. "You, my dear. I want you."

Ana wrenched her hands away, stepping back. "I'm not for

sale," she replied, through gritted teeth. "I want to go back. Release me."

But Agripin's smile didn't fade. "See? This is why I wanted to get to know you better first! Let me tell you a few things about me," he said, not missing a beat despite Ana's horrified expression. "I'm the only son of Emperor Aeron. He's a real pain in the ass, by the way. Nice, usually, but absolutely incapable of leading. I suppose that's why the Senetat loves him so much. By contrast, they hate me, because I am a *really* giant pain in the ass for anyone who tries to tell me what to do. I get that from my mother, who is, to no great sorrow of mine, no longer with us."

"I want to go back," Ana repeated, crossing her arms over her chest in a protective manner.

"I should have courted the Senetat better, because it would be far easier for me to have their support, but it was more work than I wanted to do. I have to give Aidrik some credit, here. He's right. I *should* be courting them. I should be giving them my obeisance on a big, gaudy platter. Because I will be emperor. Sooner, rather than later, if they trust I will do as they ask."

"What's your point?" Ana snapped.

"The first step in all of this is showing them I'm settling down. I'm done being an imp. Family means little to Empyreans, unless you're a royal, and then it means everything. A mate and child would do wonders toward restoring their faith in me. It would show I'm falling in line. Coming around to their delusions. Of course, I don't want a mate, or a child, so that complicates matters."

"Agripin—"

"I have no intentions of taking a mate. I only need them to *think* I have. I will craft a temporary illusion, long enough to gain the power we need to assume control."

"I have no idea what this has to do with me," Ana spat. But she did. The only thing she couldn't fathom was why.

"I need a mate, and a child. Temporarily. You can provide me with both."

Ana laughed, the sound resonating through the dream-grove in a harsh chorus. "I'm married, and evigbond to another. As duke, your options are completely unlimited. Your offer makes no sense!"

Agripin stepped closer to her. "You mistake my offer for fondness, my dear. Did you know there are already rumors of your existence? Of Aleksandr's? Claiming you as my own would create a dynamic not even the Senetat could challenge. It would be a rogue move, but it would set a precedent. And I would appease them through my agreeableness, solving several problems at once."

"But—" Ana stopped, not ready to share the secret he seemed unaware of: Aleksandr's escape. She pushed the thought far away.

"It may also be the only thing that saves your lives," he continued. "Not that I'm hugely invested in your futures, but I could use Aidrik's acumen in my cabinet. He's well-respected, or was before everyone thought he died a glorious death, and it will boost my popularity for our people to see representation from both the royal family and the Runeans," Agripin added thoughtfully, gazing upward.

"How would stealing Aidrik's evigbond and son help your cause?" Ana nearly shrieked. She was trapped in his dream suggestion, and couldn't leave until Agripin chose to release her. Walls closed in on her from all sides, suffocating her with this loss of control.

"You do know my siblings all have different mothers?" Agripin asked, as if Ana should know as much about him as he did her. "Monogamy is a wasted fixation on us. Even if our people knew you were bound to Aidrik, it would matter not at all. It's only Aidrik I need to convince."

Ana's eyes widened with understanding. "And you knew he wouldn't agree, so you thought you'd appeal to me. That maybe if I knew the threat against my son, I'd give in, and convince him it was the right thing to do."

"I really do think I could learn to like you," Agripin replied. "You think quickly on your toes, and aren't inclined to tell me what you think I want to hear. It's refreshing."

"You might be a sociopath," Ana said, still processing the conversation. He had, in all earnest, suggested she pose as his mate, his duchess, and then his empress. And for Aleksandr to pose as his son. "Wait, you're not suggesting putting my son on the throne after you?"

Agripin laughed. "I no longer bear a mark, my dear," he reminded her. "I won't die, unless someone decides to remedy that matter by their own hands. I don't *need* an heir. I only require the illusion of one, until things take their proper course."

"I'm going to repeat this, because I don't know yet whether I'm understanding your request," she said, slowly. "You want me to pose as your mate, mother of your son, and heir. You think this will lead the Senetat into thinking you're acquiescing to their ways. The fact that I'm halfling will appeal to the greater race by showing you are somehow... progressive?" Agripin nodded. "And you think that the Senetat will turn their head at this illegal slight because you're the emperor's son and they will see it as a small price to pay for your obedience?" He nodded again. "There's some twisted logic in all that, I guess. I still don't understand why it has to be me."

For a moment, Agripin's internal emotional tempest betrayed him, but he quickly righted himself. "I require Aidrik's obedience and partnership. I won't get it if the three of you die for your crimes. This move brings you close to me, and under my protection. It also helps me ensure Aidrik doesn't try anything unsavory."

Ana was positive there was more to his request than he was saying. It wasn't simply his momentary lapse of expression. His explanation only made sense in the abstract view, and there seemed better ways to appeal to the Senetat than by blatantly flaunting his disregard of their laws.

Ana also realized, with a sinking, defeated feeling, that they needed Agripin. Aidrik wouldn't have risked appealing to the cocky prince otherwise. By coming to her, he was giving them one opportunity to use his services. If she turned him away, they might not get this chance again. Worse, if what Agripin said was correct, they might already be in the mind's eye of the Senetat. Their days could be numbered.

"What if my son isn't with us anymore?" Ana ventured carefully. It would do no good to hide this, for he'd find out sooner rather than later.

Both eyebrows rose. "Well, then. No matter. In fact, perhaps a better scenario as we can flaunt your fertility and promise a new heir in time."

"If you think I am going to sleep with you, you're sorely mistaken!"

"You flatter yourself. We only need to keep up appearances. Besides, the next birthing year isn't for another decade. Or is it two?"

Ana had no idea what he was talking about, but she managed to suppress her audible relief. "Let's hope whatever we're doing doesn't take that long, then."

"I've consumed copious amounts of whiskey today, and I'm rather bushed," Agripin said, with an exaggerated yawn. "So we're going to need to wrap this up. All in favor of my plan, say aye? Aye!"

"What guarantee do we have that you aren't going to betray us?" Ana pressed.

"My dear," Agripin said, with a twist of his lips. He shifted his weight to one muscled leg. "Ask your darling Aidrik. He's known me many years. If he thought I intended to betray you, I might not be dead, but at the very least I would be badly maimed for my efforts."

Ana considered this. Aidrik had said, *He is on our side, for all that it may be worth. The challenge will be in getting him to stand up for his beliefs, rather than sit idly aside, basking in the glory of his lifestyle.*

"I need to process this," Ana said finally. "I'm exhausted."

"I'll be at that ruined castle you call home in two days' time," Agripin replied. "I will either leave with you, or without you, but that will be the only opportunity offered."

Ana nodded. Well and truly done with being studied by this arrogant creature, she wanted to wrap herself in Finn's caring arms, and forget about Agripin, the Senetat, and the danger that lie ahead. It was unfair that they had done nothing except try to seek their own happiness, and they were now targets for it.

"Life isn't fair, dear," Agripin said with a shake of his head. "But you either let it destroy you, or you take it by the balls and ride. Me? I'm an excellent horseman."

Ana felt a slight dizzying sensation and then she woke, with Finn looking down at her in concern. "Nightmare?" Finn asked.

"Only missing Aleksei, that's all," she whispered, then curled her face into his chest so he couldn't see the lie in it.

14
NICOLAS

"You coming downstairs?" Nicolas asked Mercy from the doorway to his suite. *Their* suite, he supposed, since she lived there now. Richard had been up twice to fetch her for dinner. On the third attempt, he enlisted Nicolas' assistance, with a defeated glance up the stairs.

Mercy kept her nose down in the book she was reading. She adjusted the glasses on the bridge of her nose. "Not hungry. If you leave some leftovers in the fridge, I'll wander down later."

"How the hell are you not hungry? You haven't eaten since breakfast yesterday!"

"Oh, I've snacked here and there," she lied. He knew she was lying because Richard's appeal included a list of everything Condoleezza had accounted for Mercy eating over the past week. It was a very small list.

Nicolas scrunched his forehead. "This isn't about that weight you've gained, is it? I've hardly noticed. I mean, I like a little junk in the trunk, is all I'm saying. Don't starve yourself on my account."

Mercy drew an inward sigh and lowered her book. "Thank you for remarking on something *I* hadn't even noticed myself."

Whoops. "Well, uh, anyway, you should come down. Homemade roast pot pies," he grappled, feeling frustrated he couldn't add something enticing like, *your favorite!* But he wasn't sure what her favorite food was. Come to think of it, he was pretty sure she favored a vegetarian diet. Dammit.

"Later," she promised with a forced smile. "Go on and eat before your food gets cold. We can play later."

Nicolas had no more compelling rebuttals than the ones he'd already employed, so he retreated. But when he came back later, she was sound asleep.

He couldn't decide whether he was disappointed at not getting laid after all, or if his confusion over her behavior was muddying the waters.

HARRIETT'S SILENCE ALSO BEGAN TO WORRY NICOLAS, WHO HAD NEVER put much faith in soothsaying.

Three days though, she'd been entirely silent, rendering Tristan completely distraught. He did everything he could think of to reverse whatever put her in the state. He talked to her, night and day, saying the same things over and over in different ways.

Tristan was in the midst of one such persuasive conversation over dinner the day the knock at the door came. Oz and Amelia were in New Orleans, working on launching a formal investigation into Ashley's wife's disappearance with the kids. Everyone else had succumbed to the lack of excitement and found other ways to occupy themselves as the hours ticked on with no sign of Aleksandr.

"*Monsieur* Nicolas!" Richard exclaimed, his old voice

booming through the dining hall with excitement. "We have guests!"

Nicolas wasn't the only one to rush into the central foyer. Everyone else in the household joined him, crowding so he thought he might get trampled, before they could even begin introductions.

Before them stood four individuals, none of whom they had met. One, though, did not need to be named.

"Aleksandr," Nicolas whispered, breathless. Ana's doppelgänger stood before him, in the flesh. But he was no child! He stood over six feet tall with a swash of red hair atop his smooth, pale skin, and the playful smile… why, it reminded Nicolas of himself as a teen.

"Uncle Nicolas," the young man said, and thrust forward a hand. Likely a pleasantry Ana had taught him.

"Fuck that," Nicolas declared and pulled the young man into his arms, eliciting a happy, surprised giggle from him.

"Mora said you might be excited to see me," Aleksandr revealed, as he pulled back, joining his traveling companions.

"Mother," Mercy translated for him, then stepped forward. Nicolas watched her, the way he might observe a glass with a crack down the side. *This is the first time she's been downstairs in… two days? Three?* "Astrid… is that you? And Birger?"

"How do you know us?" Astrid asked. Beside her, a young girl, young at least by Empyrean standards, fixed her gaze on Nicolas. With her wild red hair and sea blue eyes, she stole his breath. The hopeful innocence behind her eyes intoxicated him. He forced himself to look away.

"Your picture hung in the hall of Scholars," Mercy replied in wonder. Her entire countenance had come alive in the presence of Empyreans. Nicolas hardly recognized her as the same creature who'd slowly grown into a quiet recluse. "They taught us that you'd defected and were murdered for it. An example to all of us, of what would happen, if we turned our back on our calling. Like Old Aita."

"Aita?" Birger laughed. "My dear, Aita is the happiest of all of us! I'd expect nothing less of the Scholars, though. Creating their own truths was always their unique skill."

"You must be Mercy." Astrid smiled and quickly embraced her. "We know of you, and the bravery you showed in the end. Though you are the first Empyrean we've seen resurrected *after* the mark activated."

"My mora is very powerful," Aleksandr beamed. "I bet she could resurrect an entire village."

"I owe your mora everything," Mercy acknowledged, nodding at him. "And you look exactly like her."

"Where are ya' manners, child? Invite them in!" Condoleezza declared from the double doors at the end of the long hall. "Nicolas!"

"Fine, woman! Bring us some refreshments or something, shit," he called back, catching her chiding head-shake and secret smile.

Nicolas led his visitors into the receiving parlor, with the shell-shocked audience in tow. Once inside, they made quick introductions. When Eydis, the young one, clasped his hand, she gazed up at him with wide, starry eyes. *Uh oh,* he thought. *This could go very fucking badly if she's here for long.*

"We don't have much time," Birger began, as he perched on the edge of the tall, Louis XIV chair Nicolas normally claimed. "We've come to leave Aleksandr and Eydis in your care."

Eydis, too? Mercy shot a look in their direction, aware of the strange tension. *Fan-fucking-tastic.* "Maybe you can tell us what the hell is going on?" Nicolas tilted his head, and put his hands up. "Because no one else seems to be able to."

"Of course, they're welcome here," his sister, Anne, added meekly. "That's not what he's asking."

"Of course, of course," Nicolas waved her away. "Will there be others? And if so, how many? We've had a half-dozen meetings about it, but you know what they say about groups of idiots."

"You are such a shithead sometimes," Markus muttered, leaning against the marble mantle with a look of bored disgust. His eyes, Nicolas noted, were trained on the four Empyreans sitting before them. *Already studying them. And he thinks* I'm *the shithead.*

"There will be others," Astrid confirmed. She played with her daughter's hair while Eydis sat on the floor nestled between her knees. "Perhaps a dozen. Not many more, though, I would guess. So few are born these days, as many of the elders have already experienced rearing a child. Definitely no more than double that."

"There's a huge fucking difference between twelve and twenty-four children," Nicolas remarked, his voice dropping lower with each word. He had the overwhelming urge, for the very first time in his life, to ask pardon for his language.

Birger and Astrid were unruffled. Birger shrugged. "Could be less. We've seen a rash of new births in the last fifty years, but still not large numbers. You have more than enough room to accommodate whoever comes, though. And they will come soon."

Harriett looked up from Tristan's side, as if to say, *I told you so.*

Well, they were not much more useful than Ana in the information department. Nicolas was ready to kick them out, and get on with it. He longed to talk to Aleksandr, to know him. To ask him about his mother, and absorb everything he'd missed since Ana left.

"What role do you want us to play for them?" Jacob asked, pressing forward. As he did, Eydis lit up.

"Another Quinlan!" she declared, craning her neck and flashing wide eyes at her mother. "Mora, that's two in less than a week!"

Jacob's expression darkened. "What do you mean?"

Eydis appeared authentically confused. Her brows knit in worry. "Is that offensive, to call someone a Quinlan?"

"Not if they are one," Birger acknowledged, watching Jacob carefully.

What the hell is going on, and why did the room go completely still?

"We will send you someone to assist with training them. Soon," Astrid answered Jacob, observing him with the same odd intensity of her partner. "In the meantime, keep them safe. Don't take them off the property."

"No shit!" Nicolas declared.

"When will you send someone?" Markus probed.

"And bring no one outside your clan into the fold," she continued, ignoring the outburst.

"We won't," Mercy promised, still gazing at the visitors in awed wonder. Nicolas noted how her carefully constructed existence continued to be unraveled at every turn. He couldn't relate to that, but he tried to dig deep for some empathy.

"Thank you. As to your question, young Markus, we will send someone as soon as time and safety permits. Now, allow us to say our goodbyes to our daughter, and we will be on our way."

Nicolas saw Astrid and Birger out, while the others gathered with the young Empyreans in the parlor, filled with questions.

"She'll be safe here," Nicolas assured them as he was supposed to do, but this was not why he lingered. Nor the words he wanted to say.

Astrid shot him an amused, knowing look. "You're aware you're a halfling, yes? Coupling with Eydis will secure an evig-bond between you. Something I'm positive neither of you want."

"Eydis doesn't know what she wants, and is too young to make decisions for her future," Birger clarified. "What my mate is trying to say is, please keep your hands to yourself."

Nicolas put both his hands up. "Hey, whoa! You have nothing to worry about. I have enough complications in that department."

"Try to be sensitive to the changes Mercy is experiencing," Astrid replied. "You cannot know her path, or her struggles."

Nicolas didn't require, or desire, a lecture. "Thanks for bringing them. And please, for the love of Emyr and all that, send guidance as soon as you can."

"We will, forthwith," Birger promised.

"Ana," Nicolas blurted out, before they could walk away, taking their stories with them. "You've seen her, then? Is she okay?"

"Why, she's radiant." Astrid smiled. "And stronger than either of her two mates know."

"Aye," Birger agreed, but his expression was cloudy, and harder to read. "There's a power in her that even she does not yet know how to draw out. But when she does..."

Astrid nudged him, and he quickly shook his head. "Farewell, Nicolas. With luck, we will be back to retrieve our children in swift order."

15
AIDRIK

"Ana, this is completely insane!" Finn exclaimed, toppling the stone wedge he sat on as he shot straight up. "We have to find another way. No... no. This isn't an option."

Anasofiya had spent the last half-hour relaying her nocturnal conversation with Agripin. Throughout the telling, tension brewed under Aidrik's controlled surface. Agripin had visited with Anasofiya, and he'd not had an inkling.

"You say that as if we *do* have a choice," she replied. Her pale skin blazed bright with anger.

"There's always a choice," Finn reminded her. Observing the intensity between man and wife in that moment, Aidrik dropped his gaze. "We can choose to play Agripin's ridiculous games, or we can choose to find another ally. What about Birger and Astrid? They seemed to have their shit together."

"They are working with him," Aidrik interjected, realizing it now for the first time. Agripin would have known if Birger and Astrid were in proximity. And they'd have been taken into immediate custody if they weren't allies.

"He's toying with us," Finn seethed. His hands clenched into tight fists, flexing as he attempted to control his rising anger. "And by going along, we're allowing it. It was obvious from the moment we met him that he doesn't take anything serious."

"He does seem that way," Anasofiya agreed. She also attempted to force her emotions down. But where Finn's anger was relatively safe, and expected, what she suppressed sent a chill through Aidrik. "That may be how he protects himself. Or a personality flaw, I don't know. But the Agripin I spoke to was calculating his moves several steps ahead. He knows what he's doing, and his request, while ludicrous, makes sense."

"To parade you around as his mate?" Finn asked, incredulous. "That makes sense to you?"

"An unusual tactic, but I see the logic," Aidrik offered. Finn's anger was justified, and perhaps even more subdued than the situation demanded. The fact remained, to get them into Farjhem without being taken into custody, and likely executed, was going to require a miracle.

Or an idea like this.

"If he touches me, I'll kill him," Anasofiya replied, eyes trained on the fire. Her hands twisted in her lap.

Finn laughed, falling back into the wall. Dust fell, settling around them. "Oh, Ana, if he touches you, *I'll* kill him. And that's the problem. There's a huge flaw in a plan that might end up with me murdering the so-called leader of this resistance."

"Do you trust me?"

"Ana—"

"Finn, do you?" Her eyes were steady. Imploring.

His anger melted. A visible change came over him. "Of course I trust you. Ana, of course I do, silly girl." He knelt before her, untangling her hands, bringing them to his lips. "I don't trust *him*, though. How can I protect you from this?"

She smiled, but her words were hard. "I can protect myself."

Finn grinned and shook his head at her bravado, but Aidrik knew the truth behind what she said was far more potent than Finn could ever guess. Anasofiya was changing, before their eyes, and the outcome as yet remained a mystery.

"Take a jog with Forbia," Aidrik suggested, planting a firm hand on his brother's shoulder. "She's missed your companionship. The air will do you well."

Finn nodded, releasing a long breath expelling the well of anger within. "I love you," he whispered against Anasofiya's mouth, gently cradling her face with both hands. "Everything I say comes from that, and the fear of losing you again. I'm sorry if I upset you."

"Never worry about that," she offered back, her kiss passionate. "Ever. Now, go. I'll be here."

AGRIPIN WOULD ARRIVE ON THE MORROW. THE FIRST EVENT IN A chain which would lead them to their fate, for better or worse. Aidrik's unreliable seer's vision offered him glimpses of things amazing and terrible. Not knowing which would become reality was torture.

Anasofiya huddled by the fire, lost in her thoughts. This would be the last moment to tell her the truth weighing on his soul.

"Kjære, there is something I must tell you."

Anasofiya rested her face sideways across the top of her knees, watching him from across the fire. "All right."

"I should have revealed this sooner. Proper time never

presented itself. I know not where this path will take us, and so I must, now, tell you this truth."

She straightened her posture. "I'm listening."

Aidrik drew in a steadying breath.

"Back in Louisiana, the Sveising I employed saved your life. I'll not apologize for that. Now or ever," he explained. "But after, despite the bond produced between us, you wanted him still. I'll not ever know for sure if it was jealousy or pragmatism that bade me persuade you to leave Finn."

"Wait," Ana replied, catching up in her mind, "you used your powers on me? To pull me away from Finn?"

"Aye, I did. And the burden of this deception weighs heavily upon my soul."

"Aidrik, that was not your choice to make!" Her cloak fell off as her head whipped up. "You, and all your words, your wisdom, about protecting him, keeping him safe. I can't believe you would do such a thing. You, who professes to hold himself to some higher moral power. You're no better than your hated Senetat, controlling people who wouldn't follow the path you want them on!"

"I am not without flaws, Anasofiya. I never professed to be."

"I *wanted* to bring him! I *loved* him, Aidrik! Do you know what that meant for someone like me, someone who thought she was incapable of such a thing? He's the first man I've ever fallen in love with, in a pure, real way. Maybe the *only*," she added. "How do I know what I feel for you has any bearing if you can manipulate the world to your desires?"

Aidrik had predicted her anger, but not this last. "It was the one and only time I employed persuasion on you, Kjære. Once my blood ran through Aleksandr's veins, in your womb, I had no other choice. You could not remain there."

"Of course not," she agreed. The aura around her, the one

he'd noticed as of late, pulsed in a gentle, beating rhythm, as it doubled in size. "But Finn could have come. That wasn't your protection of me, that was arrogance! Selfishness!"

"I'll not disagree with that assessment," Aidrik replied calmly. Certainly more calm than he felt. Inside, his heart split down the middle. *Further reminder of why I avoided love all those years.*

"You can't knowingly hurt someone and expect an apology to be enough. You can't *rip* someone's life apart and think things will ever be the same."

Aidrik had words loaded in response; many words, as he'd had so long to think about how he might approach this with her. But the aura around her wavered, throbbing, protecting her but also shutting her off from him.

In the space of moments, and a matter of a few words, a rift formed between them.

The darkness inside her expanded, growing, encroaching. Manifesting.

Her darkness is real. An entity as tangible as she is. As powerful as I am. What will it turn into? What will it become?

What will she become?

16
AMELIA

Amelia watched in amused fascination from the doorway as Markus danced before Eydis as an over-sized orangutan. He aped and panted around the room, looking exhausted and miserable beyond words. Not the first illusion he'd woven for her on this day, by the looks of it. The young girl laughed, clapped, and begged for more.

The illusion faded and a relieved Markus greeted Amelia. "You and Oz have any luck tracking down Ashley's family?" he asked, slipping a light sweater back over his head.

"Not yet. But I trust the firm's resourcefulness," she replied. She'd promised her brother that, no matter what happened at *Ophèlie*, she wouldn't lose sight of helping him find his family.

Amelia turned toward the girl. "Do you not have illusion-ists where you're from, Eydis?"

"We have some, but they're no fun." The girl pouted. Fifty years old, she'd said, though she looked at least ten years younger than Amelia, and acted even younger than that. "They only use them when things are serious. Or when they need to blend in with Children of Men."

"They don't use it to teach you?"

"I'm not an illusionist, so that's pointless," Eydis explained.

"What is your skill, then?" Amelia pressed, slipping into the seat across from where Eydis stood, before the fireplace.

The girl's face broke into a mischief-filled grin. "Persuasion."

Markus moved to leave, but on his way out dropped down and whispered to Amelia, "Persuasion indeed. The girl is a damn siren."

Amelia stifled a giggle as Markus departed in obvious liberation. Just as well he was leaving. She'd come here to speak with Eydis alone.

"I'm sorry I missed your arrival yesterday," Amelia began, motioning for the spirited redhead to take a seat of her own. Eydis plopped down on the velvet cushions in the corner, her legs flying up. "Do you have everything you need here?"

"Oh, yes. More than I need. What a beautiful home Nicolas has!"

Amelia's empathic feelers picked up the clear infatuation from the girl, though it was also written in bold letters across her face. "Well, please let me know if I can get you anything at all. Nicolas has his hands full with Aleksandr."

A notable wave of disappointment crossed Eydis' face, artlessly unaware she should attempt to hide her interest. "Thank you, Amelia."

"Markus mentioned to me that you had an interesting interaction with Jacob," Amelia went on. "Something about the Quinlans?"

Eydis frowned. Her light brow meshed into one. "Oh, I hope I didn't offend him! I truly didn't mean to. It's just, I thought all the Quinlans lived in tribes, back in Ireland. And now I've seen more than one, and away from home. Far says I speak without thinking."

"You didn't offend him, sweetie." Truth was, she had no idea if Jacob was offended or not. He'd not mentioned anything about the interaction to her directly. "Could you tell me what you know about the Quinlans?"

"Oh, you both probably know more than I do," Eydis declared. "Most of what I know, my mora told me."

"What did she tell you?"

"Not very much. Thousands of years ago, the Quinlans and Empyreans had an alliance, but something happened that broke it. Most Empyreans won't even acknowledge the Quinlans, and others would probably kill them on sight. It's very sad." She shook her head.

"But not you or your parents."

"Oh, no. Our clan is different from all the other rebel clans out there. We live in peace with the Children of Men and the Quinlans. My far says we're rare like that."

"You said you saw another, before Jacob?"

Eydis looked confused. "Anasofiya's husband, Finn. I don't understand. Don't you know all this?"

Amelia didn't wish to give away all the secrets surrounding them, but she saw no reason to be dishonest. "The truth is, we don't know anything about the Quinlans. Jacob only recently discovered he may have this ancestry, and I had no idea about Finn. How do you detect them?"

She shrugged. "You can see it in their eyes. Can't identify the females that easily, though. Only the draoi."

There was that word again. "Draoi?"

"Male Quinlans. You weren't kidding when you said you didn't know anything, were you? Most of the Quinlan traits are passed through the female, and they hold the power, I guess. They lead their tribes, make the rules, all that. Males are pretty rare and powerful, though. My mora says she only knows of three that live today in Ireland, but she said that before she met Jacob and Finn. Before this week, I'd only met one. That's why I'm so amazed to have seen two in less than a week!"

Jacob... and now Finn. Both Quinlans. Both draoi, rare and powerful, as Eydis said.

"But what... *are* they?"

"Druids, of course. What did you think they were?"

Amelia sat before the antique vanity, brushing her hair with mindless passes. She would go to sleep tonight, and dream again of Cianán and Cerridwen, a mystery she was so close to solving but seemed equally out of her grasp.

Quinlan. Draoi. Your great-great uncle Flynn. Prophecy. Aunt Nora. You must come soon.

"We can go to Ireland." Jacob appeared behind her. "I called Oz's office. They're making the arrangements."

She turned and rose. "What changed your mind?"

"You." He slid one hand against her cheek. Her face fell into his touch. "This is killing you. Like before, but more slowly, and I can't turn a blind eye, no matter how much this freaks me out."

Now that what she wanted was upon her, the doubts crept in. "I really don't know what we'll find. Whatever it is, though, the knowing will change both of us."

"That's what's worried me all along, *Blanca.* I don't have your second sight, but my instinct tells me we won't be the same once we hear what Father O'Connor has to say."

"My great-great uncle Flynn," Amelia added quietly. She reached inside the vanity drawer and pulled out the repeatedly creased letter. "You should read this."

"He's..." Jacob's hand moved to his mouth, and he looked away. "I can't. Not tonight."

His arms came up around her sides, sliding her close as she swayed in his embrace. His lips tickled her neck. "Tonight, I want to forget everything and take advantage of my wife."

There was nothing gentle about their lovemaking. It was demanding, coarse, and tinged with a fearful desperation that left Amelia feeling drained.

She clung to him, praying she wasn't pushing them into something from which they could never return.

17
AGRIPIN

Ana sat across from him in the litter, jostling lightly, her gaze directed toward the curtained opening on the right, in defiant refusal to look his way.

Aidrik and Finn rode in the litter behind them. Aidrik and Ana were a required part of the deal, but Ana refused to leave without her husband.

"You said yourself Empyreans place no value in monogamy. He's coming," she had asserted firmly.

Agripin had known she'd cave to the request. What other choice did she have? She did so grudgingly, and in a manner that would prove to be unpleasant for all involved, no doubt. But what he did *not* expect, was that it would amuse him so.

"No wonder they're willing to share you," he said, cheekily. "Your charms are too numerous to name." Ana raised an eyebrow, but said nothing.

This arrangement would be uncomfortable, but it would at least provide some levity for him. And what did it matter to him if Finn came along? The halfling could even sleep in their bed, if it suited him, once things were established. Agripin didn't intend to lay hands on Ana himself unless matters required it.

There would be a celebration in the square, without doubt. Agripin had already sent word of his mating with a halfling, and the "inevitable offspring" when the next breeding year arrived... not that they'd still be dancing this dance when the time came. His father would meet them in anger, but when he saw Agripin was a changed man, singing the praises of their laws, he would soften. Just as the Senetat would.

And then, the *real* plans could begin.

"How long do you think this will need to play out?" Ana asked, breaking her silence.

"The thousands of years I've lived hold different meaning than the mere thirty of your own life," Agripin replied, enjoying her annoyance, "but, thankfully, I believe we can measure the time on a smaller scale. My father is already far past his prime, by the Senetat's standards. Once they see I'm a suitable ruler, they'll activate him, and we'll begin."

Ana frowned. "You talk about your father's death as though it means nothing to you."

"Should it? Mean something?"

"Appalling," she replied. "You hold yourself above men like you're some superior race. You're barely above animals."

"Can't argue with that," he agreed. "Cheer up, and be happy you're blessed to be counted among us. I would guess you're far more Empyrean than man now. And that son of yours, well he might be more Empyrean than me, if that's possible."

"Genetically, perhaps," she replied, "but the similarities stop there."

Agripin laughed in response. He could say the sky was blue and she would vehemently disagree. There would be no accord in their relationship, no matter how long it lasted.

"You're a fascinating reminder on why I've never desired a mate," he muttered, closing his eyes to catch some respite before their arrival.

He'd planned their approach under the cover of night. It would make their presentation to society that much more impactful, when no one had previously laid eyes on them. The days prior to the celebration of his return would give Agripin plenty of time to make peace with the Senetat, and his father. The former worked quickly, and the latter did whatever the former instructed.

Agripin had not been home in many years. Nearly five hundred, to be precise, and his time away had been no accident. Upon Agripin's removal of his mark, Emperor Aeron sent him away to think about his actions, and reflect on his future before he did any more damage to his reputation. After two hundred years, his father sent for him, but Agripin's time away left him more disenchanted with his father and the Senetat. He would have stayed gone until news of his father's death swept through the land, if Aidrik hadn't opened his mouth.

But it wasn't only Aidrik. The Brotherhood had come calling before that. *It is time,* they said, all of them, sending their messengers to rouse him. Well, fine.

He wondered if his sisters would be there. Oriana didn't leave the castle walls anymore, so enamored she was with her "pets," but he couldn't guess if she might emerge into the castle proper to greet him. Nerys, however, had left to travel the world as soon as she graduated from the Scholars' tutelage. He heard rumors of her adventures every now and then, as she was universally loved among her race. But none of that was useful news for Agripin, when he really needed to know if her strong heart secretly sympathized with the Brotherhood. *She is loved enough that her support would strengthen our cause.*

The litter stopped unexpectedly. Ana jolted forward,

banging her head against the small wood frame of the door. Agripin reached out a hand to steady her, and gestured for her to be still. His eyes met hers momentarily, expressing as much as he could without speaking. She offered a nearly imperceptible nod in return. He withdrew his hand.

Then, boldly, he jumped out of the litter without so much as a glance out the curtain. Outside, his Empyrean guards were arguing with what looked like other Empyrean guards, ones not his. Upon closer inspection, the bright crimson became apparent despite the night's darkness. So, word of his approach had reached their ears after all.

"Why are we stopped?" he cried out. Beyond, in the distance, he could see the craggy peaks that shielded the secret entrance into Farjhem. The smell of clean, crisp air filled him with a small burst of nostalgia.

One of the Crimson Guards stepped forward. "Eldre Brutus requests your council prior to your arrival at the castle."

"It's lovely Eldre Brutus has a request of me, but I'm going to regretfully decline this eve," Agripin replied, haughty. "While the world is our concourse, I'm sure you understand the journey from Scotland to Norway was no small one."

The guard flashed Agripin a constipated look. "I was instructed not to return without you."

"You're welcome to follow us to the emperor's palace," Agripin invited with a flippant wave of the hand, "but I'll not be entertaining visitors until I've had at least ten hours of undisturbed rest."

The Crimson Guards exchanged looks. Agripin searched their minds and found they'd been expecting his insolence, but had been ill-prepared for it. They were trying to decide whether the punishment they'd receive for coming back empty-handed would be worse than whatever fate the duke would lash upon them for further keeping him from his much-desired rest.

Remembering that winning the Senetat over was part of his plan, he said amenably, “Please advise Eldre Brutus that I’m *overcome* with pleasure at the thought of making his acquaintance again soon, and I will greet him as my first guest of the morning.”

The guards relaxed, talking themselves into the notion that Agripin was being reasonable under the circumstances. After all, he did look exhausted, and the litter had been on the road for days. “Shall we tell him after second meal?”

Agripin smiled, flashing his famous grin. “I’ll do one better. Invite him *for* second meal, and I’ll treat him to a royal feast.”

Satisfied, the guards thanked Agripin, and went on their way.

Climbing back in the litter, he observed the panicked eyes gazing back from the other side. For a moment, he considered toying with Ana, letting her believe they were still in danger. The fear in her gaze was one of the first real emotions he’d seen from her since they departed. He respected transparency. “Rest, dear. We’ll be in Farjhem in a couple short hours.”

Nodding, she closed her eyes, letting her head fall back against the damask. Her right hand clasped tight over her left, protecting her wedding ring. *Finn, I’m afraid,* he heard her think.

That took all the wind out of Agripin’s sails.

As planned, they entered Farjhem under the cover of night, finding their way through the gap in the boulder-strewn glacier by keen eyes and magic.

The litter took them winding through the sleeping valley, past shops, and commerce, up the steep mountain hill, climbing quiet and slow until they reached the town center, and finally the palace gates. They entered and eased into a small courtyard where the litter's wood and leather creaks echoed loudly off the stone walls.

"Where the servants enter," Agripin explained. "We'll not be bothered coming this way."

Ana's drowsy nod lacked entirely in her earlier impertinence. She even accepted his hand when she climbed out. Finn's arms caught her as she descended.

Agripin's own guards led the way through the wooden kitchen door. The serving staff scuttled off, clearing a path. Agripin strode in, taking Ana from Finn. "We may yet be seen," he explained, feeling the words were more than he owed him.

The royal apartments were on the third floor, but to ascend so high on the grand central staircase would rouse the attention of someone along the way. Instead, he slipped into the serving hall and climbed the narrow stairs there, stealing a torch from the wall sconce. His guests followed.

Stone faded to plush carpeting as they emerged on the third floor; medieval influence transformed to late Victorian. This had been the doing of Emperor Aeron's last mate, Isa, who died in childbed. Agripin was seeing it now for the first time, and with an inward sigh of relief, he realized these added comforts might make sleep that much more precious and restful.

He stopped before a room, suppressing a smile. *This is going to go over so well.* "Aidrik and Finnegan. This is where you'll be staying."

The halfling's reaction did not disappoint. "I don't think so."

"You'll keep your voice down unless you want to be slaughtered before I can think up an explanation as to why you're sneaking around in the middle of the night," Agripin snapped.

"I'll come for you once the proper arrangements and announcements have been made."

Ana embraced Finn with a brief kiss, whispering something likely romantic and ridiculous in his ear. But far more interesting was the scorching glance she shot Aidrik, and the lack of affectionate goodbye to go with it.

"Go. Now," Agripin ordered. He hitched a hand under Ana's elbow and guided her several doors down, to his own suites.

Opening the door, the changes were immediate and shocking. Bright red everywhere—tapestries, bedding, curtains, carpet, left Agripin confused and edgy. "Damn woman never did like me," he muttered, leading Ana inside.

"Looks like a suite fit for a murderer," Ana replied under her breath. "Charming."

"It was not my doing, I assure you." He shifted her bag from his shoulder, dropping it on the floor. "You can change behind the curtain. Privy room is over there." He pointed to the arched doorway across the room. That, at least, had not changed. "I'll sleep on the trundle, and you may have the bed, but if anyone knocks at the door, try not to look shocked if I suddenly appear beside you."

When she set her lips in a tight line, he reminded her, "You're here as my mate. You'll need to act like it from time-to-time."

Perhaps he'd worn her down after all, for she didn't argue.

Even in his fatigue, his inevitable craving for passion after a long journey rose up. It was not Ana on his mind, though, but Cyler. That incorrigible little urchin, whom he owed his mind and body to, and even some of his heart. It had been far too long since he'd had any word of him, and the wait was too much.

Others in the Dragon Empire accused Agripin of leading with the wrong head when it came to Cyler, but Agripin's cock had never clouded his judgment. Not even with beautiful Cyler, his terribly impertinent but eerily competent second-in-command.

How many of the Brotherhood would be mobilizing tonight? Birger and Astrid, for sure, on their way back from the States. Jorun, Dagr, and Trygve had only been awaiting the word. Thorvald, ready for centuries. But what of the others, like Skadi? The reclusive Brynja and Einar?

Not tonight. Tonight we relish the slumber, for tomorrow will be a royal cluster.

"When can I see Finn again?" Ana asked, just as his eyes were closing and his mind drifting toward beautiful rest. Again, she excluded Aidrik.

"I told you already, after I've made all the announcements. You can't parade around the palace as things are now."

"When will that be?"

"Whenever it is!" he snapped and turned around, done talking.

18
NICOLAS

Nicolas' day began with a naked girl disrupting his nap, and ended with the addition of one more to their rebel party.

Since the arrival of Eydis and Aleksandr, the tone had switched from sluggish impatience to excitement at the group's purpose finally emerging. Everyone fought for time with the "children," as if it were a competition. Every time Nicolas attempted to spend quality time with Aleksei, the boy was surrounded by others who plied him with questions, or shared some of their own wisdom and experience.

As for Eydis, Nicolas went out of his way to avoid her. She had a knack for appearing wherever he happened to be, her youthful face spread into what was, he had to admit, a genuinely beautiful smile. Worse than her tireless appearances, though, were her misguided efforts to get his attention. Someone had apparently handed her a book titled *Most Ridiculous and Clichéd Ways to Secure a Man* and she'd devoured it as gospel. From the twirling of her hair to excessive eyelash batting, her behavior was embarrassing. Her pouty come-hither stare would haunt his nightmares…

…and his dreams, wherein the problem rested. He wanted her, ridiculous gestures and all. To press her up against one of the library walls and demand her innocence in a tangle of sweaty limbs and desperation.

The nap occurred in the early hours, when most were still sleeping from the night before. Nicolas hadn't exactly gone to sleep, instead crashing on the couch in his study after a night at the local watering hole in Vacherie.

The incident happened perhaps an hour before Amelia and Jacob left for their open-ended Ireland trip, and about ten hours before their next visitor showed up.

Nicolas decided even before venturing into town to lay off the cognac. Yes, by choice. What had things come to? Of course, Cochin's (the first bar he saw once inside the city limits) didn't even have cognac, so it was a pointless test of his self-control. College was the last time he'd slogged down piss-water like the whiskey this place served.

He'd reached that undefined point where drunkenness turned to hangover when, as he was turning on to his back, his eyes fluttered open to the sight of a beautiful goddess standing before him. Giving the statue Venus competition, she was naked, shining with the softness of a perfect complexion and flawless body. Long red hair covered one nipple but, mercifully, revealed the other pointed north. Much like the friend in his pants, who rose with astonishing ease despite his inebriated state.

In one hand, she held a brand new, unopened bottle of Hennessy. The other rested inches from the nest of copper hair between her legs.

Is this a fantasy?

I shouldn't have consumed that cheap shit.

"Is something wrong?" Eydis' high, innocent voice chimed through his cloudy thoughts.

"I... uh..." Nope, words were still a few moments out. His jaw hung instead. The rest of him, aside from a single traitorous appendage, felt paralyzed.

"Did I get this wrong? I asked everyone what you loved, and they all said the same thing: sex and Hennessy." Eydis frowned. She set the bottle down on the table, her pert breasts bounced softly. "Did I get it *right*?"

Oh darlin', you got it more than right. Nicolas swallowed. "I thought I locked the door."

Eydis flashed a guilty smile. "You did, but then you left the key in the lock."

Nicolas' head throbbed like someone was batting it back and forth for sport. He wiped the drool drying at his mouth, sliding himself backward, away from her but also up. He had to regain some kind of control over this situation.

But she was upon him, climbing over him on the sofa. Her slender, soft legs came around either side and he was pinned, on his back, looking up at this unwanted gift. Not the first time a woman had thrown herself at him, but before now he'd never been so determined to behave. To do the right thing.

"I want to love you," the girl said, gawking down at him with those doe eyes, her hair tickling his face and neck to remind him that yes, this was happening.

"You don't even know me."

She bit her lip. Another strangely practiced move. "That's not how evigbond works, Nicolas. The love comes after."

Well, that did it. With a burst of strength, he lifted her, dropped her on the edge of the couch, and scrambled away, backing into the fireplace. "Eydis, I'm not looking for a damn evigbond!"

Her hopeful face fell. She clutched at the throw blanket, pulling it tight over her chest and lap. "Am I not desirable?"

"You're fucking stunning," he muttered, running both hands over his face. "That's beside the point."

"Markus said I looked like Ana. You loved Ana," she whimpered.

What the fuck, Markus?

"Be that as it may, I'm not in the market for an evigbond, darlin'. You've got the wrong guy."

"Have you never seen one? My parents are evigbond, and they have been happy for thousands of years. I can't imagine anything more romantic, and more perfect than that, can you?"

Nicolas didn't tell her the idea of spending thousands of years with one person sounded like the worst form of punishment. Waterboarding had nothing on evigbond. "I'm sure one day you'll find your evigbond and it will be... well, just like that," he managed. The unopened bottle of Hennessy called to him. *What in the actual bizarre fuck is going on? Last time I drink bottom shelf whiskey!*

"When I saw you, I knew. It was just like my far said, when he met my mora." She shook her head, pushing away logic. "No, Nicolas. It has to be you."

In a moment of either pure coincidence or the universe's idea of divine intervention, Anne walked in. She shot only a fleeting, curious glance Nicolas' direction, instead focusing her maternal intentions on the traumatized naked girl. "Come on, sweet girl, let's get you dressed," she soothed, wrapping the blanket tight around her and ushering her out.

Anne didn't miss the opportunity to toss Nicolas a perfect eye roll as she exited the room.

No point in trying to tell her what she'd *actually* walked

into. He struggled with believing it himself. Worse, he had a strong feeling this wasn't the end.

THE GOODBYES WITH AMELIA AND JACOB WERE UNEVENTFUL. AUNT Colleen, Uncle Noah, and Ashley came by to pick them up and see them off. Nicolas was amused to realize he'd miss his cousin. Her presence was one of the few here that didn't feel like a violation.

"Two down," Tristan remarked, with a forlorn glance at the door after they'd left. "I can't believe they're leaving us."

"I guess your girlfriend didn't see that coming," Nicolas said drily.

"What's coming at *Ophélie* is nothing compared to what will happen to our people across the world," Harriett choked out. Her voice was raspy in the process of re-discovering it.

She slipped her hand through Tristan's and led him down the hallway. Halfway, she abruptly stopped and turned toward Nicolas. "If you were thinking of napping, you'll be disappointed. Our next visitor will be here before dinner."

HARRIETT WAS RIGHT, OF COURSE. NICOLAS WOULDN'T DENY HER record was perfect, but she was utterly useless if she didn't tell them what she saw. She seemed determined to keep the worst to herself.

"If it's not too much trouble, I'd like you to remind your cousin-girlfriend that keeping secrets isn't very fucking helpful," Nicolas told Tristan later that afternoon.

"Don't push her," Tristan defended, eyes flashing. "Her visions are what hurt her. I'm not going to ask her to sacrifice herself just so we have advance notice about things we can't change anyway."

"Nihilism doesn't suit you. Why don't you try optimism on?"

Before Tristan could come up with an adequate comeback, their predicted visitor arrived.

Sindre, this young one was named. An elementalist who could conjure all four elements, which he assured Nicolas was quite rare. He hailed from the same tribe as Eydis, and in an interesting twist of events, Nicolas discovered the boy had the serious hots for her. Unrequited, however; as soon as introductions were complete, she resumed mooning over Nicolas.

There's your damned evigbond, he wanted to say, but that would require talking to her.

"We should call in Luther's twins," Markus remarked, as Sindre demonstrated his abilities in the garden. He was a natural showman, spinning vivid exhibitions consisting of loops and curls, ending with a giant lion's head above them, colored with fire, water, earth, and held together with whirling air. Nicolas considered they should keep this one around and charge entry.

"Luther has twins?"

Anne offered her second eye roll of the day. "Remy and Fleur. They're elementalists, one fire and the other water. None of us has experience with this, unless you're hiding something?"

Nicolas picked up the double meaning in her words quite clearly. "Beloved sister, would I hide something from you? And you heard what Birger and Astrid said. No one else gets brought in."

"No one outside the *clan,*" Anne clarified. "But they're kids themselves. What do they know about instructing?"

"Then hope Birger and Astrid send us an elementalist for a trainer, because this is out of our league," Markus asserted, gazing in awe at the floating, fiery tiger in the sky.

"I won't require training," Sindre boasted. The fire disappeared into thin air, and the water crashed to the ground in a swift wave, splashing the onlookers. "But I *am* famished. Might you have any haggis?"

"Sheep innards?" Anne looked scandalized.

"Whatever you have will be fine," the boy amended. He appeared as if he'd been dropped into a backyard barbecue in Kansas when he was expecting a mimosa brunch in Foggy Bottom. "Eydis, come, tell me all you've been up to. I've sure missed you."

The artless Eydis harrumphed and followed him, shooting a sidelong glance at Nicolas on her way back into the house, as if to say, *Save me.*

Nicolas decided now would be a great time to check on Mercy.

"STILL WORKING ON THE HISTORY STUFF?"

Mercy's hands flew at the keys on his laptop with furious vigor. She didn't look up when he made his presence known. "Mhm."

Nicolas gestured toward the door. "Wanna take a break? A new kid arrived. He's a piece of work. I've got money on him burning the house down."

Her eyes darted back and forth across her screen. "No, I'll say hello later."

He shifted on the carpet helplessly. The looming dark circles under her eyes seemed to grow each day, and the weight he'd teased her about had fallen off at some point without him noticing. "How about lunch?"

"Not terribly hungry."

Nicolas resisted the strong urge to take her by the shoulders and scream, *Tell me how someone cannot be hungry when they haven't eaten in days!* Instead he slowly nodded, backing out of the room.

"Maybe dinner, then."

Mercy furrowed her brow at the monitor. "Sure, dinner," she replied, in an offhand way that told Nicolas he would be dining alone.

19
ANASOFIYA

Ana hadn't seen Aidrik or Finn in nearly three days. Agripin came by exactly once, to quietly secret her away to his new private chambers, further from her mates. He'd flown through in a hurry, long enough to relocate her and remind her not to do anything foolish like try to contact her husbands, or her son, telepathically.

Ana hardly needed the reminder. She was well aware of the stakes.

The minimal fanfare on their arrival meant no one would be looking for her. Aidrik and Finn would not have the means to track her down without putting themselves at risk, and she herself was no foolish girl.

The accommodations were divine enough to house her comfortably. This came as little consolation, though. Knowing he was leaving her in such luxury meant he would be less hurried about returning with news. Or freedom.

Her meals were left in the adjoining room, behind a door that was locked until the food was safely delivered. Either to keep her from trying to leave, or protect the secret of her existence, she couldn't guess.

The only moments of liberty came in glimpses, courtesy of the dormer windows overlooking greater Farjhem. She missed the formal tour of this magical kingdom when Agripin hurried them in under the shadow of night. As she gazed down on the town square, where dozens upon dozens of redheads, all of them majestic and lovely, moved with a light finesse as they went about their business, she imagined what it would be like to see it up close. A fantasy, come to life.

The palace, from what she could see, was nestled into a tall mountain peak, which itself was positioned between two large glaciers. She saw only one road leading up the peak, to and from the castle.

Forbia, having followed the litters at a distance, paced a relentless path before her window, stopping only to occasionally run to the east perimeter. Ana assumed that must be where Finn, and therefore Aidrik, resided.

Ana had limitless time to let her thoughts wander. She thought most often of Aleksei, and of Nicolas, back home and undoubtedly in constant worry for her. It would be easy to succumb to her regret and guilt, but there was no gain in self-loathing. She couldn't change anything, and she needed to keep her mind squarely focused on their forward trajectory.

Darkness kept her sane during the cruel separation. It kept her mind far from revenge fantasies or conjuring scenarios where she could successfully break out of this jail, save her mates, and start their own revolution.

Enduring was surviving.

He will seek to separate us, Aidrik warned the night before they left Scotland. Tensions were at an unusual high in their family, which had grown smaller and colder since Aleksei's departure and Aidrik's admission. *Agripin's fondness for games is legend. Breaking you will be no more than a trifle. If you succumb, he will only push harder. Understand, we are not his guests. You are his prisoner.*

"Are we prisoners?" she mused, waving at Forbia with a smile. The pup spun in one circle, tongue wagging, and then ran off toward the east.

Ana was being fed well, at least. Better than she'd eaten in months. The feasts offered were beyond sufficient, veering toward vulgar. The clothing left for her was made of rich silks.

But the door locked from the outside.

She often wondered how Finn was faring. Aidrik could survive anything. He *had* survived through a series of life events that would have crippled anyone lacking his hardened shell. This was the crux of her inability to forgive him. She would expect selfishness of any other fallible man, even Finn. But not Aidrik. His uncharacteristic weakness for her called into question everything she knew about him, everything she trusted. She didn't know yet how to repair the break. At the moment, she didn't have the will to find the way, no more than she had the desire to focus on a way out.

Refusing to confront her doubts didn't mean she had none. They haunted her, pushing and prodding at the dark fortress around her heart. What if Aidrik and Agripin were unsuccessful in swaying the Senetat to their cause? What if Agripin had led them into a trap, and Aidrik was imprisoned? What if they both were?

I would know. If either of them were in any real danger, I would feel it. I would see the worry in Forbia.

A thundering boom filled the air as the heavy double doors swung open. Agripin stood in the doorway.

"Where have you been?" Ana demanded, spinning to face him.

"Doing exactly what I told you I would be doing," Agripin

replied, without a hint of apology. When she stiffened in anger, a familiar voice inside her reminded her to still her rage, for now. "And doing it well, I might add."

"You could've sent word," Ana chastised, tensing further.

"I could have," he agreed, "but I thought securing all our futures was more important than easing your mind. Apologies if I had my priorities out of sync."

Ana bit her tongue. Their agreement with Agripin was tenuous at best. They would be on thin ice for a long time to come, and there was a limit to how much of her ire he would take.

"You're alive, so I assume it went well?"

Agripin grabbed the tall bedpost, and propped his leg up on the frame. "Well enough. My father is dead."

Ana gasped. The cold, detached way Agripin made the announcement took her off-guard.

"Calm yourself," Agripin said with a sly smile. "I assure you, there will be no mourning in my chambers."

"So, then, you're the emperor now?"

"Only in name. It's a tedious, several step process that starts in about... two days." Agripin checked the imaginary watch on his wrist. "Which means you," he said, pointing at her, "will need to get ready. You'll be on my arm for the coronation ceremony."

"I don't understand," Ana said quickly. "You said Empyreans don't get married."

"Marriage is a contractual pile of rubbish," Agripin replied. "Means nothing except as a way of tracking asset division for men. The emperor must have a mate. An empress. I thought I explained this?"

"No, you've been pretty damn vague about the whole thing, and you never said anything about any sort of legal arrangement." She assumed the role of Finn in his absence. He would want her to say these things, no matter how pointless. "I have a husband."

Agripin waved dismissively. "Yes, and that obviously means so much to you, with how you're so graciously shared between your two men."

"I don't need you to understand our private decisions," Ana said tersely. "There is a limit to what is reasonable for this plan to work. I'm... trying to accept that my position at your side is necessary. But it's supposed to be temporary. If you start giving me titles, when does it end?"

"Men place far too much stock in titles," Agripin scoffed.

"Isn't that what you're doing, by insisting on this?" Ana pushed.

"I understand a title I give you can be as easily taken away, when the time is right. I don't require a system of laws to dispose of you. I need only do it."

"Dispose of me!"

"Dispose, dismiss, whatever. Stop reading so much into everything I say." Agripin shook his head. "We're wasting time on silly disagreements that have no bearing. I'm sending in the dressmaker. Finn will, of course, need to stay behind." Agripin's smile was only mildly apologetic. "He's welcome to watch from one of the upstairs balconies."

"Will I get to see him before, at least? You've kept us apart for days!"

"After, you will retire with me. Don't get so worked up, halfling," Aidrik said, dodging her question. "I don't intend anything that would offend you. But we need a display of harmony, and it would not do to have the empress run off to another's bed. I'm sure you understand."

She looked away. The pain this would cause Finn was beginning to finally settle in. A small, distant part of her still futilely wished she had never come into his life; never subjected him to all he now had to deal with. He'd been happy as a lobster fisherman in Maine.

But the time for regrets was long past. If Finn's love had taught her anything, it was that she could not fault herself for everything that went awry. He was a grown man, and had made his decisions. Now he was her husband, and they were facing an awful challenge, but they would rise, together, and meet it.

"All right. But I hate chiffon."

20
NICOLAS

Sindre's arrival provided Nicolas his first relief from Eydis' coquettish smiles and swooning looks. He followed the girl everywhere, insisting they receive all training and instruction together. This meant Markus carried the lion's share of the work, but he fell into the role of teacher easily and enjoyed it despite his complaints.

Nicolas was annoyed to learn her preoccupation was not the blessing he expected. He kicked himself for missing her. For seeing her disarming smile on Mercy's face in the bedroom. Not that Mercy was entirely present anymore, either.

That shit will pass, he assured himself.

Aleksandr lived in the shadows of the energy Sindre and Eydis put forth. He had equal to offer, but internalized most of what he absorbed from around him. When the other two youth got carried away, they took his vitality with them. *Energy stealers,* his Aunt Colleen explained. *No one ever means to be, they're simply born that way. Like Adrienne.*

Perhaps that was who Eydis reminded him of, his late sister, Adrienne. She'd lived her life in a series of ellipses and exclamation points. You couldn't help but love her, but it took everything out of you to do so.

Nicolas put Eydis' misplaced affections and Mercy's strange behavior out of his head, and instead focused his energies on Aleksandr.

"Mora says I am most like my far," the young man revealed as he perused Nicolas' library with shy reluctance. Years ago, Adrienne and Lucienne had spent a summer alphabetizing the many thousands of titles. Nicolas couldn't fathom the level of patience required for such an undertaking.

Nicolas disagreed with the assessment. The kid certainly inherited Finn's sensitivity to others, but the persistent and quiet introspection was all Ana. Everything you needed to know about Ana could be discovered through her impassioned scrutiny of the world around her.

"Your dad is a good man," Nicolas offered weakly. Like Ana, small-talk was a bane to him. "Look, Aleksei. One day, all of this is yours. This house, property, the money holding it up. You're my heir. Did she tell you that?"

Aleksandr slid the book he was looking at back into place, aligning the leather binding carefully with its neighbors. "Yeah. She talked about you a lot. Said that you were the only person who understood what she was feeling."

Nicolas thought of their childhood. How they hoarded their friendship with secrecy and pacts, declaring the world their oyster and their enemy all at once. That bond grew and festered through adulthood into something equally beautiful and toxic, until he could see nothing, anymore, but his unhealthy desire to keep her to himself.

It was a dangerous thing to love someone so much. And a blessing that she'd put an end to it. "The sum of your mother is stored in her mind," Nicolas said thoughtfully. "If you can get through, the reward is pretty fucking amazing."

Aleksandr smiled, leaning against the shelf. "She also told me you cursed a lot."

"Oh, don't let her fool you into thinking she's demure. I assure you, your mother can throw down profanities that make me look like I'm in charm school."

Aleksandr giggled. The effect was jarring. His beautiful, unlined face resembled a man entering his adult years, but in moments like these, Nicolas was reminded he'd only been in this world a few short months.

The development stages of an Empyrean would always dazzle Nicolas. They grew to adult form in weeks, but didn't reach maturity for nearly a century. So while Aleksandr, Eydis, and Sindre all appeared to be the same age, nearly seventy years divided oldest from youngest.

It further blew Nicolas' mind that Eydis had twenty years on him. Sindre, over double his age.

"How long until they come for me?" Aleksandr asked. "I don't like being so far away. I can sense my parents from this distance, but it's faint. Sometimes they fall off my radar for a short while and I panic."

"I don't know. They're not going to move mountains overnight though. Revolutions and shit take time." Nicolas frowned, then added, "Your parents are strong. Altogether, I imagine they're some sort of epic gestalt of baddassery."

"They should have let me come. I'm capable of helping."

"You're also capable of getting slaughtered, and I can't blame them for wanting to protect you from that," Nicolas countered. Ana's words came back to him, *I want you to guide him,* and he scolded himself for falling down on the job. "Your mother sent you to me for more than protection. You may be from some race of quasi-superheroes or whatever, but you're also a Deschanel. You need to know where you come from."

"I'd like to meet my grandfather, Augustus. Can we go see him?"

Nicolas pictured the look of indignant shock on his uncle's face as he ran through a thousand refutations about how there was no way this grown boy could be his grandson. "Baby steps."

"Shouldn't I be training? Like Eydis and Sindre? They spend all day with Markus, and I spend my time in the library, reading. What if Mora and Far come for me? I want to be ready."

Nicolas stopped short of telling him the only reason they were training anyone was from a lack of anything better to do, and could hardly be considered training. "Well, what is your ability?"

Aleksandr's face fell. "I don't know. I can sense my family, and read minds, but neither of those things are really all that special."

"Is there some kind of, uh, baking period or whatever with you folks? Are you born with your powers?"

"We are. But *I* wasn't. Maybe I don't have any."

"Bullshit. Look who your parents are. Your ability is probably so fucking epic that it will pop out when you least expect it and scare the shit out of everyone for ten miles."

This earned a smile from the young man. "Maybe."

"Like, that shit will be on the news, son."

"Okay, okay!"

"Anyway, take a seat. We've got some catching up to do."

Nicolas wrongly assumed he could sneak away without running into Eydis. He might have pulled it off, had Anne not stopped him in the foyer to ask if he had any preference for the menu that night.

His eyes moved to the stairwell, his escape. "Why are you

asking me? I can't tell the difference between duck and chicken!"

Anne's body heaved in one annoyed sigh. "Because, Amelia is gone now, and you were designated to take this task over. Instead, you've been *hiding*. Maybe this has something to do with you taking advantage of that sweet little redhead? Hmm?"

"Stop running your mouth on shit you know nothing about," Nicolas muttered. It was at that moment he noticed Eydis and Sindre emerging from the back of the house. Markus dragged behind them, shoulders slumped in exhaustion.

"God forbid they send us anymore females. Woe betide any women who come within five yards of Nicolas Deschanel!"

"Goddammit, Anne, I'm not kidding."

She laughed at his distress and sauntered off, leaving him to face his nubile stalker.

Eydis skipped over to him, stopping inches from his face. She puckered her soft lips, and cocked her hip to the left, resting her hand in the light curve. "Did you miss me?"

Nicolas swallowed hard. *Fuck me, but I sure did.* "I have a girlfriend."

She giggled, tracing her hand along his upper arm. Nicolas shivered. "No one cares about silly things like that. Least of all your 'girlfriend.'"

Nicolas looked again toward the stairs, realizing it was his head leading the charge, for once. The rest of him fantasized about pinning her against the secretary and fucking her brains out. "I don't want an evigbond."

His eyes rolled back as her hand abruptly cupped his growing erection. "There are ways around it," she teased. She dropped her voice and leaned in, breathing her hot, exquisite sounds against him. "Many ways." *Perhaps she's not so innocent after all?*

. . .

DID MERCY KNOW THAT NICOLAS' FERVENT INSISTENCE IN THE bedroom was not spontaneous, or random? If so, she didn't say, and offered the same attention as always, retreating back into her own mind when it was over.

The craving didn't pass. It flamed higher as he pictured Eydis' full, generous mouth. Recalled the firm command she took of his trousers. The girl had plenty of years to consider what she might do when the time came.

There are ways around it, she had said. *Many ways.*

Mercy already had the laptop open again, typing feverishly. He'd been pressing her for more details on what, exactly, she was doing. She finally confessed she'd been writing a version of her memoirs that could be turned into curriculum for the Runean children. *A neutral telling of who we are so they can decide for themselves who to follow. I was asked to make that choice only knowing one side. They will know both.*

He took a deep breath. In hindsight, Nicolas might never know what prompted his voice to actually say the words.

"How do you think things are going, with the children?"

"Fine, so far. It's still early."

His palms beaded with sweat. "Has it been what you expected?" *And how is she supposed to answer that when she's been sequestered in this room since before everyone arrived?*

Mercy peered at him from over the top of the monitor. "If there's something you'd really like to ask me, get on with it."

"We haven't talked about this. I thought you might want to." His nonchalant shrug didn't fool either of them.

"Let's not with the games," Mercy replied. "Talking has never been our thing, or more specifically, not *your* thing. You don't need to bait me in circles in order to reach the point."

Nicolas paused. He was outmatched with Mercy, and he

should have known that from the jump. "I was only wondering about this maturity shit with the children. They're kids by your standard, but most have been alive twice as long as me. Should we really be treating them like kids?"

Mercy's face wrinkled in amusement. "I assure you, I'm far beyond any concern *there*," she said with a laugh.

Shit. Re-route. "No, I meant..." Nicolas considered briefly that his bluff was surely to be called, but he trudged forward with his usual confidence. "Humans have laws. We treat our children one way, and adults another. I'm asking if Empyreans have the same kind of laws."

"Yes, yes," she said quickly. "You're asking me if it's 'legal' to bed the Runean children, do I have it right?"

"Well... I... not exactly..."

"This wouldn't have something to do with that pretty little Irish princess following you around, would it?"

"What? No!" *Yes, yes, yes, yes.*

"Nicolas," she said gently, setting the laptop aside, "when we agreed I would stay, we also agreed we would keep our personal freedom. You're free to do as you wish. You know that."

Nicolas liked to imagine this was the moment the invisible angel and devil popped up on each shoulder, whispering conflicting persuasions in his ear. He debated whether to plead ignorance or high-five her. He settled for a middle ground. "You're serious?"

Mercy laughed, standing. She stretched her long, nude body, an image he never grew tired or bored of, inexplicably. "I'm not like your human girlfriends. I don't harbor those kinds of sentimentalities. You fuck who you want, and I'll not punish you."

Her casual permission made him feel worse, not better. Nor did she really answer his question, though he was fairly sure he never cared what the answer was to begin with. It had been a not-so-clever tactic designed to bring them right to this very moment. But now that he was here, a part of him wished he could go back.

It's a trap. You know this. She doesn't mean a single word she's saying.

"I wasn't planning to do anything about it," he answered weakly. Her smile in response told him she knew better. His grimace said he did, too.

There is no piece-of-ass in the world worth an unwanted evig-bond, he thought.

That sentiment was immediately followed by, *There are ways around it... many ways...*

21

AIDRIK

Maddening. It was the only word potent enough to describe Agripin's storing them here without a single word of explanation.

Also intolerable was the apparent block Agripin had placed on the room. Until their arrival, Aidrik could innately detect both Anasofiya and Finn, a gift that came with his offering them Sveising.

No longer. His only indication of their safety was the presence of Forbia. She paced day and night, stopping only in two locations. Her unruffled deportment offered the only comfort of this sequester; if something had befallen either of his triad, Forbia would raise hell.

The separation came as no shock to Aidrik. The tactics were textbook. Agripin made a career from befriending conquerors throughout history. Alexander the Great, Ptolemy I, Genghis Khan, Napoleon, all received funding and friendship from Duke Agripin, in exchange for their great wisdom. Useless to him, Aidrik thought, when he refused to put the knowledge to good use.

The first evening Finn was with Aidrik. Pacing, restless. Expectedly furious. And then sometime during the night, he was removed to another quarter. No explanation, of course.

Aidrik's capacity to endure was legend. He did not possess faith in the same tolerance of either Anasofiya or Finn. Finn's quick temper had a short fuse in average circumstances, and where his wife was concerned, his anger was never gradual. Anasofiya's patience, on the other hand, would sustain her, but the burgeoning darkness within her had the potential to raze everything nearby if Agripin said the wrong word. Not strong enough to finish the task (yet), she would be summarily executed. No trial.

Aidrik banished these fears in favor of meditation. As Forbia's pacing remained calm, so did he.

When Agripin finally did make an appearance, days later, his superiority was in full form. "Ahh, Aidrik! A fine day, is it not? I'd asked the baker to bring up some fresh bread, but I see that hasn't been done. An easy remedy."

"Bread is furthest from my thoughts at present."

"A shame. You've been away from home too long, friend. Ours is some damn fine bread."

Agripin sauntered over to where supper lay, untouched. He picked at a roasted chicken, tasting it before tossing the leg back down with a disgusted frown. "Do they use different kitchens for guests? This is criminal."

Aidrik gritted his teeth. "Do you come with news?" *Or to taunt me?*

The duke rifled through the fruits. "And no pomegranates. A world without pomegranates is not to be borne!" He settled on a raspberry, plucking it and dropping the dark red morsel into his equally red mouth. "Well, Aidrik the Wise, my father is dead, I have my naming ceremony tomorrow, and... ahh, well, we *were* slated to stand before the Senetat and give testimony of your crimes and whereabouts but the emperor's death put those plans on hold. I'd estimate in a week or two they'll call us forward, but this process is sacred. I'm sure you understand."

Emperor Aeron... dead? Aidrik had not suspected Agripin and the Senetat would move so fast. But then, why were they still imprisoned?

"Eh, it's a matter of logistics." He'd quickly come to learn Agripin was unapologetic in breaching telepathic blocks. "I cannot allow any of you to roam the grounds unsupervised, and I have much to do. You'll be present for the naming ceremony, and Anasofiya will be at my side. The halfling, regretfully, will watch from his room."

"You should grant him time with Anasofiya." He dared not allow himself to long for the same gift. Not after the last words spoken between them.

Agripin propped himself against the window frame, chomping on a block of cheese. "*About* the halfling! You could have told me that Child of Man was a Quinlan!" he exclaimed.

"You're mistaken."

"Don't play coy Aidrik, you were never good at it."

Aidrik considered the words, realizing at once the strange truth of them. Finnegan's natural affinity with nature, and creatures of all walks. But it had been many years since a male Quinlan, a draoi, had been seen or heard of. Since Quinlans broke affinity with the Empyreans after the blood pact was broken.

"Ah. A surprise to you, then," Agripin concluded, with a victorious smirk. "The only thing worse than a Runean is a Quinlan. In the eyes of our glorious Senetat, that is."

"Aye. They blame the Quinlans for inciting our rebel sects," Aidrik concurred, shelving his thoughts on this news until he could reason the facets safely. "A fallacy, but the Senetat is mired in them. Finn is no threat to our cause."

"If the Senetat comes to their usual conclusion, it will throw everything we've worked for to the wind. So he remains alone. For now."

"You've told me nothing."

"It will stay that way until we've gone before the Senetat." Agripin approached him, laying a hand across his shoulder, a move of fraternity. "I have much to tell you, old friend. There's far more to the story of our cause. Years of stories. What I tell you will rock your world.

"But I'll say nothing until we go before the Senetat. Everything rides on them turning a blind eye to your crimes."

Aidrik scoffed. "My crimes! What of theirs?"

"A reckoning we'll all live to see, Emyr willing. But raising unnecessary suspicions will get us nowhere, unless you find the mines at Farskilt to be beautiful this time of year."

"If this farce must continue, I ask that you give reassurance to Anasofiya and Finn. They deserve to know a plan exists, and their patience will pay off."

Agripin laughed. "Will it? Pay off? I can't say. Anasofiya has seen me, and heard the same news. Finn, I'll confess, I've been avoiding. The halfling is volatile."

"As would any man be when the object of his heart is being cruelly kept from him without word."

"Pfft. His familiar has been pacing the perimeter for *days.* If I wanted to be cruel, I'd have the dog executed for meat." Agripin flicked at the chicken, sneering. "Might be an improvement."

22
AGRIPIN

The naming ceremony was scheduled for tomorrow. There was a waiting period between the naming ceremony and the formal coronation. He expected the Senetat would move on their request to speak to Aidrik in the lull. Assuming they didn't slice his head off on the spot—assuming they actually *listened* to Agripin's wishes and went along with them—the truce established would be tentative. Every move they made would be under intense scrutiny.

Agripin had pushed events forward at a pace that astonished him. He wondered now if he'd been foolish, and hasty, in his actions. He should have heard back from all Brotherhood's drekar, or members, by now. The Dragon Empire should be assembling. Cyler should be here again, at his side.

Not a single word from his second-in-command. Cyler had never placed much importance on communication, instead being a creature of strategy and action. His silence now was a power play, designed to leave Agripin's heart vulnerable to even the playing field.

Worse, Cyler knew Agripin would do nothing to punish

him for it. *This time, I will string him up by his balls. Teach him a goddamn lesson about authority.* Except, he wouldn't. He never did.

He hadn't been in to see Ana. She needed the rundown of tomorrow's events, to understand what was expected of her. In a way, he craved the verbal exchange of fire that would inevitably erupt between them.

Instead, he slumped before the fireplace in the old rocker, feet planted on either side of the mantle, thinking of the thousand ways his plans could go wrong.

The Dragon Brotherhood was spread across the globe with no singular means of communication. This had always been the problem with organizing and mobilizing the so-called revolution. Twelve leaders, not counting Agripin, all living under their own individually established rules, laws, and lifestyles. The more civilized ones, like Birger and Astrid, remained in regular communication. Others, like Skadi, were downright dangerous to approach without ample forewarning.

The news of Trygve's accord came earlier the same evening, a huge relief, as his following was the largest amongst the drekar rebels. Skadi's group could possibly be measured in larger numbers, but her unwillingness to accept a formal leadership position made it challenging to get a census.

They needed numbers. More so, they needed cohesion. Dagr had been unsuccessfully attempting to stir rebellion for years now, leading with his impetuous heart. Agripin once ventured to the small village outside Marrakech to talk some sense into him.

He'd lied to Dagr on that trip. Promised him, *Revolution is coming, friend. I promise, on my honor. Be patient, and wait for the word.*

But Agripin had said these words with two fingers proverbially crossed behind his back, knowing damn well he had no hunger for war. The Second Runean War had done this to him, when he fought on the side of the Senetat, disbelieving their battle cries even as he sounded them with bloody fervor. No, he would never fight again, he silently swore.

Recent events turned his lies to vows. Agripin had not yet examined the reason for his change of heart, nor did he intend to. To overthink it might lead to his rationalizing them out of an insurgency. For whatever reason, right now he wanted war more than he'd ever wanted anything in almost five millennia.

Nerys was the other wildcard. His feral warrior sister had left the palace when she came of age and never returned. Lack of any real news on her over the years, other than scattered stories of her heroism in helping Children of Men in rare and subtle ways, led to the creation of her legend. *A true princess. Savior of our ways.* And possibly, Agripin suspected, a drekar.

Aidrik inferred that Agripin was the power figure needed to stir the hearts of the rebels and non-rebels to action. Agripin understood it was Nerys, not him.

Cyler had been tasked with tracking her. This quest was the pressing reason why his lack of reporting grated on Agripin. The little runt *knew* better. He *knew* what this meant to Agripin, to all of them. This was not the time for games.

The whiskey bottles collecting at the foot of his chair was the graveyard of experiences beyond his reach. Intoxication would be such a lovely escape right now, but no amount of imbibing brought him as far as he desired. No love he'd tasted had ever lasted. Even as the duke—no, he was the emperor now! Or emperor-in-waiting. The leader of this whole damn mess, yet not truly free.

The largest tether, those imbecile megalomaniacs in the Senetat Sanctuary, still held the noose tightly at his neck. And if the inquisition with Aidrik didn't go well, it would not only be his old friend against the wall.

Agripin walked to the window, looking out at the large dais being built in the town center. All shades of glorious red and gold, from foliage to silks and banners. It was rare that the Farværdig had the opportunity to inaugurate a new leader.

Below the window, Finn's mutt pranced around, heading in the direction of Ana's room.

Ana thought Agripin cruel for keeping her separate from her men. But there was much she didn't know, and he wasn't yet ready to tell her. Or the others. Agripin's alliance with them hedged tightly on the Senetat's acceptance of the carefully crafted lie about Aidrik's defection and whereabouts. He would hold his cards closely to his vest.

A KNOCK SOUNDED ON THE DOOR. AGRIPIN BELLOWED FOR THE visitor to come in.

One of Oriana's messengers entered, clearly identified by the absence of any white in his clothing. Moreover, the vibrant full color spectrum no one else would be caught dead wearing.

"I see my sister's tastes have not changed in my absence," Agripin remarked as he accepted the folded piece of parchment from the young man's hands. "You may go."

Agripin tore the seal carelessly, unfolding the letter.

Dearest Brother,

It is with the bustle of gossip, and not a visit from you, that I learned of your presence in our palace. I must confess I expected to see you by now, and have spent my days drafting excuses on your behalf as to why this oversight has occurred.

With our father, the emperor's, passing into the loving arms of Emyr, it becomes ever more a pressing need to seek counsel with my most dearest of brothers.

I appeal to you to visit your most loyal and loving sister at your earliest, but most expedient convenience. I would have words with you prior to the coronation.

In the love of Our Father,

Oriana

Agripin noted briefly how his hands shook as he tore the parchment into shreds, tossing them into the raging fire.

Agripin had one sister who was a saint among the Farværdig. But another who was the furthest from such a definition as one could be.

Ana had accused Agripin of being a sociopath. She had not yet met Oriana.

"She can go to the mines riding Our Father's teet for all I care. Fuck her," Agripin muttered, using his incisors to tear the seal from two more bottles of whiskey.

23
AMELIA

Amelia couldn't recall any of the mundane details about their travel. She couldn't say for sure whether the flight was smooth or the food good. Everything leading up to their arrival in Ireland could be summarized as noise or roadblocks, her mind leaping between anticipation of what was to come, and a willful blocking of those same thoughts in an attempt to enjoy the last moments of normalcy.

The one thing she *was* mindful of on the voyage was Jacob. She carefully watched for any signs of something amiss. When he wasn't sleeping, he was his usual self: cracking jokes, flirting at inappropriate times, and snuggling against her on the longest leg of the flight.

In this limbo, they made the trek from Dublin to Killianshire, where both Father O'Connor and Aunt Nora anticipated their arrival. They were to report first to the cathedral, where they would be offered dinner.

Beyond that, no one would say what awaited them. Amelia strongly suspected the most vital elements in this visit would not occur within the protection of a Catholic church.

They were expediently ushered into the cathedral the moment they turned the car off, by the same young girl who served them on their prior visit. She nearly ripped their outerwear right off, as she excitedly motioned toward the back, and the private dining hall. When they hesitated, she jerked her finger forward, pointing furiously.

"I think she wants us to go back there," Jacob remarked with an exaggerated rise of his eyebrow. *Please don't let this be the last of his humor. I need him here with me, present.*

"Well, I don't know. I get the distinct impression she wants us to turn around."

"If this were a horror movie, we *would* be running the opposite direction of where the sweet young mute girl pointed."

"At least she's not directing us to the basement."

They made their way through the nave, between the pews. The sepia light pulsed from the many candles while the sun setting through stained glass colored the floors and polished wood. There were no sounds other than their tentative footsteps.

Doubts crept in as they moved together in silence. What was, really, the gain she expected from this? She'd dismissed Jacob's fears of the unknown as temporary worries, perhaps even mild cowardice. But his strength was different than hers. He'd endured physical horrors, where hers had been emotional. What if he wasn't capable of coping with things at her level? Would there be any going back? More importantly, now that they had what they wanted, why was she so eager to put everything at risk?

If we don't do this, it will hang over our lives, and our marriage for all time. It will fester, and eat away at the edges of what holds us together until we are left with rotting fabric held together by hope and a prayer.

I would rather face a cruel fate head-on, than wither away slowly.

Slipping back around the altar, they reached the door to the rectory, where Father O'Connor both lived and attended to private business. Jacob reached in front of her and opened the door. "After you."

Amelia drew in a deep breath and stepped through.

MORE CANDLES LIT THE DINING HALL, OFFERING FLICKERING LIGHT from ceiling to floor. All natural light had faded into night, but the room was ablaze.

At the head of the table sat an older woman. She wore a modest muslin dress, covered by a dark green cloak. Her hood was peeled back, revealing rich mahogany hair woven in a braid. Her face bore fine lines, drowned out by a brilliant smile.

"Amelia. Jacob. Oh, how I have waited for this day!" she exclaimed, gently tossing aside her cloak and striding across the floor toward them. "How was your journey across the sea?"

Jacob exchanged a look with Amelia. "It was fine."

"Uneventful," Amelia added.

The woman smiled, sizing each of them up. "Over twenty years since I last stepped on a jet plane. Not something I enjoyed, though I can appreciate the convenience. Come! Take a seat, and Clara will be out shortly with dinner. I apologize it may not be as satisfying as you want. We strongly discourage heavy eating prior to a ceremony. Assuming we have one, that is."

They followed her in a daze, accumulating questions.

Ceremony? Jacob mouthed.

"Where is Father O'Connor?" Jacob began. Clara rushed in at that moment, dropping their plates in front of them before scurrying out again.

"Flynn is with the rest of the clan. As is Nora, who is busy with preparations. Amelia, it is with regret I'm introducing myself to you under these circumstances, and so many years after your birth. My relationship with your father, or lack of one, is perhaps my *only* regret in this life. I am Deirdre, your grandmother."

Amelia hadn't needed the old woman's words to confirm it. Amelia's father, Noah, had the same rich, unruly hair, and generous mouth. When her face broke into a broad smile, it was Noah's face Amelia gazed into. "It's nice to finally meet you," she offered.

"You have her mouth," Jacob mused. He attacked the meat on the plate as if this were any ordinary meal back home. As if their lives were not about to change.

"I'm sorry, but I know very little about you." Amelia sipped her wine carefully, despite the urge to knock it back and ask for another. Maybe the whole bottle. "Or my aunts." Tempering her excitement was paramount if she didn't want to be overwhelmed.

"There are many Quinlans of relation to you here, my dear," her grandmother said. In the candlelight, Amelia saw many of the age lines were actually shadows. Despite her age, Deirdre Quinlan looked young enough to be Noah's sister. "Four generations, in fact. Jacob, your grandmother is not formally a part of our clan, but she is here also. Arrived several days before you did. I don't believe you've met her, either."

This roused Jacob's attention from his dinner. He shook his head. "My mother's mother?"

"Yes. Rosemary Quinlan."

Amelia's head hurt at all the Quinlans. "I'm very confused. Why is everyone named Quinlan? Jacob and I aren't... well, closely related, are we?"

Jacob shot her a look as if to say, *Ain't gonna stop hitting it either way.*

"Not any more than anyone on this Earth is," Deirdre replied. "All female Quinlans true to their past retain the Quinlan name, whether they marry or not. Jacob, your mother did not keep her Quinlan name when she wed your father, though she was careful to protect you in the ways of our tribe. She's the reason you live today."

When Jacob said nothing, Amelia asked, "What are we doing here? Jacob and I?"

"I've much to tell you in a short time. I know you'll have many wonderful questions, and if you stay, as I hope you will, we'll spend hours catching up. I would also love to hear all about your life, Amelia, and all the amazing things you've accomplished. But for now, I'd like to simply tell you about where you come from. Can we agree to this approach? And can you attempt to suspend your disbelief on the matter, for now? Until you can bear witness to the truth yourselves?"

Amelia and Jacob both nodded. Jacob looked far calmer than the emotions emanating from him: anxiousness, fear, excitement. The powerful sentiments left Amelia temporarily overwhelmed.

"Do either of you know the legend of the Tuatha Dé Danann?" Deirdre began.

"Fairies," Jacob replied right away. "Old school Irish deities."

"Sort of." The old woman smiled. "Myth and truth have commonalities, of course, but tales distort over time. The Tuatha were the original deities of Hibernia, or Ireland as we know it now, rulers under the Goddess Danu. Legend says they first appeared out of a great mist and burned their ships in order to force themselves to settle. This happened over four thousand years ago, and the earliest origin stories are from Norway, before the Tuatha settled in Ireland.

"The Tuatha were rich in magic and storytelling, tales of regular passage between our physical realm and Tir Non Og, or the otherworld. There were four ruling tribes, each with a scryer who had bound a magic item giving the tribe its virility and power. Be it a stone, bowl, or weapon, each item held unique importance to the success and prosperity of the Tuatha, who were revered as gods and treated all benevolently in return."

"So far this sounds like the fairytales we were told as kids," Jacob said. "The ones we stopped believing after the age of five."

"So far," Deirdre agreed. "The clans of Tuatha were great friends of the Farværdig, or Empyreans as they later coined themselves. The Empyreans were central to Scandinavia, and the only other divine race walking the Earth at that time. Their alliance offered mutual benefit, and they lived together in peace. Later, when the Tuatha migrated to Hibernia, they settled into being allies from afar.

"It was a perfect balance. The Tuatha had a special, intrinsic connection with earth and nature, while the Empyreans had fire and a spiritual connection to their god. The Tuatha taught Empyreans about connecting with the Earth, and Empyreans protected the Tuatha from the threat of the wider world. Both were gods, in their own right, but together they were peaceful and prosperous."

"They created a pact, bound in magic and blood, to always protect and sustain one another. Breaking such an oath came with the punishment of war and strife."

Amelia's skin tingled with apprehension. She was listening to the history of her people. Maybe both her peoples.

"Eventually, a race of men came to challenge the authority

of the Tuatha. Milesians they were called then, but have become the same race of men now living in Ireland. The Tuatha, as gods, were not prolific upon the Earth and didn't have the numbers to defeat an attack of thousands. When Morrigan, a goddess of the Tuatha, called Empyreans for help, they did not come.

"Because of this, many of the Tuatha were killed, and the rest were driven back to Tir Na Og.

"And so this group of survivors became the *Caoinlean,* or Quinlans as we are known today. Easier coming off the tongue." She winked. "Legends called us many things. *Aos si* or faeries, seems to be the most common name given to us, though our histories bled into others, such as the stories of little people. We were none of those things, though. We were so much more."

"You said there was a price for abandoning their alliance," Amelia cut in. "The Empyreans. What happened to them? They're still around today, so they obviously survived." *We,* she thought. *We are still around today. I am one of them, if only in part.*

"As an empire in shadow," her grandmother replied. "Yes, the Empyreans lived through the massacre. But this defection marked a period of strife, and eventually war, that has never ended. Their Senetat was formed, crippling restrictions were put in place, and their race grew divided: those who were willing to live under the thumb of a ruling body, and those who were not. There are many, many stories of what happened during those times, but they are not mine to tell."

Jacob shifted in his chair. "The Quinlans sound a lot like druid-types."

"Druids came later, once the Quinlans resurfaced here," Deirdre said. "Those who followed the Quinlans, who embraced the idea of balance, and of the sacred nature of the Earth, developed a way of life you know of as druid.

"They adopted many of our customs and beliefs, and founded a religious order which is very similar to ours, though not the same. Many druids went on to hold powerful positions, respected by kings for their wisdom and knowledge. But they are not us, and we are not them. The Quinlans have always lived privately, under the protection of the goddess Morrigan. All of us alive today descend from one of the four original clans of Tuatha.

"But I must move more quickly through the telling, as the others await us in the grove. Please, finish your meal. The rift between the Tuatha and the Empyreans has grown over the years. Empyreans, far removed from the origin stories, hold Quinlans responsible for the strife in their race, and thus we're considered a mortal enemy. Quinlans discovered by Empyreans have been slaughtered, time and time again. Only a handful will still ally with us. Those who know and believe in the prophecy."

"The prophecy... I keep hearing that word. In my visions, from Aunt Nora, from Father O'Connor," Amelia interrupted. Across from her, Jacob tensed, his wits ostensibly catching up.

"There is only so much I can tell you. The goddess, instead, must show you. It's time for us to go."

Amelia rose so fast the blood rushed to her head, and she sunk down again. Jacob moved to join her, but she threw a hand up, stilling him. "I need a moment."

"*Blanca,* does any of this make sense to you?"

"Yes. No. Maybe. I don't know. I need a moment."

"That was a lot," Jacob agreed with a rush of breath. "I don't know what to say. I can't even form questions right now."

"I advise you not to try until after the ceremony." Deirdre

frowned and disappeared behind the kitchen door, returning with water. "Here, drink, dear one. I forget these are truths we've held for years. Hearing them for the first time must be a shock."

Amelia pushed the water away; pushed her grandmother away. A *shock.* There were other words for what Amelia was feeling, and shock did not even register on the list. The last time she'd felt these choking hands closing in on her, she'd gone into a coma-like state for three months. *Imperiled empathy,* her mother called it, a neat and tidy definition for a personal prison.

Breathe. Inhale. Don't think about the words. Don't decipher, don't dissect. Separate your mind, and your heart, before your emotions take control.

"Amelia, look at me," Jacob implored from across the table. When she closed her eyes, he was at her side at once, his arms around her. "Come on, let's get you some air."

Amelia allowed Jacob to guide her, only somewhat aware of Deirdre leading him toward a backdoor, a quicker exit into the night air. She heard Jacob ask her to give them some time, and then they were alone, just the two of them.

A sob rose within her but she pushed it back down. "Breathe," he coaxed, using both hands to brush her hair off her forehead. "Amelia, breathe, sweetie. This isn't happening again. If I have to put you on a plane tonight, I will. Breathe."

"I'm okay," she panted. The black stars before her eyes started to dissolve and float away. "It's just all very real now. My empathic senses didn't pick up any deception from her. When she said the words, some things came together for me, but I still don't understand them. I can't pretend they're not real anymore, can I? It's all so real, and so *heavy.*"

"I'm going to carry the burden with you," he whispered, pressing his forehead to hers. She shivered as his arms came around her back, encircling her. "I'm scared, too. No, I'm absolutely terrified, to be honest. *Shittin' scared,* my Pa used to say. What your grandmother is telling us isn't the recitation of some boring family history. She's implying..." He exhaled. "Are you okay?"

Amelia nodded, shivering. Jacob pressed her tighter, resting his lips atop her head. "I'm better now. That passed a lot faster than it usually does."

"What would you like to do next? We can do this... ceremony. Or whatever it is. We could turn around and go home, and try and forget." He grinned. "Or we could kill her, if you want?"

Amelia burst into laughter, joined by Jacob. They laughed in the cold night, a merry harmony that stabilized her better than any words ever could. "Murder. Now that's one experience we haven't shared together."

"How about we go dance around the trees for a while, chant or whatever, and *then* kill her?"

Amelia smirked. "You drive a hard bargain, Donnelly."

"I always strive for compromise."

She reached for the door, but Jacob's hand stayed her. "Amelia, I love you with my whole heart. I don't say it enough."

Her heart skipped. "I love you as much. More, for taking this step with me."

"Whatever happens here, nothing will change. Between us, I mean. Nothing."

Nothing will change. Could he really make that promise?

"Nothing," she vowed, sealing the words with a kiss.

24
NICOLAS

Harriett offered a single polite knock on his study door, not waiting for an invitation before peeking in.

Thankfully, Nicolas was in the middle of a phone conversation with Oz about some legal updates and *not* thinking about his open invitation to go on a sexscapade with the delectable Eydis.

Nicolas cradled the phone without saying goodbye to his old friend. He groaned. "Are we out of hand sanitizer?"

His young cousin glided into the room in her long white nightgown, a crocheted shawl wrapped neatly about her shoulders. Her hair was long enough to tickle her waist. "Are you busy?"

Nicolas smirked. "You're talking again? Must be a fantastic affliction, to be able to shut the fuck up and no one questions it."

She ignored his sarcasm. "I've been having terrible visions. Tristan has been very sweet about letting me retreat, but he's insisted I come tell you. And I think he's right."

Nicolas sunk into his favorite Louis XIV chair. He propped a foot on his knee, watching her with an authoritative stare. "He's absolutely correct. You should have told me as soon as you started having them."

Harriett shuffled across the floor, lifting her hem as she moved. She settled on the crimson velvet Rococo sofa. Her gestures had an air of innocence bordering on meek, but her determined expression seemed a more accurate reflection of his cousin's demeanor.

"I was silent for over half my life," she replied, straightening her gown. "Finding my voice has been a bit of trial and error."

The submissiveness of her words disarmed him. "Okay, so what are you seeing that Tristan thinks I should know about?"

Harriett's hands wrung together. She looked down at them. "My ability seems to have *shifted* since I came to *Ophélie*."

"Shifted?"

"All my life, I was a precise seer." When Nicolas eyed her in confusion, she shook her head, frowning. "Let me explain that better. Most seers in our family are like your Aunt Elizabeth, or even Amelia. They get flashes of things. Glimpses, mostly. In your aunt's case, her dreams were the only time she received anything completely accurate. Otherwise, the visions were fuzzy and convoluted. It's difficult to interpret, and can drive you mad trying. I suppose it did drive her mad."

Nicolas raised an imaginary glass to his aunt. "Emyr or God or whoever, rest her soul."

Harriett smiled thinly. "Mine aren't like that. The ones I get are always precise, exact. They always come true. Always."

"Well thank fuck for some accuracy around here. It's a free roadmap to success."

"It's more of a curse than a blessing. You can't imagine

what it is to see horrible things, involving your dearest loved ones, and have no power to change them. And everyone wants to know what you've seen, while all you want to do is run away and never open your mouth again. "

Okay, he could see her point. "But you said this has shifted somehow?"

Harriett nodded, bowing over her hands again. "Instead of seeing everything, I now only see flashes. It's like going through a slideshow of pictures from a birthday party. You've captured the highlights, but everything in between is missing. You got a picture of the cake, and the pony—"

"I never got a fucking pony."

"—but you missed the moment when Timmy got his scraped knee, or why Jane is crying off in the corner by herself. Why halfway through the party Aunt Sue is no longer there. Am I making any sense?"

"So you're getting flashes of shit now, instead of the whole enchilada."

She swallowed, nodding. "The other thing is, with my ability changing like this, I don't know if there are other changes. What if my visions aren't accurate anymore? I won't know until things come true, or don't."

Nicolas waved a hand at her. "Well, you said the kids would start arriving. We've got three running around."

"I guess you're right. I did see that. And I see one more arriving tonight, too. An illegitimate son of the emperor, if my vision is correct."

Well, now. That oughta be interesting.

"I don't see the problem, Harriett. You're seeing less, but sounds like it's still accurate."

"And a halfling," she went on. "Like us. Kind of. But he isn't the only one coming." She made a strange noise, shaking her head. "None of that's important, though. We already knew visitors were coming, it's why we're all here!"

He nodded for her to continue.

When she looked up, tears gathered at her eyes. "The flashes I'm seeing are horrific. I see Ana in chains. Amelia in a place so dark she might never return. Finn losing everything. Farjhem burning. *Ophélie's* protections destroyed."

Nicolas stopped breathing. He replayed her words. "Shit." What could he say? There was no debate about the accuracy, because she didn't know.

She sucked in a stilted breath. "I know."

He recognized, with a rising sickness, that she was absolutely confident in the accuracy. Her doubts about it were misplaced bastions of hope. It was tempting for Nicolas to live in this limbo of uncertainty with her, oblivious until the bitter end.

But he was master of this house, and an elected leader of the family's magi. He hadn't acted like it, but until now the stakes had been fluid and unknown. Harriett had described their end. *In flames. Fitting, I suppose.*

"Thank you for telling me." His mouth was dry. Not the kind water could quench.

"Nic, what do we do?" Now that her brave words were out, the girl's strength faded. She rocked back and forth, eyes wild. "This isn't like the Curse, where it sweeps through and takes a few, and then goes dormant. I think... I think this is the end. Of us. Do we tell the others? Do we try to fight?"

He needed her gone. It wasn't her fault, but the ringing in his ears and the sharp pain in his chest were made worse by her presence and questions. He forced a smile and said, "You might be right. About them being inaccurate. Keep it between us for now. Deal?"

"Okay. Okay." Harriett stood so fast she faltered. Nicolas rose and steadied her.

"Take it easy today. Markus has the chilluns under control, and things are quiet for now. Tell Tristan I said to take care of you." He ushered her toward the door, the ringing growing worse. "Tell me if you see anything else."

She nodded, feet-gazing. In a quick move, she leaned her head up and pecked his cheek, then hurried off.

As leader of this clan, he'd not put them through pandemonium in their final days. Let Markus continue his tutelage as if it mattered. Let Anne thrive in the first sense of purpose she'd probably ever had in her dismal life. Mercy would compose her furious memoirs, while Oz worked through pointless legal documents on their behalf. Tristan and Harriett could snuggle by the moonlight, living in a fantasy world Nicolas had helped create. Amelia and Jacob, perhaps, would be spared so far away. *Except they hadn't escaped Harriett's visions.*

If the Deschanels were to go down, then they would go down doing what they loved.

Nicolas broke the seal on the bottle of Hennessy, and watched with resigned relief as the amber liquid poured into the crystal glass, the acute stinging scent filling his heart with peace.

Harriet was right, of course. Another Empyrean refugee did arrive that night, and he was, as she also predicted, a bastard of Emperor Aeron. His mother was human, an amusement of Aeron, and when she became pregnant, she fled Farjhem. She was discovered by one of the rebel leaders, a quiet fellow by the name of Trygve, and he secreted her away to his tribe in Mongolia. She died in childbirth, unable to bear the brutal changes brought upon her body, and Trygve adopted her halfling son, Hakon, as his own.

Nicolas heard this story the next day. For when Hakon arrived at the front door, terrified and alone, Nicolas was secreted away in his study behind a locked door, eyes glazing over as a naked Eydis looked up at him from where she balanced on her knees.

His trousers pooled around his ankles. He thought about kicking them away, but what did small details matter? Nothing mattered now. Life as they knew it was coming to a swift end. This was the time to grasp the things he wanted. Regret was pointless.

"How do you like it?" Eydis cooed, soft hand circling the base of his swollen cock.

Nicolas bit down on his lip, hard. "You haven't eaten in days. You're starving. Show me," he managed before his knees nearly gave out. Her warm tongue enveloped him as she did exactly as he asked, moaning as she slid up and down the length of his shaft with expert-level finesse.

He spilled in her mouth. All blood rushed forward; his skin was aflame. His entire body convulsed with the release, and as it left him, he reached for the couch, easing himself down for support.

Eydis made an exaggerated show of swallowing, opening her mouth like you would for a doctor when he stuck you with a tongue depressor. Nicolas grew hard again in an instant.

"Again?" she offered, eyes wide. She advanced toward him on the sofa on all fours, perfect breasts swaying. He wanted to take her nipples between his teeth, to hear her scream for more.

"Oh, yes," Nicolas breathed as she came upon him. But then he had the urge to press his face against the soft satin of her inner thighs. He grabbed her by the hips, flipping their positions, settling her back on all fours in front of him.

Nicolas ran his hands across her soft, perfect ass, settling his thumbs on either side of the pink skin, begging him to unfold it. He pressed her open, eliciting an excited gasp, and admired the glistening folds, untainted. His.

He ran his tongue from end to end, returning to the middle, he slipped inside. She tasted of sweet nectar, something you would travel to the ends of the world to find.

As she writhed before him, Nicolas thought, *Fuck it. Fuck it all to hell. That's where we're going soon anyway, right?*

What does any of it fucking matter anymore?

Lengthening his body, he looked down at her smooth, supple skin. The curve of her back and the soft arcs and cambers of her well-formed hips. Pressing the tip of his cock against her, he asked, "Do you still want this?"

"More than anything," the girl sang back. Her skin flushed in anticipation of the moment, and he grasped her consent had been given the day she walked through the doors of his home.

Seizing Eydis by the hips, he thrust inside, evigbond be damned, guilt be damned, his soul be damned.

When she cried out, he stopped, panting. "Am I hurting you?"

She swallowed hard. "Mhm."

"Do you want me to stop?"

"Emyr, no!"

He took her again and again, relishing a recovery time he hadn't enjoyed since his late teens. All her youth, her beauty, her vitality held him in delicious purgatory. He surrendered to it.

. . .

Apocalypse or not, Nicolas couldn't push away the guilt. Instead of feeling empowered and masculine, he felt like a weak and degenerate asshole.

When the beautiful girl said, at the end, "One day you'll make love to me, and it will be forever."

He hated himself all the more for responding, "Yes, darling."

Nicolas had made a lifelong career of going after whatever or whoever he wanted, remorse irrelevant. This should've left him invigorated, but the second Eydis slipped out the door with her drowsy, giddy smile, despair crept in.

Was this really how he wanted his world to end? As a man whose weaknesses were greater than his honor?

He didn't have the answer. But he overwhelmingly needed to see Mercy. It wasn't a sexual desire, but a need to be in her presence. To touch her skin, maybe catch a glimpse of her smile. All the normalcy he'd pushed away these months, he suddenly craved.

But when he entered his suite, she wasn't head-down in her memoirs. The laptop was on the bedside table, closed. Her eyes were rimmed in red, her mouth quivering.

The despair settled further. "Mercy..."

"Don't." She tightened her mouth. Her lower lip twisted, struggling to control the tremors.

"But you said—"

"I know what I said. And now I know how I feel."

She turned her head away, refusing to look at him. There was nothing he could say. No rebuttal, no further reminder she'd given her nonchalant permission, because he'd known, deep down at some level, that her words were a test. To see if he cared for her and what grew between them, or if it was instead another pleasurable diversion, a promise he'd made with his head in the clouds.

There was nothing Nicolas could say that was anywhere near the realm of adequate to what she deserved to hear.

As his heart caved from the dull, keening ache, Nicolas finally realized he'd fallen in love for the first time in his life.

And thrown it away with one careless, and characteristically selfish, decision.

Nicolas stood in the doorway watching her, rooted in place, for untold time. Eventually, she slipped under the covers and lay staring into the distance, and he sunk to the floor. Both of them eventually succumbed to sleep under their emotional exhaustion.

I love her. Mercy, I love you. Fucking shit.

They slept like this—her on the bed, him slumped in the doorway—for several hours. It was Markus who awakened them in the early morning hours, announcing more visitors had arrived.

"Not children," he added, brow set. Nicolas was too distracted and sleepy to pinpoint the exact emotion behind the gesture.

While Nicolas shook off the tendrils of fatigue, Mercy was up in a flash, wrapping her robe around her and sprinting across the room, jumping over Nicolas as she rushed down the hall, and stairs.

By the time Nicolas made it down, Mercy stood before two tall Empyreans, one male and one female, arms crossed over her chest. Unsettled.

"Clementyn. Are you going to invite us in?" the male asked with a tentative smile.

Mercy stood rooted. She said nothing.

"Well, I'm Lucia," the female said, extending a hand that Mercy did not take. Her loose blonde hair reminded Nicolas of snow; of Amelia, actually. Except hers was not the least bit natural. "And you already know Anders."

"Clementyn... Mercy... I know you're shocked, and upset. But if you'll invite us in, I'll explain everything to you," Anders said. He held his hands out in front of him, in an attempt to disarm her, but the effect reminded Nicolas of someone defending themselves from a crazy person.

Mercy still said nothing. Nicolas glanced at Markus, but his cousin watched the stand-off with quiet fascination.

"Birger sent us," Anders added with a sigh. Whatever patience he had reserved for her shock was clearly wearing off.

Mercy didn't reply, but she backed off to the side so they could enter. Nicolas remembered the name Anders vaguely from her stories, but realized, with even more regret, that he'd not paid enough attention to retain the context.

Markus gestured toward the parlor. "We can go in here."

Lucia flashed him a grateful look and led the way. The others followed.

Nicolas offered chairs, but everyone in the room, including him, chose to stand.

"We work for the Brotherhood," Anders began. "Specifically for Thorvald, but we've been under the Dragon Brotherhood for many years. Since before I met you."

"Should that mean something to me?" Mercy snapped.

"Aidrik hasn't told you?"

Mercy's laugh was bitter and hard. "Aidrik never tells anyone anything. Apparently my taste in men has always been terrible."

Lucia hid a snicker. Nicolas glared at her.

"I owe you an explanation. I know that," Anders offered. "But until now I didn't have the authority to do so."

Mercy shifted, eyes traveling between Anders and Lucia. She carefully avoided Nicolas. "So, tell me then. Obviously you didn't 'ascend,' as I thought when you left me all those years ago."

"No," he agreed. "I didn't. But you now know Ascension has never been more than a method of control. The mark on my body was removed many years ago, when Thorvald rescued me from subjugation. The one you saw when we were together was a decoy, crafted by Astrid's magic. Purely a physical magic. And only enough to keep other Farværdig from giving me a second look if they came upon me."

"You were even more devout than I was, Anders! Why pretend?"

Understanding dawned on Nicolas. *Now* he remembered. Mercy spent years with Anders as a partner, one of only a couple men she'd loved other than Aidrik. He'd supposedly ascended, leaving her alone and confused. Realizing he'd instead deceived her made Nicolas want to punt him on to River Road, but he had no room to talk, after tonight.

"We're scouts," Lucia jumped in. Her presence overwhelmed the room, reminding Nicolas of when he first met Mercy. The glow of her skin ebbed, heating the air around her. "Our task is to seek out those of our kind still under the Senetat's thumb and gauge them for fit to the Brotherhood. Most fail." She shrugged. "Many would rather live in ignorance."

"So you were testing me?" Mercy asked Anders, turning her back to Lucia with cold defiance.

"Aye," Anders replied firmly. "And you failed. But I stayed with you, long past the point I'd accepted you'd never go with me."

Lucia tossed her hair, rolling her eyes to the ceiling. "That always was your weakness."

"I can't talk about this with you. Not right now. Excuse me," Mercy said, and fled the room. Nicolas started after her, then stopped. He was the last person she wanted to see, and that was his fault. Had he not betrayed her, she would have curled up in his arms tonight, falling asleep to his comfort.

With a chill, he realized that sounded kinda nice.

"So this dragon shit. Tell us more," Nicolas said to Anders. Markus watched Lucia as if he hoped to devour her later.

"After some good, solid rest," Anders replied, glancing at Lucia. "You have my word, we'll tell you all of it. Your clan is a part of this now, whatever may come."

"We have plenty of room. You need one suite, or two?"

"Two." Lucia smiled, diverting her eyes briefly to Markus before adding, "And don't expect to see us before noon. It's been a long journey."

With the children all choosing to stay in the outside apartments, Adrienne and Nathalie's suites were still unused. Nicolas led Anders, and Markus took Lucia, giving them each the now-memorized spiel about where to find things, and to treat the home as their own.

Then Nicolas and Markus stood alone in the long hallway, gazing toward the double gallery doors and the world beyond.

"Now things will come together," Markus noted. He ran his hands through his pale hair, eyes heavy. "Finally."

No, thought Nicolas. *This is where they all begin to unravel.*

25
ANASOFIYA

Ana hadn't taken much time to consider what to expect from the naming ceremony, but if she had, she would have imagined something very colorful and theatrical, much like the painted images of the Elizabethan court. Huge, flowing dresses, high flowery collars, lots of dancing, and gaiety. Then the coronation, later, would ostensibly be twice as elaborate.

Empyreans employed an imperialist society, but their decor and practices were surprisingly austere. Red, the color of fire, was active almost universally. From the Crimson Guard, to the deep red robes of the Scholars, to the ruby togas of the Senetat. The dress Agripin ordered her to wear was modest, a long-sleeved, practical gown of—no surprise here—crimson, with simple hems and flowing sleeves.

Agripin was perhaps the one attendee who stood out amongst the sea of red. Instead he displayed his combat uniform, which was more skin than textile.

"Is that customary dress for the occasion?" Ana asked with a lifted eyebrow, as they stood on the dais before the crowds.

The town center was wedged into the mountains, and below, craggy peaks ebbed in spots where you could see the valley floor, now a sea of red. It was an assault to the senses, when all she wanted to do was make sense of the scenery, this being her first time truly outdoors in a strange and magical land.

"In the era of Emperor Agripin, customary is about to take on a far more colorful interpretation," he whispered to her, winking. He held his head high, beaming and nodding.

Eldre Servius stood flanked by two other members of the Senetat, and gave a very brief, mildly annoyed speech announcing Agripin as the soon-to-be Emperor of Farjhem and the Farværdig. Agripin grinned like an errant child who'd stolen his sibling's favorite toy.

The crowd saw a confident, smiling solider who assumed a deserved command. To Ana, who could feel his trembling legs and eagerly tapping feet, he seemed on the verge of an anxiety attack.

"Are you going to be able to speak?" she asked through the corner of her smiling mouth, surprised to realize she was teasing him. *After all he's done to me, he's lucky I haven't punted him off the dais.*

Agripin beamed wider, scanning the crowd. "We categorize speeches right up there with titles. This will be over soon. Hope you like banquets."

"Large, awkward social situations? Love them."

"You do strike me as the sort who does well being the center of attention," Agripin replied; *he* was teasing now. Perhaps later, when the crowds were gone, she could talk to him, one-on-one. Try to better understand what was expected of her, and what kind of person he really was.

But he wasn't a person. He wasn't even human. He was Empyrean. Not just *an* Empyrean, but *the most revered* Empyrean. And, by agreeing to his farce, she had further complicated her already convoluted world by adding another mate—another layer of complexity—that she could have lived without.

A year ago, she had committed an act so crippling to her conscience it drove her from her home in New Orleans, to the distant shores of Maine. A year ago, she had only just exchanged smiles with the beautiful Finnegan St. Andrews. She had still been human, or at least, her Empyrean blood had been as diluted as any Deschanel.

In retrospect, her problems then seemed small and distant compared to the ones facing her now.

Back in the days when she had lost her sense of herself, and given herself to any man as long as he would respect her need for internal privacy, she would have jumped at a chance to spend a few hours with Agripin. He was beautiful; absolutely stunning, and radiant, in every sense of the word. His deplorable personality wouldn't have been off-putting to her, as she only wanted one thing from men at that time.

"You are aware I can hear you, right?" Agripin mouthed.

Ana diverted her eyes, red-faced. She'd forgotten Agripin could get past her well-practiced mental block.

She glanced behind her, up toward the palace. Though it was colossal, jutting into the bright blue sky, she knew precisely where to find Finn. At the right tower parapet. She didn't need to scan for long before her eyes fell upon him. Shielding his eyes from the sun, he couldn't see her clearly, but she could make out his expression perfectly. Fear. Sadness. She wanted to smile, and send him a small reassurance, but he wouldn't catch it in his obscured field of vision. She would give him those reassurances, later, when they were alone.

"Not tonight," Agripin said, maddeningly still riveted to her thoughts. "Tonight you're with me."

Ana's gaze traveled across the sea of unfamiliar faces, red

hair upon red clothing, Empyreans who had journeyed from all over the world for this moment. But not one of them was her ally. From the casual observer to the glaring Senetat, even the partner by her side attempting, for once, to be pleasant.

Not even her thoughts were her own anymore.

A dark wind passed across her heart, whispering subtle promises. *Not entirely alone, then.*

Other than the sumptuous banquet. which might have given Henry VIII a run for his money, the rest of the day went by with only moderate discomfort. It was easier for her now that she'd learned to retreat into her heart. An organ she understood better every day.

Agripin, on the other hand, seemed disappointed he couldn't fawn and preen in front of his loyal followers longer. Doing so anyway, he drew disapproving frowns from the conservative Senetat and Scholars. But he assured Ana, while they stood waiting on his formal naming at the end of the day, their slight annoyance at his personality flaws wouldn't be a problem. They cared only about his obedience. On the surface, Agripin would give that.

Ana expected she would need to meet and greet with the Senetat, and other Empyreans of importance, but the ceremony was quick and sterile. Whenever anyone attempted to approach her, Agripin swiftly ran interference, reducing her role to an expensively decorated arm-piece.

She didn't miss the looks given to her by many of the attendees, however. While some were curious, most looked upon her in an awe-filled fear. The Senetat, conversely, viewed her the way a lion might approach a sickly gazelle.

Eventually, she would need to stand before them and give

her story. Convince them she was the right mate for their new emperor, and not an interloper.

When no one followed them to Agripin's chambers, Ana protested that tonight, finally, she should be able to return to Finn. She'd earned that with her obedience. But Agripin assured her that while there was no royal entourage behind them, spies were everywhere. *Never let your guard down.*

Once the large, iron doors swung shut, Agripin was already tugging at his belt, whipping it off in one move with a loud, decisive crack. Ana flinched, which prompted a smile from him. "You needn't worry I intend to beat you," he assured her, winking. "But come closer."

When Ana didn't move, Agripin grunted and progressed toward her instead. Standing before her, he ran his hands over her velvet crimson sleeves, smelling her hair. She cringed at the bitter smell wafting from his breath. "You're drunk."

"Aye," he agreed, nodding. "A rare gift. I wish I were drunker."

She craned her face away from his searching breath, but she could feel the rasp of his stubble as his breath ran hot against her neck. "Aidrik doesn't know what you are," Agripin whispered. "Should I tell him?"

"It's no great secret," she replied, stepping back.

"You're a rare gem, Anasofiya."

"Don't call me that," she snapped.

"I can't call you by your name?" His face looked entirely innocent.

Aidrik had always used her name in a way that made her feel beautiful, and good, without the flaws that once defined her. Since then, no one, not even Finn, called her that. The right was reserved for her evigbond alone.

With an ache, she realized how much she missed Aidrik.

But she said nothing. Agripin was already mentally moving

on to other things, circling her, drawing long sips from his flasks every few seconds to prolong the "gift" of being inebriated. She was growing concerned for his frame of mind. Alone with him, she had little defense against his strength.

"If I wanted you, I wouldn't need to rape you," Agripin said with a disgusted frown. He stood before her again, both hands at her waist. "You would come to me willingly."

"If you were as excellent at reading minds as you profess to be, you'd know there's no chance of that. I'm tired. Where can I sleep?"

Agripin's eyes twinkled with mischief. "You're sleeping with me."

When she opened her mouth to protest, he added, "I won't touch you, but when the servants enter to present my wardrobe in the wee hours of the morning, it wouldn't do to have you passed out on the couch."

There was no use arguing with him, Ana realized. He knew their opponents significantly better than she did. If Aidrik was around, he might be able to inflict a better kind of sense into the issue, but he wasn't, and she had to trust in her own instincts.

"Yes, Aidrik the Wise is, occasionally, still wise," Agripin agreed. He moved toward a large armoire, opened it, and pulled out a thick white gown. "You can stop wearing the rags you brought with you. You needn't suffer for your own stubbornness, as charming as it is."

She accepted the thick cotton from his hands, and moved behind a tall screen to change. Satisfied that he hadn't followed, she quickly removed her gown, and slipped the shift over her head.

Agripin was already lying back on the large four poster bed, stretched out in a similar white gown. His erection towered under the tunic, creating a tent of crude proportions.

"There is no way I am getting in that bed with you," Ana asserted.

Agripin laughed, reaching down to firmly grasp his salute. "This? Dear, this has nothing to do with you. I am the emperor! Finally! Well, almost."

She couldn't help the laughter that escaped her lips. The situation unfolding her around her was so ridiculous, so bizarre, she could do nothing else. She slipped into bed next to him, and turned on her left side, putting her back to him.

Her thoughts were blank to her bedmate, but her heart.... oh, her heart.

If Agripin could hear the gentle, shadowy weaving of plans and promises, he would not have slept so soundly.

26
AMELIA

"Do you join me now, both of you, with open hearts and minds?" Deirdre asked as they stepped back into the cathedral, rejuvenated with their commitment to one another. She held both her hands out, palms down, reaching for their hands, and they obliged.

Yes, they said. *We do.* The time for looking back, for returning to the life they left behind in New Orleans, had passed as soon as they allowed Deirdre Quinlan's words to take root.

They followed obediently as she led them into a valley beyond the church, the wind carrying her braid defiantly to the left as her layered skirts flapped tight against her. Jacob pulled Amelia close, in a protective gesture.

Before long, they entered a grove of trees, one Amelia recognized, where she'd playfully run from Jacob on their wedding night, daring him to catch her. She longed for the innocence of that night, to recapture the moment when his arms had come around her, whispering, *You cannot hope to best me in my own woods, lass.*

Deirdre led them beyond where Jacob had caught her, disappearing further in as the canopy grew so dense the night sky slipped from vision. The forest floor took on a distinct, raw wildness, as if they'd stepped into a realm where no one ever ventured.

Amelia glanced at Jacob to see if he knew where they were going, but his face stared intently forward as he worked to match Deirdre's steps, while avoiding the bubbling roots and unruly fauna in their path.

Finally, Deirdre stopped. From within her traveling cloak, she pulled out a small horn and put it to her mouth. The sound which came out was not the expected deep intonation but a clear, soft trill, like a bird at the start of spring.

At once, spots of light appeared throughout the forest around them. Torches.

Deirdre turned to them. "We've reached the last point where turning back is an option. Are you both still ready?"

"Yes," Amelia whispered. Jacob nodded, clutching tight to her hand.

"Remember your open heart, then, as we move forward into the glen, and approach not only the *crann bethadh* but also the three fountains."

"Tree of life," Jacob translated softly in her ear.

"I will lead you to the *cumdach.* Your arrival will signal the others to begin consecrating the ground and space. We've practiced for this our whole lives. You cannot allow questions or confusion to cloud your thoughts. What doesn't become evident as the ceremony unfolds, I will gladly explain after."

Jacob flashed a tentative look in the direction of the waiting torches. "What will happen? I mean, what should we do, when we are up on the altar? Did I translate that correctly?"

Deirdre smiled at them both. "I don't know, in truth. We've never been given visions of the outcome, only how to bring you through. But if you approach with your hearts open, and receive the prophecy as the goddess intends, you will know what to do. Don't struggle against it. Embrace it."

"Nothing will happen to us, right? What I mean to ask is, we're not up there to get sacrificed like baby goats or anything?" Jacob continued.

Deirdre offered a light chuckle. "No, Cianán, tonight is a beginning for you. Not an end."

Jacob's hand squeezed Amelia's several times, as he gave her a peripheral smile. She returned it with a light sigh, then nodded at her grandmother.

"Come, then, and open your hearts to the goddess."

THEY FOLLOWED THE TORCHES ROUGHLY A HUNDRED YARDS, BEFORE entering a small clearing in the forest. In the center stood an imposing tree, with a large corded trunk, and roots that stretched in every direction. Upon approach, the sheer size was overwhelming. Drooping branches, nearly touching the ground, stretched out nearly twenty feet from the base, which had a circumference of nearly five times the massive live oaks back home in Louisiana. Resembling no tree she'd ever seen, Amelia wondered at what variety as she touched the palm-sized pointed leaf, marveling at how the shade of green evolved through the color spectrum, shades of blue, orange, and even purple, as she twisted it in the dappled sunlight.

Positioned around the tree, in the shape of a triangle, were three fountains. The waters inside were still, but the light reflecting spilled a dusky hue on the ground.

At least two-dozen people gathered around the great tree, each carrying a torch, and wearing robes of various colors. A few wore the same rich green of Deirdre's, though most were in a burnt orange. Only one, a woman far older than anyone else in the glen, donned gold.

A young girl to the right of the woman in gold took a yew branch and sounded a large bell three times. Several at the perimeter began a low, rhythmic beat on bodhrans, as Deirdre motioned Jacob and Amelia forward.

The scent of sweet, smoky air swathed them, as each of the participants planted their torches in the ground, creating a circular shape surrounding the tree. They slowly backed away, as the couple was led closer to a large slab of stone covered in a lush fabric under the tree.

Jacob glanced at Amelia briefly, then took a tentative seat on the altar.

"Open your mind to me," Amelia whispered to Jacob. He nodded.

I can feel the magic of this place. What do you sense? she sent.

I don't know. It doesn't even seem like we're on this planet anymore.

There's a pulse coming off this tree. A heartbeat, but stronger. It's the lifeblood of everyone here.

Myths claim the Tree of Life is the portal between here and the otherworld.

I could almost believe that.

The old woman in gold stood before her and Jacob and studied them both. Then she placed a crown of flowers atop Amelia's head, and one of ivy on Jacob's.

Turning back toward the others, the woman declared, "*Ta muid anseo na deithe a adhradh!*"

"We are here to honor the gods," the girl in red, the one at her side earlier, translated.

"Thus completes the Consecration of Time," Deirdre called out.

The old woman walked down into the group of others,

weaving in and out in irregular patterns, circling the tree. She stopped before each fountain, cupping both hands to take a drink, allowing any remaining water to return to the fount.

All others in the group followed, weaving the same pattern, stopping before each fountain as she had. *Should we follow?* Jacob wondered.

No... they're doing this for us.

Finally, the old woman repeated her journey, settling back in before the altar.

"Thus completes the Consecration of Space!" Deirdre intoned.

Everyone in the glen then raised their hands skyward, chanting in low tones words neither Amelia nor Jacob could pick up.

"Goddess, we are here connected to all three worlds. We are as the three," the woman in gold sang. "The roots beneath our feet, the water coursing through our bodies, and the sky toward which we reach.

"Oh Morrigan, our heart, our brightest queen! Cast your blessings on to us. We are your children, and you our mother. We have brought forth your most sacred children, Cianán and Cerridwen, those who transcend space and time. Hearken unto us.

"You are the cauldron, now in our grove. Please, Morrigan, come to us! Open the door once more, between our worlds!"

Amelia and Jacob shared a moment of terror. *Is that tree going to come unearthed and swallow us? Were we crazy to come here?*

The chanting amongst the group escalated. The undercurrent filled the air as if the pressure had been removed and there was nothing but a low hum of a thousand voices. A thousand harmonies, where only two-dozen mouths sung.

A gift of joy and gladness rose within Amelia. She did not

know where this wonderful, soft blessing came from, but she empathically picked up Jacob's sense of it as well. His peace, and hope, radiating and filling her, as hers filled him.

She was smiling, and he was smiling, and the beaming bright light around them filled them with grace and joy, as if it were a physical thing growing inside, expanding, replacing their vital organs and blood vessels with a perfect, blinding light.

As this feeling took over, their physical form faded away from the chanting glen, from the great tree and the fountains, beyond the circle of standing stones.

She and Jacob, locked in embrace, stood in the same location they'd sat moments ago, but alone. No altar, no chanting crowds. No archdruid crying out for the goddess.

Amelia looked at the beautiful man standing before her. Her heart, manifesting a thousand lifetimes personified. The blood pumping through her veins. "Cianán," she whispered from her heart, understanding, finally.

"Cerridwen," he breathed back, gazing at her with the same awestruck wonder.

There were no visible time markers, but Amelia was keenly aware—was it the air? Some deep, innate knowledge?—they now stood in the middle of a time long past. When history was written upon vellum, and the world shared a central language.

Jacob, her Cianán, extended his hand and she laced her fingers through this.

They walked forward, but the clearing turned not into a grove. Rather they came upon a modest village where wood fires rose from small buildings constructed of mud and thatch. The smell of gamey meat and rich, stewing vegetation wafted on the gusty breeze.

The men and women they passed did not look up, or acknowl-

edge, instead going about the mundane tasks of daily existence.

They can't see us, *Amelia sent.*

Instinct pushed them forward, until they stood before a flap of animal skin covering the opening to the largest building in the village. A gathering house, or perhaps a seat of government.

A male and female shook hands over the still water of a fountain. Blood dripped from their hands, staining the surface. "Blood on our honor," the male said. He was exceptionally tall and sturdy, with striking red hair and smooth, opalescent skin.

"We give our own blood to the three worlds, as a symbol of our honor and truth," the female replied in kind. She wore a gold robe made of some rough-hewn fabric, her flaxen hair tied behind her in a simple leather wrap.

"They are coming for us, Birger," the woman said, after the onlookers dispersed. Attendants wrapped her wounded hand. "We have seen it."

"Rhosyn, we will stand by you. We are stronger united," Birger assured her.

Rhosyn bore a look of tragic sadness as she shook her head. "Aye, and your word I'd not question. But what of the other Farværdig? You cannot speak for them. I fear the Tuatha will stand alone when the hour comes."

Birger's troubled expression was nearly as forlorn as Rhosyn's. "If we cannot come together without a leader, I fear the leader who will arise of necessity. Astrid and I will take this mantle, insofar as it does not remove the free will of our people."

Rhosyn released a soft sigh, then nodded. "Aye. That is all you can do."

AMELIA DOUBLED OVER AS A WAVE OF DIZZINESS HIT HER. THE connection with Jacob broke temporarily as he, too, knelt in agony.

The landscape changed. Now, they stood amongst an ocean of tents, in a throng of soldiers wearing leather and preparing for battle. The cold air carried the scent of sweat and rotting decay.

"We do not fear death!" a younger man cried to his compatriot.

Another called, "We revel in it! Reincarnation is the gift of our kind!"

"We will rise again," a quiet voice added, gazing wistfully across the plains, "but at what cost?"

The faintness erupted once more, but this time Amelia and Jacob scrambled toward one another. When it cleared, they witnessed the same sea of tents now entirely razed, lying in the scorched earth littered with the fallen.

Human soldiers, the victors, moved through, surveying the damage. "We have won," a man in full red regalia said. "This land is ours."

This time the dizzy spell was quick. A mist obscured their vision, as they stood on a damp but brilliant green knoll.

A woman emerged from the mist. Her pearl skin shone, and her ember hair snaked around both sides of her face, framing it. Her golden dress swept the ground in a long train, gliding atop the surface.

She looked past Amelia and Jacob, toward two individuals standing several feet away. Their doppelgängers, hand-in-hand, the same look of shocked awe on their faces.

"Cianán and Cerridwen. Do not be afraid," her gentle, authoritative voice cooed.

"We only fear disappointing you." Cianán's voice trembled.

"You are here, are you not? You've ventured far from your homes, and all you hold dear. You did not know what you would find. And yet you came."

"We have faith, Goddess Morrigan," Cerridwen answered.

"That is well. You'll need it in the many, many cycles to come." She held out both hands as if they were a balm intended to soothe. "Do you both know where you come from?"

"I am from Findias' tribe," Cerridwen dutifully replied.

"And I from Gorias'," Ciandán added.

"Two of the four origin tribes. One half of the prophecy." Jacob and Amelia watched in enraptured silence as Morrigan glided before the other two, watching them closely. "Goddess Danu has come to me, and shown me hope. There will yet be peace for our tribe again, but not for some time. Her words should give you hope, as they do me:

"Two millennia of wars and strife which cannot be avoided, but can be stopped. One descendant from each of the four to emerge. Four become two, their offspring the peace that unites the two races again.

"From Falias, a male, draoi, pure of heart and an affinity for creatures.

"From Murias, a female, born of fire and darkness.

"From Findias, a female, reincarnated over the many moons.

"From Gorias, a male, draoi. The lover of the Findias heir.

"A son shall spring from Falias and Murias. Findias and Gorias join after many reincarnations, bringing forth a daughter. This son and this daughter will join together, in peace, uniting the Quinlans and Empyreans once more, thus ending the long days of war."

Cerridwen and Ciandán stood in a trance, hardly breathing.

"Your love is pure," Morrigan continued. "One half of our future must spring forth from this purity. The other half will come from fire and turmoil, but those stories are not for you to trouble over."

"One day, your time on this Earth will end. Your reincarnation should come as no great shock, but most of our people, when reincarnated, retain no memory of their past. The two of you will be born

knowing who you are. You will come into this world again, remembering my words, and remembering what you were tasked to do. This cycle will repeat for many centuries. A boon I give you, this wisdom. A bond you will need when the time comes for you to be reborn into a troubled world, and to return to me no longer full of knowledge, but instead filled with trust."

"We know you would never guide us false," Cerridwen insisted.

"Ahh, but it will not always feel thus in your heart, Cerridwen. Or in yours, Cianán. The time will come when your memories fade, and your hearts grow weary. And it is then I shall turn my hope to you, and pray my wisdom and faith holds as true as yours has."

"This will bring peace to our races? Our continued rebirth?" Cianán queried.

"The time will come when your cycle of rebirth will cease. When the life you enter will be your final, yet eternal, one. When the world is ready. You will bring forth a child to this world. A daughter who will join with the anointed heir of Falias and Murias. The son born of fire and strife.

"It is their union which will bring forth peace. Your reward from our Goddess Danu will be eternal life."

"We require no reward. We live in service to the goddess!" Cerridwen declared.

Morrigan's smile was benevolent. "The goddess would not ask such a sacrifice without one."

"Until that day, we will live like this?" asked Cianán.

"No lasting piece, for either race, will be known before then. Fleeting periods of respite only. Many will attempt to fix what has been put asunder by the broken vow, but only at the hour of culmination will the veil of shadows be lifted."

The two lovers' faces were troubled, but neither found words.

"Do not allow worry to consume you," Morrigan soothed. "When the goddess deigns to present a glimpse of our future, we cling to it. With hope and faith.

"I leave you now with one final wisdom: nothing is ever asked of us that exceeds our capacity. Even when things seem beyond possibility, you must grasp for the courage to push through whatever barriers your mind, or heart, construct. This will not be the last time you see me."

Dizziness, again. Jacob and Amelia were swept through one memory after another. Ones Amelia recognized from her seer's visions: Cianán and Cerridwen throughout their many lifetimes.

Morrigan's smooth voice carried across the wind. "The time will come when you can no longer remember my words. Ingrain them on your heart, to your very fabric."

...chanting once again, growing louder, resonating through her skin and bones.

Amelia gasped as the fresh air filled her lungs. She looked over at a dazed Jacob, speechless.

It was over.

The chanting ceased. The attendants in their colored robes stood quietly, waiting for something.

Amelia, I need to get out of here now. Right now, right this damn second. Jacob's thoughts came to her in rolling panic. His hand came down on her thigh. *I can't be here, Amelia, please, get me out of here, I can't—*

The woman in gold approached the altar with a look of eager anticipation. Amelia couldn't process what they'd witnessed. She thought only of Jacob, and of getting him to a place where he felt safe again.

"Deirdre! Where is my grandmother!" Amelia called out,

lacing her hand through Jacob's as he swayed back and forth in a fugue.

Deirdre rushed forward, kneeling. "What's wrong? Is he ill? What did you see? What did the goddess show you?"

"Later!" Amelia cried, grasping the old woman's cloak. "Please, Jacob and I need some time alone. Away from all of this." She let go and gestured wildly to the worried, gazing expressions. "Please!"

Disappointment crossed Deirdre's face. She nodded, briefly, and then signaled toward the crowd. A hooded observer approached, and as he removed his mantle, Amelia recognized him immediately.

"Flynn, take them to the inn," Deirdre ordered. She shook her head. "Perhaps with a night's rest, they'll be more prepared."

Tears streamed down Jacob's face as his blank gaze traveled between them, out to the crowd. His mouth hung open, but the thoughts floated her direction, *I don't know what's going on with me, Amelia. I'm going to scream, please get me out of here.*

Father O'Connor rushed them through the silent crowd and back into the thick woods. He had one hand on each of their backs, urging them forward. He said nothing, only stopping to check on Jacob periodically.

Every moment of the voyage to the inn, to safety, moved as if a heavy, lucid dream.

When they arrived, she offered a grateful thanks to Father O'Connor, and ushered Jacob inside. Their bags were waiting for them.

"Jacob, talk to me," she begged, kneeling before him on the clean but rough wooden floor.

His rocking slowed, and he pressed his forehead against hers, whimpering. "I'm sorry, Amelia, I'm sorry. I thought I could do this."

"Shh, stop. Jacob, what happened tonight was so far out of the realm of anything we've ever dealt with, I don't even know what to make of it. You have nothing to apologize for."

"I thought I could do it. I lived through my father's violence, and I thought I could handle anything after that. I wanted to do this for you." He heaved forward. "I can't breathe."

Amelia held Jacob's head at her bosom as he cried. *What have I done?*

She had never, not in over a decade, seen him like this. Whatever they'd been through that evening, their experiences, and the results, had been vastly different from one another.

As he trembled against her breast, Amelia was inundated with a flood of emotions from Jacob, most keenly his sense of guilt and hopelessness. Talking and reassuring him would do nothing.

There was only one solution, then.

Amelia closed her eyes and wrapped her hands around her husband, drawing in a deep breath. As she did so, the pressure entered from all around, through her pores, pressing against her from every side. Her heart sped as she absorbed Jacob's agony, knowing the risks, willingly accepting them to protect him.

Jacob lifted his head and as his eyes connected with hers. "*Blanca,* no..."

Her head swam with dark stars, and she felt the terrified embrace of her husband as she slipped from consciousness.

Moments later, she awoke.

She stared at Jacob in terrified awe. He stared back.

"I'm fine," she wondered aloud. "It came over me and then it was just... gone."

Jacob's hands searched her, patting her face, hair, arms with a disjointed curiosity, inspecting her. "When I realized what you'd done, I thought I was going to lose you. How..."

"I'm not sure," she replied, but she thought maybe she *did* know. They'd been so caught up in ceremony that they hadn't stopped to process how it had changed them. How they *felt.*

"Maybe we aren't supposed to question it. Like all the crazy, wonderful things we saw tonight." Jacob pulled her hands to his lips, covering them with kisses as his frame of mind shifted to the other polarity. "And a daughter. *Blanca,* did you hear that? I always accepted we weren't going to have children, but you were born to be a mother. Really. You'll make the most wonderful mother in the world."

Amelia's head spun. "We shouldn't jump to conclusions. Everything came to us at once. We need to sleep on it. I have so many questions."

"Of course," he assured her. But his eyes were already wide and searching, thoughts wandering to the moment their daughter would emerge into this world; her first steps, first words, light giggles. In Jacob's pure happiness, his guard was down and his entire mind was laid bare to her.

Tonight was not the night to tell him she'd never bring a child into the world, no matter what the goddess said.

Tonight, she only wanted to thank heaven and Earth for pulling Jacob through, so they could face whatever else may come, together.

For her seer's sense had made an appearance tonight, screaming at her. And the words were loud:

If you push down this path, your life will be forever altered. The world as you know it will cease to exist.

The one left in its place will be like nothing you've ever seen or known.

PART TWO
BROTHERHOOD OF THE DRAGON

"There are many events in the womb of time which will be delivered."

William Shakespeare

27
AIDRIK

Aidrik stood at Agripin's side, awaiting the inquisition with leaden dread. He was prepared for their questions. For the most part, his answers would be honest reflections, and what remained beyond that, Agripin had counseled him on thoroughly. He was confident he could parry any attack thrown at him.

What nagged were the unknowns. He did not share Agripin's confidence the Senetat was already past their anger. The soon-to-be-emperor's arrogance impeded his better judgment. Agripin remained unconcerned at how easily the Senetat had accepted his explanations, and the unorthodox halfling mate.

He'd yet to be reunited with either Anasofiya or Finn, despite Agripin's continued reassurances it was "coming." Meanwhile, they'd sent their son across the ocean, to a fate Aidrik must trust in because communication of any kind was unwise. Aleksandr's future hinged on keeping *Ophélie*, and the protection she offered, completely clandestine.

Aleksandr's existence was the other secret Aidrik insisted

on protecting, but Agripin reminded him the Senetat was not keen on surprises, and they were shockingly competent at seeing through constructed lies.

I will not reveal his whereabouts. I'll force them to kill me first. It would destroy the ward, but I am not the only individual who can weave one.

Agripin did not want to hear Aidrik's doubts. In his mind, the plan was solid. Aidrik imagined that, should their situation falter, Agripin would assure himself it was part of the greater good, bringing things toward their proper conclusion. He had never known a creature so wise, and yet so foolish.

Senetat Sanctuary was a sterile, yet also peculiarly opulent structure. The mammoth, domed room was made of pure marble, ceiling to floor, the color of stark alabaster offsetting the painted figure of a phoenix in the arched ceiling. Bold red, with unclear edges as if the dye could not be contained within the art. A rumor circulated once that it had been painted with the blood of Runeans. Aidrik knew better, but he also overheard Eldre Brutus ruminate on how he wished they'd thought of the idea.

The Senetat shuffled in. Their slippered feet made light *swoosh swoosh* sounds as they glided across the slick marble, their crimson robes dusting the immaculate floor as they passed. Nine leaders. An odd number to ensure a true majority; a farce of democracy.

The Senetat stopped in a v-formation, creating an arrow pointing at the assembly. Those most senior in rank stood closest to the front. Eldre Brutus, who had requested their presence upon arrival in Farjhem, stood in the middle of one arm, signifying his prominence was moderate compared to others standing before him. Agripin shifted in annoyance as they assembled.

Grand Eldre Servius settled in at the front of the V. Servius, then, their new leader. Aidrik tensed. There were few eldres who had fundamentally disagreed with Aidrik more than Servius. At the time, Servius had been a novice eldre, scrambling for even small vestiges of power or intrigue, selling secrets to the highest bidder. Times had evidently changed.

Other than three—Brutus, Servius, and Cassian—the faces were alarmingly new. The order usually guarded their members closely, and seldom replaced them.

"Grand Duke Agripin, future emperor of this realm," Eldre Servius boomed. His voice carried and bounced off the marble in repeated echoes, with no furnishings or tapestries to provide absorption. With an ugly smile he affected a low, cartoonish bow, making no attempt to hide his disdain.

When Agripin nodded, Servius rose, and turned to Aidrik. "Aidrik the Wise, Cheater of Death. Wielder of Forbidden Secrets and Magic."

"No great secrets or magic," Aidrik replied carefully.

"Yes, we're privy to the crude story of how you sundered the maker's mark using a scullery dirk," Servius rejoined, turning his nose in disgust. "I can't portend to understand this foolish decision. You could have lived forever in our ranks. In luxury. Choosing the life of a vigilante is beneath you. Yet not entirely surprising."

"My choice was not as desirable as you're suggesting. It was either die at the hands of black magic disguised as Ascension, or risk death at my own hand. I'd rather choose the hour of my passing," Aidrik replied with forced blandness. On his right, Agripin released a small warning huff, which he ignored. "You'd not have allowed me to live, had I stayed."

"Aye," Servius agreed, his skin stretching into a long, slow smile. Despite the everlasting youthfulness of Empyreans, Servius had the look of disintegrating parchment. "I'd have activated you myself."

"So we understand one another."

"No, we never did," Servius replied. "Who else knows of your defection?"

Aidrik was surprised at this question. Either the Senetat did not know the answer, or they were hoping to catch him in a falsehood.

Knowing that some of them, like Agripin, might possess the ability to get past a telepathic block, Aidrik had ceremonially cleared his mind before the meeting, pushing aside any thoughts of the Deschanels, except Ana and Finn. He would have kept them from under their purview, as well, but that ship had sailed.

"My evigbond, and her husband," Aidrik replied.

Eldre Cassian snickered. "A human evigbond, with a husband. If you wanted her so badly, why not eliminate him?"

"Or," Servius thundered, "eliminate her, too. She is an affront, and an abomination, to our laws! We should execute you for this law-breaking, after allowing you to watch her and her lover writhe on the dais first."

"That won't be necessary," Agripin replied, breaking his silence. "Aidrik's evigbond or no, I care not. She is *my* mate now. My *chosen* mate and the future empress of this realm. She will remain unharmed."

Servius' jaw clenched, but he recovered his frustration well. Aidrik could not penetrate his rival's thoughts, but it was apparent Servius saw the benefit in having Agripin's full cooperation. A secret halfling, one no one needed to know about, was a small price to pay to keep things harmonious.

"On sight, Anasofiya looks as Empyrean as my own family," Agripin went on, less to convince, and more as if he were waxing for the sake of the esteemed audience. "Finnegan, her partner, could easily be passed off as one of Oriana's 'pets' if an explanation became necessary."

"I can't pretend to understand why you chose this halfling when you could have claimed any pureblood in all the race," Servius replied with a suggestive eye roll. "But why you keep her mate around completely defies comprehension. Is there something we should know?"

"Other than my dearest enjoys having toys of her own, and I aim to please her? Nothing at all," Agripin replied, with a winning smile.

Aidrik said nothing. He was unhappy with the manner in which Anasofiya's reputation and person were being bantered. But Agripin was selling this profane situation better than Aidrik ever could.

Servius stared at Agripin evenly for several long minutes. It reminded Aidrik of the solemn, judgmental looks the Scholars gave fledglings who dared to ask a question in contradiction to their teachings. Finally, he turned back toward Aidrik.

"Other than your halfling toys, you've encountered no other Empyreans, no other beings who know your identity, and what betrayals you've committed?" he pressed. Aidrik could not discern if his skepticism was of a rhetorical nature, or if he truly could not grasp how Aidrik had managed to escape detection.

"I am adept at remaining hidden," Aidrik replied.

"For over a thousand years?"

"I managed to prevent knowledge of my existence from reaching your ears," Aidrik replied with a touch of defense.

"What Aidrik means to say," Agripin started, stepping in, "is his word is his bond. If he says he has not spoken with others, he has not. And it wouldn't have benefitted him to go flaunting his status. He would have been captured, and straightaway executed."

Servius searched for a means to dispute their claim, perhaps even a way to justify slicing Aidrik's head from his shoulders at that very moment. When he did neither, Aidrik was far more worried than relieved. He'd rather know his enemy than guess at intentions.

"If we discover otherwise, we will have no choice but to exact the punishment that you as yet deserve," Servius said, getting the last word. "The fact remains we must decide what to do now with you."

Aidrik noticed the muscles under Agripin's robe flex, the only outward sign of his agitation. "As we have both graciously agreed, Aidrik's services are necessary. He will be my first-in-command, and my right hand."

"What of that twit Cyler? He'll be disappointed to lose his station," Brutus said with an oily smirk.

Agripin tensed at the mention of a name Aidrik was not familiar with. "Cyler is young and inexperienced. He will understand and appreciate the opportunities I've given him."

Another eldre grunted. "And how will we explain this to the population? Aidrik 'ascended' and now has come back?"

"Of course not, Eldre Felix," Agripin replied. "We wouldn't want to undermine the significance of our beloved Ascension." Aidrik hoped he was the only one who could hear his heavy sarcasm.

"Then *what?*" Servius asked, sighing with affected weariness.

"Would it not send a powerful message if Aidrik had been on Earth all along?" Agripin began, strutting out before the Senetat. "How powerful for you to claim the much beloved Aidrik the Wise had been on special assignment for the Senetat?"

The shock on Servius' face was immediate and amusing, but Aidrik knew better than to smile. "It may appease the questions, yes. But it does not excuse the behavior."

"Grand Eldre," Agripin said, kneeling on the platform in

feigned supplication. "Pulling Aidrik back into the life he fought so hard to leave is punishment enough, I should say."

"For now," Servius conceded.

Servius then bowed, saying no more, and the v-formation of eldres reversed its direction, momentarily forming a W, as he moved to depart, the choreography precise. Reminiscent of a flock of birds changing direction.

Aidrik understood consequence had not been avoided. If he made an ill move, not even Agripin could shelter him. *Pray we do not need long.*

"That went fairly well," Agripin chirped, once they had left the sanctuary and emerged back into the crisp mountainside air.

"Aye," Aidrik agreed, inhaling the healing scent of his homeland. That, at least, was welcome. "But we'd do well to practice expedience unless we want to be dangling from a rope in town hall next week."

"I should give you special accolades for not shifting into insurgent mode and attempting to massacre them where they stood," Agripin acknowledged as the carriage arrived. "Though that would have made for a stunning display."

"It is not only *my* neck I must be concerned with." He waited for Agripin to ascend into the buggy and then climbed in after. Small touches, such as Farjhem's refusal to adapt to man's technologies, to remain firmly rooted in a simpler time, were among the things that made Aidrik wish he were home in better circumstances. He'd never stepped foot in a car. Never would. "Now that the inquisition is behind us, I request congress with Anasofiya and Finn immediately."

Agripin stretched and yawned, lazing back into the plush satin seat. "Congress is an amusing term for your triad's arrangement. Yes, of course. But perhaps later tonight. First, a nap. This emperor business is exhausting!"

28
LUCIA

Lucia hit her second wind about ten miles downriver, past where the Mississippi bent into a near hairpin. When she'd asked Nicolas last night, after he'd shown her and Anders to their quarters, where the good running routes were out here in plantation country, he'd shrugged and said she'd better stick to the top of the levee.

Fine. She'd certainly run worse routes. The South American rainforest came to mind, when they were tracking one of Jorun's folks in the Amazon wild. Her unique gifts meant very little when held against the forest's predators.

Exercise wasn't the pull anyhow. She got enough of that in with the scouting, whether it be trekking across the barren Russian frontier or climbing walls of red rock in Utah. Escape was the motivation behind the marathon-length sprints. It was her only tether to sanity. Her method of grounding herself.

Wandering had been in her heart since the very early days, when she was still under the deceptive thumb of the Scholars in Farjhem. In the beginning, her story was not so very different from Mercy's: ripped from her parents, forbidden from seeing them beyond the scheduled holiday events in town center, and force-fed propaganda like it was a core food group.

When Mercy was faced with her first test, she chose blind faith. When Lucia saw her opportunity to bolt, she took it.

She'd been under instruction at the Scholar's Temple for over half a century, though it hadn't taken but a sliver of that time for her to start questioning their stories and motives. Tales of Old Aita, wandering the Earth in agony. Of Birger and Astrid, executed for their myriad sins. Most of the students responded as the Scholars expected, with sad head bobs and exaltations of the rebel's foolishness. But Lucia's rogue heart ignited to full flame when she thought of the bravery they showed. To be that free!

Secretly, she also suspected none of it was true. She wanted to believe Birger and Astrid were still out there, being the amazing creatures they were born to be. That Old Aita was having the last laugh, always. Lucia spent the first fifty years of her tenure waffling between the two sides. If the Scholars were wrong, and the rebels were in fact thriving, she could find her way to freedom and live a life of her own choosing. But if the rebels *had* been executed... if Aita *was* miserable and regretting her defection... Lucia would sacrifice everything on this miscalculation.

In the end, she decided it was worth the risk.

On Fardag, or Father Emyr's Day, while all the lambs were bent in supplication to the phoenix idol, and the guards distracted, she slipped out a hidden entrance, to freedom.

Lucia's passions often lived in the moment, or no more than a couple steps beyond her current destination. She'd given appropriate thought to how to get out of Farjhem, but the moment she stepped on to Norwegian land, she immediately realized the folly in her plan.

So she ran. One foot after the other, and she didn't stop until her feet bled through her boots. She slept only a few hours at a time, ate what she could forage, and continued running until she ran into an Empyrean with a presence so overwhelming she was at first convinced the Senetat had caught up to her.

Thorvald's strong arms came about her, and he whispered with his full, generous mouth, "You're safe now, *mi belleza*."

How he'd known where to find her, he would never say. He took her to his settlement on the *Costa del Sol* in Andalusia, a city built in the cliffside fifty miles from Malaga, forged from the ruins of a 12th century Moorish alcazar. Here she learned of the rebel's pure hearts and unwavering strength; of the greater Dragon Brotherhood, "Runean" only a slur invented by the Senetat, another means of marginalizing something they feared. Thorvald's people were not only rebels, but warriors. Not the heathens the Scholars preached about, they were preparing for war.

Every tomorrow became the day they would reclaim Farjhem. *Most of the Brotherhood do not share our thirst for war,* Thorvald told her, when she exclaimed they needed to rouse the world to this cause. *But one day, they will. That is the day we prepare for,* mi belleza.

Lucia quickly fell to loving Thorvald, who towered over seven feet with monstrous limbs to match. Powerful words behind smiling eyes and easy gestures inspired her to his cause. Not just for freedom anymore. For *him.*

Her greatest and deepest fear was that the Scholars and Senetat would eventually catch up to her, find her, and drag her back. But they never did. *The fools either think you're dead, or have disregarded you as a risk. It's a damn good thing they don't see in you what I do, right* mi belleza?

Thorvald always knew exactly what to say to put her at

ease. On their long walks across the rugged Spanish coastline overlooking the Mediterranean's cerulean waters, she could listen to him speak for hours. Stories about his own past, and how he came to be a force within the Brotherhood. One of the oldest Farværdig walking the Earth, he claimed, and she believed him.

It didn't bother Lucia that Thorvald didn't see her through a lover's eyes. Her love grew vast enough for both of them.

Lucia's rare and potent shamanistic powers were immediately put to use in the settlement. Though an empath, her strength was not in witnessing the emotions of others, but in transferring and soothing them. Lucia could assuage drekar with a simple touch of her palm. What made this gift special was that it caused no harm to Lucia whatsoever. She was never at risk of being imperiled, like other empaths when they attempted such a transfer.

The soft nature of her healing skills felt like the universe's idea of humor at times. Lucia was born of fire! She should have been an elementalist, manipulating the earth with her fingertips. As consolation, it was her unique gift which made her valuable to Thorvald, and later, unfolded into the opportunity to be one of his scouts.

Thorvald's sole purpose was preparing for war, and that required bodies.

His scouts were an elusive bunch, and a role among them was coveted. Always on the move, always working, Lucia rarely saw one in the encampment. And when they did show up, they were gone before next light.

The thought of being separated from Thorvald was excruciating. Yet, the promise of seeing the world exhilarated her!

She was partnered with Anders—they were never, not ever, allowed to scout alone—a create who was, from the start, hard to know. But he was sharp and quick on his feet. His gift of magic detection spanned miles, and his extended silences were often a crucial part of avoiding danger. In the two hundred years they'd worked side-by-side, she had not once feared for her life when Anders was by her side.

WHEN THORVALD DEMANDED LUCIA AND ANDERS RETURN TO Andalusia, at first she'd been horrified, thinking they'd done something wrong. There was no reason for a scout to return to the settlement once deployed, unless something serious happened.

There was, of course, that time Lucia tossed a sailor over the bow of his own boat, but should she have let him continue that business with his hands and the whiskey bottle? Promising not to meddle in the affairs of Children of Men only counted when men weren't meddling in the affairs of her body.

Thorvald pulled them far from the group, to a cave where Lucia remembered he often retreated to think, and there he'd revealed their time was coming near. *Agripin has finally ascended the golden saddle. Aidrik the Wise yet lives, and the two have partnered together. Can you imagine a force such as theirs? We must prepare for the inevitable battle on the horizon. We must protect our Livia. Others in the Brotherhood have youth as well. There is a safe house in the Americas. New Orleans. Aidrik has placed a mystic's ward on the estate land that has held for over two centuries. We've been advised to send our fledglings there, for protection, until the war has passed and victory is ours.*

He may as well have thrown the words up in her lap, for she couldn't have prepared herself for the shock of them. Despite her fervor in aiding Thorvald's war preparations, deep down she'd never truly believed the day would come.

Her and Anders' specific role was revealed shortly thereafter. *You are to go to this safe house and train them.*

Lucia choked back a laugh. Except, Thorvald never said anything he didn't believe and mean, and he'd already moved into the topic of mobilization.

They were to leave immediately, with Livia. But as Liv's situation was so precarious, they were commanded to assess the situation at the safe house before bringing her into the mix. Had Thorvald not commanded this safety precaution, Lucia would have insisted upon it anyway. Livia, being a halfling, couldn't pass as Empyrean with her lovely olive skin and glossy teak hair.

Anders accepted the assignment with unusual fervor, and went to rejoin the rest of their peers for the brief reunion they were granted. As he pushed past the guard, Lucia could hear the empowering words of their war ballad wafting on the warm Spanish breeze:

We all have our secrets
We all have our scars
Hiding all our shadows, locked inside our hearts
Face the evolution
Written in the stars
Force a revolution, for us
Awaken at dusk

But Lucia had questions. She always had questions.

Thorvald... isn't now, if we're finally serious about battle, the time where we should be increasing our scouting efforts? If the house is safe, why not leave them there and let it be done?

Lucia, mi belleza, *you are always thinking only as far as tomorrow. We don't advance in this fight with spears and guns. Our weapons are something less tangible, and numbers will only stretch as far as our leadership can span. Are our youth not also weapons?*

Then why not bring them with us? Why bother shipping them away?

His hard expression confused her when paired with such a beautiful smile. *They are not ready. But you,* mi belleza, *can make them ready. If Emyr holds us, we may not need to call on them.*

Thorvald's protectiveness of his clan could turn to cold detachment the moment it needed to. Should she, also, learn to separate her emotions when bigger issues were at stake? Well, she *had*, to be fair. Many times. But there was something ominous and deeply unsettling about the gleam in Thorvald's eye when he suggested the children might become pawns in their war games.

Thorvald had never steered her wrong, though. He'd saved her, and bestowed upon her the freedom she'd craved. Given her a purpose in her scouting role, and at times, a fatherly love.

Now he was asking something in return. She wouldn't let him down.

Anders declared their first morning that not only would they be training the refugees, but also the halflings living under the roof. *You're only safe here as long as Aidrik lives. He's one of the last mystics capable of producing powerful wards. Since I don't see any Quinlan draoi here, we have an "area of exposure."*

She'd expected the halflings to put up a fight, but they all jumped at the chance to learn more about themselves, and what they could do. All but Mercy, but what was she? A Child of Man? Tension burned between her and Anders, and Lucia had *no* desire to know the sordid details.

They divided the group evenly in half, splitting the work. Lucia was furtively pleased to find Markus in her group. She'd rarely found herself in the bed of a true Child of Man, but a halfling? She was not at all opposed to trying, especially not with this rare Nordic beauty.

After their first full day of getting to know the trainees, Anders came to her with a look of intense concern.

"Lucia, I'm going to call on you to shoulder the burden of training most everyone. I wouldn't ask if I didn't think you could, and if it wasn't necessary."

"Are you leaving me?" she'd demanded.

"Far from it. Thorvald failed to mention we have a youth here who is born of a halfling, a draoi, and a pureblood Farværdig."

Her face must have expressed sufficient shock that he continued on without waiting for an audible response.

"He also failed to mention this child, Aleksandr, is a powerful mystic. Lucia, I could see the power physically radiating off him. He was producing a damned electrical charge powerful enough to light up the neighborhood. And he has absolutely no fucking idea."

"Stellar. You can teach him, then."

"Can I?" Anders ran his hands across the growing stubble on his chin. He was normally fastidious about hygiene so this uncharacteristic abandon of it intrigued her. "I don't know. Hell, we were told mystics were dying off, that no new ones had been born in what, two thousand years? And now, I'm sitting in a house with two of them. One thirty years old, the other a few months."

The gravity of what Anders was getting at increased Lucia's annoyance with Thorvald's mission. "You're asking me to take everyone else. Allowing you to focus on two."

"Lucia, if the world finds out these two exist... no, well, they can't. We won't allow it. But they can't be kept from their potential, nor can either of them be allowed to know that potential without the proper training!"

"That answers my question, then. I'll look after the kiddie pool while you solve all our race's problems."

Her group was so diverse she didn't know where to start. She had Tristan, the telepath; Harriett, the seer; Anne, the arborkinetic—*like Nerys,* thought Lucia; Markus, the illusionist; Eydis, the persuader; Sindre, the elementalist; Hakon, the bestiakinetic; and Livia, the empath.

Their first training session resulted in one big battle of the egos. Sindre would not stop making grand bonfires in the sky with one hand, and extinguishing them with bolts of water from the other. Anne grew perturbed by this and sent half the parterre garden after him. Harriett made implications they were all headed toward a gory, fiery doom, because Eydis wouldn't stop persuading her to spill her guts. Hakon and Livia watched from the sidelines, overwhelmed.

Patience extinguished, Lucia gave them each tasks. Homework. *Tristan and Eydis, practice reaching for a specific person, not in this family, and breaching their thoughts. Harriett, attempt to see into a specific point in the future on your own, before a vision comes to you. Anne, try to summon the plants when calm, dear. Sindre, tone it down and create a list of practical applications. Hakon, work on communicating with that cat, Miss Kitty. Livia, observe each of them and gauge their frame of mind. Report back on the results.*

As they dispersed, Markus hung back. "And what would you like me to do?"

Lucia tossed her head back. "Oh, Markus. I think you know."

A WEEK INTO THEIR TRAINING, SEVERAL THINGS WERE CLEAR.

Tristan was far too concerned with Harriett's frame of mind to focus.

Whatever Harriett was seeing freaked her out so badly she stopped coming to training.

Anne lived in a constant stage of agitation. Therefore, so did the plants at *Ophélie*.

Eydis was so focused on winning Nicolas' affections as to not be useful in any other capacity.

Sindre had razed not one, but two buildings.

Hakon kept sending Miss Kitty running to the barn in fear.

Markus had been practicing his skills all his life and she had nothing new to show him—at least not where illusions were concerned.

And Livia was so overwhelmed with reading it all that the girl slept half the day.

In other words, Lucia was failing miserably.

"I give up," she told Anders. "I'm a scout, not a trainer, dammit."

"No, you're an impatient wench who can't keep her hands to herself," Anders grinned. "You think I haven't noticed?"

Lucia didn't rise to the bait. "There are no rules about it in our world. And the whole *automatic evigbond* bullshit is a scam by the Senetat. We don't have the mark, so it doesn't apply to us."

"He's distracting you."

"The ineptitude and immaturity are distracting me."

She was shocked when he shrugged, dropping the matter. "Lucia, let them swim to the Gulf for all I care. Training them was never the objective anyway. I know that now."

Lucia flipped her hands to her hips. "Oh, really? So you're in contact with Thorvald, are you?"

Anders pressed his lips into a tight line. "He's trusted us for centuries to bring him the best recruits. Well, we're about to bring him the biggest and best recruits of all. Sindre burning down some ancient barn, and Anne zapping the nutria with bougainvillea, won't even be a blip on his radar."

LUCIA WANTED TO BE RELIEVED AT NOT HAVING TO SPEND HER TIME herding cats, but instead she felt neutralized. She'd never been relegated to the background in all their travels, and it left her with an awful, sinking feeling not even Markus' adept attentions could dissolve.

She sat pondering this one afternoon, in the study, when a Child of Man entered the room. A new face.

The dark-haired, emerald-eyed man dropped his gaze but offered a polite handshake, which she returned and immediately felt flashes of his pain course through her. *A tortured soul, this one.* "Oz Sullivan. I'm the attorney for the Deschanels, here to work with Nicolas on some estate business. Were you in the middle of something?"

The heaviness of this man, as if even the skin on his back felt too substantial to bear, was overpowering. She could fix it, as she had done so many times before. Except... no. Not this time. There was a process, an evolution, and this tender creature resided somewhere in the middle. To interrupt would not be a mercy, but a cruelty.

"Nothing worth continuing," Lucia had replied. She gave him her name, and then said, "Nicolas is tied up for the foreseeable future. Maybe I can help?"

29
AMELIA

Getting to know the Quinlans was akin to stepping into another world entirely, a realm where things seemed and felt vaguely familiar but were interlaced with wonders she had before only believed as fantasy.

Growing up a Deschanel, the part of her brain equipped to suspend disbelief was well-calibrated. She'd never seen a vampire, for example, but if someone insisted they were real, it would be no great stretch for her to accept it, once she saw it with her own eyes.

But life as she knew it—her life, and Jacob's—had fundamentally changed. Their lives had meaning far beyond anything they could have ever imagined. That they were reincarnated, many times over, and together, was something they both slowly moved to accept. As the days passed, the belief evolved to a deeper sense of *knowing* this to be an irrefutable truth, at a very organic level. Amelia no longer had visions, but *memories*. The ceremony had awakened them in Jacob as well, allowing him to see her through the dual lens of both Jacob and Cianán.

If the bond between their hearts had been strong before, it now forged unshakeable. Jacob's soft hands laced through hers were no mindless gesture, but one they'd shared a thousand times over, across many lifetimes and countless experiences. When he said he loved her, he was speaking not of Amelia, but of the soul rooting her current body to this Earth. Her heart was full to bursting, and she wished everyone could feel this kind of love, this indescribable sense of spiritual fusion and purpose. A joy no one had the power to tear away.

On only one topic were they divided: having a child. With all the excitement and discoveries coming at them, the discussion had been relegated to *We'll discuss it later. We have time.*

But time would not change the Curse. Though it had become mercifully quiet in the past month, it would return. Amelia had no doubt, nor did her mother or any of the other family leaders. *The Curse is only a tiny element of a much larger picture,* her Aunt Nora had said. *The Deschanels have Empyrean blood running through their veins, and so they, too, suffer from the Empyrean's defection of the vow. You must solve the root of the problem, not attack the symptom. Fulfillment of the goddess' words will rectify both concerns.*

It was a circular argument. Amelia wouldn't bring a child into the world for fear of the Curse, and the Curse would remain as long as no child existed.

And no one, no matter how many times she asked, could explain how they were supposed to find this other couple... the other half of the prophecy. Without them, the idea of having a child remained inconsequential.

She'd wrapped her mind easily around all the rest they'd learned over the past week, but the topic of a child remained stubbornly sidelined. *We have time,* Jacob reminded her, and she would take advantage of that promise.

• • •

THE MORNING AFTER THE FATEFUL CEREMONY, THEY'D AWOKEN wrapped in one another's arms, the scent of the forest and smoke still potent and heady against their skin. While they'd slept, someone brought in a full breakfast, accompanied by a note from Deirdre to return to the glen once they'd eaten and showered. *You'll know where to go. From here on out, you'll always know your way to us.*

Amelia's grandmother was true to her word. After breakfast, she and Jacob ambled over the hills and entered the forest, stepping along the path as easily as if they'd walked it a thousand times. When they emerged into the tribe's glen, Jacob remarked how different it looked in the daytime.

The valley floor was blanketed in a bright green moss, which stretched up and over the roots of the great *crann bethadh*. The leaves of the tree held colors so varied it reminded Amelia of the crystal prism her father used to dangle from the rearview mirror of his Mercedes. As light hit the foliage, the colors changed. Developed.

All around them, flora and fauna pulsed with life, in colors Crayola surely hadn't yet defined. Beyond, the water of the three fountains remained still, with an opaque blue surface that looked painted with a soft brush.

Unlike the prior night, there was no Quinlan presence to be seen. Jacob pointed out something they'd not noticed before, far in the distance, beyond the fountains: a small village.

"I must've wandered these woods a thousand times as a kid, and I never remember stumbling upon two dozen wooden huts," he remarked.

"You never found the glen either. I wonder if it's like Farjhem, where the average person can't see it with the naked eye."

He smiled, and took her hand. "Yeah, well, there's certainly nothing average about us anymore. Except, your cooking, that hasn't improved much."

Amelia sagged her head sideways in mock offense. "How would you know? I haven't had a chance to try lately."

Jacob kissed the tip of her nose with a playful smirk. "No amount of voodoo druid magic will fix your tendency to start fires making toast, *Blanca.*"

He traced his tongue along her bottom lip, a feeling that was as electric and alive as the woods around them. Her skin tingled with desire, traveling in a wave from her neck to her toes. *Want him. Now. Always.* She cupped his inner thigh, loving the way his eyes widened as if he *hadn't* expected it, and how his expression swiftly turned to hunger.

"Ahh, you're here earlier than we expected!" Deirdre's voice sang through the glen. Amelia felt the blood rush to her face, and saw the same in Jacob. She wondered if the woman had sensed what was about to transpire on their sacred ground.

If Deirdre knew, she didn't let on. "Come, I'll take you back to our settlement. It isn't much by the standards either of you are used to, but we've never needed much. Our world lives in here." She touched a fist to her heart. "I'll take you first to the sacred hall, our only formal structure in the village. Seara, Nora, and Rosemary await us. We will see how you feel after, and if you're up to it, I'll introduce you to the others. All in all there are fourteen of us. Everyone serves the goddess in their own way."

Jacob and Amelia followed. On closer inspection, the buildings appeared to be some kind of canvas, stretched and sealed with a strong bond, possibly cement. Built to last, and to withstand a range of elements. Each structure was the same tan shade, though they'd been customized to the dweller. One had an ivy plant stretched over the top, another had some handmade chimes representing the sun and moon. Subtle changes from home to home made the marked difference between boring uniformity, and the sense that everyone's unique personalities had a place.

They passed several Quinlans as they moved through the small series of buildings. The night before they'd all been hooded so Amelia couldn't match the faces in the light of day.

A young couple smiled broadly as they walked by. The man affected a light bow, and his female partner scolded him, but never stopped smiling.

"Regan, Padraig. I'll introduce you later," Deirdre told them, then ushered Jacob and Amelia forward, toward a building three times the size of the others. "I'd like to say we're above being star struck, but, you see, we've all waited so long for this. You'll forgive the others if they're excited to see you. Maybe even afraid."

"They've nothing to fear from us," Amelia said, because it was the right thing to say. But as the words left her, she thought, *What do they know about us that we don't yet?*

A painting of a large sapling, done in black dye, marked the double door opening to the sacred hall. Inside, a broad raised platform sat near the back (*Not all gatherings are in the glen,* Deirdre explained), but the majority of the space was decked in an enormous woolen rug. Oversized pillows were spread across the carpet, and in the very center sat three women of varied ages. Arranged in a circle of pillows, three empty between them.

Amelia and Jacob each took a pillow when prompted, and Deirdre took the last one.

"Four generations of Quinlan women," Deirdre began. "Those of us in this tribe are descended from the line of Findias, though we have one Quinlan from Gorias, with us today, as our tribes will soon need to unite toward our common cause."

One of the women nodded, and reached a hand toward

Jacob's arm. His expression went white. "Rosemary Quinlan. Your grandmother, Jacob. So very pleased to see the fine man you've become."

Amelia loosely recalled mention of Jacob's grandmother in their initial talks the day before, but hadn't considered they might really meet her. For a woman in her seventies, she was quite striking; her black hair had only glimpses of the aging white strands, and her green eyes—Jacob's, Amelia realized—had a dazzling, youthful effect.

"I don't remember you, I'm sorry." Jacob couldn't look at her. His eyes stayed trained on her bony hand resting tenderly on his forearm.

"You wouldn't, dear. Your mother made her choice when she was very young. She wanted a normal life for you and your siblings, even though her seer's eye told her your truth was already long established."

A biting sadness gripped Amelia as she thought of all Jacob had been denied. In stories, the hero was prone to suffer many hardships until their destiny lay before them. Jacob almost certainly fit this mold. In comparison, she'd had her share of losses, but her life had been full of love and family to bring her through.

"My life *has* been full, because of you, *Blanca,*" Jacob whispered. She'd forgotten their minds were now open to each other after last night. No secrets.

Amelia smiled and tightened her hold on him.

"Jacob, I hope you'll spend some of your time with us getting to know your grandmother. Just as I hope to do with my Amelia," Deirdre said with a warm smile. "But let's begin with introductions." She gestured first toward a woman Amelia recognized as the leader from the night before, the one who'd been wearing gold. Last night, she would have guessed this woman was no more than sixty. Now in the light of the day, with the soft age spots and gently sagging skin, she was clearly thirty years beyond that original estimate.

"My mother, your great-grandmother, and leader of our tribe, Seara," Deirdre finished.

Before Amelia could think to speak, Deirdre then motioned toward the younger woman. As her eyes locked on the dark-haired woman, she didn't need an introduction. "Aunt Nora. You look just like my father."

"You resemble Noah strongly as well," Nora said, as her eyes took her in. "Though I see plenty of Colleen in you. You've grown into an absolutely beautiful woman, Amelia."

It settled over Amelia that she was sitting in the same room with her great-grandmother, grandmother, and aunt. An entire branch of her already prolific world had opened up in an instant. The familiar tingle signaling tears surfaced, and she bit them back. "I'm turning thirty in a few days, and more than anything else, I'd like to understand why I was never allowed to know any of you."

"That is Deirdre's story to tell," Seara answered. Unlike the strong voice of the ceremony, her tones now were gravelly and strained. *The goddess speaks through her in the glen,* Amelia realized.

Sensing the emotional unrest brewing within her, Jacob moved closer and his strong arm came around her waist. The move was as much protective as stabilizing.

Deirdre settled into her pillow, crossing her legs over the soft chemise. "I met your grandfather, Kellan Jameson, in school in Killianshire. You see, though we're raised here with the tribe, we are still sent into town for our academic education.

"Over time, we fell in love. The story of our courtship is not terribly interesting, except to say that, for an Irishman, he was dreadfully close-minded. I thought we could get past that, though, the way young lovers often think their problems are easily overlooked when the heart is doing the thinking. My mother cautioned me, but I'm sure you can guess how well *that* went."

Seara's wrinkled mouth tightened into a smile. "My free spirit. And you wonder why I skipped a generation and chose Nora as my successor instead."

"I've never wondered, Mother." Deirdre smiled sweetly and Amelia saw the first evidence of a fracture in the relationship. "After I had my daughters—Nora, Nevina, and Niamh—I began to miss the simplicity of the tribe's daily life. I felt disconnected from our goddess, and from nature. I tried, at first gently, coaxing Kellan to return with me. But from the very first word, he was adamantly against it."

I'm so grateful you've always accepted who I am, and where I come from, Amelia sent silently to Jacob.

How else was I going to get you in the sack? Jacob cracked a tiny smile, sharing a glance from his peripheral. *There was never a question,* Blanca. *To love you is to love everything that comes with you. Bad cooking, crazy-ass family curses, and a heart that took me in.*

And now this.

Yes. Contented sigh. *And now this.*

Deirdre went on to explain how the chasm grew wider between her and Kellan. She could no longer talk about her family without a fight. She didn't blame him, not entirely. He was a kind man, but his parents had sheltered him from the wider world, raising him to believe that anything different was to be feared, not embraced. Kellan had loved Deirdre so much that he'd thrown these beliefs aside initially, but they re-emerged when the initial romance faded.

Deirdre shook her head. "He threatened to take all four of my babies away from me! What else was I to do?"

One evening while the house slept, Deirdre planned to spirit her children away from the house, and deliver them safely to the tribe. She left with the girls first, because Noah had a fever and his transport would require more attention.

Once Nora, Nevina, and Niamh were sleeping soundly with their grandmother, Deirdre returned to retrieve her son. But when she arrived, all she found was a note.

"He said he knew what I'd done, and he'd hate himself forever for not seeing it coming. He'd hate me forever for taking his daughters. I'd never see Noah again. That was my punishment."

"Neither of your decisions were very wise," Seara intoned. "You or Kellan." The younger girl they saw on their way in, Regan, entered to bring her a mug filled with a steaming liquid. She nodded in thanks. "At the core of our beliefs is the need for balance. I did not agree with your decision to marry someone so close-minded, but in making that decision you chose to take the good with the bad. There can be neither without the other. Both of you forgot this balance when you separated your children."

Deirdre bowed her head with a sigh. Nora placed a hand of comfort against her arm, but her expression was hard.

"However, we must also remember Morrigan's words," Seara continued, after a careful swallow of her drink. "If Kellan had not taken Noah across the sea, he'd have never met and married Colleen Deschanel. Amelia's birth was foretold. Of course, you do not get to take credit for helping fulfill this prophecy, as we know your overriding desire was not spiritual in nature."

Amelia didn't understand why her great-grandmother chose now to scold her daughter, when the wrongdoing was nearly half-a-century old.

"My letters to your grandfather went unanswered. Likely

destroyed," Deirdre said sadly. "He sent none in return. When your father grew into an adult, with the ability to decide for himself, I wrote him many letters. Hundreds! But I never sent a single one."

"Self-punishment does not wash away a crime," Seara chided. "But we didn't come here today to renew your guilt, daughter. What's done is done, and we are now, after many years of waiting, celebrating the coming together of Cianán and Cerridwen, for the final time. This is a most joyous event! Amelia, are you satisfied on the subject of your grandparents, for now?"

"I suppose so. Though, I wish my father could see all of you, together now. He used to say the greatest gift in marrying my mother was inheriting a large family," Amelia replied. The joy of his face at Christmastime, as he played Santa or snuck around in the middle of the night filling stockings, were among her favorite memories of him.

"Perhaps one day," Seara replied. Her ancient face cracked into a broad leer. The effect was not warm, but unsettling. "The son of Kellen is unlikely to accept these revelations about his daughter's past and future."

"My father is more Deschanel than Jameson," Amelia countered, with a touch of defensiveness. "He's probably more Quinlan than you think."

"Nay," Nora said. "He is not a draoi."

"Isn't that a male Quinlan?"

"Maybe someone should explain to us what that is, exactly, since you all keep slapping that label on me," Jacob added.

"All females of our blood are Quinlan," Deirdre explained. She seemed to be recovered from her swirl of self-recrimination. "But it's rare for a male to share our traits. So rare that their powers are far beyond any of ours. Those are the draoi."

"Jacob is a draoi then," Amelia said, processing. "My father is not. What about my brother, Ashley? He can kick up a crazy storm, but I guess he could have gotten that from my mother."

"Ashley is not. Nor was your other brother, Benjamin," Nora replied. "We have two in this tribe: your great-great-uncle Flynn, who you know as Father O'Connor, and Padraig, the husband of Regan. Padraig came to us from another tribe of Findias descendants, joining ours when he chose Regan as his mate. And, of course, if males are born into this tribe, draoi or not, they are welcome to stay."

"It is considered a blessing, and a great honor, to bring a draoi into this world," Rosemary added. Amelia had forgotten her, she'd been so silent. "I knew the moment Enid birthed you and you drew breath, Jacob, what you were. I also knew she would attempt to shelter you from the knowledge, and that she would die before she could reveal your truth."

Jacob's face went blank. His hands drew into fists, then released, but the tension remained. "You knew, and let it happen?" Amelia sent him calming thoughts, but carefully. He deserved to feel this, and to ask his questions.

"The curse of a seer is being given a horrible vision we cannot change," his grandmother replied with a gentle sigh. "I knew you would not die, that the goddess would intervene. And so I appealed to Seara to send Flynn to Killianshire, to look after you. He'd been living in a monastery near Shannon, a quiet life, but he didn't question when we asked him to be of service in the cathedral.

"It was Flynn who received the vision from the goddess that your place was in New Orleans. He arranged with Sister Agnes to have you sent and brought up there. She was told to watch over you and not let you fall into a place you couldn't return from. To give you safety to grow into your own decisions. She did not know the future that awaited you. That Amelia was a part of it."

Jacob wrinkled his mouth. "Let me guess. Sister Agnes is a Quinlan, too?"

"No, only a dear and trusted friend who asked no questions."

A silence came over the group, one that seemed to say, *Where do we go from here?* There were a thousand unasked questions, and that number only grew as the answers unfolded.

It was Jacob who finally ended the pause. "I feel like two people right now. On one side, I'm still the kid whose father went insane and murdered most of his family. No matter how long I'm with Amelia or how good my life gets, I can't shake that heartache. I see him when I look in the mirror, or when I walk past a kid on the street with the same gleam in his eye. He's always there."

Amelia squeezed his hand.

"Now I'm also this other person. At first I thought it was Amelia who had given me this happy confidence. Except she was only part of it." *How can I ever really know who I am if the foundation keeps shifting?* he added, to Amelia only.

You're my Jacob. My Ciarán. The other half of my soul. And you were these things long before we ever stepped foot into this strange land.

"You may continue to experience that over the coming days, though I hope the feelings move from prevalent to transient as you come into your memories. *And* your powers," Seara responded.

He lifted an eyebrow. "I have no powers."

"Ahh," Nora replied with a broad grin, "but you will."

It had been nice to spend the next few days settling in with the tribe. Amelia and Jacob were moved into their own tan house—one that, everyone insisted, had been reserved for them since before they were born—and quickly learned the unique customs.

The *crann bethadh* remained the spiritual center of the Quinlans, whose ways were similar to what Amelia knew about druids, but somehow simpler and more tuned to nature. They spent each evening in the shelter of its leaves, rooting their souls and appealing to the goddess for wisdom and faith.

It was more than simply a connection to the gods, and the otherworld. If a branch was cut for firewood, that branch grew back. Fruit grew, and was replaced faster than they could eat it. It provided a never-ending bounty of anything they might need, in a constant stage of growth and replenishment. The Quinlans didn't eat, or consume in other ways, what they couldn't get from the world around them. And they needed nothing the earth couldn't provide them.

The ceremony had removed the last of Amelia's skepticism, and so she accepted glimpses of nature's magic with a comforting reserve. With enthusiastic curiosity, she and Jacob took in the stories from the tribe's bard, Nevina, who had inherited the memories of the Old Ones. Even the others, who'd heard these tales a hundred times before, listened, enraptured, as if absorbing the dazzling words for the first time.

When the leaders led the tribe in rousing songs of the Tuatha, Amelia and Jacob joined. No one was more surprised than Jacob to find himself dancing soft, fluid rhythms before the swelling bonfire.

There's a definite appeal to living this kinda life, he'd said, the first night.

Maybe one day we'll call a place like this home.

Home for me is wherever you are.

The celebrity factor wore off by mid-week, and getting to

know her relatives became an easier and more enjoyable task once everyone stopped the slack-jawed staring. Seara's days were approaching an end as the archdruid of their tribe, and she'd chosen Nora as her successor, skipping all three of her daughters.

Philomena, Seara's oldest, possessed an ugly bitterness about her position in the tribe. When she'd birthed a son, years ago, and he was not a draoi, she'd left him in town for a stranger to raise.

Meara, the middle daughter, wore her peaceful joy in every smile, every step. Her mind, however, was on another plane, existing in a world apparently more beautiful and magical than theirs. The tribe protected her, and Amelia too, discovered a defensive love for her great-aunt, within hours of their first meeting.

Amelia's thoughts on Seara's youngest, Deirdre, her grandmother, remained undefined. She tried not to let the bad blood between Seara and Deirdre cloud her own feelings, and yet, she didn't know if she could forgive her grandmother for tearing the family apart. Even if the outcome had been one everyone agreed was appropriate.

And there were others, so many personalities surrounding them, that it was a chore to take stock.

Regan's husband, Padraig, was the draoi earmarked to help Jacob learn more about who he was, and what he could do. *Once the truth settles in. We don't want to rush it,* the young, sturdy redhead assured them.

They were so caught up in these new discoveries, both of extended family and way of life, that they hardly had time to make sense of it as a couple. At the surface, Amelia grasped how much her love for Jacob had grown over the past days, and she knew his had developed in equal measure.

Neither could find the right words to externalize this

evolution. They relied on secret, internal communication, which became easier the longer they fell into it.

The subject of a child, a daughter, remained securely on the fringe. She sensed hints from Jacob's thoughts, but they were only that, hints. If her refusal still bothered him, he showed no signs.

HER THIRTIETH BIRTHDAY STARTED WITH AN OFFERING TO THE goddess, and ended in the arms of her husband.

Amelia nestled her head into his chest, as his hands played across her hair. There never had been, and never would be, a place safer than she felt with her head against the beat of his heart.

"I have a surprise for you," Jacob professed, pressing his lips to her forehead. His heart and mind were, for the first time in many months, at perfect ease. *How did we get here? How did we skip the part where Jacob runs away screaming, and I have to lull him back into comfort?*

"I already have everything I could ever want," Amelia replied. Her hands danced lazy circles across his abs, trailing lower.

"That won't stop me from giving you this," he replied, as he reached his hand into the drawer next to him, and drew out a powder blue box of a brand she recognized immediately. "I bought it before we left because I wasn't sure how long we'd be here."

"Jacob!"

"Well, open it," he urged.

Amelia took the Tiffany box from her husband. Inside was a solid silver chain bracelet, with a thick heart locket of rose gold dangling from the links. Etched on the back were their initials, *A & J*, above a tiny keyhole.

"This is... the most beautiful thing I've ever seen," she said, breathless. Jacob tenderly latched the chain over her wrist. The weight of the gold heart felt so solid, and real, the way every moment with him always had.

"Haven't looked in a mirror recently, eh?" He grinned, running his fingers across her wrist.

"Those cheap one-liners won't work on me, Donnelly."

"No? Explain the last ten years, then."

She rolled on her back, her laughter fading to a smile. "Even a month ago, I never could have imagined us here. Not in my wildest dreams."

Jacob's hand stopped. "Tell me more about these wild dreams of yours."

Amelia flipped over so she was atop him, gazing down at his contented smile. *There is no place, here on Earth or in the heavens, more satisfying, more beautiful than the creation of our yin and yang. My Jacob. My Cianán.*

She let her hair trail across his chin, tickling on down to his chest. His growing hardness ignited the flame within her. "Haven't we already established I'm much better at showing?"

30
ANASOFIYA

Ana paced the length of her room, awaiting news of Aidrik's inquisition. Every footstep outside the door pushed her heart into her throat. Were they here to escort her to her execution? And Finn? Only Forbia's calm kept the dark swirl at bay. *I could do it. If I wanted to, I could separate that iron door from its five-inch hinges.* Whatever grew inside her was not yet at its potential.

If Finn had been harmed, Forbia would've gone ballistic. If Aidrik had walked into the Senetat Sanctuary and never emerged, the pup would have raised hell. They must all know this applied to her as well, that Forbia was their well-being barometer. For now, all of them were safe, but that was only a small consolation. Her instincts warned of terrible things on the horizon.

Then Agripin appeared, sashaying in with the airy nonchalance of someone who was simply passing through. As he had on all prior visits, he went straight for the silver tray of food, popping an oversized grape between his teeth without bothering to close his mouth. "I moved your paramours into the adjoining suite." He went for a triangle of cheese.

Ana froze. "What?"

He didn't bother with the cheese knife, using his teeth to separate a hunk from the orange-red wax. "You'll stay here in mine, with me, but you may slip next door at your pleasure and do whatever it is you do with those two."

"Finn and Aidrik are next door?" Ana wondered if he was enjoying her incredulity. Why did she not already know this... sense this? How could she not have known they were several feet away?

"I believe that's what I said."

"That arrangement works for your plan?" Ana continued. She tensed, alert. This was far too easy, too convenient, after all they'd been through since arriving. "So, why, then, didn't you arrange us this way to start with?"

Agripin pulled on his crimson jacket. "Aidrik was incapable of focusing on his meeting with the Senetat if you were a distraction. Now it is done." He adjusted his lapels, smiling. "And I needed to see how *you* would act under pressure. You managed not to cry too much in your sleep, and you handled my erection with finesse,."

"You were toying with me. Instead of, I don't know, *communicating* with me, telling me the plan."

"My dear," he said, as he buttoned the last of his two-dozen buttons, "we're facing an extremely precarious situation. I needed to know you could handle whatever comes."

Her dark spirit stirred. She closed her eyes, steadying. *Breathe.* "Now you know."

He gave her an admiring, but mildly dismissive look. "Well, I'm off to meet with my newly appointed cabinet members. In the middle of all this intrigue, I nearly forgot there was a kingdom to run!" He pointed to a small door. "You'll find it unlocked. They're waiting for you."

Then, he left. Ana stared at the door he exited before turning, slowly. *Breathe... your anger won't help you here... calm.* Her eyes scanned past the full-tester bed with the four iron posts, beyond the changing wall, then stopped on the tiny red door. The one she'd assumed was the entrance for the serving staff, as they always snuck in without her detection. The one that had been locked.

Oh, Finn. If Agripin has harmed even a single hair on your head... even one. If your eyes bear the look of a man who has been questioned for too long, or seen things you shouldn't... I will kill them all.

And Aidrik... the ache building inside, fighting for placement with the dark gift... it burned for him too.

Ana reached for the door.

Ana made only one step through the door before Finn rushed toward her, scooping one strong arm across her waist, a careless and desperate gesture full of anxiety and disbelief. She pressed her head to his chest as her jerky breaths intensified. His own soft gasps were muffled by her hair as he whispered unintelligibly. *My safe place.*

Then she was pulled from his arms. Aidrik, uncharacteristically pushing Finn aside and taking his turn, showing a surge of emotion nestled in rare impatience.

"Kjære," he murmured, pulling back long enough to take in her face. His glassy, tortured eyes appealed to her fractured heart, and Ana realized she had never, before this moment, seen tears from him. She equally knew they wouldn't spill, he would never allow such a thing, but seeing them there, for her, culminating evidence of his very real fears, left her nearly swaying on her feet. He caught her, and pressed his lips against hers in firm possessiveness.

Before she could protest, his sturdy arms hoisted her. *Mine,* the gesture said, as he carried her toward the bed. She gave up any struggle and allowed his flash of dominance, giving a languid look over his shoulder at the threshold where she'd entered moments ago, no idea what to expect when her hand reached for the knob.

Finn watched, processing. Saying nothing. He turned and closed the door, which clicked once with the lock.

Aidrik eased himself on the bed, placing her on the carpet before him. He lifted her nightgown, exposing her, and tugged at her panties hard enough to tear them at the hip. Behind her, Finn's arms were at her waist, and his kisses rained against her neck. Her husbands.

Then, Aidrik was lifting her again, saddling her over his lap in one swift, aggressive move. His cock pressed into her, and before she could wrap her mind around this abrupt and delicious assault, he was filling her, all of him, moaning in an ecstasy such as she had never heard from her unyielding evigbond. This was not the same creature who had indulged her own need for pleasure, time and time again. He was someone else entirely, a being who existed, at this moment, for nothing more than ardent surrender.

As Ana rode him, folding herself over his length in slow, delectable strides, Finn's hands guided her hips, not only permissive but encouraging. Her head spun with the reality of it all, but this was not the time for analyzing. For thinking of anything beyond the blood rushing to her head as both her men loved her in this primal way.

One of Finn's hands slid up over her breasts and then down again, through to the mound between her legs. His fingers tickled that sensitive bundle of flesh as his kisses against her neck turned to bites, driving her further toward the cliff of whatever this—this wonderful and dangerous reality—was.

Beneath her, Aidrik's hips thrust upward, creating hungrier, needier motions from her. Finn cupped her face, tilting her head back toward him, filling her mouth with his tongue as he pleasured her, as she rode Aidrik. As she made love to them both.

When Aidrik's cries grew louder and more desperate, Finn's fingers worked faster, first kneading and then pinching, bringing her close to conclusion. Aidrik reached out and grasped her thigh at the moment he released inside her, shuddering in one powerful spasm as he cried out.

A blinding pleasure washed over her when her own body rocked with a powerful orgasm. She moaned into Finn's mouth as his hand moved back up over her body, caressing her gently. "I love you," he whispered, holding her sweaty torso with one strong arm.

Finn lifted her from atop Aidrik and laid her gently on the bed beside him. He climbed up and over her, entering before she could recover from her first incursion, engaging in quick, hurried strokes that were as desperate as Aidrik's had been. Silently, Aidrik moved around the other side of the bed and knelt where her head rested, setting kisses upon her forehead and cheekbones. Her eyes closed with this sensory overload, her men, both her husbands, making love to her in unison, a sharing she never thought possible.

When her head rolled to the side, her eyes opened. She saw Aidrik's hand fold over Finn's briefly. Their first two fingers twined around each other's with a light squeeze, and then retreated. It was one, single moment, and then it was gone.

Finn's release came moments later, so powerful his head fell upon her chest, panting something incoherent against her neck.

The only sounds in the room were their exhausted, ragged gasps, as their minds struggled to catch up with all their bodies had done.

A WHILE LATER, THEY LAY SIDE-BY-SIDE ON THE LARGE BED, THE MEN flanking Ana, each wrapped around a side of her.

None of them attempted to put voice to their actions, and Ana wasn't sure they should. When Finn and Aidrik came to their understanding those months ago in Wales, that they would share her, and she accepted, they'd only loosely defined the boundaries of the arrangement. It came with promises to respect one another, and to communicate, never keep secrets. The subject of precisely what the *sharing* entailed had never been fully explored. They had never once discussed what it might mean to truly, and completely share her. To the contrary, there seemed to be a lingering, unsaid promise that they would not bring in this element to the relationship.

Yet they had. And, despite Ana's swiftly beating heart and raging storm of emotions, the world hadn't ended. Both men were still here, both glowing in the aftermath of their hungered lovemaking.

Whatever it was, it won't happen again. Not because it shouldn't, or because it was wrong, but simply because it won't. This single act will have strengthened us, but to repeat it would probably do the opposite.

Slipping her hands through those of both men, Ana closed her eyes and fell into the sleep she needed but had not been able to achieve for many nights.

31
NERYS

Nerys flew through the jungle with the fluid grace of a cheetah. Her red hair, wound into several heavy braids, trailed behind. A clear path in the overgrown brush opened up before her as the flora responded to her mental commands, peeling to the right and left as she approached her endpoint.

She abruptly stopped. Her eyes flashed as she took in her new surroundings, processing them with astonishing mental agility. The luscious vegetation came to a temporary end before a stagnant body of water. Pooling from a recent monsoon, most likely.

At last, Nerys' gaze settled on the path's continuation. Backing up several feet, she wound her limbs and leapt across the pond, landing in a running sprint as she continued on. Reptiles, spiders, and small rodents scattered out of her way, though not out of fear but respect. Many years had passed since Duchess Nerys had come through Ecuador, but memory of her left an imprint on all inhabitants. They knew her as they knew the rain, and the sun, and the powerful biota they thrived in.

Nerys wished she could spend time with all the beautiful creatures and life bursting around her. In the past, she'd lingered years on end, disappearing from the greater world without regret or notice. She was beholden to no one, loyal to all who chose harmonious balance over chaos. When she would, on occasion, cross the path of another Farværdig, their first question was inevitable: Where does your loyalty lie?

I exist in the light of Our Loving Father, Emyr, was always her answer. It had been her personal truth since the day of her birth. Alliances, rebels, revolutions, blood feuds... these things were noise, polluting their world with unnecessary politics and intrigue. Had the Senetat's intentions remained in the light, Nerys could have curtseyed to their requests. But neither had she dabbled with the other side, the Dragon Empire. They were often as misguided as their nemesis, their personal desires and spiritual ones diverging in years past. There were two sides to every story, and history was penned by the victors.

Nerys had no time for any of that.

Until now.

JORUN WAS HARDER TO FIND ON THIS VISIT. IN THE DAYS WHEN THEY could still call Rome an empire, Jorun had kept her drekar close to her breast, living communally amongst old, viney Mayan crumblings, cloaked from detection. Reclusive even then, she'd been quick to help any who asked, but her retreat from the society of her creation began before she was even designated the Brotherhood leader of their region.

In time, she'd moved her dwellings away from the ruins, emerging only when necessary. Eventually, the drekar of Ecuador became the drekar of South America, scattering to the winds in the shadow of their leader's need for solitude. She'd not defected from society due to a lack of love. Jorun loved all creatures. She just loved those on four legs more than those on two.

The rustling of the fauna clearing her path halted, and Nerys stood before what, at first glance, looked like a tangle of bushes that had the misfortune of all growing in the same direction. Nerys' eyes narrowed, then widened, as the picture came into focus. She smiled.

A mass of blazing, matted hair and tattered sun-bleached leather stumbled out. The figure hunched forward, muffling grunts.

"Jorun," Nerys sang. She pressed forward and embraced her old friend, but only briefly. Her need to show appreciation was not as important as Jorun's craving for separateness.

Jorun's eyes darted back and forth; anywhere but in the direction of her visitor. Years as a hermit had left her resembling the very animals she loved. Always a risk with a bestia-kinetic.

Nerys wondered, briefly, if Jorun's years away from others had left her without a voice. Then in a low, raspy growl, she said, "Thorvald's men already paid visit."

Nerys half-smiled. Thorvald was *always* ready. A good man, and one of her oldest and most trusted friends, even if she could not—would not—see the world through his blood-speckled lens.

"What did they say?"

"Your brother sent signal. War coming."

With a frown, Nerys remembered Cyler's words. *Only track down the wild ones. Ferret out their willingness to come if called. But do nothing yet! We can't risk raising suspicion.* Further evidence as to why the Brotherhood had always suffered without a central leader. *Too many cooks in the kitchen*, as Children of Men would say. "Agripin sent the signal. You sure?"

Jorun grunted, shifting back and forth from one leg to the other, eyes still fixed on the ground before her. "Thorvald said."

Well, Thorvald would say anything to put gears in motion. "Do nothing yet, Jorun," Nerys counseled, keeping her tone low and soothing. She kept her own thoughts close to her vest, not yet ready to reveal them to anyone. Least of all, anyone in contact with her brother.

Jorun ceased her nervous shuffle. "No contact my people? Weapons coming, he said."

What kind of weapons would Thorvald think appropriate for such a cause? "Store the weapons when they arrive. Wait for word from me. No one else." When Jorun diverted her attentions to a coral snake slithering between them, Nerys added, "No one, Jorun. You understand? Not Thorvald, not Cyler. Do you trust me?"

Furious nodding. "Aye. Aye."

"Good." She extended her hand, looping it behind Jorun's back. "Shall we break our fast? I promise, I won't stay long. But I would very much love to pass the morning with an old friend."

32
TRISTAN

Tristan's nightmares started when he was still running around playing with plastic trucks and Lincoln Logs. They weren't the fantastical kind other kids had, involving monsters and things not possibly real. No, his were a sequence of events so closely mirroring real life that no matter how many reassurances his mother showered upon him, he struggled to discern the difference between a real memory and one his mind had twisted in his sleep.

As the nightmares intensified, Tristan's young mind grew so confused his father wanted to send him to counseling. His mother balked at the suggestion, and took to sleeping by his side, her long legs hanging off his tiny bed. Tristan remembered this gesture more than anything else from his childhood... the time his mother had truly been a mother.

Tristan, you have to decide what's real. Your mind has to reach out and seek it. Think about the one detail, the one thing that feels just a wee bit off to you. And then latch on to what you know, what never changes. Find your constant.

It was a big, complicated concept for a kid barely out of

kindergarten. But he understood. If he went to bed on a Wednesday, and *Full House* played in the background, that was a wee bit off. The clock chiming six times when the short hand was on the eight wasn't right, either.

Finding his constant was somewhat harder. When his mind was trapped in a world so similar to his own, what could he trust?

You have to tell your mind to do it, Tristan. It won't know if you don't train it.

What am I supposed to tell it, Mama?

Pick something. Anything. Something you can trust in.

And so Tristan had picked his mother. None of her disappearances or neglect leading up to that moment mattered, because she was there *now,* doing motherly things. Helping him figure out the most confusing thing he'd ever dealt with. He asked his mind to use his mother to help him understand when he'd fallen into a dream.

From then on out, whenever he'd been caught in that suspended limbo, disoriented, all he needed to do was look at his mother. If awake, she would be doing what she always did. But when asleep, his mind prompted the vision of his mother to put her book down, press a finger to her lips, and smile. *Not real.*

But his mother, his constant, was gone now. Conveyed into heaven or hell, or somewhere in between, he wasn't even sure what he believed anymore.

His life had once again fallen into an upheaval, where the lines were blurred between what was real, what felt real, and what was simply his mind playing tricks. And so he'd remembered his mother's words, and how he'd manipulated his young brain to be on his side. Except his problems were no longer dreams this time, but the onslaught of a reality he was still adjusting to.

Once more, he sought out a constant.

He found one in Harriett.

When a scent is closely tied to a memory, the transporting effect is greater the further back the memory lives. The smell of date bars brought Tristan back to his toddler years, plopped before the television playing with his car collection. Lemon verbena conjured memories of Aunt Colleen picking him up from summer camp, plying him with questions in the back of her town car when it should have been his mom, or dad, there to do it. Burning rubber would always remind him of the day Danielle died. It would carry him to that moment, back turned, the world ending in the street a few feet away. Everything before him would haze, no longer real, or anywhere near as real as his tiny feet glued to the front porch while his sister died.

The morning Tristan woke up at *Ophélie* to the smell of burning rubber, his scream carried throughout the house in violent echoes.

The world spun. His ears rung. Burning rubber scorched his nostrils, and he thought, *Don't turn around, don't turn around, don't turn around, don't turn around.*

"Turn around," Harriett whispered. And he did.

"You're safe now." She pressed a kiss to his forehead.

The terrifying scents from earlier in the day intensified throughout the afternoon, when Tristan finally pulled himself out of bed. There was little reason to rise before then in any case, as Lucia had all but given up on training them, and all the focus was on Aleksandr and Nicolas.

"Sindre sent all the old farm equipment up in a ball of

flames," Harriett explained, gazing out the double doors of the bedroom. She shook her head. "Markus said they didn't want to call in the fire department because of the attention it would bring, so they've been hauling water from the house and the old kitchens. Sindre refused to summon any himself because he's pouting. Can you believe it?"

"Someone needs to smack that kid," Tristan muttered. The acrid smell burned stronger than ever, but Harriett's presence was a balm. "Before he burns the whole place to the ground trying to show off for Eydis."

"It's lost on her," Harriett replied with another thoughtful gaze toward the carnage. "Just like her charms are lost on Nicolas."

Tristan snickered, slipping nude from the bed. "I wasn't the only one who heard their show in the study."

Harriett turned. She frowned. "He's human, like you and me. We've all made mistakes, and he certainly regrets this one. But I'm afraid there's nothing he can do to rectify it."

"You've seen something?" *Something else,* he almost said, thinking keenly of the dreams she'd shared before. Explosions and doom.

"I don't know. It's unclear, but..."

He shrugged a t-shirt over his head and slid on boxers. Sidling up behind her, the scent grew stronger, but he pressed his face into her chest, closing his eyes. "You know you can tell me."

Harriett tugged his arms around her. She pressed one of his hands to the side of her cheek. "I can't see Mercy's future."

"Does that mean anything, though? You've said before you only see what the visions send."

"It might."

Tristan recalled the petty way his mother used to hoard information. Like it was a commodity, and its exclusive possession bestowed upon her some rare and important power no one else had. Harriett, on the other hand, kept her information close because it was her only means to protect her loved ones.

It was with this knowledge in mind Tristan asked, "Are you going to tell Nicolas?"

She spun, breaking free of his arms with a gentle pull. "And say what? I don't see the woman you wronged in your future? Actually, I don't see her future at all?"

"You told him the entire family was going up in flames. I don't see how this could be any worse," he replied before he thought to censor himself.

Her expression darkened, but he detected no anger. "You know I didn't tell him everything. I didn't tell him about Ana."

It was her decision, but he hoped she never would, about as much as he hoped she was wrong.

He wrinkled his nose. Stomach churned. "Someone needs to force Sindre to summon a damn wave and get this over with. I can't handle smelling this all day."

"Why don't we invite your father to lunch? He's left several messages." Her wide chocolate eyes implored without judgment. If he said no, she would smile and suggest something else. Always easy, Harriett. It was never through her words that she pushed him to be more, or better. Her presence alone, soft and thoughtful, was enough to accomplish that all on its own.

He wanted to argue, to insist they had so much do. But with Lucia proverbially throwing her hands up and declaring her job irrelevant, and Anders tunneled in with the other two, the house felt stagnate; devoid of purpose. Sindre lighting farm implements on fire merely a symptom. Eydis' attempts to persuade Richard to give her the key to Nicolas' master suites another. Even Oz's visits seemed compulsory, coming out only because he felt he must. The excitement they'd all borne when this project began, had slipped slowly into the walls and floorboards.

But there was a bit more to it than that, wasn't there? That one little detail—or maybe not so little—he'd kept from Harriett without really understanding *why* he felt the need for confidentiality. In the weeks they'd been together, he'd laid out every dark secret of his life, without any hesitation.

Those disclosures had been things he'd had time to contemplate, process. Label. He had no idea what to make of the conversation he had with Anders two afternoons ago.

Any particular reason you're wasting your talents lazing around in the swamp? Anders had asked in an offhand way, as he poured coffee from the carafe into a tall wine flute. Tristan had been preparing to point out how strange drinking coffee from stemware was when the question came up.

Are you talking to me?

I don't see anyone else in the room wasting their talents.

Defenses rankled, Tristan was readying some of his best comebacks when Anders smiled. A knowing smile, like one might give if they already knew exactly what you were about to say and thought it adorable.

I don't have time to train you. You know what you can do, yet you don't seem keen on flexing those muscles. A damn shame, too. I've never seen a telepath quite like you, and the Brotherhood could really use one with your skills in the field. You really are wasted here.

If you thought I was all that important you'd be training me with the others, he'd countered.

You don't need training, halfling. You're ready. Skills-wise, at least. You need to stop hanging on to whatever is tethering you here like a babe to the teet. If that time ever arrives, come see me.

And like all mysterious discussions, it ended with those last words trailing behind Anders as he exited with his unconventional coffee cup. Tristan was pretty sure he'd been given some kind of recruiting pitch. More importantly, he was surprised to discover the idea excited him.

A lot. And more so as the idea permeated.

"Sure, let's call Dad." Tristan sighed, and offered the warmest smile his distracted heart could muster.

33
ANASOFIYA

Ana and Finn stood on a rocky trail around the castle, gazing down at the hazy valley below the craggy peaks, beyond their reach. Surely they'd passed through it on the way in, but they were forbidden to venture down there now. Forbia was nearby, likely hunting.

From their strangled vantage point atop Farjhem, Ana felt a keen sense of déjà vu.

When she was fifteen, Aunt Evangeline and Uncle Johannes invited her along on their family vacation to Sweden. Very likely there was some pity involved, as Ana's father rarely took a day off from work, and so one aunt or another would often bring Ana along like a well-loved third wheel.

Uncle Johannes was from Sweden, and they'd not been back since their children were born. Markus was six at the time, and Katja four, and they were bringing them to spend time with their grandparents.

After the first couple of days in Stockholm, Aunt Evangeline asked Ana if she would like to accompany her and Uncle

Johannes on a train trip to Bergen, Norway. When Ana asked what was there, they'd simply responded, "Oh, mountains, fishing, fjords," and shrugged as if those things were specific enough. But she didn't belong in the slender brick townhouse with her giggling cousins and their grandparents, and so she set her heart toward adventure.

Norway had been as she expected from the books she read, but amplified on such a grand and awesome scale that she eventually gave up trying to capture the beauty with her disposable camera. Sweeping fjords and mountains carved from glaciers, with air that felt, more even than crisp, clean. As if a few days breathing here would clear the body of any malady.

Every village they passed through was virtually the same: fjords and inlets, bodies of water supporting communities dotted by red and yellow homes built on the lakes, on stilted stands, and into the cliff sides. Sometimes she would spot the ruins of a castle deep and high into the mountains, standing sentry.

What would Farjhem look like from afar, she wondered?

Their newfound freedom came with so many limitations that it felt like their prison cell had expanded, not opened. Agripin was only slightly less anxious than Aidrik about the relative silence from the Senetat since Aidrik's inquisition. Until that confident swagger waned, Ana hadn't realized how much she took a strange comfort from it. If Agripin was worried, then they all should be.

Ana had questions. Many questions. Most were for Aidrik, but since his "exoneration," Agripin had kept him busy on official palace business. He was frequently off playing bodyguard to the soon-to-be-emperor, or acting as messenger, returning exhausted, and solemn. Agripin couldn't relax with the coronation imminent, but still a week away. A lot could go wrong in a week.

The farce seemed to take a greater toll on Aidrik than anyone. One night, Agripin and Aidrik had returned after fourteen hours away. Agripin's energy levels were at an unusual peak, and whatever Aidrik had left after the long day had been absorbed into his new master. *Did you see the way Valerius flubbed his prayers at sunset? My kingdom to see it again!*

The returned look from Aidrik, pointedly aimed at Agripin's stretching back, had not been annoyance, but hatred.

Aidrik was powerfully resilient. He'd endured four millennia by *not* giving into his overriding emotion in less-than-ideal circumstances. Ana understood this, and she tried not to ask too many questions when he would return each night, slipping quietly into bed bedside her and Finn.

They all slept that way now, three in a row, refusing to be separated again. Nothing had happened like that first night—they hadn't even discussed it, to Ana's relief, as discussion might somehow detract from how it had brought them back together—but neither were there any more rules about who had Ana. She was theirs, and they were hers.

"Aidrik wasn't joking about the baking bread. I've smelled it everywhere here," Finn remarked. His warm breath furled in the air before them. He wrapped his arms snugger, the cable-knit from his sweater tightening around his shoulders. Curiously clean-shaven for a fisherman usually, he'd let his sandy hair grow, the longest curls reaching his brow now. His five-o-clock shadow had become the makings of a beard.

This rougher exterior seemed a fine match for the firm resolve taking root within him. The Finn of a year ago had seen no more than the average man's tragedy. He'd embraced the strange and wonderful world given him, one that turned his old life on its head.

"Aleksei would love it." Ana closed her eyes and breathed in the crisp Nordic air and warm yeasty scents. "He never stopped talking about your grandmother's bread after we left."

"Maybe we shouldn't have. Left."

She watched him. "You don't mean that."

"No. Not really."

Ana allowed herself to indulge wondering what Finn's life would have been like had he stayed in Maine, trapping his legendary lobster, taking different women to bed without commitment. He'd said to her the day they met that his life was simple, and this was how he liked it. He traded all that for something far from simple. For her.

Finn gave her a troubled frown. "Don't listen to me, silly girl. I'm not myself right now. Missing Aleksandr and wishing we could give him an easier time of things. But if our lives were easier, his life wouldn't have been possible. I know we're right where we should be. Working to make the best life we can give our son." He brushed the hair back from her temple and pressed his lips against it. "And my wife."

Ana smiled. She gestured down toward the bustling valley. Life, everywhere, but they were too far away to make out the important details. "What do you think would happen if we took the road down there?"

"I think we'd be back up here in shackles before we could ask about that bread."

She'd already known the answer, but small talk felt safer and easier than asking what he thought their odds were of making it out of Farjhem in one piece.

They wandered down the rocky path further, toward the sound of running water. The crunching of their shoes summoned Finn's wolf, who seemed content to stay close now that she'd inspected the nearby forest. A break in the mountain revealed several tranquil falls that slowed into the Farvann River below. Finn's expression seemed to indicate he was debating whether they'd make it down in a barrel from Agripin's wine stash. "You've read *The Hobbit* too many times," she teased.

His eyebrow shot up. "Can a man not admire his surroundings without being accused of plotting shenanigans?"

"Glad to see you both taking in the palace grounds," a velvety, measured voice spoke from around the corner. Coming into view, Ana observed the crimson robes. One of *them,* and she recognized her as the one and only eldre who hadn't been ready to devour her at the naming ceremony. "If you'd like an escort to the valley floor, and the town, I can help arrange it."

Ana tensed. Finn appeared at her side, flanking. Forbia stood on the other side of Ana, protective but not alarmed. *No immediate danger then.*

"Eldre Maxima," the woman introduced herself, with an abbreviated bow. Her red locks were tightly coiled to her head, in a wreath of tiny swirls. Woven throughout were gold-coated laurel leaves, coming to a point on either side of her face. *Once the Romans came along with their empire, everything changed. Everyone took new names, new customs. They fancy themselves Cicero,* Aidrik told her once.

"Ana and Finn," Ana replied, voice tilted with hesitation. Every word, even the innocent ones, must be guarded against this enemy.

"I know who you are," Maxima answered. She lifted her robe and stepped closer, revealing golden gladiator sandals. "The empress-to-be and the halfling, paraded around under false pretense. This must be very different from your traditional accommodations. Do you have all you need? Has Emperor-in-waiting Agripin seen to you appropriately?"

They both nodded.

"I'll not attack you. Not with words or arms," Maxima said, circling around them. She knelt by the falls and dipped her hands in, cupped as if preparing to take a drink. Then her hands rose up from the current, the water arcing from her palms, back and forth like a slinky.

Standing before Finn, she twirled her hands and the water took a new shape, falling into place as a ship. "Forbia." She offered it to him with a broad smile, as if offering a child an elaborate balloon animal.

Finn's jaw went slack. He reached forward, then yanked his hand back in sharp retreat.

"No?" Maxima looked more amused than disappointed. The water shifted once more, landing softly in her hands in the shape of a kitten with wide eyes. This she offered to Ana. "Cocoa... do I have that right?"

Ana's stray cat, adopted and sent to live with her Aunt Colleen before her life went into chaos.

Ana looked away. Inside her, something stirred gently.

"Perplexing. Are we not on the same side? What horrid things has Aidrik said about me that scares you so?" Maxima teased with a peripheral glance, but was back to her water tricks.

She released the water into the air, backing away slowly. The molecules first separated into a million drops and then immediately reformed, creating the outline of a man. The details came into focus; sharp cheekbones, full mouth. Wide laughing smile. Aleksandr.

Ana's breath caught. The swirl inside her heart rose, forming, higher. Dark. She could push it forth and send this maniac hurling over the falls into the craggy rocks below. Maxima would never see it coming, and even if she did, the burst of black strength would overpower her for the time needed to do it. She could. One down. Eight to go.

Finn's hand traveled to her lower back, steadying her. "Impressive," he managed through a tight frown. "Is there a point?"

"You miss your son," Maxima noted. The water crashed loudly to the ground in a puddle, splashing Forbia before running back through the rocks to return to the source. "You fear you won't see him again. That Agripin won't follow through on his promises."

"You can't know or understand my fears," Ana asserted, throttling the familiar anger whispering to her, *Come on. It would be so easy. So, so easy.* "And the duke is my mate, and soon to be our emperor, so I'd appreciate you watching your words."

Maxima's snicker and eye-roll indicated a shared secret, as if she saw through their farce. "You'd do well to take care around Agripin. You've known him a few weeks. I've known him since before the symbol of the cross you gave your son had any meaning. There is not one man under that surface. He can be whoever he needs to be, whoever you need him to be, and then back to another when it suits him.

"He will only allow you to see your son if he finds some strategic advantage in the offer. Can you think of one? It would be far more expedient for him to get a child on you, and claim his own heir. Maybe more than one."

"I couldn't bear more than one child even if I wanted to," Ana argued, frustrated at herself for entertaining the discussion.

"Myth," Maxima scoffed. "Childbirth for us is by no means easy, but it doesn't have to be a solitary experience. Agripin knows this, though I suppose he never mentioned it."

Finn's discomfort brought her stirring back. "Again, what is your point?" he fumed.

"If you want to see your son again, leave Farjhem. Only ruin awaits you here." Maxima lifted her robe again, moving to depart. "If you decide to take me up on the tour of our beautiful town, please don't hesitate to send a messenger."

When she was out of sight, Ana looked at Finn, staring wordlessly.

34
NICOLAS

Nicolas and Anne sat at the dining table with Aunt Colleen and Luther, running down the events of the endeavor thus far.

No, they had not heard anything more from Ana.

No, they didn't know how many more children were coming.

No, Anders and Lucia hadn't shared anything beyond some colorful histories with them.

No, Amelia and Jacob had not given a return date.

No, Nicolas did not know why Mercy had selected Anne to be her proxy at this meeting. At least, he wasn't going to entertain the reason.

No, they didn't need anything. Not extra hand sanitizer. Not a menu refresh. Not guidance from their elders, either, who meant well but were reminding the siblings just how outleagued they were.

"I don't understand," Colleen was saying, rifling through her day planner as if it contained the answers to the universe's greatest mysteries. "Mercy made it sound like you'd be running a refugee camp here. We spent a good deal of money preparing the property, and it seems to all be wasted."

"A Deschanel wasting their wealth on trivial expenditures? Unheard of," Luther quipped. When Colleen shot him a vicious look, he slid a hand across the table and brushed hers. "Leena, take a deep breath. No one would have handled this any differently. We always prepare for the worst, and hope for the best. Always."

"I know, but..." Colleen closed the planner. The crescents under her eyes were a badge of all she'd weathered in the past year. "Are you sure you haven't heard from Amelia?"

Nicolas and Anne shook their heads.

"She hasn't called Ashley, either," she replied, shaking her head. "So unlike her."

"When they left, she said they might be awhile. Didn't know how long, and I told her to take her damn time. It wasn't like we had a barrage of shit to do here," Nicolas said.

"I'm sure she's fine," she replied with an offhand look toward the other side of the room. "In any case, it doesn't appear you're in need of additional resources."

"Hell, feel free to take some back!" Nicolas declared. Anne swatted him.

"You could assign the children to menial but fruitful tasks. Is anyone keeping daily ledgers?" Luther asked. "We should be chronicling these events for the formal record."

"I could," Anne volunteered, perking up.

"We're fine," Nicolas asserted. His jaw ached from the past hour's tension. "Really."

Markus appeared in the doorway. "You can count me out. At least on a consistent basis."

His already pale face had gone stark white. "What's the matter, dear?" Colleen asked, rising immediately.

"Katja called me. She wants me to come see her."

Anne spun in her chair. Nicolas couldn't help doing the same. No one had heard from Katja since the twins were born... since Alain had taken his life and tried to take hers as well. Their cousin Olivia had taken on the duty of caring for them, at Katja's request. Katja hadn't even spoken to her own mother.

"What? Just now?" Colleen fumbled with her planner, shoving it in her oversized purse. "Is she okay? We can leave immediately."

"No, Aunt C," Markus said patiently. "She asked for me. Only me."

"Oh. Oh, I see." It had been a long time since Nicolas had seen his aunt so flustered. "What about your mother?"

Markus shrugged, glancing toward the door. "I don't know. I'm guessing she hasn't called her, or you would know. Right?"

"I suppose so."

"But she's reaching out at least. And I don't care if we had a thousand rebel kiddos rolling around on the property, I'd still go to her." Markus quickly embraced his aunt, then nodded at the others. "I'm sorry. Depending on what she needs from me, I'll pop in when I can, and help where I can. Call if there's something I can do from New Orleans."

"Don't sweat it. And you tell your sister, she's welcome here anytime. Anything she needs," Nicolas said. He thought of how he'd offered Katja and Alain his Quarter apartment not so long ago, and how badly their story ended there. But how could he have known?

"I will. Thanks."

"What should we tell Lucia?" Anne chimed in, with a pert look on her face. "I assume you haven't said a proper goodbye?"

"Nothing to tell her. She knows it wasn't a permanent deal," Markus replied evenly.

"It never is," Nicolas added, with a knowing nod.

. . .

NICOLAS WAS FIXING A SNACK IN ONE OF THE KITCHENS WHEN HE spotted Hakon sitting by himself under a live oak to the rear of the property.

It was easy to forget this quiet youth existed. He moved through the property without words, and it seemed his only friend was Amelia's cat. But Nicolas remembered what Anne told him. The illegitimate son of an emperor, whose mother avoided death at his father's hand, only to die in childbirth.

Even Nicolas could muster some sympathy for the kid.

"If you're talking to the birds, maybe you can ask them to stop shitting on my sports cars," Nicolas called, as he approached the shelter of leaves.

Hakon jumped in place. His head rolled forward, and then snapped back. "Sorry. I didn't see you coming."

"Do they talk back? The birds?"

"They don't *talk*. They're birds," Hakon replied. His face broadened into a shy smile. "It's more like I can interpret their thoughts, and communicate with them on their level."

Nicolas dropped his head to the side. "Yeah, but... why? Do you learn something?"

Hakon shrugged. He reached his hand into a small grain bag beside him and tossed a handful off to his right, where a group of birds waited. "You have scientists who study the brain, and the changes in weather, or the pathology of disease. But none of them can talk to animals, right?"

"Did you get this talent from your father?" Nicolas ventured, wondering whether it was true about him not knowing his background.

"I never knew my father," Hakon said and dropped his gaze. He tossed another handful at the birds. "Or my mother."

This kid has no idea his father is the emperor, or that his mother wasn't an Empyrean. No clue who he is, or that he could be one of the most powerful of his race.

Bullshit. It's his right to know these things.

But not Nicolas' place. If the information was kept from Hakon, Trygve probably had his reasons, whoever Trygve even was. And since Anders and Lucia hadn't offered, he was likely to create a shitstorm beyond his own comprehension if he took it upon himself to enlighten the kid.

"You know you don't have to hang out here by yourself."

"Yeah. I know."

It's okay, kid, I couldn't stand to constantly be around the energy suckers the Brotherhood sent our way, either. If we hadn't promised to take care of them, I'd ship Eydis and Sindre to the next parish. Fuck, the next state.

At least Eydis had backed off her game.

"I saw Livia wandering around the gardens earlier. Maybe she could use the company." Nicolas offered his hand. Hakon blinked a few times, hesitated, then took it. "She can't talk to birds or any of that, but she's pretty cute." *And quiet.*

"I'm too young for a mate," Hakon said quietly. "But if you want me to protect her, I will."

"What is it with Empyreans and mating? I just said talk to her!" Nicolas rustled Hakon's strawberry hair. "Look, who knows how long this stuff overseas is gonna take. There's only so much chatting with crows you can do before boredom sets in. Why not find a friend?"

Hakon blushed, nodding. "All right."

"Good boy."

As he watched Hakon shuffle off toward the gardens, Nicolas wondered what had prompted this sudden rush of paternal effort. Pep talks and 'atta boys were part of Oz's repertoire, not his.

Whatever caused it, another, more potent thought was

weighing on him now that he was alone again: *They've sent us more than just the children of rebels. We have someone here who could be in the line of succession. This could change the entire game. Am I crazy to wonder why no one is more worked up about this?*

The one person he felt he could ask this question to was no longer talking to him.

He would fix it. He would. Just as soon as he figured out *how.*

35
AGRIPIN

Cyler arrived late. Agripin was equally displeased and relieved. He was convinced something had befallen him, when the young Empyrean burst through the doors, covered in the dust of his travels.

"Where have you been?" Agripin demanded, but his resolve had already begun to crumble as he saw the object of his desire standing before him, clothes askew, blazing red hair a mess.

"Doing exactly as you asked, Aggie!" Cyler cried, dropping his filthy cloak to the floor. He then stood before the fireplace, propping one muscled leg upon the chair. This move completely exposed Agripin's favorite parts, as the younger Empyrean insisted on wearing a kilt, sans undergarments. Agripin felt a strong stirring beneath his own leather.

"I asked you to report back on the status of our Brotherhood leaders," Agripin intoned, doing his best to maintain a semblance of command, frustratingly absent around Cyler. He'd hoped separation might dull the desire so they could continue in the professional rank and command relationship they should be enjoying.

"Aye, you did," Cyler agreed, smiling as he soaked up heat from the fire. Agripin remembered the day, a hundred years ago, when he'd seen Cyler standing on the dais, taking his mark. How proud and defiant Cyler had been, accepting the symbol right on his derriere and then laughing when the Scholars complained the real estate was too small. *Well, spread it across both cheeks, then, I don't care!*

That was the moment Agripin knew he needed him. Selfishly, he took him under his wing, and insisted Cyler be a member of his personal guard. It did not take long before Agripin began to see there were other benefits in having the fledgling at his side.

Young and unpolished Cyler may be, he was also a brilliant tactician. Agripin was revered for his military knowledge and prowess, but even he could not formulate plans dozens of steps in advance. It was as if Cyler was playing a complex, multilayered game of chess in his mind, always. Youthful confidence demanded he always win, and so his mind continuously searched for every possible move, every variable. Even with his inexperience, he was an invaluable battle tool. In a thousand years? He would be unstoppable.

That is, if Agripin could focus more on teaching him than fucking him.

"Report, then," Agripin commanded.

"As I predicted, Birger and Astrid have roused the support of nearly the entire Brotherhood," Cyler boasted. He bowed and flexed his legs, stretching, and Agripin had to look away as his kilt flipped higher. "I find it fascinating the peaceful ones were the most successful in pulling together a war."

"Do we have an accurate census yet?" Agripin asked. He carved a piece of the oxen that was now long cold on the oaken table.

"As accurate as we're gonna get," Cyler responded. He

mercifully dropped his leg, and sauntered over to the table, pouring himself a tall mug of ale. "Ready to be pleased?"

Agripin frowned, frustrated at the intentional double meaning in Cyler's words. "How many?"

"Don't choke on your meat, Emperor, but I believe we have as many Empyreans living as drekar rebels as we do under the Senetat's control," Cyler said. His face erupted into a sly smile as he added, "Emperor. I could fucking get used to saying that, aye?"

"Grand Emperor," Agripin corrected, coarsely, though they were both wrong. The looming coronation nagged at him. "And that is ludicrous. There's no way our population is double what we believe it to be. The Senetat would have gotten wind of that!"

"Oh, aye, because they're all so eager to be caught and slaughtered!" Cyler laughed. "You know how long Brynja and Einar have stayed hidden. No one has seen those two for many thousands of years!"

Agripin wrinkled his nose. "Then how do we know they still exist?"

"They're in regular communication with Trygve, and he's as old as they are. It took me awhile, Aggie, but I eventually traced my way to most of the leaders, despite Birger and Astrid making it difficult by not volunteering the info. Don't look so worried! It wasn't as easy as I'm making it sound. You know I'm an especially skilled tracker," Cyler boasted. "When I found them, the result was the same. They all want in. Do you hear me? They want actual freedom. What Birger told us is true."

Agripin processed that, trying to hide his thoughts from his protégé long enough to decide how to respond. "How many then? A thousand?"

"More," Cyler responded, in dramatic fashion. "But about a thousand willing to fight. And that's not accounting for those with marks who might step up, if stirred by events. All that's been lacking is a competent leader."

"Excuse you all the same, but you've not met Runa," Agripin argued. "Or Erikr. Neither were terrible leaders."

"Failed leaders," Cyler boldly corrected.

"Timing and luck," Agripin countered.

"Precisely," Cyler replied. "Timing is on our side. The Brotherhood has had time to propagate, and grow their population. Runa had no more than a score on her side when she attempted her insurrection, and Erikr maybe double that. We can match them, head for head, and probably best them."

"Wipe the smirk off your face. It won't be that easy," Agripin replied gruffly. He was tired, and still miffed at the cavalier way Cyler had sauntered into the room.

Cyler stopped smiling. "Aggie, don't be such an old man. The Senetat's days are numbered. They know it. Why do you think they're activating marks so much earlier now? Why they've been thinning their own ranks? They're afraid of something exactly like this happening. It's right about at a thousand years when Empyreans start to get bored, and curious, and sticking their noses in places they don't belong. But there's nothing they can do about the scores of us who don't have a mark. Speaking of which..."

"No," Agripin replied. "Not yet."

"Do you know how comfortable it is to have a phoenix singe your arse and drawers?" Cyler countered, shaking his head. "Not very."

"If I remove it now, they'll think you've died. You'll have to stay in exile until this is over." Agripin added silently, *I need you by my side.*

"When, then?" Cyler pressed. "If we wait too long, they might activate me. Do you want that?"

"Soon," Agripin replied, refusing to commit to anything. He

was well aware of the risk in waiting, and didn't need his insolent lover reminding him. It was the one bit of control he still held over Cyler.

"Though," Cyler mused, "I've heard tell your new empress is a resurrection shaman."

"Where did you hear that?" Agripin snapped, spinning toward him.

Cyler smiled and pointed at his temple. "You got lazy."

Damn it all to Farskilt. Agripin's primary weakness was his inability to multi-task under emotional distress. Even at his age, he sometimes let his guard down. And now, Cyler had been in his head, hearing all of it. Why, that meant...

Cyler sidled up before him, reaching down between Agripin's legs with a gentle squeeze. "Aye, I heard it all. Want to rule me, do ya? Tired of my insolence?"

"Very," Agripin agreed, spinning Cyler around until the boy was pressed against the table. Lifting Cyler's kilt, Agripin finally took that which he had been wanting from the moment Cyler left his side.

36
AMELIA

Jacob spent his days with Padraig, the draoi from another Quinlan tribe who'd married Nevina's daughter, Regan. Jacob's grudging disappearance into the small hut each day was marked by disappointment it was this young naïve man, and not his trusted Father O'Connor, teaching Jacob about his capabilities.

I'm too close to you to be an objective help, the old man said, but reasoning did nothing to help Jacob's mood. The initial wonderment and thrill of this new life had begun to slide past the honeymoon phase for him, as all things in life do, and Jacob's natural doubts crept back in.

What if they're wrong about me? Maybe they slipped us some good acid that night. Is there such a thing as good acid, do you think?

I'm just a ragtag orphan from Ireland, Blanca. *They've confused my epic skills with fists for magic. Easy to mistake, I suppose.*

I refuse to believe any of this rubbish until a friendly, misunderstood giant shows up to declare, why, 'yer a wizard, Jacob!

At least his humor still made appearances from time-to-time. His temperament had always served as something of an early warning system for Amelia, beyond her empathic senses. When his wit still came out to play, the turmoil was transient.

"Do you think they'll come out and join us for repast?" Nevina asked, with a disapproving shake of her head. They sat in Nora's small home, around a table that appeared carved from their great tree. Most likely it had been, and then quickly regenerated.

"Padraig will make sure he eats," Niamh's timid voice answered. She looked not at her food, but away, toward something in the distance only she seemed to see. Her black hair fell from a messy ponytail. Every hour or so, Nevina would wrench it free and re-tie it, mumbling annoyances under her breath.

"Regan tells me Jacob hasn't manifested yet." Nevina dropped the stone bowl in the basin. "I guess that's true, Amelia? You would know."

"Nevina," Nora warned. The eldest of her aunts, Nevina made no secret of her belief that Amelia and Jacob were too "modern" for the job, and thereby ill-equipped to rise to all the demands of the prophecy. But rather than having a solution for this, she instead expressed her skepticism through continued pointing out of events that may indicate things were not going perfectly to plan. Constant undercurrents of *I told you so.*

"Well, I haven't either," Amelia reminded them. Had they expected it to all just fall into place? One night of revelations would set everything on the right course? "I'm still limited to what I inherited on my mother's side."

"The Empyrean blood running through your veins." Nevina wrinkled her nose and drew in a sharp breath. "Maybe it's tainting the process somehow."

"Without it, she wouldn't be the right one," Nora reminded her. She nudged her younger sister Niamh, attempting to steer her attentions back to the stew before her. Niamh smiled and took her spoon. The sweet woman was older than Amelia's father, but her mind enjoyed a simpler time. All the women tended to her like a child requiring their protection, but a part of Amelia thought, *It's a blessing, maybe, to see the world through those eyes. To not have our worries.*

"Once all is said and done with this, I'd prefer we go back to our own corners of the world and pretend they don't exist," Nevina replied. "Empyreans have caused us nothing but grief, for centuries."

"Who knows what will happen when the peace is restored." Nora wiped broth from Niamh's chin, who was back to staring intently into the corner. Her head tilted in mild amusement at some invisible prankster. "No one knows. Perhaps it simply restores our choice in the matter."

"Maybe the timing is wrong," Amelia speculated. Her mind traveled back to the other side of the world, to the events facing her other family. She would tread carefully, not sure how much she should reveal, even to kin. "I think the Empyreans may be on the verge of a civil war."

Nevina snorted. The clay bowl clanged in the ceramic basin as she furiously scrubbed it clean. "When are they not? They only have themselves to blame. They are the cause of all their heartache. And ours."

Throwing up her hands, Nora dropped her cloth. "Generalizing is a behavior of the ignorant. Don't forget the alliance we've formed with Astrid and Birger."

"Birger was the one who signed the blood oath they later broke!"

"He came when the others didn't. It is no fault of his the others refused."

Nevina stopped scrubbing the long-clean dish with a drama-filled pause. "Deception runs in their blood."

Amelia dropped her spoon. "I suppose it runs in mine, then."

"Enough," Nora asserted. With a smile in Amelia's direction, she added, "I know the war you speak of, child. Birger has informed us, and that your loved ones are involved. I do not know how, or even if, this bears weight on your role here, but we must proceed separate of those efforts." She removed the bowl in front of her sister and stood. "You've asked us a lot about how our tribe operates. You've asked about your family history. But you've asked almost nothing about what comes next for you and Jacob."

Because I know what you're going to say. "The visions seemed clear enough."

"Do you understand what the goddess asks? I'm sure this all must feel tremendous."

When Amelia gazed at the table, Nevina flipped around and said, "Goddess, Nora, just ask her! Are you and Jacob trying yet?"

The heat rose to her alabaster cheeks. Amelia wasn't ashamed or embarrassed about her sex life, but discussing it in the context of clinical procreation was another matter entirely.

She still took her birth control pill, meticulously, each night before bed. She had no plans to stop, nor plans to share this information with her aunts.

"That's their business. Between them and the goddess," Nora bailed her out.

"Jacob and I aren't the only ones who have expectations on us. The goddess mentioned another couple, from the other tribes," Amelia said. "Do you know who they are?"

Nora shook her head. "One step at a time."

"Nora, if they're not even trying then these two may as well go home and return to their pretty little world of obliviousness," Nevina pushed, tapping her feet against the wood floor.

"Don't give me that look, sister. Noah might not have known, but do you think Colleen Deschanel was ignorant to her daughter's lineage? Nothing gets past that meddling woman."

Amelia shot to her feet. "I've been tolerant of you talking about me like I'm not sitting three feet away, but I draw the line at you speaking badly of my mother! She gave me the life you talk so frivolously about. I would be *nothing* without her!"

Before they could attempt to assuage her, Amelia fled the house, emerging to find a red-faced Regan who had obviously been eavesdropping.

"I apologize for my mother," she mumbled, contrite. Shuffling.

No, the sympathies are all mine for having to grow up with such a negative creature. "It's fine, Regan. Really."

Amelia wandered in the direction of the grove, and the *crann bethadh*. She couldn't say why she was drawn there, but the moment she arrived, she knelt at the base of the great tree, placing her hands on the bark in submission.

She didn't belong here. She'd thought she had—God help her, she'd been so sure, her surety had been the key in convincing Jacob to put his old life behind—but the *wrongness* of everything multiplied with each interaction. This was not her battle... or at least, not one she was equipped to fight. Maybe Jacob was right. Maybe they had it all wrong.

She wanted him. To call out to him in their secret way and have him appear at her side to proffer the comfort only he could provide. Take him away from the instruction she'd forced upon him so she could tell him how sorry she was. Release him from the commitment of facing these truths.

"Lass." The cracking voice of Father O'Connor sounded behind her, as his robed shadow came over her. "Ye are troubled. I see it. Ye and Jacob both. But did ye believe, truly, tha' a trouble this old could be solved wit' somethin' easy?"

Amelia dropped her hands. She pivoted, looking up. "Why won't you train Jacob?"

"'Tis as I said. I canna be objective."

"But he trusts you. He came back here, because of you."

The old man's face cracked as he attempted a smile. "No, lass. He came back 'cos of *you.*"

Amelia didn't return to her aunts. Instead, she called Nicolas, who told her everything was fine, and no, they weren't needed. *Do your shit, cuz. We have more than enough meddling Deschanels running around here.*

Has Oz had any luck tracking Ashley's wife and the boys?

No, but he's the most persistent son-of-a-bitch I've ever met. He'll find them even if he has to enter a wormhole.

And Miss Kitty?

Getting in everyone's way, and Condoleezza spoils her rotten. Same old, same old.

That's a relief. Say hi to everyone. We'll be home... well, when we can.

She wandered through the woods for a couple of hours, waiting for nightfall. Each step, the crunch of vegetation beneath her slippered feet, focused her thoughts toward a clearer path, steering her emotions forward, beyond the words. The heavy heart on Jacob's bracelet nestled into the base of her palm as her hands swung with her strides.

When she peeled everything away, a single truth remained: Whether they stayed here and pursued the goddess' direction, or returned home, Jacob's steadfast love would remain. Constant. Persistent. Knowing this most critical piece of her heart would not change, not alter, returned her courage to stay.

As with the night after the ceremony, her direction

remained true, and she had no trouble finding her way back to the village. Head clear, she was ready to curl up in her husband's arms and forget again until tomorrow.

Approaching the small abode she shared with Jacob, she detected movement inside. She stopped at the window and looked through the small crack in the curtains.

Jacob was poised in the corner, shirt draped over a chair. Sweat poured off him as he swung his arms, fists clenched, shoulders flexing. Shadow-boxing an invisible opponent.

For Jacob, this was equivalent to a recovering addict indulging in a sip of whiskey after life threw another curveball too challenging to handle alone. Only a sip. Only a punch.

Amelia's heart sank. One punch was all it would take.

37
ANASOFIYA

Agripin generously allowed Ana to sleep with her husbands most nights, but on some evenings he required her presence. The decision seemed a whim of his erratic moods, rather than anything strategic. On grumpier days, he preferred solitude. When riding a high, usually after obtaining the upper-hand in a childish debate or an afternoon with Cyler, he insisted on her company, ushering her into one of the plush chairs while he regaled her with tales from his day. She listened, alternately exhausted and amused, understanding this creature better every day.

She hadn't forgotten Maxima's words, of course. But when two people came to you separately and told you not to like or trust the other, it was a fair assumption you could trust neither.

His eyes were saucers as he double-fisted whiskey from the mountain of bottles at his side. "It is all falling into place, my dear. All of it."

Ana smiled obligingly.

"I'll confess, I never presumed the odds were in our favor.

Herding cats, I believe, is the expression men use to describe organizing discord? Well, we herded some cats, dear, we herded a lot of cats, and the Senetat is none the wiser!" He emptied the bottle in his right hand, gave it a curious glance, then moved to the one in his left.

His confidence was back, at least. Though more hubris than anything useful, he hadn't survived this long by being an idiot. Maxima's knowing looks and toying gestures left Ana wondering how covert their operation actually was. If the eldre had even hints of what Agripin planned, they were all in a lot of danger.

She thought of mentioning her concerns. She hadn't told Agripin about the meeting at the falls, and the strange exchange with the enigmatic Maxima. There were only two men she'd confide everything to, and he was not one of them.

Agripin broke the seal on another bottle, paused, then offered it to her. She shook her head. "Are you going to explain what that means, or should I continue to eat football-sized grapes, and gaze longingly out the window?"

"It meaaaaaans..." Agripin dropped his legs and leaned forward. "It means tomorrow I can tell you everything. The Brotherhood, all of it. Oh, don't purse your lips at me, you dark, strange creature. Yes, I know all about what grows inside you. In fact, I know more about it than you, dear. I may be the only one who can help you understand what is happening."

Ana stiffened, shifting in her chair. Useless to play dumb when the man was capable of reading any thought, any feeling. "But you prefer your secrets and intrigue. No fun to actually play straight, right?"

His golden red hair caught the light as he leaned back. His tongue flicked over his lower lip, pausing in the middle. "Sometimes. You're wrong about this, though. I can teach you, my dear. I *will*." His teeth caught the tip of his tongue. "Our war is far from over. Your war will go on. Mine will never end."

She said nothing. His rambling was often a mix of something useful and so arbitrarily peripheral that to attempt sense from it was futile.

Agripin's eyes went glassy. One bottle dropped to his side, hanging half out of his fist. The other settled between his legs. "You think me heartless."

"Self-serving," Ana corrected. "Not heartless."

"A heartless man couldn't love you. But I do. Love you. Not the way your men do. Not the way I once loved Aanya. The way I might have loved Oriana had she not become a total psychopath. Or Nerys had she not run from me."

He rose from his chair and stumbled forward. Ana quickly caught him, knees buckling from the weight of the man and his elaborate dress. From across the room, Forbia started, alert.

"Ohh," Agripin moaned, sagging against her. "I may, finally, be drunk."

"You think?" Ana struggled to support him, looking around the room for something to change him into. She considered, briefly, calling for Aidrik or Finn but both men would react with rage to see the scene unfolding.

Ana tugged and shuffled him toward the large four-poster bed, heaving him atop it with one powerful shove. He groaned and rolled over, exposing the laces on the back of his uniform. She pulled at each one, and the armor slowly loosened. With one more grunt, she turned him back over, pulling the plate off, dropping it to the floor.

"And my tunic?"

"I'm not touching it. You have a strange habit of getting erections for no reason."

Agripin rolled to his back, slipping one hand above his head, dropping the other on his chest. His grin was boyish, genuine. "I would never let harm come to you, Anasofiya. Do you know that?"

"I told you not to call me that," she chastised, but tentatively climbed into the bed beside him, leaving adequate distance between them.

"You and your inane sentiments." The arm above his head came down around her shoulders, pulling her against his chest. The lines there were hard, sharp, in stark contrast with the soft strength of Finn's muscular build. *He'll be asleep soon.*

"You don't trust me. No point in arguing, not that you were going to." He chuckled, using his pinky to twirl her hair. "You're right to be guarded here. 'Twould be foolish to trust blindly, my dear. And you're far from foolish."

His heart-rate began to slow; his breaths grew spaced. "You can... you can trust one thing, though, Anasofiya. I would never, ever harm you. On my life."

Agripin's hand fell away as he succumbed to sleep, the sharp whiskey wafting from his breath in light snores. *I would never, ever harm you.*

Ana stared at the faint light falling through the curtain, realizing he'd made no similar promises about Aidrik and Finn.

38
CYLER

Cyler waited until the first of Agripin's snores echoed in the dark room before slipping away. His master's post-coital sleep was beyond disruption. He would not be missed.

The palace halls were cold this time of night. Most were wrapped in layers of furs and blankets, safe asleep. It was nearly impossible to keep the castle heated at night. The staff would be up and about before the sunrise to start the arduous process of warming it up again before the royals arose. But Cyler knew there was one room in the palace that always stayed warm, morning and night.

Cyler spiraled down the long staircase, descending so many levels it gave the impression of journeying right into the center of the Earth. With each step, the warmth from The Menagerie grew and eventually, between exertion and environment, Cyler no longer shivered.

As he descended the final group of stone stairs, two Crimson Guards flanked the entrance to the Ivory Hall. Beyond them, double doors made of ivory and pearl marked the entrance labeled in gold script, *The Menagerie*.

"Speak the entrance code," one guard intoned.

Cyler groaned and rolled his eyes. They should know him by now! "Watered silk."

The guards said nothing, but stepped back against the wall, allowing him passage. Cyler strode down the hall confidently, but slowly. He was not always a follower of rules, but he carefully heeded those ordained for The Menagerie. He would not be allowed to return if he broke them, even once.

Please proceed at a leisurely stroll, the sign with ivory inlay read. It sounded like a polite suggestion, but every suggestion was law in The Menagerie.

Cyler approached the tall doors, and slowly opened them. As he did, his view grew awash with bright and colorful lights, as The Menagerie came alive.

Almost immediately, every one of his senses were overwhelmed. His ears took in the sweet sounds of a hundred birds trilling and singing, while his eyes, as usual, began to catalogue the uncountable variety of flora and fauna that decorated this Garden of Eden. Many of the plant species had been developed right here in The Menagerie, the botanists brought in for their specialty in creating the most colorful, and vibrant hybrids.

All around him, Children of Men, male and female, wandered without a stitch of clothing. They were afforded a blanket for rest, but otherwise were not allowed a single item of apparel upon their arrival into The Menagerie. Many balked at this rule initially, but very few ever left. *Utopia*, they called it. And why not? They were treated like royalty, and given every comfort and pleasure they could ever desire. If Cyler had the misfortune of being born human, this is where he would have desired to end up.

Many of them smiled in his direction, as he meandered down the ivory floor, toward the large throne at the back. Some greeted him by name, and suggestively inquired whether he was staying long. He returned their smiles and greetings, but coyly refused to answer.

The Menagerie existed as the ultimate affront to Empyrean law. It was a crime, punishable by death, for Empyreans to copulate with men, but The Menagerie existed solely for that purpose. It was a veritable harem, and only the duchess' closest chosen confidants were invited to taste.

Cyler had been coming here since his days under the Scholar's tutelage. Agripin had not been the only child of Grand Emperor Aeron who took a liking to Cyler. Oriana's scouts discovered him, and he was summoned to her private chambers for inspection. While the duchess didn't mate with other Empyreans, she would allow only the most beautiful, and hence most worthy, of her race in to enjoy the fruits of her illicit garden. Oriana's stamp of approval was given immediately, and he was welcomed into the succulent, elite world that same day.

Agripin didn't know, and Cyler wanted to keep it that way, clearing any thought of this paradise from his head when they were together. The duke, now nearly an emperor, could be very possessive. Cyler enjoyed his elder's affections, and shared them, but despised the double standard. Agripin could enjoy the bed of anyone, at any time. Cyler was expected to save himself.

And there was the matter of the hard feelings between brother and sister.

Cyler figured his unwavering loyalty in politics and battle was enough. What he did to satisfy his other urges was his business, and his alone.

As he pushed through some orange and purple palm

fronds, his view opened up to a gargantuan throne made of millions of tiny pearls. Upon it, nestled amid thick animal pelts, the always stunning Duchess Oriana sat, attended by several of her most beautiful humans.

Cyler took a moment to drink her in. Her cascade of red hair looked like a waterfall of fire against her white gown of watered silk, and snow leopard furs. Long, slender arms were bedecked in pearl bracelets, from wrist to elbow, her neck covered completely with an ivory bone choker that ran chin to breast. The Snow Queen, she was sometimes called, by her pets. She was the only being in The Menagerie allowed to wear white, and other than the pearl and ivory accents flanking the escape, no white foliage or decor were allowed either.

"Ahh, Vakkar!" Oriana cried with pleasure, extending her long, jeweled wrist for Cyler to kiss. After, he rose, and sat on the silk-covered stool she patted, next to her.

"We've missed you," she purred. "Pray, where on Earth have you been?"

Cyler watched as the nude Children of Men fanned her with a rainbow of multi-colored fronds. Another human scuttled to her feet and began tenderly washing them in rosewater. "Agripin had me on assignment," Cyler said, cautiously. He was more than happy to have Oriana's Menagerie attend to his physical needs, but he wouldn't share his master's secrets, even with her. Especially her.

"I do believe you mean Grand Emperor Agripin. Soon, anyway," she replied, with a coquettish drop of her eyes. "Don't look so surprised. There may be little love in our family, but he is still slated to be my ruling emperor. I would be nothing if such designations were not respected."

"Understood," Cyler replied, contrite.

"Must have been important for him to send you away for so long," Oriana pressed gently. Cyler knew she was fishing for information, and he would need to tread even more carefully now that she was expecting something.

"My own foolishness kept me away so long. Truth be told, he's angry with me for extending my assignment." Cyler grinned.

Oriana giggled, shooting him a punishing look. "A little rebel, aren't you, Vakkar. I should start calling you a Runean!"

Cyler's heart seized, but he quickly recovered himself. The reference was clearly a coincidence; there was no way she could ever know what he, or Agripin, were up to.

"Call me whatever you want, just don't change the pass-code on me!" Cyler exclaimed, then let out his breath when she smiled playfully.

"Never," she promised with a light, airy wave. "Tell me more about my brother. What brings him back to the palace? I hear he's brought some amusements with him." She dropped her voice. "That must sting."

No, it stung not at all, but he wouldn't say that. Cyler had yet to fully understand Agripin's intentions with the halflings, but whatever his play, they weren't his lovers. "You know how he is," Cyler replied with a shrug.

"Indeed," she replied, drawing out the word. "But you haven't answered my first question."

Cyler paused for only a moment, before saying, "Your father's passing, of course. Agripin had to take over as emperor."

"Ahh, but he did not know that when he arrived," Oriana said, with the tone of someone who has caught another stealing from the cookie jar. "Ascension is unpredictable, is it not? Only Our Father Emyr truly knows the time and place."

Cyler pressed his tongue against the roof of his mouth, in an effort to hide his discomfort. "Grand Emperor Aeron summoned him," Cyler lied. "Beyond that, I'm unaware of the details."

"I see," Oriana replied, though her tone suggested exactly the opposite. "Well, I do hope he's not getting any foolish notions in his head. I'm hearing rumors that Nerys is planning a return."

Where did this woman get her information? For someone who never left the lower levels of the palace, she seemed to know as much, or more, than everyone else. "I hadn't heard that," Cyler lied again. Of course he knew about Nerys. He'd recruited her.

"I suppose the truth will surface in due time," Oriana said knowingly. Cyler found himself fixated on her eyes, which were lined in black kohl, to resemble a cat's eye. It was the only bit of color she wore, other than the natural red of her hair.

"The truth is usually rather boring," Cyler added, realizing too late he should have let it go with her last statement.

Oriana raised one jeweled brow. "I've been awfully good to you, my darling Cyler. If something exciting were going on, you would tell me, wouldn't you?"

"Of course," he said.

"Because," she went on, drawing in a the scent of a turquoise rose that had been placed in her lap by one of her pets, "for as good as I am to those I hold dear, I am equally, and more so, a danger to those I do not."

From her honeyed voice, the threat sounded musical, melodic. But her words were clear. She knew Cyler was keeping something from her. If she found out what, he would pay. Cyler knew enough about Oriana, and The Menagerie, to not doubt her will or ability. He understood that all the visual beauty around him was an elaborate illusion designed to mask the cruelty and darkness under the surface.

"But, the night is growing old, and you have just arrived!

Go find your amusements, Vakkar! And don't wait so long between visits this time," Oriana sang, and then went back to distracting herself with one of her pets. The gesture was final. He was dismissed.

Cyler pushed the danger from his mind and went forward toward his enjoyment.

39
LUCIA

"Remind me why it was necessary to run miles from the house to have this discussion?" Anders panted as they raced along the top of the levee, his complaint muted as he kept fair pace with her.

"Because I needed the run and you've barely left that study since we arrived." Lucia shot ahead of him, sprinting long strides courtesy of a killer second wind. When she reached the chain-link fence topped with barbed wire at the petro plant—the *No Trespassing* sign didn't shake her, but the armed guards a hundred yards in did—she shuffled down the grassy hill toward the riverbank, and a small dock. Anders was behind her, not without a few exasperated grunts.

"You have my undivided attention." He stood over her, like a scolding father, refusing to sit.

Lucia rolled her eyes. "We haven't heard from Thorvald even once. Remember what he said before we left?"

"Try not to kill anyone this time, *mi bellezza*?"

She whacked the back of his calf. "About sending for us soon. He said the assignment could be measured in weeks, not months. Don't you find it strange he hasn't sent us *any* word at all?"

Anders shrugged, looking away from her, into the choppy river. "You know how he is. Not sentimental. And not good with pleasantries."

"I'm not looking for pleasantries, Anders. We're going to *war*!"

"Maybe," he replied, unruffled. "I'll believe that when it happens. For now, we have a job to do, Lucia. Questioning why Thorvald hasn't given us better communication has no place."

"I'm not questioning him. I'm worried."

"For what? He never set us up with expectations he'd send regular correspondence. That's an expectation of your own invention."

Lucia dropped her head. She tickled one of her sneakers in the water below. "You're right. But I know him."

Anders' laugh was drowned out by a steamboat emerging around the bend. "Still not over your childish love for him? Lucia, he is your *leader*. He will never be more than that, no matter how many cute nicknames he bestows on you to retain your loyalty."

"You know nothing." Her stomach sunk at the truth of his words.

"Luc, why do you think he paired you with me?" Anders' voice was softer now, turning on the soothing tones of an adult speaking sense into the inexperienced. "You have big ideas, always have. You're impulsive and passionate, and a fantastic fucking scout. But you can only see three feet in front of you. Think, even for a minute, about what you're saying. The reason he hasn't contacted us is obvious."

The answer wasn't obvious to her at all. But Anders loved saying things like that. She suspected it gave him power over her, though why he needed it she could never guess. "And that is?"

"Your war is closer than you think." Anders seemed pleased with himself. "He may even have his clan marching to battle as we speak. Which means, we can't lose focus, getting silly and emotional about letters from home."

Oh, he could go to the mines for that remark! "Then you better hope you have your two little pet projects ready to go," she murmured.

A brief flash passed before Anders' gaze. "Aleksandr's power is buried deep, and I'm still working to unearth it."

"And Nicolas?"

"Stubborn," Anders replied, frowning. "More stubborn than you, I'm afraid."

Lucia didn't rise to the diversion. "I really have no interest in knowing the details of what happened with you and Mercy, but is that why he's distracted?"

"I don't think he knows of my past with Mercy. Or cares. His screwing around with Eydis is the problem."

"Then he should stop screwing around with Eydis."

"He has, I think. But the damage was done with Mercy, who has always been terrific at holding grudges." Anders shook his head. "I'm not here to sort through their drama. I need Nicolas to get his head on straight. When he does, the boy will follow."

"She's depressed," Lucia replied. "Deeply. I can sense it so strongly in her that it overwhelms me to even be in her presence. And I think it's more than Nicolas' straying."

Anders gave her a pointed look. "Tell me you wouldn't be depressed if you were killed and brought back as a damn Child of Man? That ever happens to me, Luc, you *leave* me dead."

• • •

Anders gave Nicolas and Aleksandr the day off and disappeared. To where, Lucia could only guess. He seemed to need his own head-clearing. She imagined him slipping into the swamp, chasing nutria and wrestling gators, and chuckled to herself.

She went to check in on Livia, and was surprised to find her and Hakon huddled in a corner, sharing a private joke. If it had been Sindre instead, she'd have gone in and put a stop to it. But Hakon needed the kinship as much as Livia, and their ease warmed her.

A part of her missed Markus, and the companionship he offered, no matter how fleeting. But if they'd played their games much longer, the connection might have strayed past diversion and into attachment.

Lucia didn't want a mate. Not now, not ever. Not unless his name was Thorvald.

Venturing into the study in search of something to read, she ran into Oz again. The lawyer. Before him was a mountain of paperwork and folders, but his eyes were glassy and fixed on something in the distance.

She moved into the room slowly, unsure of where his mind currently resided. Interrupting a man at the wrong time could lead to problems. "I'll come back."

He waved at her, shaking his head to clear himself. "You caught me daydreaming on the clock."

"I won't tell the boss," she promised, cracking a careful smile. He was being playful, sort of, but if she told him she could actually hear the torture in his soul, the black pain eating at his heart, she didn't think he'd appreciate it much. "Our secret."

Oz smiled, but his expression was muddy. "Secrets have never done anything except bring misery." Then he sighed, shaking his head. "I'm sorry. That was heavy, and you didn't ask for it."

"You lost your wife," Lucia risked. She couldn't say for sure why she started there, or why she seemed intent on discussing this with him, but there was a draw and she followed. "Recently."

Oz nodded, closing a folder. He didn't ask how she knew. This was a man who'd grown up around people who knew things without being explicitly told. "Brain tumor. A secret she kept from me until the very end, to protect me. See what I mean about secrets?"

"I'm sure her intentions were good." Lucia said these words because they were the right thing to say, but also because her mind was busy searching his. She didn't like what she saw: a man intent on torturing himself, unable, maybe unwilling, to move on and crawl out of his misery. For as awful as he felt, he seemed to invite it, to burrow in the angst. It occurred to her a strong backhand might be a good first step in curing him. Thorvald's voice stayed her. *You can help him,* mi belleza.

"Aren't they always?" He flashed a pitiful smile.

Lucia approached the desk, leaning forward on both palms. The look she gave him was not the pity he probably expected, but arrogant determination. "I can help you. I can actually take this pain and make it disappear, just like that. I'm not going to, though, because I get the strong sense this is how you handle your problems every time they come up. And that's a bigger issue, if you plan to survive in this world. Seems to me you need to live since you have children and all. Am I making any sense?"

Oz watched her. Gave a slight, tentative nod.

"Good. Great. So instead, you're gonna talk to me. And when I sense you getting too far down the pity hole, I'm going to smack the hell out of you and get you back on track. Before you ask why, I have nothing better to do, and I'm bored as hell, so why not solve two problems at once?"

"What if I don't want to talk about it?"

Lucia flopped down in the chair opposite him and crossed her arms defiantly over her chest. "Then I'll sit here and watch you pretend to do paperwork."

40
JACOB

"I've seen enough *Harry Potter* to know it's not supposed to be that easy," Jacob said from the small settee in the corner of Padraig's home. "And if it *were* that easy, I'd have done it a thousand times by now."

Padraig offered a patient smile. "I said it was simple, not easy. The power of the goddess, and her nature, has been in you since you were born, Jacob. You've likely used it many times without ever realizing, but I'm trying to show you how to use her gift to your fullest potential."

Jacob glanced toward the door, then back at his mentor. "Just ask, you say?"

"With all your heart."

Jacob closed his eyes. His knuckles ached, but the sensation was more pleasant than a distraction. "Goddess, please bring me a million dollars. And a new car. A Lambo will do nicely, but I reserve the right to upgrade with the newest model year."

"Jacob," Padraig said placidly, "you know that's not what she's here for. Or what we're about."

It wasn't what Jacob was about either, but humor was a

much safer place than disappointing Amelia, who looked at him with expectant, hopeful eyes each night. He'd tried to tell her he thought this whole thing was one big, huge mistake, and that they had him confused with someone else. Every time the words started rolling off his tongue, they'd turn into a joke. She'd smile, and that was that.

He *did* remember Cianán's life, somehow, for whatever that meant. But he and Amelia were students of science. There were plenty of explanations, involving the brain's many defenses and chemical phenomenon, that were a lot more likely to be true than he and Amelia being reincarnated over hundreds of years.

It was a romantic thought, but not a realistic one.

Except for the way you look at her and see someone you've known since the dawn of man, not high school. How when you take her hips in your hands and look up at her flushed face, she represents a beauty older than religion.

"Okay, fine. But you're acting like the goddess is our own 'on demand' cable channel, and that doesn't make much sense, either," Jacob countered.

"You're asking with words. You need to ask with your heart," Padraig clarified. "It isn't about what you want. She knows your needs, and now that you've let her into your heart, she'll never ignore your call."

Jacob wondered briefly if Padraig used his charming gift of language and gratuitous use of heart references to woo Regan.

"I don't need anything, though."

Padraig walked into the kitchen. He grabbed a small wooden bowl and returned placing the dish before Jacob. "You haven't eaten since supper last night, right? You said earlier you were hungry. You asked for lunch. Your hunger is one of your most basic, and important needs. We eat nothing here that the goddess cannot provide."

Jacob didn't amend that he'd actually asked earlier for a steak and mashed potatoes. Padraig said they didn't eat proteins that couldn't be found in the grove.

Padraig led Jacob, carrying the bowl, out into the small village and then beyond, entering the grove so they stood before the *crann bethadh.*

"Ask the goddess to fulfill your need," he commanded gently. "In this case, your need of sustenance."

Before Jacob could do anything, two red apples appeared in his bowl with a *thunk,* fallen from the branches above.

"Okay, yeah, that was a cool parlor trick," Jacob conceded, blinking at the fruit. "But I could have picked those apples myself."

"Not from this tree," Padraig replied with a wink. "I wasn't trying to astound you with this demonstration, Jacob. Only attempting to show you how the goddess senses and responds to your needs. You didn't even have to ask."

I wouldn't have asked for apples, Jacob thought. "I still don't understand the point of this lesson."

Padraig took one apple, and nodded at Jacob to take the other. He tucked the bowl in his satchel, and laid his free arm over Jacob's shoulder. "The goddess understands your needs, both large and small. Sure, you can pick your own apples. Forage your own kindling, and purchase your building materials from any store. And I wouldn't discourage you from doing those things, if that is what you wanted to do.

"But the goddess lives in your heart, in the breaths you breathe through your lungs, in the blood flowing through your veins. It's when a need you can't solve on your own arises that this blessing will emerge and you'll understand the true power you inherited as a draoi."

"This is all too vague for me to appreciate," Jacob replied. "I need some framework."

"Aye," Padraig answered, taking a bite from the apple with a crunch, "but your abilities will come to you when you most need them. She will be sure of it. All you need to do now is trust in this truth, and remember it when you find yourself with a problem you can't solve on your own."

JACOB LEFT PADRAIG EARLIER THAN PLANNED. LOOKING AT THE TIME, he had a couple hours before he needed to meet Amelia for dinner, where he'd have to face his own disappointment and frustration in being so much less than she was hoping for. Meanwhile, he'd pretend he was okay to table the ever-important discussion of the one prophecy element she refused to acknowledge.

He decided to venture into Killianshire and see if he could find that same kid again. The one with two shiners and a jaw that hung too far to the left.

Ye sure? he said the last time, outside the pub when Jacob's curiosity got the best of him. He knew the look in this lad's eyes; knew where he'd been. *I cud show ye the place. T'ain't far.*

Maybe next time, Jacob had answered, hoping he had the wherewithal to prevent a *next time*, while realizing that *next time* was closer than he wanted it to be.

Just this once, he promised himself, knowing it was a lie, and venturing forward anyway.

41
AIDRIK

Long past the witching hour, the only lights were flickering candles they had carried down to the armory.

Their destination was connected to the palace by a narrow stone corridor nearly a half-mile long. The uneven passage was filled with cobwebs and vermin, making it apparent the path had not been trod in many years. *The armory is more for show than anything else,* Agripin confirmed. *More than likely we'll find nothing ahead but rusted metal.*

It had been many years since the blacksmith "ascended," and he was the last Empyrean to craft weapons or armor. The thought of seeing his mentor's handiwork desecrated caused a twist deep in Aidrik's bowels.

He was then pleasantly surprised to see the swords and armor had held up well over the years, much like his beloved Ulfberht. After a cursory examination, Cyler pulled against a dusty sword rack. It swung inward with a creaky groan.

"We're not stopping here?" Aidrik asked.

"This tunnel leads us outside Farjhem," was all Agripin

would say as he ushered them along, holding his torch to light the path.

The vines and stench grew denser the further they moved into this new corridor. Trafficked even less than the path to the armory, they spent the trek untangling their shoes from weeds or avoiding piles of rat excrement.

No one voiced a complaint. All his years in Farjhem, he'd never seen or heard of any hidden path, beyond the armory, leading out of the city. The lack of control over their destination unsettled him. He experienced a moment of regret they'd left Forbia outside the castle, and not found a way to smuggle her inside to join them.

Anasofiya stifled a cry as she connected with something jagged. Finn's quick reflexes caught her, and he helped her regain an even stride. Agripin and Cyler did not look back.

A dim light appeared ahead. It expanded, slowly, as they continued forward. At last they reached the source.

The rough entrance opened into a large open space; a cave, Aidrik deduced, applying his directional senses and memory to determine where on the map they might have emerged.

"Don't strain yourself, old friend. You won't find this location anywhere near Norway. Stian's portail has taken us across the globe. Fiji, yes, Stian?"

A tall, well-tanned Empyrean, red hair lightened by sun exposure, nodded from across the musty cave. Belatedly, Aidrik noticed the other half-dozen Empyreans gathered around a tall fire. Ancient ones.

"A terrakinetic," Aidrik whispered.

"What the hell just happened, Aidrik?" Finn muttered from the corner of his mouth.

"Stian here is a terrakinetic," Agripin explained. "From the dumfounded look on Aidrik's face, you can probably deduce he's never seen one in the flesh."

"Stian of Africa?" Aidrik wondered. He grasped at pieces, attempting to create order of confusion.

"Aye," Stian responded, with a light bow.

"A terrakinetic... he manipulated the Earth to create a portal? Somewhere on the path we exited Norway and stepped into... Fiji?" Anasofiya queried, her wide eyes illuminated by the flames in the center of the room. She stepped forward, away from Finn, toward the fire. "Is that right?"

Stian's deep brown eyes glimmered. He gave a diagonal nod, never taking his eyes off Anasofiya.

"Holy shit," she whispered.

"What is the cost of this?" Aidrik demanded. Stian's light forward slump was reminiscent of Atlas bearing the weight of the world on his shoulders. Aidrik realized Stian was keeping the portail open with tremendous focus.

"Whatever the cost, it's worth the reward," Agripin asserted.

"My powers... your powers... will be weakened when you return," Stian pushed through a clenched jaw.

"For how long?"

"Depends," Stian replied, then dropped his head, straining.

Agripin perched on the edge of a stone outcropping. "Aidrik, Ana, Finnegan... you wanted answers. You'll get them tonight. But first, introductions. Everyone here already knows who *you* are, thanks to Cyler." He flashed an annoyed glance in his protégé's direction.

Cyler stood near the corner, arms crossed in an unreadable gesture.

Anxious, unreasonably so considering this assemblage was his doing, Agripin stood, moving before the fire. "Those assembled here are leaders of the Brotherhood of the Dragon. Our *real* moniker, in contrast to what the Senetat calls us. The

Dragon Empire is spread across the globe, and we are not nearly as disorganized as they would like to believe."

Finn started with a question, but Aidrik stayed him. *Listen.*

"We have ten recognized regions. Nine of the ten are represented here before you, which is a phenomenon in itself. You'll have to take my word for it, but it's been centuries since we assembled, and never more than eight of us at once."

Anasofiya huddled close to Finn, whose strong arms enfolded her. Their attentions were raptly focused on Agripin.

"You know Birger and Astrid, who reside in Ireland." Two familiar faces stepped forward, smiling warmly.

"How is Aleksei?" Anasofiya blurted.

"Delivered safely to Nicolas," Astrid assured her. "Who is also doing well."

Anasofiya closed her eyes, whispering her thanks. Finn released a breath he seemed to have been holding since before arriving in Farjhem.

"As I was saying," Agripin went on, "we also have Dagr, here from Morocco. Aidrik, I believe the two of you met when you were wandering around contemplating the meaning of life."

Aidrik said nothing, but offered a slight nod in Dagr's direction. The last time he ran into Dagr, the latter preached of revolution. Not one word about the Brotherhood, though.

"Then we have Trygve from Mongolia, who hails from the first days. He was stomping around with Brynja and Einar when they escaped into the wild." Agripin approached the solid Trygve, who stood taller than any Empyrean Aidrik had ever seen, past or present. "I'd hoped you would persuade them to our cause now."

"Who said I did not?" Trygve's low voice boomed across the cavern walls. His hair was the dark, deep red of the ancient ones, not a hint of highlight, let alone silver. Height was an

Empyrean attribute that waned over the years, but Trygve stood near to seven and a half feet tall.

Cyler snorted, gesturing around before re-crossing his arms with a smug grin. “I don’t see them here. Agripin, do *you* see them here?”

“Hush,” Agripin commanded with a quick snap of his neck, then returned his attention to Trygve. “Are they coming?”

“I’m representing them, and will carry the message after we adjourn. If the plan is solid, they will lend their support.”

Brynja and Einar, the oldest living Empyreans. Dubbed their “Adam and Eve,” by many, they escaped when Runa’s rebellion fell, and hadn’t been seen since.

At least, to Aidrik’s knowledge, but it seemed his knowledge had been severely limited, despite his wisdom.

“I should hope so. This plot isn’t like the others,” Agripin replied. “Then this fine fellow is Thorvald, hailing from the *Costa del Sol* in Spain. Thor here sent resources to your family in Louisiana. When this is over, I suggest you thank them.”

Anasofiya’s face brightened. Aidrik bristled when Thorvald smiled back at her. Another Empyrean he’d never met, but heard tales of. A warrior, through and through, but he had a reputation for something else entirely.

Two female Empyreans stood apart from the group, both looking wild for different reasons. One had a gleam in her eyes that indicated some kind of bloodlust, or mania. The other, with hair tangled and matted, gaze directed at her feet, seemed more animal than Empyrean.

“Skadi the Ruthless from Bulgaria,” Agripin said with a nod toward the warrior, “and Jorun, of Ecuador.” Skadi stood rigid at the introduction, hand fixed on her body-length spear. Jorun shuffled from one foot to another.

“Yiva from Thailand is a bestiakinetic, like you Finnegan. When matters are over, she may be able to teach you a thing or two. And Leif comes to us from the Caribbean. He was once a member of the Senetat. We have within our ranks three ex-Senetat members, in fact, though far more have defected." With a nod, he added, "The others were activated before they could make their escape."

Anasofiya and Finn silently observed, transfixed. Aidrik contemplated how this entire organization of rebels could have escaped his notice. Not only him, but the Senetat.

"Shocking, isn't it?" Agripin voiced Aidrik's thoughts. "But here you have the leadership of the Dragon Brotherhood. Or most of it. They represent the drekar spread across the world, which are a mix of Empyreans born outside of Farjhem, as well as some who escaped. Now that you all know of our clandestine organization, you all are drekar as well."

"Who's the leader?" Finn asked.

All eyes fell on Agripin. He grinned. "I suppose I have no choice in the matter."

"The emperor of two worlds," Yiva alleged with a wolfish smirk.

Agripin stopped smiling. "But only one of them matters."

Agripin nominated Birger to lay out the history of the Brotherhood. "Runeans they called us after Runa fell. Shortly thereafter, many of us came together, and we formed the Dragon Empire. How we've escaped detection, I believe, comes down to their blind arrogance, and a lack of any meaningful way to track us. They can't fathom the existence of a body of Empyreans that could possibly hold any threat to them. In some ways, both Runa and Erikr's failures reinforced that belief."

Birger explained the Brotherhood was formed by Erikr, who, emboldened rather than discouraged by Runa's fall, felt the time for cohesion was immediate, when their fallen brothers' blood still ran through the lands.

"Erikr was a personal confidante of Alexander the Great. Alexander and Erikr conspired to join forces, appealing to Alexander's lust for conquest and Erikr's desire for survival. Alexander died before the dream would be realized, but Erikr was not deterred.

"After Alexander's empire was divided, most of his generals would not give Erikr the time of day. Seleucus told him not a one of them ever agreed with Alexander's whims, and the best our race could hope for was not being wiped off the map. He met similar words from others, until he sought out Ptolemy I, in Alexandria.

"Ptolemy equally did not want to be involved, his empire being the most self-sustaining, but also the most isolated, and he had very little land resources in Europe or Asia. But he was willing to help Erikr create the framework for what would become the Dragon Brotherhood.

"Trygve and Thorvald were among the first to take the oath. Astrid and I came along soon after. Over the years, additional rebels with a strong pull toward cohesion emerged.

"Erikr chose the time of his rebellion on his own, not long after the Brotherhood's formation. His fellow drekar not only advised against it, but begged him to reconsider. They weren't yet ready, not organized enough. Erikr could not be dissuaded, his ideas still far beyond their ability to execute, and thus his small uprising never stood a chance. Those who foolishly stood with him perished, and Erikr was encased in a block of ice. One that still stands in Farjhem."

According to Birger's narrative, from that point on, there was no central leader among them. Between their dislike of government stemming from the Senetat's rule, and Erikr's decision to fight without accord from all, they had no taste for falling subject to another's direction. They maintained their secret alliance with the Ptolemies through the remainder of that dynasty, ending with the death of Cleopatra VII. From that point on, the Brotherhood maintained no formal alliances with the Children of Men.

"Our goal, above all others, has been survival," Birger concluded. "Our dream is to see the Senetat removed from power, and a true democracy formed. One where leaders can uphold very basic, minimal laws all Farværdig can agree to and stand behind."

"And you think now is the time to act on that," Anasofiya said softly.

It was Thorvald who answered. He'd watched her with unusual intensity throughout the entire telling. "We've waited long enough. Our numbers have never been greater. Our force, never stronger. Now that Agripin is assuming the throne, it will only be a matter of time before they reveal his loyalties. If that was to happen, everything we've worked for, for thousands of years, would be thrown to the wind."

"I agree, but I don't have your history," Anasofiya replied, stepping out of Finn's arms. She gazed into the fire, warming her hands. "I suppose my reasons are more selfish."

"I see no flaws in you," Thorvald countered. Finn rolled his eyes. Aidrik's hand traveled to Ulfberht.

"Sheath your sword, Thor," Cyler quipped.

"Am I the only one here not thinking of bedding the halfling? Does she have an enchanted womb? Even Skadi's mouth is watering. This defies logic," Yiva griped.

"Never mind that," Cyler retorted, jumping forward. "Our last guest has finally arrived. Late, but better than not."

All eyes snapped to Cyler, and then scattered to scan the room. The only sounds were lapping surf beneath the base of the cave, and the crackle of the fire.

Cyler turned toward the path that led them there, and standing tall and proud, hand instinctively pressed over her chest, fingers touching her bow, was the Duchess Nerys. In contrast with her posture, her red hair was held with a simple leather scrap, and not a stitch of vanity was evident in her attire.

Aidrik had not seen the youngest royal child for many years. He recalled her graduation, and release into the world. Her eagerness to roam far and free from Farjhem. How she had wanted to spend her time exploring the land, and cultivating her deep love of nature. There were legends among men about the tall, crimson-haired nymph who roamed the forests of Europe. She was said to bring good luck and fertility to the lands. This wasn't untrue. Nerys was a known arborkinetic, who could both speak with, and influence, the flora.

Outside of nature, Nerys' values remained an enigma. Despite her tendency to keep her own company, she remained most beloved of all Empyreans. They believed in the purity of her heart, and her commitment to always doing what she felt was right. Her popularity was no doubt the reason Agripin recruited her into the fold.

Aidrik was wary of her presence, knowing she could either be a tremendous ally or a formidable enemy.

"Brother," Nerys greeted evenly, with a touch of fondness. "Our Father's blessings on your new assignment. May our father Aeron thrive in His loving arms."

"Our Father of Light, Our Father of Fire," all Empyreans in the room responded.

"You'll forgive me if I put aside pleasantries," Agripin began, studying his sister carefully, "and accept my promise to catch up on lost time later. But I need to understand where your allegiance lies before we go any further."

The cave went ominously silent, all focused on Nerys and the words she would speak next.

"I am a humble servant of Our Father, and through him, accept you as my new emperor," she said innocently.

"Blah, blah, blah," Agripin replied with a roll of his eyes. "Nerys, you know what I'm getting at."

"I don't," she insisted. "Why does this suddenly feel like a trap?"

"Have you been aiding the rebels, or not?" Thorvald exclaimed, stepping forward.

Nerys' face darkened with suspicion. "Are you accusing me of treason?"

"Nerys, come on," Cyler pressed, sighing. "Just tell them. You weren't this difficult in Bali!"

Agripin shot a warning look at his young lover. "Whatever your answer, sister, you'll walk away free. But speak truthfully, for I'll know if you do not."

Nerys straightened her stance, but her eyes bore the look of a cornered, and angered, animal. Her gaze paused on Jorun. The silence in the room wove a thickness in the salty air.

Finally, Nerys drew in a breath of courage and announced, "My heart belongs with the best interests of my people. As of now, I believe neither group to be purely innocent, but the Senetat less so. So yes, brother, I sympathize with the rebels, but you should already know this, as you sent your lover to recruit me. I was wrong to trust his intentions, and to trust the intentions of any present. You may punish me as you see fit, but I shall never, ever reveal the whereabouts of any of my people."

As Aidrik relaxed, he could hear the other collective sighs of relief from around the room. Agripin's smile, though, spoke for all of them. "Welcome, sister. We have much to fill you in on."

. . .

While Agripin caught his sister up, Aidrik stepped over to where Anasofiya and Finn had been observing silently.

"Are you all right, Kjære?" Aidrik asked.

Anasofiya looked up at him with drowsy eyes, but behind them he felt the intensity of her focus. "I'm fine, just anxious," she said.

What she did not say, but was apparent in both hers and Finn's eyes, was that she was sick over missing Aleksandr. Aidrik knew acknowledging it would draw the pain out unnecessarily, so instead he reached one hand and touched her face briefly. "Aye," he agreed, "we all are."

"I know this is all positive news," Finn added, nodding at the group talking across the room, "getting Nerys on board, and confirmation the Brotherhood is greater in number than we thought. But I can't help feeling like the clock is running out, and that all of these things working in our favor are too good to be true."

Aidrik shared those worries. He did not know what the future held, and if things escalated, he needed Finn to take Anasofiya and run. "That is a common fear when events become serendipitous," Aidrik counseled. "I believe there is much going in our favor. Not the least of which will be the element of surprise."

"I still don't entirely trust him," Anasofiya whispered with a slight nod in Agripin's direction. "He has little to gain and everything to lose. He doesn't strike me as the type who does things purely on principle."

"To the contrary," Aidrik gently corrected, "he is absolutely a being of strong principles. And equally stubborn. He believes in this cause, and won't stop until he achieves it."

"A lot is riding on you being right," she warned.

"We trust Aidrik," Finn assured her. "He's never steered us wrong."

Anasofiya said nothing to correct his faith, instead diverting her attention to Cyler, Nerys, and Agripin, who had finished talking and were looking their direction. All three were smiling. Aidrik allowed himself a brief moment of relief.

"What is the conclusion, then?" Aidrik ventured.

"We are in accord," Agripin said with a proud smile. "And we need to act fast."

"That's for damn sure," Finn agreed, as he and Anasofiya slid off the ledge and moved to join the group around the fire. "I have a sense things are not as secret, or as smooth as we think."

"Explain," Dagr challenged.

Aidrik nodded at Finn. The young man was mildly empathic now, and all senses, all observations were worth consideration. "I don't think the Senetat is completely blind to the fact there are rebels plotting something," he replied. "It's just a feeling. My gut tells me we don't have time to waste." Finn shared a look with Ana. Aidrik observed there was more Finn wasn't sharing.

"Unless your gut has a strategic advantage, or wields some sort of magical power, it would do well to keep its opinions to itself," Agripin replied, tartly.

Finn's jaw tightened.

"Whether you consider Finn's warning or not, Agripin's arrival and coronation plans have caused quite a stir in Farjhem. And, obviously, his choice in pets," Anasofiya said, grimacing at the last reference to herself and Finn. "I don't think anyone is confident the Senetat took your explanations at face value."

"I knew there was a reason I chose you as my pet," Agripin teased her with a wink. "Right you are. They are skeptical at best. Mutinous at worst. No matter what they are, I'm an impatient fellow ready to get on with it."

Cyler dropped a handful of ancient daggers on the dusty cave floor. He then arranged them into a crude shape. "We have our Brotherhood leaders engaged. We need to get their followers here, undetected," he said. "None of them bear the mark, so they can't be tracked that way. However, the Senetat has scouts everywhere. Some likely right under our noses."

Aidrik sensed there was more than coincidence behind Cyler's last statement. Aidrik wondered what Cyler knew, and was not saying.

"Brynja and Einar need to get on board," Agripin affirmed. "Without those two, we may as well turn it in."

"You said that about Nerys, and I brought her," Cyler boasted.

"I will bring them," Trygve vowed. "As I said I would."

Agripin snorted. "You'll pardon me if I'll believe it when I see them standing before me."

"They've been enjoying their freedom longer than any of us," Aidrik reminded him. "They would be foolish to give it up without some assurance of support."

Agripin began to argue, then stopped, instead frowning at the daggers. "Fine. What else?"

"What do you mean, what else?" Cyler looked indignant. "I brought you everyone!"

"Except Brynja and Einar."

"Come *on,* Aggie."

"You'll address me appropriately, or I'll flog you for insubordination!" He brushed imaginary dirt from his uniform, then breathed in, shaking off his flare of rage.

"The safe house has a handful of our children," Birger chimed in. "There's room for many more if needed."

"Leaders on board. Children safe. This was altogether too easy," Agripin said with a mischievous smile. "What am I missing?"

"We refuse to battle," Yiva declared. She shot a disgusted look at Thorvald and Dagr. "Most of us, that is."

Agripin raised an eyebrow. "How do you expect this to play out, then?"

Cyler smirked, lifting one leg up on the table. His kilt lifted with it, exposing him. He seemed to know, and did not care. "For being the leader of a non-militant race, you sure are bloodthirsty. If I didn't know better, I'd say you were a Child of Man," he accused, adding a subtle, but not missed, eye roll. "If enough drekar show up, we won't need battle. Besides, these lovely relics of the Blacksmith are useless. The Senetat is filled with powerful telekinetics, and mystics. What is the saying? Don't bring a sword to a magic fight?"

Finn snickered.

"Trading magic for swords doesn't make it any less of a battle," Agripin countered.

Cyler shook his head impatiently. Aidrik thought to himself that this pretty young fledgling might be the only one who could get away with such impertinence. "When it comes to numbers, magic is no different. We would have hundreds, possibly thousands, of drekar on our side. Very dangerous drekar. Their powers haven't been squelched by that wretched mark, remember? They've roamed free, mated, and created more powerful Empyreans. Hell, Aggie, we could probably bring in a dozen and it would be enough."

Agripin glared at him. "I still don't understand how this doesn't result in battle."

"Negotiation," Anasofiya jumped in. "The Senetat will have two choices, really. Be destroyed, or accept some kind of pardon, and release off into the world. Even if they choose to be destroyed, which seems unlikely given how much they have enjoyed their power over the years, it still wouldn't be a battle so much as an execution."

Thorvald eyed her thoughtfully. "The halfling has a point."

Agripin glared at the warlord.

"There is a risk," Finn added, frowning, "that we could do more harm than good with his plan."

"Please, go on," Cyler said with another exaggerated eye roll.

Finn ignored the slight. "No one wants to hear that the Senetat may be on to us, but, if I'm right, then they could be looking to desperate measures. If they suspect what's coming, what's to stop them from activating everyone with a mark, and destroying half the Empyrean race?"

Agripin looked at Cyler, and Aidrik briefly caught the pang of fear in their leader's gaze. "Well, we have a resurrection shaman, do we not?" he demanded, pointing at Anasofiya.

"That will not work, for many reasons. The most obvious is that the Empyreans are spread across the globe. More important, is that it took nearly all of Anasofiya's energy the last time. Planning for her as a resource is only reasonable if one or two fall. Not an entire race," Aidrik explained.

"It's a risk," Agripin said, thoughtfully. "But there's always risk involved when change is desired. For now, we keep any plans to this group only. Leaders, inform the others about our safe house. Stian will need to open many paths."

"Aye," Stian nodded.

"So now, we wait. In several days, there will be a new regime."

42
AMELIA

Amelia always guessed Jacob's placid acceptance would end, or at least fade. He was riding a high, she knew this, but she'd hoped when he finally came down he would settle somewhere in the middle.

When shadowboxing turned to him hiding bloodied knuckles, or a bruised jaw, she understood whatever had pushed him forward into this new life had abandoned him.

Did she own a piece of what drove him to sneak off, when he should have been with Padraig, to pursue his old escape? She'd emotionally blackmailed him into coming on this trip, only to decide she'd pick and choose the pieces of the story to accept and follow. Turned her back, or changed the subject, whenever he ventured down a path she wasn't comfortable traveling. How was that any different than what he'd done in refusing to come to begin with?

The best thing would be to talk the situation out, to lay everything on the table. But they both protected their fears through isolation. Her by avoiding a topic she knew would end in an argument, and him by releasing his frustrations elsewhere. She waffled between trying to find a passive way to help him, and addressing their discord head-on, forcing the rest of the discussion. The potential of either outcome was daunting.

These defections of his made her crave his presence more, though. After a grueling session with her grandmother—her first step in Quinlan training involved asking for an offering from the *crann bethadh*—she set off toward Padraig's home, in hope of finding Jacob finishing his own lesson.

Even before she lifted her hand to knock, she sensed he wasn't there. Before she could turn away, the door opened. Nevina wore a hand-sewn apron, her hands pruned. *My mother likes to show up and help care for the household. Unasked,* Regan told Amelia abashedly a few days prior.

"He didn't show at all today," she barked, wearing a look bordering on pleased. "That *is* why you're here, right?"

Amelia clenched her teeth. "Sorry to bother you."

Nevina unwound her apron, and tossed it on the wooden table near the door. "You didn't come here thinking this would be easy, did you? You and I both know where he is, and we both know why. I told Nora you can't just pluck kids out of the city and expect them to be one of us. She never listens, though. Thinks she doesn't have to, since she's Seara's successor. But Seara isn't always right, either."

Amelia recognized the resentment in Nevina's words, but she couldn't find any sympathy for her negative aunt. She could hardly muster the courtesy her mother taught her. "Jacob is fine. We're both fine. But thank you for your concern."

Nevina snorted. Her arms crossed over her chest, and she shifted her weight, watching Amelia with a curious expression. "Go on, then. Go pick your husband off the floor of the church basement."

The door closed in her face before Amelia could think of a reply.

JACOB DIDN'T RETURN UNTIL AFTER MIDNIGHT.

Before, he'd made attempts to hide what he was doing. At the very least, this told her he understood it was wrong.

His late return indicated blatant flaunting of his behavior. Daring her to challenge it.

When the door to their small house opened, Amelia fixed her gaze out the window, unable to find words in her anger.

"Not going t' say anything to me?" Jacob challenged.

Amelia didn't look up; didn't take the bait. One glance at his eyes and it would unlock her frustration. She felt strongly if she let go of her fury, if she stopped caring, it would cause them both to spiral further away from one another, maybe to a point they couldn't return from. "What should I say? Good on you for taking your frustrations out by submitting to an old weakness? Or would you prefer I chew your ass about it?"

"I'd prefer tha' I was able to talk to ye about things, instead of havin' to find another outlet. Tha' anytime I brought up havin' a kid ye wouldn't change th' subject on me."

"Are you looking for an apology?"

"Aye, something would be nice."

"Fine. I'm sorry for providing a convenient excuse for you to go off acting like a juvenile. Will that work for you?"

The door slammed. The action caused all the windows in the tiny cabin to rattle, and a chair to topple. "Dammit, Amelia! You are the most stubborn creature I've ever known!"

"I won't take responsibility for your weakness, no matter how many doors you slam, or accusations you throw around!" She finally stood, rising to the challenge. The smell of sweat and dirt rolling off him only incensed her further, a feeling that grew exponentially as she observed his split lip and the light flare of his nostrils.

"This is what I ha' to do to get your damned attention!"

"Spending the last two weeks in Ireland with you hasn't been enough, then?" She marched toward him, inspecting his wounds with the back of her hand. "You can tend to your own damage this time."

"I would no' *deign* to ask," he seethed, pushing her hand away. "One of many topics I can't seem to discuss wit' my own wife these days."

She splayed both hands on her hips. "I can't read your mind when it's closed to me." Only as she said the words she realized they hadn't listened to one another's thoughts in days. Her heart sagged. "If there's something on your mind, say it."

His tongue danced along the wound splitting his lower lip. "Aye, you'll listen this time? It takes me gettin' my face beat in to grab yer attention?"

"Oh, you've certainly grabbed that!"

He shed his jacket, dropping it on the floor with a soft thud. "I don't know what ye want from me. I've believed every las' thing you've shared with me, about your family, who ye are. All of it. And I came to Ireland to learn th' truth about me, despite tha' it sounded like bloody insanity. And now tha' we know, ye just want... to ignore it? Where does tha' leave us?"

"We are only one *half* of this prophecy Jacob! Did you hear them give any indication they even knew where to find the other two supposedly involved? I've been trying to take this one day at a time, so we don't overwhelm ourselves!"

"By all means, don' overwhelm yourself."

Amelia's nose crinkled in disgust. "You've been drinking. Go to bed before you say or do something you might regret."

He pressed closer to her in one rapid move, acrid breath hot against her face. Her flinch made his nose flare wider. “I would never hit you.”

“The rage in your eyes says different,” she spat.

“Then ye don’t know me at all.”

“Right now, I don’t want to.” Even as the words left her lips, as the anger grew rather than subsiding, she knew they were words she’d come to regret.

“Aye. It’s mutual. Why don’t ye go stay with yer aunt tonight.”

She hadn’t expected this. “If I walk out this door...”

His response was to turn away and raise a hand, dismissing her.

43
ANASOFIYA

Hardly a day had passed since the meeting at the end of the magical tunnel. Ana still couldn't force her mind to accept they'd started their journey in Farjhem, and ended up in the South Pacific.

Their return home had been as eerily smooth, back in Farjhem in a matter of minutes. None of this was possible, yet she couldn't deny it had happened.

As they'd emerged from the tunnel into the neglected blacksmith shop, a harried-looking Empyrean—one Ana didn't recognize but Cyler and Agripin immediately greeted with wary frustration—declared Eldre Valerius had been searching for Agripin all evening and was nonplussed to discover him nowhere to be found.

They know, Finn had whispered from the corner of his mouth, so only she could hear. She wanted to challenge his fear, but wasn't sure he was wrong. The Senetat only seemed to come in search of them when they were engaged in unsavory behaviors.

Agripin scoffed he had better things to do than answer the

call of the Senetat. After an annoyed exchange, they learned the Senetat had invited the four of them to dine in their hall the following evening. *Whatever, whatever* Agripin dismissed, either ignoring or not seeing the look of alarm on the others' faces.

After a sleepless night, and a morning of separation—Finn off on an errand with Aidrik, while Ana was fitted for yet another ridiculous gown—Finn returned to spirit her away for a walk to clear their minds before the night ahead. Forbia faithfully watched their backs.

"Aren't you tired of this same trail by now?" Ana said as they moved down the mountain path they'd tread nearly every day since being given their limited freedom. "Maybe we should take what's-her-face up on that offer to go down to the village."

"The trap you mean?" he teased with an amused glance. "I suppose we can leave that in as Plan D."

"Do we have a plans A through C yet? I don't recall any solid marching orders coming out of that meeting last night."

"I got the feeling most of the important conversation in that cave was the parts we couldn't hear," Finn lamented. Ana had the same suspicion. If they could open a portail across the world, surely someone in that room could open a private communication channel. And what was the point of the meeting if not to formulate their plans?

"What do you suppose is the meaning of tonight? Just a dinner or something more?"

Finn stopped before the top of the falls, where they'd met Eldre Maxima. "Nothing is *just* anything here. I guess we could talk about it, and try to develop our own strategy around how to handle ourselves tonight, but if we try too hard, they'll know it. If we block too hard, they'll know that also, right? We could pray, but the God I prayed to my whole life doesn't seem to have much to do with Farjhem. You know?"

Ana nodded. She kept to herself that her real fear was no longer the Senetat, but those they'd come to consider their allies. She didn't clarify her suggestion to travel to the village, and perhaps get the hell out of there, was not facetious.

"I have a better idea." His worried look faded to a crease of mischief. "Come on."

THE CREST OF THE WATERFALL WAS SEVERAL HUNDRED FEET ABOVE where they stood on the craggy trail. Not reachable by foot, or any means other than perhaps some very adventurous rappelling. Where they stood was what they'd always called the top of the falls, because it was, for all practical purpose.

From where the cascade fell before them, there was nothing to break its powerful fall, freely dropping toward the river Farvann below. Whereas looking north, there were sharp mountain shelves slowing and re-routing the path, converging before where they stood into a thin veil before continuing on.

It was this veil where Finn aimed himself as he stretched a hand back toward her.

"Are you crazy? You don't know what's behind there," she chided, though she slipped her hand easily through his. The words felt requisite, her fears centered around things far less involved than what lay behind a waterfall.

"I do," he corrected. "And you can stop playing demure. We both know better."

Ana knelt down to cup some water intending to splash him, but when she looked up, he was gone. Craning her head right and left, finally she saw his hand snake out from behind the falls, beckoning.

With a half-second's hesitation, Ana closed her eyes and leapt.

Her feet hit the soft earth with a light thud, and her balance teetered, but Finn's arms were around her, steadying.

Ana looked over his shoulder at the small enclave, no bigger than her bedroom back home in New Orleans. No footprints, no evidence of use.

Finn pressed her into the dusty cavern wall, running his lips across her chin and neck, whispering her name into her skin with hot breath.

Intimacy had been last on their minds with the peril of the situation, but Ana set her anxiety aside and surrendered to her husband. Her hands tugged at his waistband, and traveled to his grizzled face, unable to make up their mind which she wanted to touch more.

She knew the Senetat probably had eyes on them, and she didn't care. Let them watch. Let them see something pure for once. She was not ashamed of the love she bore this man.

Finn knelt before her, trailing kisses down her torso, beneath her lifted wool sweater. When he looked up, tears pooled in his eyes. "I love you, Ana."

Ana wound her hands gently through his hair. Her own tears prickled. "Finn... my heart..." Her voice caught. *My safe place.*

Her pants were off before she could regain her words. Finn lifted her, balancing her against the wall, inside her in the next moment. She gasped, her head falling back as he thrusted, moaning her name, over and over, her hands gripping his ass, digging in.

The first time she'd slept with Finn, it had been love. Nothing gradual, no leading into these powerful feelings. She loved him in that very first moment of connection, a feeling which had spiraled into something near obsession. How easy it had been to push her own needs aside in the face of all the dangers in Farjhem.

As he filled her, body and soul, Ana cried, a carnal sound yet also a song of her spirit keening for the other half of her heart. *I love you. Always.*

After, he didn't let her down. He held her, pressing her face to his damp chest, where she could hear his swift heartbeat and feel safe, even for a moment.

Ana expected an ostentatious show from the arrogant leaders of Farjhem. Gold plating, silks, ornate china. Tapestries made of the finest threads.

The dining hall of Senetat Sanctuary was the opposite of opulent. White walls, floors, tables. A stark and noticeable absence of color of any kind. The stemware, plates, and even utensils were all clear. Not a single item of decor on the walls, and only a simple bouquet of white flowers in the center of the massive marble dining table.

"This thing must weigh a ton," Finn remarked as they were seated at the far end.

"Aww, you were thinking of running off with it," she joked, tossing him a light elbow. "Not even you, my Poseidon."

"It would look good in *Ophélie*, though, you gotta admit."

Agripin was seated at the end of the long table, flanked by Aidrik and Ana at the first seat on either side. Finn sat next to Ana. Behind them, several of Agripin's officers, Cyler included, stood in silent guard.

They were the only ones in the clinical room.

Ana forced her heartbeat to slow to a normal pace. Beside her, Finn was less successful.

“Still yourself, halfling. It’s their way, to make us wait,” Agripin groused. His look in their direction was shared sympathy.

“They make the Deschanels look inhospitable,” Finn dry-panned.

“Did I say they were hospitable?” Agripin returned.

Agripin’s prediction was correct. They waited an hour, in silence, before the blood-red robes swished through, cutting a startling contrast through the pure, clean room. Blood flowing through an ivory corridor. *Well, now I know why they went with white.*

Their seating was a matter of choreography, as with anything else they did. Grand Eldre Servius took a seat at the other head of the table, as the remaining eldres stood, awaiting their turn. In a blur of crimson, one after the other took their place. *According to rank,* Agripin whispered to her when he caught her gaping. When all had taken their seats, a large gap remained between their party and the Senetat. Ana wondered if they would need to shout their words across the monolithic slab.

She needn’t have worried. “A blessed evening!” Eldre Servius’ voice reverberated off the blank walls, creating an echoing acoustic. “We thank you for joining us!”

“The pleasure is ours,” Agripin responded, with a brief nod. Ana, Aidrik, and Finn nodded in kind.

No apologies were offered for the delay. Sections of the wall came open, revealing hidden doors, where the wait staff hurried out with trays of food even more involved than the spreads left in Ana’s room.

Eldre Maxima flashed her a small smile and a wink before lifting her wine glass to her cherry-red lips.

More silence permeated the room as everyone was served, and began to eat. Ana chewed her food with great effort, unnerved by the way all the eldres watched her, never dropping their eyes even as they cut their meat or swirled their food on to fork.

"At last, we lay eyes again on the specimen who has Agripin forsaking everything he's come to learn and believe," Servius began, setting down his fork. The other eldres followed suit, despite some of them only being half-finished with their meals. "How are you finding your stay in Farjhem?"

As if this was the Holiday Inn. "Fine," she managed.

"You hail from the subtropical Gulf region of the Americas. I regret we cannot offer you that same heat, and the menu, I'm sure, required adjustment."

"This isn't my first trip to Norway."

"Ahh. But you are not in Norway, my dear."

She looked toward Aidrik and Agripin, but their gazes were focused at the other end of the table, as was Finn's.

"No, of course not," she said.

"And you." Servius turned his eyes to Finn. His lips were stained red from the wine, leaving the effect he'd just drunk the blood of some unfortunate soul. "Truly, the only Quinlan we've permitted to live within the limits of our haven. How fortunate you have the protection of our future Grand Emperor."

Finn opened his mouth. Closed it. Released a half-breath.

Why is Agripin saying nothing?

"Well, look at them, Servius! I might be persuaded to break some rules to have them in my chambers. And our dear emperor-in-waiting has always favored both the fairer and darker sexes," Maxima cut in. Her eyes twinkled with amusement as she watched Ana and Finn.

"A testament to your dying faith, I'm sure," Servius grumbled. Brutus snickered, shooting Maxima a gratifying look.

"Now that you've seen them once more," Agripin replied, annoyed, "we thank you for the supper."

"If my aim was only to witness them, I could have done that without the trouble of serving a meal," Servius replied, draining his wine. With a light clink of the glass, another servant appeared from behind the false wall, refilling his cup to the brim. "This is a meal of official business."

Agripin pushed his wine away. "Oh?"

As Servius enjoyed more of his drink, Valerius took over. "The sentiment of our people was first one of shock, when you presented your mate and her plaything. However, there are those who are... reformist enough they embraced the idea. But all are awaiting the next steps."

"Next steps?" Aidrik jumped in, leaning forward.

"She has not yet conceived!" Valerius declared, as if stating the obvious. "If you plan to usher in this new era of yours, you will need an heir, and soon."

The sound of Finn's dropped fork reverberated around the room. He set both hands in his lap, breath caught hard in his throat.

Ana felt much the same. Her heart slumped like jelly. "Not for lack of trying," she choked out, setting one hand over Finn's. Squeezing.

"Your strength is apparent, despite still possessing some Child of Man within you. Try harder."

She managed a smile, reaching her free hand to Agripin's. He at first looked upon it like a foreign object, then took it. "Of course. We're just as eager as you to see an heir."

"Good," Servius said, turning his wine glass upside down. "Then we are in accord. If an heir is not upon the empress-in-waiting by next moon, we shall engage in a fertility ceremony."

"It's not a birthing year," Agripin pointed out. The light,

nervous tap of his foot shook his chair. "Not for another decade. Or is it two?"

Servius' smile stretched across the width of his placid face. "Those rules do not apply to you, as you're well aware."

Servius stood and shuffled out without another word. In perfect composition, the rest of the Senetat followed in their order. The large door shut with a deep thud.

"What the hell is a fertility ceremony?" Ana demanded, releasing a choking breath.

Agripin's color faded. He straightened his cloak, refusing to meet her eyes. "As you know, the more fathers a child has, the stronger he will become."

"And?"

"Kjære, they mean to put you on the dais and allow every male Empyrean of power to mate with you. To ensure not only a progeny, but a powerful one."

After he spoke the words, Aidrik nearly stumbled from his chair as he fled the room, leaving the others in stunned, helpless silence.

44
TRISTAN

While the rest of the house waited, Anders continued his mission to uncover the wonders that lurked within Nicolas and Aleksandr. If Tristan had a dollar for every time he heard how "rare" it was to have two mystics under one roof, he wouldn't need his trust fund.

Tristan and Harriett spent most of their days exploring the property. For as long as *Ophélie* had been in his family, he was ashamed to say he'd not spent much time outside of the Big House. They wandered through what had, at one time, been a self-sustaining village, filled with everything the Deschanels would have needed to survive. They took naps under the rows of live oaks. They got to know each other, something a young couple normally did *before* falling in love.

Harriett had little to say of herself. Her years of silence kept most of her experiences in her head. But Tristan loved hearing about the directions her imagination could go. His own imagination was equally limitless.

He told her about his sister, Danielle, a death he had never completely processed. He also shared the ambiguous love he had for his late mother, something he'd been afraid to say out loud for fear of betraying her in some way. Harriett told him she had an idea about that, but refused to say what, for now.

Tristan was in love, for the first time. What he'd shared with Emily was tainted with his misguided motivation. The handful of other women he'd been with were even deeper escapes. Harriett offered a beacon of light. A way out of the darkness.

He enjoyed every moment with her. That was, until Anders summoned him into the elusive training room.

Nicolas stormed out, brushing past him without so much as a greeting. Aleksandr sat on the couch, face buried in a worn copy of some Dostoevsky novel. Tristan couldn't read the title, it was so old.

"Have you thought about our conversation?" Anders asked Tristan, motioning for him to close the door.

Tristan shrugged. "I guess. A little, yeah."

Anders crossed his arms, and leaned against the book ladder. "That doesn't inspire much confidence. Have you or haven't you?"

Every word exchanged with Anders weighed as some kind of critical test. No incidental or extraneous words. "I have. But, I mean, I dunno if you've got the wrong idea about me or what. Telepaths aren't anything special."

"No," Anders agreed. "You are no ordinary telepath, though. You know this, so why are you acting like you don't? Modesty? Fear?"

Tristan lifted his shoulders for another shrug, but stopped mid-gesture, conscious of Anders' close analysis of every move. "Probably more a lack of experience. What I have is special for a Deschanel, but I don't get how that measures up to the creatures you've come across. I'm just a kid who can read minds long distances. That's all."

"That's a lot!" Anders crossed the room, flipping Aleksandr's book closed with a teasing smile. He stopped before Tristan, his gaze traveling up and down the young man's figure. Whatever he was looking for, Tristan couldn't guess.

"It amazes me how some members of your family seemed to have escaped ability dilution entirely," Anders mused. "You, for example. Your cousin, Nicolas, if he could get over himself and stop whimpering over Mercy."

"What about Aleksei?" Tristan nodded at the young man, who was again immersed in his tome.

Anders grinned. "The most substantial powers are always the last to surface. I have a feeling your little cousin is preparing to blow our minds."

Tristan looked over at Aleksandr, who seemed oblivious to the discussion. "Why am I here?"

"I want to teach you how to breach a telepathic block."

"You said I didn't need training."

"Not for what you can already do. I want to train you to do something you may not know you can achieve."

"Excuse me?"

"You heard me. You can reach across any distance to read minds. Do you have any idea how invaluable you would be to the Brotherhood if you could also breach a block?"

"You don't have anyone else who can do this?"

"Not on our side," Anders replied. "The Senetat does. We've been searching for our own for many years, but none of the telepaths we've come across could span the distances you can. Now, there's no guarantee you can get past a block. Most telepaths can't. But I have a... well, let's call it a hunch, that you're the one who can."

"So if I can, then what?"

"Then I hope you'll join us."

Tristan frowned. He dropped his eyes to the floor. No one had ever looked to him as someone special. Someone who could make a difference. He thought he wanted that, but now he felt sick. "What does that mean? I don't even know what it is you do."

Anders smiled patiently. "We explained that already. Lucia and I are scouts for Thorvald, one of the foremost Brotherhood leaders. I don't know what Thor would have in mind for you. My guess is he would want to keep you by his side. Maybe even his right-hand-man. You can't imagine the honor."

"I'll take your word for it. What if I don't want to go?"

"Why wouldn't you?"

An image of Harriett filled his mind, and Anders immediately smiled. "Ahh. Of course. You could bring her, you know. We aren't mercenaries, Tristan. She's your mate, and would be welcome."

Anders' words had an immediate calming effect on Tristan, one he found unexpected and welcoming at once. A way out of New Orleans. An important role, one that might involve making a real difference in the world. Harriett by his side.

Anders grabbed two antique chairs, and sat them facing each other in the middle of the room. Aleksandr looked up for a brief moment, then went back to his reading.

Tristan took a seat across from Anders. Immediately, his heart did flip-flops. Moments ago, he'd wanted to walk away, go back to his quiet naps with Harriett. Now he badly wanted to make Anders proud, to pass this test.

"Don't be disappointed if this takes a few tries. Some require months to learn. We will keep at it until you succeed, or get frustrated. And if that happens, we'll try again tomorrow. Okay?"

Tristan nodded, swallowing.

"I've never done this myself, so I can only suggest what I've heard from others. I'm going to throw up a block, and then I need you to focus on breaking through. How you do that depends on you. Most telepaths create some relative pattern they equate with the reading. Do you have one?"

Tristan considered this. To him, telepathy had been reaching into a sky full of stars, looking for the right star. "Yeah. I do."

"Use that. In the same way you search for a mind, search for a crack in the wall. A flaw in the design, if that makes sense?"

Tristan nodded again. "Okay."

Anders drew in a deep breath, straightened his shoulders, then looked square at Tristan. "Block is up. Now, take it slow. Don't frustrate yourself on the first try."

Tristan closed his eyes, and conjured his night sky. All the many stars burned, but those closest to him, those in the house, burned the brightest. He knew if he focused hard enough, he could find Amelia and Jacob across the sea. Maybe even Ana and Finn.

But they weren't the assignment. Anders was. No surprise, he did not see Anders' star.

Tristan bit down on his lip, scanning the dark sky. *A flaw in the design.* How was he supposed to find a flaw in space?

"Remember. You created this design, Tristan. It is yours to bend, or break, at will."

"My design," Tristan whispered. And that was true, wasn't it? He wasn't *actually* staring into outer space. He came up with this when he was a young boy, something that made sense to him and kept his thoughts from spinning out of control.

His mind sky adjusted, becoming a two-dimensional space. A poster. He imagined himself reaching out and tearing at the corner. As he did, the sky folded forward, revealing another sky, even darker than the first. Behind it, many stars burned, twice as bright as the others.

He gripped harder, his knuckles white against the seat arms. "Tristan, calm," Anders warned.

But Tristan would not be calm. He had done something wholly new, something that would be huge if he could tread further.

There were many, many stars here. It took moments for Tristan to find the one he was looking for. Anders. His mind's eye reached forward and grabbed hold, closing his fist.

Across from him, Anders jumped. "What the fuck?"

"Oh. Sorry, did that hurt or something?"

"You've done this before," Anders accused, face darkening with suspicion. "You already knew you could. And you said nothing."

Tristan stood, but the blood rushed north, and he fell back into his seat. "No! I swear, I had no idea until you told me I should try. I just did as you said, and looked for a flaw in the design."

Anders watched him. His eyes appeared to tremble in their sockets, an effect that was either rage or fear. "Do it again."

Tristan sighed, closing his eyes. The sky conjured forward once again. The tiny tear. The new sky. And Anders, again.

"Hell, that was even easier this time!" Tristan declared, clapping his hands in delight. "Wow!"

"Tristan," Anders said. He went silent, looking up at the plaster ceiling. "I'm not going to force you to come with me. But I need you to."

"Of course. I'm excited! And Harriett... well, she will be too, I think. We've been talking about getting out of New Orleans. We were thinking Baton Rouge, but—"

"This isn't a vacation," Anders cut in. "What I'm asking you to do is to put your life at risk for a cause that involves only one-half of your blood. And Harriett's."

Tristan smirked. "Yeah. Ever heard of the Deschanel Curse? If this doesn't get me, that probably will."

Outside, a powerful explosion shook the house. Then another. Books flew from the shelves, vases shattered to the floor.

"What the hell?" Tristan gripped the desk.

"One of the runts," Anders grunted, toppling back over Aleksandr, who'd finally put his book down. "Goddamn Lucia needs to be more attentive!"

A third explosion sounded. This one sent a sinewy crack down the center window.

Dust trickled from the ceiling. Then, the sound of creaking metal. There was no time to react, as the chandelier came crashing down, right where Tristan stood.

Tristan looked up as the chandelier halted above his head. In the next moment, he was on the floor several feet away. Safe. Untouched.

The chandelier shattered.

Aleksandr stood with his hands forward, panting, sweat pouring down his cheeks.

"Holy Mother of Emyr," Anders whispered, pulling himself up. "A time shaper."

"A what?" Tristan asked.

"You can thank you cousin for saving your life later," Anders said. "Tristan, I need you to leave us."

"Why?"

Aleksandr's legs went to jelly, knocking together like a cartoon character. He sunk to his knees in the carpet, hands still trembling.

"Because I need complete silence to calm him or he's going to go off the deep end."

45
LUCIA

Anders had balls of steel! The nerve of him, marching in while she enjoyed lunch, demanding to know what the hell Sindre was up to with the explosions.

Well, how on Earth was she supposed to know? According to Anders, training the rest of the household was as pointless as swimming upstream. Instead, she was relegated to wandering around the property, or offering to help Condoleezza with the household. The latter was so offended at the suggestion, Lucia never brought it up again.

"Get him under control, and do it now!" Anders declared, both palms flat on the dining table. Lucia kept her eyes on her meal, ready to take his anger and fling it right back at him.

"Who?" She played dumb.

"Who. Right." Anders stood, whistling a gust of air, gazing at her with stern disapproval. "They're your responsibility. Fix it."

"I can't imagine what you're talking about," she muttered, running her knife through the thick slice of ham. "I have no responsibilities, according to you."

"Now isn't the time to give me your usual flippant bullshit, Luc!"

The high rise in his tone caused her to look up. Her fork paused in mid-air. Her partner was drenched in sweat, his face a blurry mess of confusion and excitement.

She dropped the attitude. "What's gotten into you?"

"Aleksandr. He manifested today, finally, and... not now. I have to get back to him. But it's big. Bigger than I imagined in my wildest dreams. Can you please just silence that little hell-beast so I can calm the boy down!"

Lucia nodded, breath catching. She wanted to ask so many questions, but now wasn't the time.

She rushed outside, leaving the rest of her lunch untouched.

Oz, the grieving lawyer who showed up once a week to push some papers around and scold Nicolas for this or that, beat her to the punch. They stood in the rear garden, Sindre leaning back with his arms crossed over his chest, Oz taking an animated, but authoritative stance.

"My mora and far said I would be able to practice here!" Sindre pouted. "Back home, I would be rewarded for these feats!"

"Well," Oz began, drawing a deep breath, "you're not in Ireland amongst fellow, er, magicians. You're in South Louisiana where everyone owns a twelve-gauge shotgun and looks for an excuse to use it. I suppose Nicolas didn't share that we're trying to keep attention *away* from the property while y'all are here?"

Sindre twisted his lips in a half-circle. "He did. But I wasn't told we were answering to a Child of Man."

"I think the term you use is halfling," Oz corrected with a

diplomatic nod. "Even so, this is his home. He's the master of this property. Do Empyreans own property?"

The young one snorted. "Why bother? We take what we need."

Lucia stepped in. "Sindre. Really. I know your parents won't care much, but if Astrid and Birger heard about how you're acting, they wouldn't be pleased."

Sindre's façade cracked slightly. "They're off fighting the war we weren't ready for. I hardly think they have time for this."

"I talked to Astrid just today," Lucia lied, convincingly. "She asked for a progress report, and I left out your past destructions of property."

Sindre rolled his eyes. "Old decrepit piles of—"

"But I won't lie for you next time. You either respect this household and property, or I let her know we're shipping you off and someone else can deal with your tantrums."

He marched off in a nonchalant stomp, but not before she saw the fear flash through his eyes. Message sent.

"I guess threats work as well as reason," Oz laughed, shaking his head.

"I don't think Sindre possesses the good sense to appreciate your reason," she returned, watching to make sure the boy didn't wander off into more trouble. "I suspect he will be at it again by dinnertime."

"Kids..."

Lucia nodded. "Kids." She turned back to Oz, smiling. "You look better today. Brighter."

"Keeping busy. Took the kids to Biloxi Beach for the weekend. Naomi kept trying to go further out into the water than I allowed, and Christian kept telling on her. So, later, she crushed his sand castle." Oz laughed. "Sorry, you don't want to hear about my lame daddy stories."

"I've nothing else to do," she replied. She understood in the circles of Children of Men, this was usually droll conversation. But Lucia couldn't envision a life anything like what Oz led. She had a curiosity about it. "Care to walk?"

He looked surprised at her invite, then held his arm out as an after-thought, looking embarrassed. "Sure. Yeah."

Lucia took his arm, listening to the man's emotions. A thick, hard grief settled within him, but the outer layers were peeling back, allowing these small glimpses of function... kids at the beach, attempts at work. Seemingly safe conversation.

Oz had found her on each of his visits. *Saying hello,* he'd announce, but then they would end up talking about Adrienne. Lucia had the natural effect of others wanting to open up around her, but it was more than that. She'd opened the door for him to share, and he'd walked through it, feeling she was safer as someone he had no ties to.

"So, Naomi destroyed Christian's stunning architectural masterpiece. What then?" Lucia asked.

Oz stumbled when he went to respond, trying to determine whether her question was genuine interest or polite conversation. "Uh... well... he stole her towel and threw it in the Gulf. Which, sad to say, we were not able to recover. I gave her mine, and then she gloated all the way back to the hotel room." Oz quickly added, "Mine was bigger."

"I see," Lucia responded, mind drawn between Oz's story and keeping an ear out for Sindre. "Your children have two different mothers?"

"How did you know?" He stopped, re-routing them through the row of live oaks. "Never mind. Dumb question. Yes, Naomi's mother died when she was a baby. And Adrienne... as you know..."

Lucia frowned, giving him a wry smile from her peripheral. "Wait. You mean you killed two of your wives?"

Oz missed a step. "Excuse me?"

"You heard me. One of them dying, well, that's tragic. But two? Obviously you murdered them."

"That is the most messed up, horrible—"

"Relax!" She threw her hands up, then slid one back under his arm, which was as tense as an oak branch. "I was playing with you, Oz. You could use someone willing to tease you about this stuff. Your grief isn't going anywhere with you mired in it."

Oz's face stared incredulously forward, careful not to look at her. "Teasing me about my dead wives? Are you serious right now?"

"Yes."

He stopped abruptly, and she jarred forward, nearly losing a step. He lightly dusted her hand off his arm, as if brushing away a crumb. "I'm going to not hold the complete inappropriateness of your words over your head, being as you're not human and maybe don't understand the basic rules of social decency, but this conversation is over, Lucia."

"Nope."

"Sorry... did you say *no*?"

"I did. You're still standing here, so methinks you doth protests too much." She frowned.

Oz's mouth flapped, searching for words, coming up short. "You are... I don't know what you are. There's no word for it."

"Your language is vast, Oz. I'm sure there are many words for it."

Oz looked past her, for an escape. "I really need to go pick up the kids."

Lucia grinned, blocking the path. "Do they get out of instruction this early?"

"School?"

"Whatever."

"No, but I have things to do." He brushed a hand through the air, flustered. "I have to go!"

"Then go."

The two stood in the path, silent, watching one another. He wasn't nearly as offended as he pretended to be. Her amusement at his discomfort was equally feigned.

A flutter played in her heart as she studied the grieving man, whose wallowing at first annoyed her, later intrigued her, and now drew her in for a closer look and feel.

"Tell Nicolas I'll be back in a couple days," he mumbled. One hand brushed her shoulder briefly before he shuffled back toward the house, leaving her smiling at his back.

46
AGRIPIN

Agripin chose to be alone on the eve of his coronation. Cyler offered to keep him occupied, but, for once, his presence was an unwanted distraction.

The coronation was the final step to securing his place at the helm of the royal family. Though everyone was already granting him the respect of titles, all the Farværdig, especially the Senetat, knew they meant nothing until he was given the sacred crown of Emyr and spoke the blessed vow before the eldres.

After this, there was nothing, short of outright murder, the Senetat could do to supplant him. He bore no mark, and the early word around Farjhem brought excitement at the fresh ideas Agripin offered.

Anasofiya would be at his side, to be crowned empress. A halfling. A first in the history of their entire race. Many emperors had bedded and seeded halfling, and even human women, but none had put a crown on their heads. Ana's power would be second only to his. And knowing what she was, this seemed a significant gamble. She was beholden to him now. It might be the reason she'd not attempted to kill him, yet.

Or maybe she had wanted to ride him into tomorrow.

Agripin smiled at the audacity. He drained his whiskey bottle as a knock sounded against his door.

The obnoxious color scheme in the young Empyrean's dress indicated he was a messenger of Oriana. *Again. This makes twelve separate summons from my sister since I've returned.*

This time, she didn't bother with a personalized note. It simply said: *Grand Duke Agripin, your dear sister requests your presence immediately.*

Agripin threw the note into the roaring fireplace, watching it blacken and curl with pleasure. "Psychotic bovine."

As the words disappeared into flames, he thought of the shift in tone of her notes. The earliest ones dripped with her usual disingenuous pleasure, and had slowly evolved toward a more formal approach. This time, she was not asking.

He could smack her for such insolence. Or have her sent to the mines. Even better!

Agripin was not yet emperor, though. The crown of Our Father had not yet been bestowed; he'd not spoken the sacred vows. And the real reason he'd been avoiding her summons was the very reason he suspected now, in this final hour, he might be well-advised to finally answer. It was not only likely, but probable, she was in political bed with the Senetat.

After tomorrow, he wouldn't need to see her again. He could fail to even acknowledge her existence and no one would do a damn thing about it. He could go just short of having her killed without anyone batting a lash.

But it was not yet tomorrow. He was not emperor. And his demented sister was a threat he had not spent enough time assessing. A foolishness he had no choice but to rectify.

With a grudging sigh, Agripin left his suite and descended toward The Menagerie.

THE SINGLE STAIRCASE LEADING DOWN TO THE MENAGERIE WAS A winding, crumbling relic of the castle that had never, in the years since it was built, been updated. The number of accidents on the stone steps were no longer tracked or counted. Only his cracked sister would insist her visitors take such a dangerous path to reach her "den of delights."

Agripin didn't know either of his sisters well. Oriana was born two centuries before he left Farjhem, and half that time was spent with the Scholars for her required instruction. Nerys came into the world right as he was leaving.

Most of what he knew came from the words of others. But where the stories of Nerys reaching his ears were about her goodness, kind heart, and warrior spirit, Oriana's contained flickers of fear and disgusted reverence. No one loved Oriana, but they shamelessly vied for a spot in her inner circle.

Cyler thought Agripin was oblivious to his forays down into The Menagerie. Which was good, because that's what Agripin wanted him to think. If he knew his master knew what he was up to, it would force Agripin to do something about it. He didn't care, truly, where Cyler dipped his wick, so long as he remembered where his loyalties lay. If Cyler had betrayed him, he would know.

Even as a student of the Scholars, Oriana's eccentricities were well-surfaced. She challenged the rules forbidding copulation between man and Empyrean, and more than once had drugged unsuspecting humans smuggled in by lackeys. She once pulled Scholar Saxon by his hair, down the crag, the power of her twelve fathers coursing through her, dangling him over the edge toward the Farvann. His crime? Denying her bread and honey in the middle of his instruction.

If she were anyone else, her behavior would have earned her a trip to the mines for rehabilitation. But she was the emperor's daughter, and no one was willing to risk their necks for an insolent student who wouldn't be their problem forever.

She then missed the day of her graduation, not only refusing to attend but denying she was required to take the mark. By then, her beauty had helped her obtain many minions willing to do anything in exchange for a smile or a brief look in their direction. *She is our Helen of Troy,* they would say. And so she took up residence in the bowels of the palace, and had it turned into an obscene array reminiscent of a bad drug trip.

Immediately, her dreams of flaunting the race's most sacred rules became a reality. Dozens of men were brought in and taken to The Menagerie, where they lived only to give and receive pleasure. Not a bad existence, Agripin had to admit, but the cost for angering Oriana was not worth the price of admission.

Her first sacrifice was a young man, not likely more than twenty years on the Earth, who dared to fall in love with another young Child of Man in The Menagerie. Rules strictly prohibited men mating with one another... they could only receive their pleasures from the visiting Empyreans.

Oriana ordered him drawn and quartered, before all her other delights. She then demanded they all dip their hands in his blood and smear it across the stark white walls. *This place could use more color,* she was reported to have said.

The dried walls of The Menagerie were now a solid dark red, nearly brown. Testament to the other, more important, half of Oriana's nature. A visible reminder of Agripin's lack of desire to find a place for her in his life.

He reached the bottom of the stairs. *Please proceed at a leisurely pace,* the sign read. Agripin rushed forward with a rebellious grimace, toward the guards blocking the ivory door.

"The duchess awaits you in her private chambers," one said, not bothering to address Agripin with his proper title. Acting as if it were Oriana, and not him, who should be given honor.

He wasn't in the presence of mind to deal with the rudeness at the time being, but he noted it for later action.

Agripin was led through the jungle of loud colors, past nude forms of men picking fruit from bushes somehow cultivated in this dungeon, or servicing the Empyreans who'd come to visit. Many likely oblivious that the walls were painted with the blood of their own.

There were few things in life Agripin felt too vulgar for his tastes, but this strongly sat on the border of that line.

They passed beneath a trellis of purple and orange, rounding a path protected by more guards. At the end, another ivory door, also well-guarded.

He was stopped at her door.

"The passcode," one demanded.

"You must really have an ache for the mines!"

One of the guards flanking Agripin coughed, nodded toward the entrance. The other's eyes widened as he stumbled mid-bow, backing away.

Agripin pushed open the heavy double door.

HIS FIRST THOUGHT UPON ENTERING THE PRIVATE CHAMBERS OF HIS sister—his first time there, and also, he predicted, his last—was how closely they resembled the Senetat Sanctuary. Everything was a stark white, from ceiling to floor, couch to rug to fixtures.

The shock of red in the center of the room had a startling effect. Oriana's hair flowed in gracious waves down her white gown. She lay sprawled on a settee, engaged in nothing except waiting for him.

"Brother," her chocolate voice spoke.

"Grand Duke," Agripin corrected. He squared his stance. "Soon to be Grand Emperor."

She tilted her head to the side, widening her eyes. An effect that must send her many minions into a tailspin, but only incensed Agripin further. "Must we adhere to such formalities? Are we not beyond that?"

"You know we're not."

Oriana straightened herself, eyes imploring him. "It saddens me we view our familial bond through two very different lenses, apparently. I'd hoped your return to Farjhem would portend an opportunity for us."

Agripin sneered, gesturing toward the door, and the madness beyond. "I have no time for what you have to offer."

The corner of her upper lip rose. "Your dearest one does."

"You think I don't know Cyler comes to visit? Nothing escapes my notice."

"A bold declaration. Maybe a dangerous one," Oriana said, eyeing him as she rose. She approached a white altar, lifting an ivory vase filled with wine. She poured a small amount in an alabaster fluted glass. Agripin was not offered one.

"Your spies are legend," he conceded. "But mine are better."

She smiled, a gesture boldly sinister. "That is the hope, at least."

Her determination to get the last word was maddening. Almost more than her apparent lack of respect for his station. "Why am I here, Oriana?"

"Our shared relation isn't reason enough?"

"No."

Her laugh this time was far more aligned with her cold demeanor. "Fine. I need you to discard your playthings, brother."

Agripin shook his head in disbelief. "You need me to... I'm sorry, you *need* me to what?"

"Discard the halflings. They're an abomination," she responded evenly.

Agripin threw his head back in laughter. "No greater hypocrisy has ever been recorded in the history of our people!"

She set her goblet of wine down on the ivory table. The lack of color in the room was distracting; near blinding. "Let's cease to discuss rules and instead venture into politics. Would that be all right with you?"

Agripin rolled his eyes. Nodded.

"There are two types of rule-breakers in society, dear brother. *Grand Emperor.*" She affected a crude bow, flashing a sardonic smile. "Those who do so in the shadows, and those who do so in the open. The shadowy rule-breakers are equally guilty in the eyes of the law, but it is not their eyes which matter the most. The view of our people is who we must cater to. A sinner who sins in the shadows is a necessary evil, one people are accustomed to believing must be borne and cannot be stopped. But one who sins in the open..."

Agripin gaped at her. "You are a special piece of work, Oriana. So we're both sinners, but yours is somehow more acceptable than mine because you're underground? I suppose next you'll say the blood on the walls was the idea of your interior decorator?"

She grinned. "We both have our ways of keeping order."

Looking around, he realized he had no idea where the door was. White, everywhere, was all he saw. "You needn't worry, sister. I have no plans of shutting down your hedonistic brothel. I may even work to have it no longer be a violation, our mating with men."

"You misunderstand me!" She sashayed across the room, stopping inches before him. "My aim is to *keep* the practice illegal. As long as it remains illicit, The Menagerie will thrive. If you open it up to the masses..."

Agripin waved a hand, searching again for the door. "Fine. I won't. Personally, I have no care in the matter. I can take a halfling empress without changing the rules."

"You cannot continue to flaunt her, or other rule breakers will emerge!"

"Like you?"

"Now we are talking in circles," she hissed, turning her head. "You are making enemies, brother. More than you know or have guessed. You have no friends in the Senetat."

"I *need* no friends in the Senetat." *And what the hell do you know about it,* he nearly added, but stopped himself. She'd given herself away. She was not simply a basement pimp minding her own business. He'd guessed it all along, and now he knew.

"You think me cruel," she said. Her countenance took on an injured look that nearly appeared genuine. "And maybe I am. I care not what others think, even you. But I didn't invite you here to win you over. I'd hoped we could find common ground."

His desire to leave grew heavier. Buried within was a burgeoning realization he'd boldly ignored so much. Too much. "Our ground is common enough, Oriana. I won't get in your way, and I expect the same."

"I'm not who you should fear," she replied gently, guessing at his thoughts. "And you are not yet emperor."

"Tomorrow."

"Ahh, but the night is long."

. . .

Agripin's heart did not truly begin its race until he was safely ensconced in his own quarters. Next door, his empress and her mates slept. Or didn't sleep. No concern of his.

What *was* a concern was Oriana. Why had he waited so long to hear her words? He'd underestimated her, and he didn't yet know what the cost of that would be. That she was aligned with the Senetat was unquestionable. Her warnings held weight.

But the night is long. Yes, it was. And Agripin would remember every grueling moment.

47
CYLER

"Have I not earned my peace this night?" Agripin boomed, smashing his whiskey bottle into the fire. Flames roared higher, the sound whistling through the room with quick force.

"You taught me to always be vigilant," Cyler argued. When in this mood, he would get nowhere with either Aggie the lover, or Agripin the leader, but he had to try. "And so I am."

"If vigilance includes fucking your way through The Menagerie, then perhaps my instruction fell short."

Cyler paled. "I didn't think you would care," he lied.

"Bullshit. But you're half-right, because I *don't* care. You'd have been strung up by your testicles if I thought you were sharing secrets." Agripin rifled through his bottles, finding only empty ones. He smashed another against the wall with a frustrated grumble.

With a sigh, Cyler pressed on. Amidst all else, he loved Agripin and he would save him from himself, if he could. "We need to move to the backup plan," he suggested calmly, for the third time since arriving in his master's chambers. "They know. I don't know how, but they do, and they will take you down in front of all of Farjhem, Aggie. This, I'm sure of."

Agripin turned to him, waving a bottle. His hair was a frightful mess. "You're so sure, and I'm only hearing about this tonight?" He snorted, laughter ringing across the bottle as he held it high, hoping for a final drip from the bottom. "You and Oriana."

Cyler narrowed his eyes. "What about Oriana?"

His master dropped the bottle with a grin. "Aye, there's that temper. Are you upset I shared a drink with her tonight?"

"No one shares drinks with Oriana. I think her wine is poisoned."

Agripin cackled. "Not bloody enough."

Cyler sighed and rolled his eyes.

"Fine. I'm tired. Tell me why you're here. Specifics only, as I've no energy for more banter."

Cyler straightened his spine. The most important of all lessons he'd learned from his master was a confidence in delivery. "Eldre Maxima requested my presence tonight."

"That creature!" Agripin boomed, mouth hanging. "What have I told you about her? She's a Senetat wench! Why do you insist on trusting her?"

Cyler pursed his lips, steeling himself. "We must agree to disagree, Aggie. She's been my single best source of intelligence this entire time. Nothing she's given me has proved false."

"A convenient battle tactic to lure in her enemy with false loyalty," Agripin accused. "One of the oldest strategies we know. Cyler, Cyler, Cyler. Have I truly taught you nothing?"

Heat rose to Cyler's face, and he swallowed back a stinging retort. "She knows, Aggie. She knows our entire plan."

Agripin thundered across the stone floors in his direction,

spittle flying as his words came out in loud booms. "DID YOU TELL HER?"

"Of course not!" Cyler defended. His master's hot, pungent breath assaulted him, but he would not drop his eyes. "I would never tell her a thing, and you know it. My relationship with her has been one-way information sharing, with me being the only benefactor. But she knows, nonetheless."

Agripin's eyes were a blaze of suspicion. Searching his mind, no doubt, but Cyler had never cared about this gimmick. He had no secret worth keeping from his master. "So you did not. I believe you."

"You should." This time, Cyler did wrench away. "My thoughts aren't capable of lies."

"How does she know, then?"

"I told you, I don't know."

"They have no block-breachers in their ranks. Or their employ, so far as I know," Agripin speculated aloud, his thoughts spinning. "Or do they?"

"Maxima wouldn't say. But she's on our side, just like Leif was before, and all the others. She has a plan to help us, but we need to postpone the coronation—"

"Absolutely not! I will not postpone it a day! Not a single hour!"

"Aggie—"

"Cyler, my patience wears thin. You'll call me by my proper titles, even in privacy, or so help me..."

"My apologies, *Grand Emperor.*" Cyler affected a sardonic, sweeping bow. "As I was saying—"

"You can stop talking," Agripin said. "I won't postpone anything. The longer we wait, the higher the risk."

Cyler swallowed. "There is one other way. You won't like it, I'm afraid."

Agripin sunk back into his velvet chair, looking up. "A fair guess. Tell me anyway."

Cyler told him.

48
JACOB

Jacob's anger flared to a peak as Amelia slammed the door and marched off.

It faded briefly to curiosity as he watched her venture not toward her aunt's home, where he expected her to go, but in the direction of the far woods. Neither of them had ever wandered in there.

And then he was incensed again, at her foolishness in meandering out of their known world. She was always doing this, going boldly forward, without fear.

Nothing ever seemed to faze her, a trait he sometimes found adorably endearing and others, like now, maddening. He could declare unicorns were washing up on the Cornish shores, and she would only ask when they'd leave, and would they be home in time for dinner.

Accepting that they were descended from *druids* had come so damned easily for her. Sure, her whole family were sorcerers. But druids, too? Really? Next they would learn she had a vampire uncle somewhere. Maybe she was even the heir to his vast fortune.

She embraced everything thrown at them in the Quinlan world... all except one thing. *The most important damned thing of all!* Her stubborn unwillingness to accept this critical, show-stopping element of their role, was the first big crack in the foundation of Jacob's sanity.

He wanted to share her courage, but her selectiveness had the opposite effect. It caused him to see her easy acceptance as convenient rather than foundational, and strong. Then he started to do the same, because he wasn't raised with her convictions. Jacob was a survivor, and surviving meant finding the closest route to shore.

It wasn't her fault, but it also was. If she'd only said, *I'm afraid.* Just admitted it, even once! Instead, she acted as if their child was a silly notion, an inconvenient piece of the puzzle that might go away if they ignored it.

In the beginning, Jacob sat patiently while Padraig attempted to indoctrinate him in what it meant to be a draoi. It reminded Jacob of the folklore his friends passed around in their youth. Fascinating, but far from grounded in reality.

The days grew longer and his attention span, shorter. Feigning headaches, he would retire early, and throw some punches at an invisible opponent. One who understood the root of his struggle. One who wouldn't judge him for it.

Then he discovered the local boys in Killianshire who gathered occasionally in the cathedral basement. If Father O'Connor knew about it, he never let on.

Jacob hid it at first, careful to protect his face from damage. But when he came tonight, he'd *wanted* Amelia to know. He wanted his face to say what his words could not. To force the discussion, and resolve things, or at least find common ground.

The situation escalated quickly and violently before he could think to correct it. And now she was gone, with so much unsaid.

. . .

AFTER WAITING AN HOUR, HIS ANGER THAWED, HE SNATCHED HIS jacket up and went off to find her. The moment Jacob entered the far woods, he noted a physical change in the air. *We've wandered outside the Quinlans' magic protection.*

He wouldn't have guessed how much comfort he took from this shield until he no longer had it.

Unlike the woods that led from Killianshire into the Quinlan lands, these were darker; the foliage appeared steeped in heavy shadows, the ground curling and dying around the gray roots of trees in their final days.

His breath swirled before him. A chill passed through the decaying path. He pulled his jacket tight.

"Amelia?" he called out, conscious of the tremor in his voice. How the woods seemed *aware* of him. Not in a good way. He was a parasite to their unwilling host.

Every step felt heavy, laden with an unseen weight. *The forest trying to expel me,* he thought, then shook it off. He needed to find his wife, then get out. It was as simple as that.

Jacob's eyes caught a shimmer on the ground. Kneeling, Jacob saw Amelia's Tiffany bracelet, one link shattered, as if ripped from her wrist in a hurry. His breath caught. "Amelia!" he cried, louder this time. "*Blanca,* let's go home!"

No response. *Something's happened. Something bad. She's hurt.* Heedless of the danger to himself, he rushed forward at a quicker pace, pushing down his fear, calling her name every few steps.

The path grew thicker. The oppressive air had Jacob gasping for breath, but he pushed forward, driven by his fear and love, crying out for his wife with her bracelet clutched firmly in one palm.

All at once, the path opened to a clearing. The air offered a slight relief, and he gulped in greedy mouthfuls, bent over his knees.

When Jacob rose, he saw Amelia standing in the middle of the clearing. She was not alone.

Behind her was a creature who rose nearly two feet taller than his Amelia. Pale, sturdy, with a mane of red hair atop his cruel face.

One of his arms was looped around her midsection, trapping her. The other held a knife, pressed hard enough into her throat to leave a thin trail of blood trickling down to her collarbone.

Fear stewed in Amelia's eyes, but she didn't struggle. *Turn around! Go back, go now, please Jacob. You have to go back, he means to kill us!*

I would never leave you in a million years, Blanca.

"You left me waiting a good long while!" the creature called, in the playful tone one might expect from a teasing friend. "The Farværdig are bred for the cold, but that does not mean we enjoy it, sir!"

Jacob put his hands up, to show he had no weapons. "Aye, well I'm here now. Hand back my wife. Whatever it is you want, you can have."

The creature nodded down at Amelia, then at Jacob. "I do have it now. Or will, soon. I must confess to you, I have no intentions of unhanding your mate. That is, not until you've both given me what I'm after. But! Tis' cold out here, would you say? Let's retreat to someplace warmer."

Without waiting for Jacob's reply, the creature pivoted and headed up a short hill. Amelia gasped, her feet flailing as she struggled to keep up.

Jacob followed in a daze, holding Amelia's bracelet tighter. On his lips a prayer to God, or the goddess, or whoever might be listening.

. . .

THE CREATURE ENTERED A SMALL CABIN. HIS, JACOB GUESSED, AS IT was well-lit and a fire burned in the hearth, smoke billowing into the night sky.

Before Jacob could enter, the door was slammed in his face. He tried the handle. Locked.

Sounds of Amelia's cries echoed inside, mixed with the sound of metal and wood shifting. Finally, the door opened again.

"Won't you please come in?" the creature offered with a beaming smile.

Jacob's eyes immediately fell on Amelia. Her hands were suspended in cuffs above her head, looped through a thick hook in the ceiling, the kind used to hang meat in a butcher's locker. A gag ran through her mouth. Too terrified for the mind talking, her panicked eyes implored him to go, to leave.

"Now, then! Have a seat." The creature snatched a chair and shoved Jacob into it. "I know *what* you both are, so let's forgo the slew of denials. What I don't know is *who* and you're going to tell me."

Whatever he says... whatever he does to me... tell him nothing, Jacob. NOTHING!

"You want our names?" Jacob asked. Blanca, *what does he want?*

The back of the creature's hand connected to Amelia's face with a crack. Blood flew from her mouth as her head snapped to the side. Jacob started forward and was pushed back down in his chair. "Names! I apologize, I have not yet introduced myself. My name is Baldur. And she is Amelia, and you are Jacob. We can stop with the games now. WHO THE HELL ARE YOU TWO?"

Jacob's words caught as he watched his wife, swinging from a meathook, mouth full of blood. *This is not happening.*

Jacob, it is happening. He's a madman, an Empyrean who is

hunting both the rebels and Quinlans, and he won't stop until he bleeds us dry. You can't tell him anything, I'm begging you.

I won't watch him kill you!

If he finds my family because we led him there, you may as well rip the heart from my chest.

Baldur approached Amelia, running his hands up and down her torso with a soft lover's touch. His tongue flicked out, licking the blood from her lips. "Mmm. My favorite, and never enough. More where it came from."

Amelia flinched and shoved her head away, but Baldur snaked a hand up, roughly forcing her to face him. "Amelia. You won't survive this night. Nor will your mate. But if you tell me what I want to know, I will make your death quick and unmemorable.

"However, if you make me work for it, understand that my patience is legion. I will slice every limb. Fuck every hole. And then I'll do the same to him, and make you both watch. Do you want that?"

"Fuck you!" she cried and spat blood on his cheek.

"You will. Worry not," Baldur responded pleasantly, then lifted his hand and dealt another cracking blow to her other cheek. This one knocked her unconscious.

As Amelia dangled, bloody, before him, Jacob was willing to reveal anything, do anything, to save her. But Baldur's words, *You won't survive this night* felt true. This creature meant to kill them, no matter what they told him.

Stall him. Use yer wits, lad, his mother's voice sang in his head. *Like I taught ye, Jacob.*

Jacob closed his fist around Amelia's bracelet and looked up into the face of the creature.

49
ANASOFIYA

Sleep was impossible when the morning held such dire circumstances. All the Brotherhood leaders would begin to arrive, in shadows and secrecy, and whatever plans they had in motion would begin. There would be no time to slow down, and reconsider. No time to assess. No time to change course, if things did not go the way everyone hoped.

The crisp breeze chilled her, but Ana welcomed it. She wished for any sensation other than fear. Inside their room, the two men whom she loved with all her heart slept. It might be the last night they slept near each other. She knew she should go in, and soak up every last moment, but the pain was too fresh, and deep. And with her son across the world, her heart felt bruised and weary.

It should give her strength, to know her son was away from the danger ahead. But it wouldn't matter, if they failed. If they were discovered before victory was secure, they would undoubtedly be executed. If Aidrik died, his protection over *Ophélie* would fail. There was nothing that could be done for Aleksandr at that point, or the rest of the Deschanels.

Ana realized, with a sense of dreadful finality, that her entire family could be gone in the blink of an eye.

It would be very much like the old Ana to look back and reflect on all she could have done differently, blaming herself for putting them on this path. But the new Ana, the one who had finally accepted sometimes the world spun forward even without her involvement, understood the threads of fate had woven this way all on their own. Despite all the trouble ahead, she had never, not once, been so complete in all her life. As a mother, as a wife, and an individual.

I wish I could have shown you this land through my eyes, Anasofiya, Aidrik said to her earlier in the prior day, with a light, remorseful sigh. *I would have liked to share that with you.*

You will. Once this is all over.

Aye. Of course.

A welcome interruption to the cold, she felt first warm breath, and then warm hands, encircle her. Finn. His face came to a silent rest atop her head, and he nearly crushed her to him.

"I can't sleep either," he confessed.

"Is Aidrik awake?" she asked.

"He hasn't said anything, but I can hear him moving around. The guy never sleeps though."

She allowed a short chuckle. It was true. Aidrik was always at the ready. She once wished he could learn to relax, but she had come to understand this was an integral part of him.

She leaned back against Finn's strong chest, allowing him to hold her, finding the silence a comfort. Vulnerability used to terrify her. Allowing someone to strengthen her was harder still. But she'd let that barrier down with Finn, and allowed him to share her burdens.

"Ana," he said finally. "I want to talk about changing part of the plan."

She turned to face him. "It's a bit late for that, don't you think?"

"I need you to listen," he pleaded. Resting his forehead against hers, he added, "I never ask you for anything. Ever. But you're my wife, and the mother of my son. I need you to listen to what I'm going to ask, and really, really think about it. Not just say no, because you don't like it. Consider what I'm asking, and why."

Ana nodded, as a sense of growing dread spread through her.

"If my instincts are correct, and I hope they're not, but if they are, Aleksandr will need a head start. So will the others. Nicolas. Your father. But we can't give them that here," Finn said. "You should stay back from the event tomorrow. If things go wrong, you will know. Forbia will come tell you. And then, you go Ana. You run, and you get to your family, to Aleksei, and you tell them what's happened and you get them to run, too. I don't know if it will do any good, or if it will just delay the inevitable, but we can't sit here and not try."

Finn was right to qualify his speech beforehand, as Ana's first reaction was indignant rage. Why would he ask her to go? Why would he think his sacrifice was more important than hers? But she realized, in the next heartbeat, he was right. Aleksandr, Nicolas, her father, and all the others she loved, were sitting blindly back in New Orleans without even a sliver of knowledge about what might befall them.

Ana had a demand of her own. "Only if you go with me," she breathed.

"Ana—"

"I can't lose you both!" she screamed, the sound bouncing off the palace's stone walls. She didn't realize she was crying until Finn pulled her closer, steadying her.

"Okay," he agreed. "I won't leave you."

A sensation of abhorring his selfishness washed over her at the ease in which he acquiesced, but it was quelled by the relief that she would not lose both of them. Then, guilt immediately followed as she realized she was allowing the hope of Finn's safety to make up for what might befall her other love.

The truth was, she couldn't live without either one of them.

"I'm terrified," she admitted. The tears had nearly frozen against her face, and she welcomed the cold, hoping it would override the pain.

"I shouldn't say this, but I'm afraid too," Finn admitted softly. He drew her in closer, and she could both hear and feel the heavy, fast rhythm of his heart. She had been so caught up in her melancholy she hadn't realized Finn was just as scared, and in just as much pain.

"Whatever happens—"

"You don't have to say anything like that—"

"I do," she insisted. "Because I've never said it and if the chance escapes me, I won't live with knowing I gave up the opportunity. I need you to know, Finn. The only real regret I've ever had was leaving you in New Orleans. Everything ended up as it should, but I need you to know I love you. Really, and truly. I didn't marry you because of Aleksei. I married you because you are the love of my life."

"I do know, silly girl," he said, but she didn't miss the tears in his eyes, or the relief behind them.

"And I can't live without you. Maybe that makes me sound weak, or like a dumb girl, but it's the truth, and so you need to not do stupid shit that might get you hurt," she went on. "I need you to look me in the eye and promise."

"I promise," he said, without hesitation. "I would lay down my life for you Ana, but I won't do anything that isn't absolutely necessary."

"Okay," she said, and pressed her lips to his. "That's as much as I can expect."

Aidrik joined them on the balcony. Ana stifled a giggle at his full dress and sword at the ready. "Apologies if I've interrupted a private moment."

"It's fine," Finn assured him. "We should probably fill you in on our slight change in plans."

"No need," Aidrik replied, drawing in a deep breath of cold air. "I hear more than my share." He looked slightly guilty as he added, "And the door was open."

"What are your thoughts on the change?" Ana asked.

"A practical suggestion. One I'd have made myself if I didn't think you would slice my head clean off," Aidrik said with a tight smile. "I would send you both tonight if it didn't risk suspicion."

"Unfortunately, you're right. I'm supposed to be at Agripin's side."

"You'll attend the event," Aidrik went on. "Depart before our guests arrive."

"Do we know when that will be yet?" Finn asked.

Aidrik shook his head, then nodded, confusingly. "They will arrive for the reception, following the coronation. My suggestion is the two of you leave prior, one at a time. Not together. Set up a waypoint outside of Farjhem, and meet there. Alone, neither of you will draw suspicion, but together, you may. Don't tell me where your waypoint is. Last thing I want is someone pulling it from my head."

Ana nodded. "Do we wait for you?"

Aidrik shook his head, this time vehemently. "No, Kjære. Go straight home, to New Orleans. Gather the family at *Ophélie*, under my protection. If we are successful, I will come for you. If we are not, you will know soon enough."

"It has to be successful," Ana said. "We can't live in a world where our son is in constant danger."

"Aye," Aidrik agreed. "I hope tomorrow night to join with Agripin in the celebration of not only his coronation, but the redress of the Senetat."

"Do you have faith things will really get better? Trading one government for another hasn't always worked so well for us Americans," Finn said.

"Rebuilding will be a long, arduous process," Aidrik agreed. "Empyreans will live in freedom, absent of their mark, and we will never again allow any body to have absolute power."

"That's how you feel, but politics are polarizing," Ana said, continuing Finn's doubt. "No two people will ever agree."

"One step at a time," Aidrik replied. "Finn, may I borrow you for a moment? I'd like your help with something."

Finn flashed Ana a bemused grin and went off to help Aidrik.

Ana remained behind, watching the clouds pass over the dark sky, across the moon, realizing she was losing the battle to contain what lurked dormant within her.

It would emerge, sooner rather than later.

PART THREE
EMPIRE OF SHADOWS

"Hell is empty
And all the devils are here."

William Shakespeare

MORRIGAN'S PROPHECY

Two millennia of wars and strife, which cannot be avoided, but can be stopped. One descendant from each of the four to emerge. Four become two, their offspring the peace that unites the two races again.

From Falias, a male, draoi, pure of heart and an affinity for creatures.

From Murias, a female, born of fire and darkness.

From Findias, a female, reincarnated over the many moons.

From Gorias, a male, draoi. The lover of the Findias heir.

A son shall spring from Falias and Murias. Findias and Gorias join after many reincarnations, bringing forth a daughter. This son and this daughter will join together, in peace, uniting the Quinlans and Empyreans once more, thus ending the long days of war.

50
FINNEGAN

For once in his life, Finn didn't rise with the sun. He wasn't much for delaying the inevitable, but he never wanted to forget the way the light peeking around the velvet curtains hit his wife's wavy red locks. How her light, easy breaths burned against his heart.

Aidrik sat across the room, dressed in his full regalia, the absence of Ulfberht glaring. He peered into the darkness, not looking at anything in particular. His words last night to Finn had been surprising. Finn hoped they weren't also true. He'd come to see Aidrik as more than a requirement of the deal. They were brothers, in ways they'd only begun to explore and appreciate.

Aidrik nodded at him. He nodded back.

Finn felt Forbia's presence outside. She was always standing guard, alert to the presence of all three of them. What a gift Forbia had been... more so than he'd ever expected when he ruffled her pup fur and declared her importance in his life. And tonight, she might play her most important role of all.

"It can't be morning," Ana lamented with a light groan,

burying her face deeper in his chest. Her hand played mindlessly at the old scar bisecting his torso. "Say it isn't so."

Finn grinned down at her. "It isn't so."

He felt her smile stretch across his skin. "Liar."

"You can rest longer, Kjære," Aidrik said. "Your presence won't be required until after lunch."

Finn ran his hands across the soft skin of her back. How he loved her, this strange and beautiful creature he'd married. So unlike the women he was drawn to back home. Ana was perfect in his eyes, despite the flaws which dotted the landscape of her tortured soul.

"I think I'll just lay here." She yawned lazily, nuzzling further into him. "And pretend I'm not about to get crowned the empress of Narnia."

"Are Finn and I your concubines then?" Aidrik asked. A small smile played at the corners of his set mouth. Finn cocked his head with a mystified grin. *Aidrik. Teasing. Well, I'll be damned.*

"You're lucky I only have two," she replied. "I've seen a lot of very striking young men parading through the town square."

"Kjære, they are probably as old as the Vatican," Aidrik returned. He nodded at Finn. "I assumed your tastes tended toward... younger men."

"Well," she said tartly, rising with the sheet clutched to her chest, "I have one of the oldest men in the world on one arm, and a younger one on the other. Maybe I'd like to settle somewhere into the law of averages."

Finn rolled over the top of her, pinning her to the bed. "Don't be greedy, now."

Aidrik appeared at the side of the bed, hands resting sternly upon his hips. "Must Finnegan and I punish you, Anasofiya?"

Her eyes widened into saucers. She traced her tongue along her bottom lip slowly. “I *have* been very bad.”

The silence then spoke louder than any words. Finn worried where this was going, a part of him exhilarated at the potential, the other part terrified.

The pounding upon the door broke the spell. The messenger was for Aidrik, who was summoned by Agripin.

“Tonight,” Aidrik assured with a nod as he disappeared through the tall door frame.

“Tonight,” Finn agreed, his heart surging.

51
JACOB

"Unhook her and I'll tell you everything you want to know," Jacob lied.

"I don't think so," Baldur parried. He pressed a hand to Amelia's cheek. Her unconscious form stirred. "Perhaps my earlier words were overly harsh. I don't *have* to kill you. Those weren't the orders, only my preferred interpretation of them. Tell me what I want to know, and maybe the two of you walk away." Baldur's face was at first stoic and then he burst into laughs. "*I* might let you walk away, but the escape would be temporary. Rebels and Quinlans catch a fair price."

Stall him. Keep him involved in his self-indulgent rant as long as you can. "Orders? Who do you work for?"

"Not very keen, are you?" Baldur asked. "Who do you think I work for?"

"Someone powerful."

"Aye, that's obvious. Are you daft, or..."

Jacob's heart raced. Every word was a test. He didn't know whether it was better to play dumb or to act like his knowledge was greater than it was. "You get your orders from Farjhem."

There, that was safe. Broad, but also sounded strangely official. Like what he might say to a decorated general. "How did you know where to find us?"

"I was following rumors of warded Quinlan and Empyrean rebel camps when your mate wandered right into my arms. You might say fortune smiled upon my soul this evening!"

At least he wasn't specifically after the two of them. Jacob didn't know if that made things worse or better, though. "You're a bounty hunter then?"

"Something like that."

Jacob nodded, searching desperately for something else to say, something that might prolong the discussion until he could formulate some kind of escape.

"That established, you're going to tell me everything I want to know. Deception will cost you. Or her, more likely." Baldur nodded at Amelia. "And if my mood is merciful, I may let you both go. You'll be caught by assassins, without doubt, but you may find that more sporting than dying undefended." Baldur pinched one of Amelia's nipples. She awoke with a gasping start. "I'm tired of talking. Your turn."

Amelia's cheeks had started to swell, the red bruises rising to prickle the surface of her cold flesh. They would soon fade to purple. At least one of her cheekbones was broken. It was gut-wrenching to look at, but he owed it to her not to look away. She was in danger, but she wasn't alone.

For once, he would lead with his head. If he let his impetuous fists guide him, they'd never leave alive.

"You'll have to kill me," she sputtered, slowly returning to consciousness. His *blanca,* full of fire, even in distress.

Don't egg him on, Amelia! He's a full-on psychopath. He isn't dealing with a full deck. Not even you in infinite therapy sessions could help this mad son-of-a-bitch.

He's going to kill us no matter what, Jacob!

"Aye, I can do that!" Baldur exclaimed. He brandished the dagger from earlier and cut her shirt away, tossing the tattered shreds to the ground. Her bra snapped off with another effortless nick, the blade was so sharp. The edge of knife danced around her left nipple. "But it won't be quick."

"You sick fuck," Amelia barked, coming further to her senses. She writhed in her bindings, scissoring her feet toward him.

Baldur caught one foot and twisted it with a quick snap. She howled in pain, but bravely kicked out her other foot.

"Feisty little rebel," Baldur murmured with pleasure. He yanked her pants down and over her broken foot, causing her to whimper pitifully. Tears poured down her cheeks, but her eyes were ice.

Baldur ran the tip of his knife down her inner thigh, millimeters from her femoral artery. Blood instantly beaded on the surface of her pale skin, and then Baldur was on his knees before her, drinking from the inside of her leg, as she dangled naked from the meat hook.

Jacob shot up in quick rage before he could restrain it, but Baldur was on him in a flash. Stars swam in his eyes, as he swayed in the chair. Then everything went black.

WHEN JACOB CAME TO, HE WAS ON THE FLOOR, BOUND TO A THICK post that extended from the foundation of the small cabin, through to the ceiling. He yanked with a burst of strength, but the post didn't flex at all.

Peering through his damaged eye, he saw Amelia dangling, battered and bleeding, eyes closed. The gash on her thigh had begun to clot and dry, but the crude knife work left her entire leg swollen. Baldur was nowhere in sight.

He mumbled something about his commanding officer. I don't know where he went. Or when he will be back.

"He isn't here, *Blanca.* You can talk," Jacob said gently. His eyes scanned the room, darting from window to door, looking for anything that might aid their freedom before the psychopath returned. His gaze settled again on his wife in helpless agony.

Trying to conserve my energy. So I can kill the motherfucker when he returns.

Jacob smiled. Tears sprung to his eyes. "Not if I kill him first."

I've seen what you can do to men. Poor Baldur would never know what hit him if we unleashed you.

I'm serious. No matter what else happens, I'm going to kill him, Amelia.

Remember those movies we used to like? The ones about those kids who escaped death but then death was like, "Sorry, not so fast."

We watched the hell out of those silly films. Well, you watched and I tried to make out with you.

I sorta feel like that right now. I keep thinking, maybe I wasn't meant to survive the Deschanel Curse. That when Oz intervened, he was going against the natural order of things, and every moment after that was borrowed time.

You know how ridiculous that sounds, right? Using a silly horror flick to describe what's happening?

Does this not feel like a horror flick to you?

No, it feels worse. Because this is really happening, and so we have to figure out a solution. Mostly me, because we already know you can't pick locks with your brain. Unless you've been holding out on me?

I love you, Donnelly. If I thought we had a chance of getting out of here, I'd spend the next however long working with you on a plan.

But right now I'm so tired... wake me when he comes back, will you? I don't want him to take pleasure in catching me asleep.

"I will."

"Good," she whispered. Her eyes slowly closed.

I love you, Amelia. I've loved you forever.

I know.

This was not the end. He couldn't accept they'd come all these years, all this way, for it all to conclude like this.

Jacob closed his eyes, and, for the first time since opening his mind to his wife, he subsequently closed it, going to work on a plan. She needed her rest, and he needed to hold fast to his hope.

Leaving Amelia alone, even temporarily, was out of the question. Baldur could disappear with her, and they might never track them. She was here, feet before him, and any plan for escape had to include both of them getting out, together.

Alive.

JACOB FAILED IN HIS PROMISE TO WAKE HER, AS HE HIMSELF WAS roused to the sound of Baldur's taunts.

The creature's hands were on his wife's breasts, squeezing, whispering things in her ear that made her face bright with rage. Her nostrils flared, spittle fresh on her lips.

"There's nothing you can do to me that will make me betray my family," Amelia spat. "Unlike you, I can't be sold to the highest bidder."

"That's the Child of Man in you, halfling. Struggling for your conscience in a puddle of false nobility." One of Baldur's hands traveled south, over her smooth belly, disappearing between her legs. Amelia gritted her teeth, but didn't cry out at the crude violation.

"Enough!" Jacob cried, yanking at his bindings, twisting so hard they cut through his skin. "Turn your brutality on me!"

Baldur continued his assault, smiling at Jacob. "But why, when *this* is what gets your attention?"

Amelia, I'm sorry, I can't do this, I can't watch him hurt you like this. I have to tell him, even if you hate me forever.

Jacob, no!

Baldur lifted his fingers to his nose. Smelled them. Then slipped them in his mouth, closing his eyes as he moaned. "Sweet. Like honey."

Then the creature sunk down, to where Amelia's legs were now bound spread apart. He lapped at the dried blood on her thigh, then his tongue moved north, sliding along her smooth skin before settling where his fingers had been moments before. Tears slid down Amelia's cheeks.

The pressure rose so fast in Jacob he nearly passed out. A boiling rage radiated to every limb, one unlike any he'd ever known, even in his most intense days in the ring. This time, when he pulled at the post, it caved in the middle. With a second furious cry, the post splintered and Jacob was free.

Without a backward glance, Baldur's hand shot out and Jacob flew into the wall with a powerful thud, the force stealing his breath.

Baldur rose, making a show of wiping his mouth with the back of his hand. He approached Jacob slowly, his sinister grin spreading wider with each step. "Let's get a few things clear, Jacob of the Quinlans." He threw a hand out, a wave of power knocking back the table in his path. "This is going to end, soon. Your mate is with child. If you do not tell me what I want to know, I will fuse my seed to your unborn daughter, forever binding her to me. I will claim your child as my own, and you will never see her, or your mate, again. Not in this lifetime.

When I'm done, they won't want to meet you in the next, either."

Jacob... Amelia couldn't find words. Neither could he.

Baldur kicked a chair, knocking it into the wall. He pressed his boot heel against Jacob's throat. "Don't listen to the bitch. I know she's in your head. All women get there, right?" Baldur shook his head, as if they were sharing a moment. "Tell me what I want to know."

52
NICOLAS

"You have to stop thinking like a Child of Man."

Nicolas leaned back against the velvet settee with a baffled grin. Orange beams from the setting sun creased the center of the room, reminding them they'd been at it most of the day. "What the fuck does that even mean, Anders?"

"Yeah, Uncle. Stop thinking like a Child of Man. Sheesh!" Aleksandr mimicked. Nicolas threw a decorative pillow at him.

Anders paced the thinning carpet. "You haven't manifested because your mind can only think as far as its prescribed limitations," he explained patiently. "And you won't, until you can break down those barriers."

"Bullshit. I'm a mystic. I can do nested visions, and some other random shit," Nicolas argued. "You keep talking about manifesting, but I already have."

Anders smiled. "*Bullshit.* Nested visions are a lower tier ability for a mystic."

"I don't know what the fuck that means, either."

"It means you can do better," Aleksandr said smartly. He dodged an invisible pillow.

"Oh, you think *you're* hot shit, now that you can stop time?" Nicolas volleyed back.

Aleksandr nodded. "Aye."

"Why am I even here?" Tristan piped in. He lay on the carpet, staring at the ceiling. "I've already mastered my skill."

"You breached my thoughts when I was a foot in front of you. Your skill is useless until you can do that across the globe. Keep at it," Anders countered, shooting Nicolas a look as if to say, *Some kids.* "Look, whatever is going on with you and Mercy is clouding your head. I don't want to know what happened, but you need to set that tension aside. Work it out with her, or put the relationship behind you."

Nicolas turned his eyes toward the ceiling, but the shit with Mercy *was* distracting. He didn't know where things stood, because she wouldn't talk. She wouldn't talk to him because she wouldn't get out of bed. And she wouldn't get out of bed, because she was experiencing one of the biggest defects of being human: depression.

It was tempting to blame only himself, and his romp with Eydis, but Mercy's downward mood started within weeks of her resurrection. Nicolas supposed that might be a real downer for him, too, if the roles were reversed. Comforting words never having been his forte, he'd only known of one way to improve her disposition, but even that had diminishing returns. And now she wouldn't let him within ten feet of her.

"Think on that," Anders concluded. "While I work with Aleksei for a bit."

"Sure, Dad," Nicolas quipped. Only after the words were out did he appreciate the irony. These few words of advice from Anders were more parenting than he'd ever had from his own father when he was alive.

Not that *any* of this mattered. The family was destined to go up in flames. Harriett saw it, and the girl was as reliable as the taxman.

Still, he couldn't help feeling relieved that the afternoon with Eydis hadn't led to an evigbond. He was initially baffled that he wasn't glued to her, after the event, by cosmic forces beyond his control, until he cornered Lucia and she laughed at him, explaining it was a phenomenon tied to the Mark of Emyr. For those not bearing one, it was possible, but not a guarantee, though sometimes parents told their children that to scare them. Birger and Astrid were trying to keep their daughter chaste, but instead all they did was break her heart when she found herself not mated to Nicolas.

I don't understand... it was supposed... we were supposed...

Sorry, sweetheart. I don't make the rules. And no encores.

To his tremendous relief, whatever lust he'd felt toward Eydis disappeared in the moments following the tryst. It wasn't the girl's fault. He blamed his cold, dark heart. Only upon completely sabotaging the relationship, did he realize he loved Mercy.

ANDERS TOWERED OVER THE COUCH, CASTING A LONG SHADOW OVER the young boy and his book. "Aleksei, you can wipe that smug look off your face. It's your turn."

"Careful, you'll interrupt his quest to read through the entire Deschanel library," Nicolas muttered, grinning at his nephew. Cousin, really, but Ana had told her son to consider Nicolas his uncle, and so he did. "He's only on C, so that would be really cruel."

"I got one!" Tristan interrupted, shooting to a sitting position. "In Metairie!"

"Where is Metairie?" Anders asked.

"Uh, about twenty minutes from here. Thirty or forty in traffic."

"Keep trying."

With a flop and a sigh, Tristan went back to it.

Aleksandr slid the bookmark carefully in the old copy of *Crime and Punishment* and yawned. "I think it was an accident. The time thing."

Anders took the book from his hands with a searching look. "No, that kind of thing does not happen by accident, kid. Sorry. An ability like that is indescribably dangerous if we don't help you learn to control it."

"How could stopping time be dangerous? I kept Tristan from getting squashed to death!"

"Thanks again for that," Tristan called from the carpet.

Anders sighed. "Don't you Children of Men have movies and books about this stuff?" He shook his head then, stopping. "Actually, better you didn't watch whatever nonsense they put out. It's probably wrong."

"I don't want to hurt anyone," Aleksandr said, face open and earnest.

"You wouldn't on purpose. But if you don't learn to control it, if we let you continue to spawn the ability when one of your cousins is in danger, we're going to have a real problem on our hands."

Anders raised both hands in the air, twining them together. "This is how time looks to us now. One contiguous path, moving forward. Every single one of us goes down this path, together. Think of it as a thick piece of rope.

"Now, when you stop time, as you did, it doesn't really stop. What happens is, the thread we are all on is what stops, and another thread fringes off from the bigger one, creating two threads with identical pasts but possibly different futures." Anders unwound his hands, creating a V shape with his palms connected. "With me so far?"

All three students nodded.

"The problem is, once you restart time, those two strands weave themselves back into the single rope. This can create a paradox, as both of the futures that occurred during the break will merge into one." Anders relinked his hands.

"Mind blown," Nicolas said.

"If time is stopped for a few seconds, no harm is done. Usually. It only impacts the immediate area around the time shaper. But the longer the threads are separated, the greater the chance of confusion and other problems when they are reunited. While one reality takes precedence, both realities will continue on as the true ones. Tristan... how have your dreams been since Aleksandr saved you?"

Tristan frowned. "Fucked up. I can't stop dreaming about the moment I looked up and saw the chandelier coming at my head. But in the dream, it actually hits me and I... uh... die."

"Sorry to hear that, but precisely my point," Anders replied, nodding his head toward Tristan. "In the original strand of time, Tristan *did* die. In the second, of course, Aleksei saved him. His mind believes both versions happened. Over time, this could drive him insane."

"What?" Tristan gaped.

"Hopefully it won't," Anders said, in a not-so-reassuring tone. "Thankfully, the thread closed quickly. But I suspect you'll continue to have these dreams for months. Maybe always."

Tristan contorted his mouth. "Swell."

"The effect is far worse when a thread is open longer. The range of the split widens, to include people further away. Imagine what it might do to an aeroplane in the sky? Or even something as simple as someone using a dangerous piece of equipment in their everyday job? The ripple effect one action will have on another." Anders ceased, the excitement flush on his face.

He drew a breath. "Fascinating for those of us interested in the scientific aspects. Devastating in practice. History only tells us of one other time shaper, and they died young. It's rumored his time shaping prevented the residents of Pompeii from escaping in time."

"Dude," Tristan whispered.

"Of course, there have been others, but it's hard to pinpoint what changes in history have been predestined, or changed."

"Was he trying to help?" Aleksandr asked.

"Is this going to be like one of those movies, where I was supposed to die but cheated death, and now death is coming after me?" Tristan mused. "Because those guys didn't win."

"I'm sure he was," Anders replied, addressing Aleksandr. "Just as you were trying to help your cousin. And you did help him. He's alive because of you, even though his mind still thinks he's impaled." He winked at Tristan. "But you didn't *know* you were doing that, and this is what concerns me. The time shaping manifested as a result of your distress, and your mind took over. That can never, ever happen again! We were lucky this time."

Aleksandr perked. "I definitely don't want to cause problems! How do we do this? You want me to try to make it happen on my own?"

Anders shook his head. "Negative. We can't risk things going wrong when you're still new to this ability. We are *all* new to this ability, as there isn't anyone I know who has actually seen a time shaper at work. We're going to try something else. It's called, practicing backwards. Tristan, you can help. Nicolas, you're excused."

"Practicing backwards?" both young men said in unison.

"That's what I said. I'm going to introduce dangerous situations where Tristan is put in peril, and Aleksandr is going to practice *not* time shaping."

Tristan put his hands up. "Uhh... yeah, I don't know about this..."

Anders lifted his palm, and Tristan flew back several feet. "We don't need a time shaper to save you from danger. Calm down."

"Y'all have fun," Nicolas declared and left them to their crazy games.

HE ASCENDED TO THE THIRD FLOOR, TO THE MASTER SUITES. THE door to the room he shared with Mercy was closed, possibly locked, but Nicolas had the only key.

She was sleeping, as expected, her silver hair peeking out from under the top of the blanket she was buried beneath. His heart flipped. He wanted to hold her, to snuggle up behind and reassure her. Who the hell was he becoming?

"Go away," she murmured from her cocoon of blankets.

He went around to her side of the bed and tentatively sat on the edge. "This is my room, you know," he said lightly.

Mercy threw the blankets off in a flash. "Fine. I'll go."

Nicolas reached forward and gripped her shoulders, forcing her to look at him. "I didn't say that."

She dropped her eyes. A tear slid down one cheek. Her messy hair matted the side of her head. "I shouldn't be up here sleeping anyway. I don't know what I'm doing anymore."

Nicolas brushed her hair back. She flinched. "None of us do," he said. "It's been a clusterfuck of epic proportions."

"My fault, I suppose," she sighed. "This whole thing was my idea."

"Mercy, that isn't what I meant."

Her laugh was bitter. "Why are you up here?"

Nicolas swallowed, then lifted her chin to meet her eyes. "Because I love you, Clementyn."

Mercy's mouth dropped open. More tears surfaced at her glistening lash line. Then she pushed his hand away and lay back down, turning away from him. "How unfortunate for you, Nicolas."

53
JACOB

A daughter. A child. They were going to bring a child into the world, together, as foretold. As he'd always dreamed, secretly, despite knowing it was a dangerous business bringing any life into the cursed Deschanel family.

"Tell me what I want to know," Baldur repeated, his heady breath, now tainted with Amelia's scent, repugnant as he leaned over Jacob.

Is it true? About the baby, Blanca*?*

I had no idea. I wouldn't have kept a secret like this from you.

I know, Amelia. I know, baby. We're going to get out of here. I don't know how, but we're going to be okay, I can feel it.

"The bitch still in your head?" Baldur sighed. He stood and moved back to where Amelia dangled, lifting her off the hook with one arm. In a flash, she flew across the room, hitting the window and shattering it. Her body and heavy cuffs hit the floor with a resounding thud.

"STOP!" Jacob cried. Baldur shot a hand out and pinned Jacob down again.

Amelia moaned, dragging herself away from her approaching assailant.

Baldur was upon her, and again Amelia's body rose in the air and was hurled toward the other side of the room. This time, when she landed, she made no sound.

Amelia, say something. I need to hear your voice.

Nothing.

Amelia, if you can hear me. I promised you I would say nothing, but it doesn't mean I will do *nothing.*

Jacob rose slowly. Padraig told him, in what seemed a lifetime ago, that Jacob's abilities would come to him when he most needed them. The problem was, his abilities could be anything at all. He didn't know what to ask of the Earth, how to appeal to Morrigan. It was like shooting into the dark night sky, aiming at a single star.

In a move so quick it reminded Jacob of a B-movie vampire, Baldur had him bound with chains heavy enough to hold a car, and was hoisting him up on another hook, one feet from where Amelia's was. "This is your final opportunity to tell me what I want to know, Quinlan."

Jacob bit down on his cheek and said, "Aye, you've been saying tha', ye shitting bully. Ye all words, then?"

Baldur's smile sent a dark chill to Jacob's belly. This was it. He'd invited the end, a glimpse of hell. *Padraig, you better not be wrong.*

The creature went to Amelia and flopped her over his shoulder. She still made no sound or movement, but her rasping breaths—he recognized them from when he'd had punctured lungs in fights—told him her fight hadn't left. There was yet time.

Baldur placed her again on her hook, giving Jacob full view of the damage. Her lung was punctured, several of ribs poking up and out of her sternum. The knee above her broken foot was unnaturally bent. Her beautiful alabaster hair and porcelain skin was covered in blood.

I will tear this beast limb from limb, put him back together, and do it all over again, and again, and again.

Baldur pulled her bloodied hair back, stretching her neck. "Take a good look, Quinlan. You did this. I'm going to kill you, but not before I claim her and the child as my own. Scream all you want. I'll enjoy the sound."

Please let this be the end, her voice weakly called in his head. These weren't the bold, brave words from earlier.

Blanca, *be strong just a short while longer.*

No response.

Baldur's buckle snapped, and his pants dropped. The crisp sound followed by the creature holding his cock in his hand were more real to Jacob than anything that had happened this night. He was done. This was over, this... *being* was not going to hurt his wife a moment longer.

Amelia's tears cut a path down her blood-stained cheeks. *Don't watch this,* she implored. *Please, I don't want you to see me like this.*

I won't let you go through this alone.

She gasped as Baldur entered her. Until this moment, she had borne every attack with brave whimpers and soft cries. But this sent Amelia into shock. She screeched and bawled, pivoting so hard on the hook that dust filtered down from the ceiling.

"Not quite the way your mate does it, eh," Baldur grunted, pulling her hair back as he continued the rape of Jacob's wife. A patch of hair came out in his hand.

Amelia's screams rang across every beam of the cabin, and echoed through the chambers of Jacob's heart.

A fury started in Jacob's toes and radiated in ferocious spirals, passing north toward his heart. When it reached its destination, an explosion filled every limb, and everything before his eyes went white.

The room disappeared. The only sound Jacob could hear was the raging thrumming of his heartbeat.

His soul surged forward from his body, appealing to Earth. His heart lurched at the separation, but it didn't hurt. Rather, the feeling was soothing, as if his soul were headed exactly where it needed to be.

Jacob's spirit swayed across the white space, then rocketed back into the dark woods. A black bear stood at the edge of the tree-line. They regarded one another, the bear and his soul. The bear blinked once, bowed its head. Jacob's soul surged forward.

A whoosh, and then his soul saw through new eyes. The bear—Jacob—adjusted to the intrusion and then reared up, issuing a roar that started from its cavernous belly. With a jostling heave, they pummeled back through the forest, hurtling toward the small cabin.

In the now shared bear form, Jacob crashed forward through the door with a giant leap, landing flat on top of it inside the cabin. Jacob's body hung limp, eyes rolled back in his head. Amelia's eyes had closed since Jacob last looked upon her. He had but a brief moment to hope she'd found a retreat from this atrocity before rearing again on his hind legs, and signaling intent to Baldur.

Baldur's glance flashed between Jacob's limp body and the bear. Understanding dawned. "Aye, a warg then." He reached down, drew his dagger from the boot he still wore, and plunged it deep in Amelia's belly just before Jacob tore his throat out with borrowed claws.

. . .

Jacob felt his soul turning as it exited the bear and floated back to his dangling figure. Now, he could see the bear through his own eyes. The bear ambled over, and with one bloody claw, knocked Jacob from the hook. With his teeth, he carefully pried the chains up over his fingers.

Jacob and the bear regarded one another a final time. Then the bear ambled off, back toward the woods.

Trying to stand was torture, but he immediately remembered this was nothing compared to the pain his wife was in. Stepping over the mutilated Baldur, Jacob lifted his dying wife from where she hung. She collapsed atop him. Blood gushed from her mid-section. He reached a hand up to her neck, felt a pulse, and drew an inward sigh of relief.

"Amelia, hang on sweetie, I'm going to get help." But even as he said the words, Jacob knew: there *was* no help. She was going to die without immediate intervention. He wouldn't make it back to the edge of the woods.

The words hit him all at once. His wife was going to die. His Amelia, his *blanca,* the one thing in his life that ever mattered, was going to cease to be.

Unless... was she a healer, too? Like her mother?

"I can't," Amelia sputtered. Foaming blood gurgled from her bruised lips. "Never have."

Jacob ripped dirty sheets from the bed, tying off wound after wound, pressing carelessly wadded strips to stop the bleeding. "Oh, God. God, no. No, no, no, no, no. Maybe you can, maybe it's like a thing you have to manifest in a time of need too." Every piece of linen he used was stained red in moments. He went off in a panicked search for more, but Amelia lifted a battered hand.

"No time," she whispered. "You're a draoi, Jacob. Nature is yours for the commanding."

If that were true, she would already be healed!

"Ask..." Amelia instructed, and then succumbed to her pain.

"Ask who?" But he knew. He'd asked the Earth to bring him a tool to destroy Baldur, and it had.

Clutching Amelia's hand, Jacob let his grief carry him this time, rather than his rage. The room faded to white, and he stood before the image of the *crann bethadh*. He dropped to his knees, face raised to the sky, beseeching the goddess.

"Anything," he pleaded. "Anything you ask. Anything at all. Anything you want is yours if you help me save her. Anything."

The goddess obliged, filling Jacob with golden warmth as he was carried back to the bedside, to the sensation of his wife's limp hand in his. The stained wad of cloth still covered her belly.

"My turn to save you," he whispered. Laying a kiss against her forehead, Jacob transferred the swirling, fluorescent power to Amelia. A green, iridescent light surrounded her, lifting her from the bed in a jolt.

A long, yawning sigh filled Amelia's mouth as she drew in the healing energies. Gashes in her skin slowly closed over. Her ribs retreated, snapping back into place.

She is not out of the woods, Morrigan sung in Jacob's head. *Seek out the tribe of Birger and Astrid. You must make haste.*

"Aye," Jacob whispered, clutching Amelia to his chest as he finally allowed his sobs to break free. "Aye, Goddess."

54
ANASOFIYA

The crowds before them undulated, an endless living sea of crimson and pale faces. They stretched so far the sanctuary doors were pinned open, attendees spilling out into the courtyard, down the mountain, and into the town square. A rare event despite their extended lifetimes, Empyreans had arrived from all over the world to witness the coronation of Agripin and his halfling empress.

Gilded crimson velvet draped the stark-white walls, creating the effect of blood dripping from the ceiling. *Probably not too far off,* Ana thought. Other than the gauche splash of color, and decorated thrones, there were no other ornaments of the occasion. The stories-tall statue of Emyr, as a phoenix rising, had been taken apart and re-assembled in order to bring it through the large double doors. Perched in the center of the room, the spread wings nearly pierced the walls on either side.

Ana's dress weighted her to the jeweled throne. Layers upon layers of crimson silk and gold cloth, which made her feel like an over-wrapped Christmas present. The garment was another reminder she was yet a prisoner here.

To her left, Agripin sat on a throne even more ornate than her own, his smile plastered on. Every time she tried to make small talk, he'd speak to her from the corner of his mouth, keeping his eyes rigidly ahead. His refusal to look at her made her stomach flop.

On her right, Duchess Oriana perched upon a smaller throne, her first public appearance in over fifty years. The small chair was a slight from her brother no doubt, but no one would guess she was annoyed by the way she bestowed her slight, feminine nods, and coquetting smiles, upon all her adorers. Her red hair cascaded from braids and wraps, a gold crown of a phoenix wrapping around her forehead and through to the back of her coiffed design. Visually, the duchess was a delight, even to Ana, who knew to be wary.

Nerys was notably missing. Hopefully a sign she was rallying the other leaders to action on Agripin's behalf. Without access to Forbia's cues, and the crowds a blanket of faces and noise, Ana had no way of knowing if all the moving facets were coming together according to plan. She was forced to trust things would turn out, when nothing about her experiences here gave her the confidence to do so.

Ana couldn't actually see Aidrik, but she sensed his presence behind Agripin, next to Cyler. The emperor's personal guards. Finn had taken a seat in the upper mezzanine, in a box with several of Oriana's favorite "pets." He'd be unnoticed there, and his escape, with any luck, seamless. Hers, on the other hand, would require some creative finessing, perhaps assistance from Agripin, if she could ever grab his attention. Even her bathroom breaks required an escort.

The eldres assembled before the elevated thrones in their traditional V-formation, first facing the royal court. They dropped into a light bow, and then in perfect synchronicity, pivoted to face the throngs.

"Brace yourself, dearest sister," Oriana purred, never dropping her saccharine smile. "*Everything* is about to change."

The low din of casual conversation rose to a roaring call to prayer, as all in the room sang out in unison, *Our Father of Light, Our Father of Fire, We are Yours in the Flames!*

Agripin's contribution was the most enthusiastic of all, as he stood and flung his arms skyward, yelling the verses. Ana rose tentatively beside him, dutifully mouthing the prayer. Over and over the chant went on. She lost count after the twentieth round.

When at last the voices faded, Grand Eldre Servius addressed the onlookers. Agripin's foot tapped in nervous excitement beneath his robe. "We, the humble servants of Our Father, have gathered you on this joyous occasion to witness the coronation of Agripin, son of Aeron, son of Theda, and his empress, Anasofiya, daughter of Augustus, daughter of Ekatherina."

Ana cringed inwardly at the obvious sneer from Servius when he named her and her parentage.

"Our Father of Light, Our Father of Fire," the crowd intoned in response.

Ana snuck a glance northward at Finn. His tense, bearded face softened briefly and he offered her a light smile. *No matter what else happens, he has to get to safety. He has to get out of here, and to Aleksei, and Nicolas, and my father.*

Servius held his hands out, reminding Ana of a picture depicting Jesus feeding thousands. "As you know, we are a modest race. We opt not for the pomp and circumstance of men, but instead offer you our emperor and empress, in the simplest of ceremonies, as they take the vows of Our Father and swear fealty to His name and honor."

The crowd murmured in solemn agreement. Oriana tittered.

The V-formation pivoted again, a crisp snap of robes filling the air as they turned to face the royal court.

Agripin, stop ignoring me. You've never told me what I'm supposed to do!

His internal sigh was audible. *Because there was nothing to tell. They'll say words, you'll repeat them. How difficult is that?*

How difficult was it to tell me that?

I have other things on my mind, dear.

The same things that are on my mind, I should hope.

He didn't respond. Servius lifted his robe and ascended the court stage, the other eldres remaining behind in stiff formation. Most watched Ana in morbid curiosity. Maxima, normally coy and playful, looked as if she might be battling with her lunch.

"Do you both agree to recite the sacred vows of Our Father?" Servius asked, his glance traveling between Ana and Agripin.

Ana looked up in time to see Finn disappearing into the curtain. She had no watch, and there were no other timepieces in the sanctuary, so she focused on counting down the seconds, which would also, she prayed, keep Agripin out of her head. She couldn't block him, but she could muddy the waters. *Thirty minutes. If I don't make it to him by then, he leaves without me. He promised, so he better.*

"Aye," Agripin said.

"Aye," Ana repeated.

Her toes curled in her satin heels, Ana's equivalent of biting down on her tongue to keep calm. Finn was gone. She was about to be crowned the empress of Farjhem, a title that would likely strip her of power rather than granting any. Aidrik was nearby, but she couldn't see him, nor use his solid face for strength, in this moment when all she wanted to do was run.

Twenty-eight minutes. Ana couldn't let Finn leave without

her. It would crush him. She promised, the most important promise of her life. How long would this take? For all she knew, the ceremony would go on for days and involve ritual animal sacrifice. She knew as much about what to expect as the guy who bagged her groceries in Jackson Square.

Come on, come on, come on!

"As the imperial leaders of the Farværdig, do you solemnly vow to govern our people from the seat of Our Father, Farjhem, extending this leadership to all corners of the known world, and according to the laws laid out by Our Father by way of his sacred vessel, The Eldre Senetat?"

"Aye, I solemnly do vow," Agripin said.

"Aye, I solemnly do vow," Ana repeated.

One down, Ana thought, until the crowd erupted once more in an untold number of *Our Father of Light, Our Father of Fire.*

Twenty-four minutes.

"As the imperial leaders of the Farværdig, do you solemnly vow to adhere to the wishes of Our Father, that the Eldre Senetat be the singular entity for the creation of the laws of the Farværdig, and to honor their position as blessed by Emyr Himself?"

"Aye, I solemnly do vow," Agripin said. His foot tapped faster.

"Aye, I solemnly do vow," Ana murmured, holding her breath in hopes there would not be another round of prayers.

Our Father in Light, Our Father in Fire, Our Father in Light, Our Father in Fire...

Twenty-two minutes.

"As the imperial leaders of the Farværdig, will you be swift in your support of justice? To uphold your power for the good of Emyr even in times of strife, or when doing so would be unsavory or unwelcome?" Servius' glance landed on Ana. Her mouth parted as she realized, *He's talking about me. I'm the unsavory and unwelcome piece of this equation. This creature may very well be asking Agripin to execute me. Or for me to execute myself.*

Ana meticulously counted the seconds down, letting each one roll through her mind, blocking her fears, which would do her no good surrounded by so many of her enemies. Her toes clenched.

Then Agripin and Servius were both looking at her, the former with an expectant rise of the brow, the latter with abject annoyance.

Say your damn vow! Agripin intruded her thoughts.

"Aye, I solemnly do vow," Ana said quickly, wondering how long she'd been lost to her counting. Oriana affected a light, ashamed sigh.

More chanting. More counting. Finn, I'm coming, just a few more minutes. Hopefully this is almost over...

Seventeen minutes.

Two more vows, each near identical versions of the last. Each a slightly different way to say, *We will obey you, Senetat.* Not a one of them speaking to the true good of the people, and sustaining the beauty and wonder of the race. *I was wrong. The emperor has no power here. Everything is a beautiful illusion. His role is as benign as the Queen of England.*

Seven minutes. Ana's heart was beating so hard she feared it was visible to everyone around her. It blurred her vision, stunted her breathing. Seven minutes would hardly be enough time to leave the castle, let alone make it out of Farjhem to meet her husband. If she was going to do this, she had to do it now.

"Our Father, Emyr of the Light, Emyr of the Fire, has conferred upon me the authority to bless this union in His eyes, and His glory. With that power, I crown thee Agripin, Grand Emperor of Farjhem and the Greater Realm."

Agripin bowed his head to accept the gilded crown of flames. He rose to thundering applause. Only Ana could hear his long, controlled breath as he exhaled throughout the presentation.

When Servius turned to Ana, his grin widened. In his eyes was a malice that stopped her racing heart for seconds. "Our Father, Emyr of the Light, Emyr of the Fire, has conferred upon me the authority to bless this union in His eyes, and His glory. With that power, I crown thee Anasofiya, Grand Empress of Farjhem and the Greater Realm."

With held breath, Ana slowly leaned forward to accept a smaller version of the flaming crown. It settled on her head with a heaviness that caused her neck to sag. The metal was cold, the edges hard.

Ana closed her eyes and drew in a long gust of air, filling her lungs, petitioning her dark traveler for strength. Her familiar obliged, rising forward and pushing her up, until she was standing before her subjects.

Her lower lids filled with tears and she choked back a sob. *Three minutes.*

Finn would be leaving without her.

Servius looked around, as if expecting someone. He tripped on his words as he announced, "The... grand emperor and empress will be... hosting a reception in the palace within the hour. All are invited, and for those who cannot fit inside the palace walls, refreshment will be served in the town square."

A flurry of excitement caused everyone to turn toward the left side of the crowd, where a Crimson Guard made his way purposely toward the throne stage. Servius' grin returned, though he moved quickly to disguise it. Maxima turned away.

The guard hurried to Cyler, whispering something Ana could not hear. Cyler then knelt behind Agripin, passing the message.

Agripin's expression didn't change, but his face lost all color. He nodded at Cyler, who conferred again with the guard.

Agripin stood and faced the crowd, countenance solemn. "I regret to announce that we are placing Aidrik the Wise and Empress Anasofiya in immediate custody for the charge of treason!" He marched off the stage, toward a private exit, Cyler in tow.

The blood rose so fast to Ana's head that when she stood, she slumped. A guard caught her, and a second appeared, jerking her up and forward. *This isn't really happening... this has to be part of the plan.*

But as she was dragged away, Ana caught the pleased looks from the Senetat. Not a one was shocked... each had the satisfied expression of someone who was witnessing something they'd waited a long time to see.

All except Maxima, who flashed Ana a sad smile as she passed.

55
NICOLAS

The entire household went to hell in a matter of days.

Harriett ceased speaking altogether. Not to Tristan, not to anyone. She retreated back into the safety of her mind, a place barricaded so tight Tristan couldn't so much as send her a message. Before she went dark, she'd said one thing: *Call the family together. Here.*

Nicolas thought about it. Maybe if she hadn't declared the whole mission an abject failure before they even had a chance to fight, he might have rallied the Deschanels together for one last big hurrah.

"What aren't you telling us?" Anne asked, her searching eyes more suspicious than usual, which was quite the statement.

"I could make a list, but it might take me a while," Nicolas responded with a shrug. Was tempting to tell his pig-headed sister the truth and watch her innocent jaw drop, as she blubbered silly suggestions that made no difference. But she was his only remaining sister, and he loved her. Better she, and all the others, spend their final days in a state other than terror.

"That would require *literacy,*" she quipped, hiding a pleased look at her insult before pivoting and sashaying from the room. Amateur.

Aunt Colleen had come by earlier to check on everyone. She asked him roughly the same question Anne had, but he hadn't lied. She'd see through it, and maybe she'd have a helpful suggestion. *Hey, here are some suicide pills. Quicker and cleaner.*

Instead, she'd pulled the adult card. "Darling, Harriett is very young. She's afraid, and her imagination may be getting the best of her. Am I suggesting she's wrong? No, I suspect there's truth in her visions, but they're being clouded by these outside influences. Remember, she's only recently reconnected with the world."

"So... you're saying we're going to be fine?"

Aunt Colleen pulled a surprisingly classic rookie liar's move. She blinked. "Of course. Focus on keeping your household together, Nicolas. That's all you can control anyway."

She'd left in an awful hurry after that. Never did say why she came by. Didn't need to. Her departure spoke to Nicolas pretty clearly.

Then Sindre took off. Not for an afternoon stroll, either. No one in the house could detect him at all, as if he'd fallen clean off the face of the Earth.

"He doesn't like it here," Eydis pouted, still refusing to meet Nicolas' eyes after his clear rejection. She shrugged. "Can't say I blame him."

Hakon used his bestiakinesis to connect with a hawk and search for him. But he grew exhausted before he made much progress.

"We can't just *leave* him out there! He isn't protected!" Anne shrieked when Nicolas declared the boy would come back when he came back.

"He knows that and went anyway. Sounds like his problem

to me," Nicolas replied. "Anyway, leftover jambalaya for dinner. Condoleezza has the night off."

Anne gaped at him, slack-jawed, hands gripping her hips.

"Nic is right," Markus agreed, clearing his throat. "We can't risk ourselves for someone who gives his own life no value."

Anne was incredulous. "What do you suggest, then, Markus? We do nothing?"

Markus made a face at her. "Did you have a better idea?"

"Suicide mission," Anders piped in, entering the room with one of his bizarre coffee-in-a-wine-glass concoctions. "If Sindre wants to be a cowboy, let that be his decision. The rest of us stay here."

"And what if I don't agree?" Anne pushed. "What if I go after him?"

"Your funeral," Anders and Markus replied in unison. They exchanged a look. A mental bro-fist transpired.

"Anne, calm the fuck down, okay? Have a drink. Unwind your panties." Nicolas put an arm around his sister's neck.

She shrugged it off and shot him a disgusted look. "It's not even noon!"

By one, Anne, Eydis, and Hakon were gone.

"We had one job," Nicolas lamented as he and Markus searched the property.

"You thought this was going to end well?" Markus cracked, giving him a peripheral frown.

"Well, I didn't think we'd lose the majority of the goddamn kids, no. Maybe one or two."

Markus stopped and gave him the oddest look. Then he burst into laughter. After a moment, Nicolas joined him.

With disaster looming, and half the household off God-knows-where, laughter was all they had to keep them going.

. . .

Anders dumped the leftover jambalaya into a casserole dish and tossed it in the oven. Lucia was right behind him, turning the oven on, mumbling something about what a wonder it was he could secure his britches every morning.

Everyone took a bowl and scattered to their own room, or preferred corner of the house. No one had the heart to eat at the table, where they might feel compelled to talk about the hopelessness of the situation, and the lack of familiar faces.

Nicolas stayed, as did Anders. "I heard what you told your aunt today," the latter said, in between spoonfuls.

A day ago, this would have unnerved Nicolas. What did it matter now? "You don't sound surprised."

"Harriett isn't the only seer in the house," Anders answered. He held his spoon clutched in his fist. Nicolas wondered if he was raised in the wild, by baboons.

"You saw us all dying a fiery death too?"

Anders dabbed a napkin at his lips, a dainty gesture when compared to his barbaric eating. "Not exactly. Harriett is limited by one version of our future. She might be seeing a broken strand of time, one that has come un-fused." He lifted the bowl to his mouth, and drained the stew, throat ebbing as he swallowed sausage and rice without so much as a single chew. *Maybe cheetahs.* "I've seen several outcomes myself. One matches hers."

Nicolas choked off the hope he felt at the words. "And the others?"

"Harriett shouldn't have told you what she did," Anders answered. "A trained seer knows better. We're taught to keep our premonitions to ourselves, because it's impossible to know which piece of time we might catch. Some seers happen to catch the true version of events every time, and so they falsely believe they will never be wrong. Harriett is one of those, I suspect."

"Why the hell would you want to keep that shit to yourself?"

"Because you can't alter the course of time, Nicolas," Anders explained patiently. "I've seen four versions of our future. All dramatically different. One of them *will* come true. This is a certainty, not a guess. But I can't control which one will happen anymore than I can dictate the terms of the tides."

Nicolas dropped his spoon on the table, considering. "Can you tell me if one of these outcomes has us succeeding?"

"What does success look like to you?"

"Living. Surviving this mess."

Anders nodded. "If you're asking me if all hope is lost, then the answer is no."

Nicolas' hands tingled with furious relief. "Why didn't you say something sooner?"

"You didn't ask."

"I didn't know you were a fucking seer!"

"Again, you didn't ask."

Nicolas groaned. "So, what do we do, then?"

Anders stood. He grabbed his bowl. "What we've been doing. Train and prepare. Because I'm personally not a fan of Harriett's version."

"You're saying this is all up to chance? We're playing time roulette."

Anders turned toward the main kitchen. "I said we couldn't change the future. I never said we couldn't influence which one comes to fruition."

Nicolas jogged to catch up. "How can I help?"

The scout laughed. "I've been telling you for weeks, Nicolas. You didn't want to listen."

"Yeah, well. I thought we were all gonna die."

"We might."

"Make up your mind!"

Anders dropped his bowl in the soapy tub Condoleezza had left in the sink. He turned. "If you want to help, do as I've asked, and focus on figuring out what it is you bring to the table. Because if a nested vision is the best you have to offer as a mystic, then Emyr has one hell of a wicked sense of humor."

After dinner, Nicolas peeked in on Mercy. Sleeping again. The urge to wake her and talk was not as great as his fear of the same, so he gently closed the door, retreating.

He descended to the second floor. Lucia stood in the center of the long hallway, gazing toward the double doors that led to the gallery facing the river.

"You lost?" he asked.

Lucia shook off her daze. "Thinking is all. Trying to put myself into the mindset of Sindre and the others who went off after him."

Nicolas snorted. "Good luck. The kid is a psycho, and the others are foolish little girls."

She grinned. "Maybe. But Anders and I came to help, so that's what I'm trying to do. If Livia had gone with them, you couldn't have kept me here."

"That's admirable, really. But unless you're fluent in mind control, I don't see how you're going to get them back." Nicolas' gaze was thoughtful. "Anne isn't stupid. She'll come back soon."

"The others?"

Nicolas shrugged, considering that this was further evidence why fatherhood was never a solid idea for him.

"Where's Anders?"

"Dunno. He wandered off after dinner."

Lucia snickered. She turned back toward the river view. “Figures. He’s probably not concerned at all, since his prize recruits are still safely ensconced under this roof.”

Nicolas had a strong suspicion Lucia could run on all night about the complexities of her relationship with Anders. He turned and started down the staircase when she stopped him.

“How’s your training going, Nicolas?”

“Well,” Nicolas said, turning to look up at her, “your partner insists I’m some kind of superhero mystic, but has yet to show me how the fuck I’m supposed to figure that out.”

Lucia’s brow arched. A mischievous smile spread across her face. “He’s been here for weeks and still hasn’t been able to draw it out of you?”

Nicolas shook his head.

“I think I know exactly what your skill is. Care to indulge me?”

NICOLAS TOOK HER TO THE THIRD FLOOR STUDY. SOMETHING ABOUT doing these exercises on the ground floor felt like a betrayal to Anders, which was ridiculous, because the dude had done absolutely nothing to further Nicolas’s learning.

He took a seat on his Louis XIV chair near the windowed door. Lucia stood with her back against the marble mantle, watching him. Smirking.

“Well?” he demanded.

Lucia started a slow pace across the Oriental carpet, watching him. “I began to suspect about a week into our visit. Mostly from collecting stories from your sister and cousins. No terribly complicated detective work, just casual conversation.”

“What are you going on about?”

“I picked up some things from Oz’s mind, too. Your poor friend isn’t even bothering to block anymore. Did he ever? Did your sister teach him?" She shook her head. "Doesn't matter. I tried to talk to Anders but he insisted he had everything under control. Guess not."

Lucia stopped and knelt before Nicolas' chair, gripping the wooden arms. "It has to be. You're pretty on the eyes, no doubt, but not enough to explain this… phenomenon."

"Christ, Lucia, just say it!"

"I think you might possess a form of illusionment called seductive influence. Ever heard of it?"

He shook his head. "Sounds kinky."

"Some illusionists have the power to influence others. I'm sure you have some in your family?"

"My uncle. Ana's dad, Augustus. Markus can make people see things. There are probably others, too, I don't know."

"Right. So you get the basics. Someone with the power of *seductive* influence though, uses sex and sensuality to accomplish the same result."

Nicolas laughed, sagging in his chair. "So, let's get this straight. You think I'm controlling women with my cock, simply because I've bedded half of South Louisiana? Am I tracking?"

Lucia didn't rise to the bait. "Think back on all the women you've been with. Men, too."

Nicolas threw his hands up. "Just women."

"Whatever. Has any one of them *ever* turned you down?"

Nicolas considered this, dragging his thoughts across over fifteen years of memories. "Does my sister count?"

Lucia blinked. "Come again?"

"You're asking me to recall a hell of a lot of different conquests, Lucia," Nicolas replied. He ran his hands through his hair, still thinking. "I can't remember ever having to fight for it, but I'm not a rapist."

"I'm not talking about rape. I'm asking if you ever wanted a woman who didn't want you back," she replied evenly.

Nicolas squinted his eyes, going even further back. So many women. The chase had always been fun for him, but quick. Easy. Sometimes they played along, knowing that's what he liked, but they always gave in. "No, I guess not. But I'm a Deschanel. There's not a woman in this state who wouldn't get on her knees for my money."

Lucia raised her hand. "I could not be less interested in you *or* your money, Nicolas. Which is why I'm going to let you test this on me."

"Test what?"

Lucia pulled a chair from behind her, sliding it across from him. "I believe you've had this power all your life, but you've been using it subconsciously. Without realizing."

Nicolas narrowed his eyes. "Yes, I know what subconsciously means."

"Aidrik's protection kept you from major demonstrations. But it's hard to fully temper a mystic's powers, and so your ability surfaced in smaller, less potent ways."

Nicolas couldn't stop himself. "You're saying being a slut was never a choice for me?"

"Everything we do is a choice," she replied. "Bringing us to the present, your abilities are no longer diluted as you've been exposed not only to Mercy, but also to Aidrik, myself, Anders, and so on. Which means, you're capable of realizing your full potential."

"And what is the full potential of a seductive influencer? I entrap women with my steely, irresistible gaze, causing an instantaneous orgasm, thus prompting them to reveal all their kinky secrets to me?"

Lucia rolled her eyes, but smiled. "I need you to answer something honestly for me. Your answer won't offend me."

Right, that's what all women say. "Sure."

"Are you attracted to me?"

If it feels like a trap, it probably is! "Yeah, I mean, you're hot."

"That isn't what I asked. Remember, honesty."

"Well..." Nicolas frowned. "Not really. No offense. You *are* hot. Just not my type, and also, you're banging my cousin. Never been down with other people's property."

Nicolas flinched, dodging the inevitable smack to the face. Instead, she looked relieved. "Good. Now I'm going to clear my mind, Nic. I'm going to stop blocking you, and I want you to focus on whatever it is about me that *does* interest you. Then I want you to decide you want me. To make a conscious decision that you're going to have me."

"Uhh. For science, right?"

Lucia groaned. "Can you do this, or not?"

Nicolas nodded. It wouldn't be a significant stretch.

She closed her eyes, drew in a breath. A calm came over her. "Okay. I'm ready."

Nicolas cracked his knuckles. Rolled his neck. He'd certainly had worse assignments over the years. *Focus on what interests me. Her tits are spectacular. Those nice white arcs cresting from behind her leather jer... okay, yep, I can do this.*

Before Nicolas could start his usual charismatic propositions, Lucia was on top of him, straddling her muscular legs over each of his, tongue jammed down his throat.

"Whoa!" he cried, tossing her off. She hit the floor with a thud, peering up through hungry eyes. She panted as her tongue flitted over her lips.

Nicolas made a definitive choice to find her about as unsexy as he could fathom. A gust of air escaped her lungs. Her hands traveled to her flushed face. *She asked for it!*

"Well, then," she said, standing. She brushed invisible dust off her pants. "I think that's enough for one evening."

"That was fucking incredible!" Nicolas exclaimed, as the events of the last minute caught up to him. "You just *threw* yourself at me!"

"Yes, yes I did."

"Holy shit!" His mind was racing. So many moments from his life made perfect sense now. Recent events with Eydis... it wasn't his fault!

Sorry, that's too convenient.

Lucia started toward the door. "Be careful who you practice that on."

"Wait... that was pretty fucking cool, but what is the... er... practical use? Why the hell would Emyr give me the ability to seduce someone?"

"I don't know," she answered with a short sigh. "But when the time comes, *you* will."

56
FINNEGAN

Finn reached the rendezvous point within ten minutes. He timed it, because he'd already decided to add that time to the thirty minutes, giving Ana adequate time to get to him. If she yelled at him later, so be it.

Patience had never been something Finn excelled at. As a lobsterman, he laid double the traps of other seamen, determined to get quicker results. He was last to retire for the winter, and earliest out in the spring. When idle, his mind went to unhelpful places, where his imagination spun up ludicrous notions.

The next thirty minutes would pass very slowly.

Forbia had run ahead of him, marking the path as she leapt in zigzags. The pup had been busy these weeks alone, exploring all of Farjhem. Finn liked to think she had gathered knowledge that would be useful in the future. Whatever the truth, her job would be to watch for Ana, and help guide her once she escaped.

Now, she paced before her master, hackles half-raised. No

immediate danger, she told him, but she didn't like this plan. Not one bit.

"I know, girl. I don't either," he mollified, running his hands through her thick white fur. The tender gesture was as soothing to him as her presence. If Finn could think about how Forbia needed a hot bath, and perhaps a nail trim, he might buy his mind some relief for a few minutes.

The meeting place was a small cave, if one could call it that. Nestled into a mountainside, it was more of a concave shelter from the elements for someone passing by. A thicket of trees covered the entrance, and unless someone specifically knew to look there, he'd remain undetected. As a second defensive layer, the fauna would respond to his presence, offering further protection.

Finn shook his wrist, rotating his father's watch. "Five minutes. Is that all? Are you kidding me?"

Forbia whined in sympathy, and went back to pacing.

The day he first laid eyes on Ana, he'd had one of those classic romance movie moments, double-take and all. On the eve of winter, her fresh face and fiery hair lit up his view coming back to shore from a long day on the Atlantic. Her tentative waves and smiles etched themselves to his soul. And this was even before they said hello.

Not your type? he'd asked when she politely rebuffed him.

No, you're exactly my type, Finn. That's the problem.

Finn only wanted Ana to love herself, and see herself through his eyes. He'd never ignored or glossed over her flaws. In his mind's eye, he could see them, all of them, decorating her like thin scars. When he made love to her, he'd run his lips over these scars, healing them each time. *I don't care what you've done, Ana. It makes you who you are. My heart, my first safe place.*

Romance was a nice change of pace for Finn. Entirely

foreign, but it suited him, like putting on a tailored jacket for the first time. He still didn't know how to navigate the waters. He didn't think girls went crazy over flowers anymore, and besides, he didn't want to give his wife something that would wilt and die. That custom seemed so morbid. Everything he gave her would be a representation of his commitment. Eternal. Unflinching.

Nothing would ever be a greater representation of those things than their son, Aleksandr. Finn never wanted to be a father, but the moment he learned Ana was pregnant, he had never wanted anything so much as to be a parent with *her*.

Watching her with Aleksei doubled a love he didn't think had capacity for stretching. To see her teach him, so patiently. Her soft smile when he made her proud, which was always. If she could only see herself as he did.

"Why didn't I say these things to her last night?" Finn muttered to an empathetic Forbia. She sat and watched him, tilting her head. "I suck at words."

Forbia growled, chased her tail in a circle, then plopped back down, tail wagging. "Yeah, yeah, yeah. I know, I'll tell her in...." Finn checked his watch again. "Fifteen minutes."

The two companions sighed in unison.

Finn checked his cloak once more for the item he'd been entrusted to take back to *Ophélie*: Ulfberht. Still safe and sound, sheathed tight against him, Aidrik's final words buried somewhere deeper, unprocessed.

THE SUN HAD BEEN SETTING WHEN THEY LEFT THE CASTLE, AND THE sky began to darken as they arrived at the rendezvous spot. Now, with five minutes left, stars lit up the canvas above.

She's sure taking every minute. It occurred to Finn their plan hadn't been as sound as they thought the night before. They hadn't discussed whether the thirty minutes included travel time. If not, she was already late. They weren't made for this life on the run, plotting and planning for their very survival. He only hoped it wouldn't matter.

Forbia went alert, the hair on her back rising in a menacing arc. A rustling in the woods. Leaves crunching. *Not Ana.*

Three Empyreans emerged from the woods. Forbia peeled her lips back in a rumbling growl, but Finn stayed her. "Duchess Nerys. Stian… and, I'm sorry, I forgot your name." *No, I didn't forget. I just didn't like the way you flirted with my wife, you shameless son-of-a-bitch.*

"Thorvald," the third said quickly. Stian fell back, scouting the area.

"We have to go, Finnegan. Right this minute," Nerys ordered, moving closer. Forbia tensed, sitting on the top of Finn's feet.

Finn shook his head. "I'm meeting someone here." *Don't be an idiot. They know why you're here or they wouldn't be standing in front of you with those terrified looks on their faces.* He slumped against the rock wall. "She still has five minutes. I'm going to give her every last second."

Nerys reached a hand out toward Finn, saw his look, then instead rested it on Forbia's head, stroking her mane. Forbia thumped her hind leg, stretching her snout into a satisfied smile. *Disloyal mutt.*

Thorvald rushed forward and snatched Finn's arm. "We can't delay. She isn't coming, and unless you want to meet the same fate, and abandon your son to the Senetat, who *will* find him now that—"

"Thor!" Nerys snapped.

"What the hell are you talking about?" Finn ripped his arm free, backing away. Forbia stayed with him. "She *is* coming."

"Something terrible has happened," Nerys added in a cool

voice. She slipped her hand over her quiver of arrows. "Stian is going to get us out of here immediately, and then we can talk. But for now, we must go!"

Finn's body shook with indignant rage, the blood rising violently toward his head. "I'm not going anywhere without my wife!"

Thorvald groaned, drawing his sword. "For the love of Emyr, you insensible halfling!"

Nerys' hands shot out and cupped the side of Finn's head in one quick move. His vision blurred and he faltered, but Forbia was quick at his feet, guiding him slowly toward the ground. Yes, the ground, where all he wanted to do was snuggle against the soft moss and sleep...

FINN AWOKE TO THE WORLD SIDEWAYS, THE UNDERGROWTH OF THE forest floor cutting his vision in half. Somewhere, people were arguing. His eyes struggled to regain focus.

"I can't do it. My magic is blocked," the darker skinned Empyrean was saying. Stian. The world traveler.

"You saw me sedate the halfling with no problems. How is your magic blocked?" Nerys cried. Her calm bearing earlier was starting to crack.

"A lesser magic. Why would they block that?" Thorvald gruffed, glancing back toward Farjhem. Toward whatever had become of his wife and Aidrik. Toward...

"Ugh," Finn groaned, trying to sit. "Ana. Someone go tell Ana I'm here. Ana, my wife." When he shifted, he felt Forbia's reassuring weight, tucked against his back.

Thorvald shot an aggravated glance at Nerys. "Do you want to try again, or should I handle it this time?"

"Don't you dare," she seethed, then glided toward Finn, kneeling down. "Finnegan. Something very, very bad has happened. Anasofiya is not coming, and I have no words to soothe you right now. But if we do not leave immediately, Aleksandr and your entire clan will be in mortal danger. Do you understand?"

Finn's jaw went slack as he nodded, slowly. *Why did I let her talk me into going first? It should be me in there, facing whatever punishment.*

"Stian was going to open us a portail, but his magic has been blocked. We will have to journey back to Louisiana the long way, out of sight as much as possible. I do not know if we will get there in time, or what we will find. But it is the only path. We must protect Aleksandr."

Why would they care about my son? Why are they here? Who betrayed us? Finn's questions flowed in faster than anyone would answer them. He knew that without opening his mouth. Words were lodged in his throat anyhow, where his heart stuck. He nodded.

57
JACOB

Thank God for the wheelbarrow. Even if Jacob could have carried Amelia, it likely would've resulted in further injury to her. Whatever healing he'd offered, she needed more. A lot more. He'd pulled her back from the brink of death, but she wouldn't survive without the help of someone far stronger than he was.

He'd found a cupboard of unsoiled linens and padded the metal bottom with a colorful quilt, a riot of colors in no particular pattern or shape, before gently laying his wife inside. She didn't wake, even when her head bounced against the front lip, her legs swinging between the wooden handlebars. But she was breathing. He would focus on that.

And her bracelet, in his pocket, which he'd picked up off the cabin floor before leaving. It had led him to her once. She was alive because she had the good sense to tear it from her wrist.

There was no path through the dark woods that Jacob could find. He had the strong sense that when he started into the woods after Amelia, the point where he emerged was a far distance from the beginning. A troubling realization, and one he knew better than to dwell on.

"Almost there, *Blanca*," he sang, as he looked around for any signs of the direction he was supposed to go. *Come on, Goddess. You said to find Birger and Astrid's folks, but you didn't bloody say* where.

No sign appeared, and so Jacob closed his eyes and picked the direction with the least resistant foliage, praying simultaneously to his Catholic God, and his Quinlan Goddess, that his direction would be their salvation and not their end.

AMELIA WAS NOT ESPECIALLY HEAVY, AND THE WHEELBARROW SHIFTED her weight in a way that made pushing her no burden, even with the rough terrain. But as the day wore on, and the light faded, everything on Jacob, from his clothes, to his arms, felt laden.

He stopped, wiping the sweat from his brow with his bloodied sleeve. He hadn't thought to bring water, he only wanted out of there before whoever Baldur reported to went looking for the missing scout. He would do anything in the world for a sip. And Amelia surely needed hydration.

He rested his hands atop his damp head, taking in the horizon. Every direction looked exactly the same. For all he knew, they'd been moving in circles the whole time, and were back where they started. He feared looking down and seeing Amelia's chest no longer rise, but her breaths were there. Slow and long-spaced, but there.

Jacob closed his eyes for a moment. He only needed one, a second to stabilize himself, to find the strength to push further into the unknown, to forget that his wife was slipping away from him and that if he chose wrong, he would lose her forever.

When he opened his eyes, two figures stood before him. Jacob pitched back, startled, and a third person caught him.

Tall, red hair, skin like fire. "Empyreans," he mused. The one holding him didn't feel like a threat, but he couldn't have broken away even if he focused.

"Aye," the old woman said with a gentle tone. "Though different from the one who did this to you."

Jacob's eyes traveled between her, and the other figure, a man with a worried but welcoming smile. The wave of sobs started somewhere low within him and then rolled forward until he was gasping, long before the tears erupted. "God, thank God," he cried, before exhaustion rose up to meet relief, and together they overcame him.

JACOB AWOKE IN THE ROOM OF ANOTHER CABIN, NOT UNLIKE THE ONE where they'd been held captive. A wool blanket covered him on a small cot, the smell of basil and mint dense in the air.

He rolled his head to the side. Amelia lay in a bed to his left. Her hair had been pulled back and braided, and someone had cleaned her of all the caked blood.

"*Blanca,*" Jacob whispered, rising so fast his head spun. He blinked away the confusion, trying again.

"She's resting now," the old woman said. She dabbed a washcloth at Amelia's forehead. "For how long, I don't know. The elders came in and healed her physical wounds."

He could have collapsed all over again. "She's going to live?"

"Her body continues to heal as we speak. Her mind is another matter."

Jacob struggled to catch up to all that must have transpired while he slept. He started to ask, but all he could manage was a ridiculous question about how she could be an old woman Empyrean.

Her leathery face cracked into a wistful smile. "I once bore a mark, like so many. I died trying to remove it from my neck when I sliced into an artery. Foolish, but I was desperate. Birger restored me, but as a human, I aged."

"He brought you back to life?"

She nodded. "A resurrection shaman."

"I know a resurrection shaman," Jacob said, thinking of Ana.

The old woman flashed him a knowing glance. "Aye. You do."

Jacob wanted to climb into the bed with Amelia, as he had when she was imperiled, months ago. But he was terrified that if he pulled the blanket back, he'd see the gash in her belly, where Baldur had buried his dagger.

"This is Birger and Astrid's clan?" Jacob asked.

"Aye. You're safe in our protection, Quinlan. But your place isn't here."

"Where is 'here' exactly?"

"You'll not find it on a map," the woman responded. She wrung the cloth out, setting it back in the basin. "Nor would you ever discover it on your own."

Jacob had no doubt she was telling the truth. If she had said she and her cohorts appeared out of nowhere, like magic, he might believe that, too, because that's exactly what it seemed like.

He remembered the Quinlans, regretting how they'd left without a word. "Is there a way to send word to someone?"

"Seara's clan, you mean?" She stood, and he imagined he could hear her old bones creak. "They've been made aware. I expect our scouts will find them wandering sooner or later and bring them back."

Jacob breathed out in relief. One less thing to worry about. "Where are Birger and Astrid, then?"

"You'll be gone long before they return," the old woman said. She hobbled toward the door, reaching for a stout knobby branch she used for a cane. "I'll leave you two. There's naught more I can do for her."

"I don't understand. What's wrong with her?" But he did understand. He knew.

The woman surprised him with her answer. "She's not imperiled. An imperiled empath hides in the blanket of protection their mind conjures to keep them safe. Amelia's mind may have tried to give her that protection, but if it did, it didn't work."

Jacob turned away from the woman, looking down at Amelia. Her skin was fresh and smooth, as if none of the events in the cabin had ever happened. "If she isn't imperiled, then why won't she wake?"

"She's past the help of her mind, dear Jacob. Whatever horrors befell you two were too much, even for a creature with her defenses."

"What are you saying, exactly?"

"Your wife is dying because she's willing it so."

When they were alone, Jacob set aside his fears and slid under the covers, resting his head against Amelia's chest. Her heartbeat was strong, and this filled him with a surge of hope. If her body could sustain her, he could fix the other. He knew unequivocally that he could, because she'd been saving him every day for a decade. He wasn't the same man anymore.

He wasn't the same as twelve hours ago. Yesterday, he'd shared souls with a bear. Yesterday, he'd laid hands on the woman he loved as she breathed her final breaths, and brought the life of the forest into her, healing her.

Their roles were reversed now. "I'm here, *mi bruja blanca.*" Jacob pulled her limp hand to his mouth, holding it there, drawing strength from the warmth of her skin. "I've loved you forever, and I'll love you longer still."

58
ANASOFIYA

The world flipped and turned as Ana was hooded and dragged out of Senetat Sanctuary. Hands from everywhere reached out to grab her, touch her, pinch and smack, prompting the guards to yank her forward and rush faster.

Voices all around declared her a traitor, spewing the word *halfling* as if there were no worse affliction in the world. All the kind words from the past few weeks melted away, forgotten. The focus shifted to the *schadenfreude*-like excitement of seeing one punished.

She couldn't see Aidrik, or even sense him in all the commotion. When thrown into the back of a carriage, she was flanked by several guards. Four or five, but it was hard to tell with her senses on overload. *How many strong men does it take to subdue a woman?*

The vehicle was wrenched into motion with a jolt, and she flew back against the seat. Hands tightened on her arms, bruising her. She heard the slicing sound of a sword being drawn.

A stern voice offered the first words. "Silence your magic. If you attempt an etheric summoning, your head will be removed from your body without a second caution."

Ana refused to answer, intent on some degree of dignity in this untenable situation. Nor did she have any idea what an etheric summoning was, or what possible threat she could offer five Empyreans equipped with strong magic and ancient swords.

"Do you understand me, *halfling*?"

Drawing her shoulders back, she hoped she was facing him directly, despite her covered eyes. "I understand you're afraid of me."

He laughed, and the others joined in. Nervousness tinged the edges of the sound, and Ana's hearing was hyper-sensitive with her vision compromised. "Of a *halfling?* Afraid you might taint our line even further, perhaps!" They erupted in more laughter, but it felt perfunctory. They *were* afraid of her. But why?

She was pressed back into the seat as the carriage began ascending a steep hill. She searched her brain for all she knew of Farjhem's geography. They'd passed the palace, and beyond that was... only Farjus Temple, which sat at the peak of the mountain, the highest point in the land. Beyond that would be a descent to the Scryer's Temple.

What did she know of Farjus Temple? Aidrik's wry assessment came back to her. *The most devout sojourn there to pray. You'll not ever see the Senetat there unless it is part of a festival. But Farjus is also the entrance to Farskilt and Farsengel. Farskilt, where the Farværdig disappear for punishment and never emerge. And Farsengel, where they are sent for trial. You never want to find yourself in either locale, Kjære.*

Farsengel, then. She and Aidrik would be tried for treason,

and likely executed. She wondered if she would get the chance to learn the details of her charges, though it wasn't hard to guess the source.

Agripin.

They'd been played for a fool after all.

Ana blocked out the guards' taunting and closed her eyes, disappearing down into herself, into the darkness, where she could push away fears and conjecture. Where she could face the prospect of her own death with bravery.

SHE WAS STILL LOST IN HERSELF WHEN THE CARRIAGE CAME TO AN abrupt halt. Voices echoed from behind, and she imagined the angry mob carrying torches up the mountain. She nearly smiled.

Inside the temple, she was dragged to a platform and they waited, as the guards worked as much to restrain her as they did to fend off angry onlookers.

Where are you, Aidrik?

A rumble of machinery roared to life and she had to steady herself as the floor jerked and dropped out, descending. An elevator of sorts. *Taking us to Farsengel, after all. Or maybe Farskilt. They might just forgo the trial and dispose of us.*

The urge to laugh was stronger with that image. She bit her lip, but a snicker escaped and one of the guards elbowed her. *Is this what it feels like to lose your mind?*

The old, rusty metal creaked and clanged as they descended further into the base of the mountain. It was slower than those original elevators her dad had at Deschanel Media, the ones he was too cheap to replace until someone had an accident.

Dad... I'm sorry. I hope Finn makes it home, and he can explain everything. He knows the things I wanted to say but couldn't. I think the man knows my heart better than I ever did. And I guess ever will. Please accept Aleksei. He will need his grandpa, and you're the only one he has. Bend your disbelief, just this once.

"Jesus, does this thing go any faster?" Ana exclaimed, before she could stop herself.

"In a hurry to die, are you?" Another guard, not the one who'd harassed her earlier.

Ana shrugged, then laughed. Her nonchalance was the epitome of hilariousness to her. These assholes were *still* scared of her!

She waited, expecting at least one of them to throw a punch or run their sword over her, but they went quiet. A noticeable thickness filled the air, as the light disappeared. They were close to the bottom.

They landed with a thud, as presumably a cloud of dust choked her escort. *Y'all need to fire your cleaning crew.*

Ana was led down a long hall, and then they emerged into an open area. She couldn't see the space, of course, but she sensed the change in air pressure. It felt similar to stepping into an old cave.

Someone removed her mask with a crude tug. She squinted to adjust to the dim light.

A dungeon. Circular, with a hollow center extending stories tall. The outer edges were lined with prison cells, as far as the eye could see. Before she could attempt to count or make sense of the size, she was shoved into a cell, stumbling back into the wall as the metal shrieked closed. A heavy bolt slid into place.

"You can laugh until you pass into oblivion," a new voice snapped, somewhere beyond the door. Though a small window offered a glimpse outside, Ana had no desire to see the face behind the words.

. . .

Ana awoke to the sound of construction. She shook off the light doze and rose, gripping the crossed bars on her prison and stretching to her tiptoes to get a glance.

At the base of the dungeon, a scaffold had been erected. Before she could consider the implications of this—or make inevitable comparisons to Anne Boleyn, whom she remembered had famously watched her own scaffold being built on the eve of her execution—her attention was diverted to the far side of the arena, where crowds were vying for entrance.

"Patience!"

"Not so fast!"

"In due time!"

Guards attempted to subdue the bloodthirsty Empyreans who were, apparently, here to watch the show. *What is this, Ancient Rome?*

Agripin's face abruptly blocked her narrow view. She gasped, backing away from the door.

"For Aidrik," he said, nodding toward the center of the arena. He kept his gaze there, away from her.

The humor from earlier faded from Ana's disposition, with such a rapid decline that she couldn't imagine where it had come from to begin with. Her evigbond was going to die before her eyes, and there was nothing she could do to prevent it. She wouldn't have the chance to say goodbye, or fully repair the rift in their bond that started with his loving lie.

They'd trusted this creature, followed him to Farjhem and supported what they thought was a shared dream of a better future.

"Fuck you, Agripin." She re-approached the door. A fire started somewhere, deep within her, somewhere near the darkness whose form was no longer nebulous but very real. "If you expect me to plead for my life, I won't. I won't plead for

Aidrik's, either, because he wouldn't want me to. I'm not going to ask you *why,* though you owe me an answer. I don't want it. I don't want to know what sick, depraved scum covers your heart. But I have something *I* want *you* to know before you take my life."

Agripin half-turned, so only his profile faced her. He looked weary of the whole business. *If you had the balls to start this, you'd better find the balls to finish this, you sick motherfucker.*

"Speak your mind, Ana," he said in a tone so low she hardly heard him.

Ana pressed her face into the bars, so roughly her skin protruded. *Look at me, motherfucker.* "You said before that you knew me. Knew things about me even Aidrik and Finn didn't know."

Agripin affected a slight nod. She noted he hadn't breathed out in nearly half-a-minute.

"Then you should know you can kill me, but you'll never be rid of me. A part of me, the part you're afraid of and *should be,* will live on, and haunt you. I'll be the passenger you can never get rid of. The parasite you can't kill. This part of me knows no restrictions like patience or failure, Agripin. I'll be with you until the sun goes supernova and kills every last person on this Earth, and even then, I won't let go of your soul. I will crush it in the infinite darkness that lives in me and will live on when you snuff my life away."

Ana shot her hand through the bars and gripped his robe, yanking him into the bars with a snap. "You will never, ever know peace again."

As she released him, a force issued forth from Ana that threw Agripin back. His head snapped as his body bent toward the bottom of the arena. Two guards quickly flew forward to right him.

Ana did not drop her eyes. As Agripin rose back up, he met them, for a moment, with a look that left her utterly perplexed.

Sadness.

59
NICOLAS

Emboldened by his new discovery, courtesy of Lucia, Nicolas decided it was time to move through the rest of his list of things he'd put off.

Most ideas flew into his head, and then out, unless it somehow brought him pleasure or amusement. Better, both. But two goals stayed prominent in his mind: the education of Aleksandr and reconciliation with Mercy.

Negligence in the Aleksandr matter was not entirely due to his own avoidance. As the days went on, Aleksei pulled further away from the household, burying himself in books. The kid, plain and simple, missed his parents. He didn't want to hear about second cousins thrice removed, or a retelling of the Deschanel emigration from France. For that matter, neither did Nicolas.

As a consolation, Nicolas would lay a hand on his shoulder when walking by, or tease him about inconsequential shit, but he was otherwise helpless.

Newly empowered with the knowledge he wasn't some

failed mystic, he committed to Aleksandr's tutelage with renewed focus.

Lucia didn't stir his nerves at all. He didn't inflate with ego, or dissolve with shame. He was, frankly, indifferent to her. As he was most women, unless he wanted to bed them. Maybe this seductive influencing had something to do with that. Even he had to admit the comedy in his ability coming forward as being a sex god, in so many words.

Now that he'd reclaimed his position as head of the household, he felt he could come to Mercy with something other than pathetic excuses.

He found her somewhere other than the bed. This seemed like a good sign, but her mind had always been a mysterious place to him. For a woman who was often straightforward, she guarded herself well, a trait Nicolas both envied and found frustrating.

The double doors off the third floor study rested open. Mercy was stretched out on the chaise lounge, eyes closed with a subtle smile.

"Hey," Nicolas said.

"Hey," she repeated, without opening her eyes. As she stretched, Nicolas realized she was sunbathing. *Sunbathing!* Oh, how her human life had come along, in the strangest ways.

"I'd like to talk. Now, if possible."

Mercy propped a hand above her eyes, shielding them from the sun. She looked at him. "Sounds serious, Nicolas."

Mocking him. Not that he didn't deserve it, but this stalemate wasn't doing either of them any favors. "Yeah, well, that's because it is. Can we talk?"

With an exaggerated sigh, she pulled herself slowly to a sitting position. "I have some things to say, too. But you first. I'd hate to see you injure yourself by wearing that expression too long."

Nicolas perched himself at the end of the lounger. Reflexively, she drew back. "I told you when you decided to stay that I wasn't any good at relationships."

Mercy smirked. "Well, when you put it that way, how could any woman have resisted?"

"You agreed," he pressed, already annoyed with her snarky defenses. *Chill. You can be the champion of comebacks tonight or you can get your point across.* "You told me we shared those beliefs. You know, that commitment isn't for us."

"Oh, yes. I did."

"I didn't mean to hurt you with the Eydis stuff. I'm not gonna make excuses though, and throw your words back at you. I wasn't looking for loopholes."

"Weren't you?"

Nicolas dropped his eyes to his hands, which twisted uncomfortably in his lap. He'd never been so nervous. "Look, I'm not just terrible at relationships, I'm shitty at family, too. You know about my fucked up father, twisted mother, and the long line of dead sisters. I'm not gonna cry about it, but I don't think I understood the impact on me until my family started to come together. Here, to *Ophélie*. I've never had so many people need me."

She slipped her cardigan off the railing and draped it over her shoulders. Her silver hair shimmered as she pulled it free. His heart leapt. "What are you looking for, Nicolas? Sympathy?"

"No, and if you tried to give it to me, I'd tell you to fuck off," he retorted. "Sympathy is for assholes who want some kind of free ride or exception. I want neither."

"Then what?"

"I'm not justifying my actions. I'm explaining them. I've never had anyone in my life I cared about enough to fear losing except Ana, and we both know that shit was never healthy."

Mercy raised an eyebrow, but generously said nothing.

"I don't like the feeling. Fucking understatement... I hate it. *Hate* it. You know why I'm still here? Because I looked fate in the eye and told that bitch to go eat shit. You want my father, you crazy whore? Take him. Take my mom, too, and my three sisters who I never really knew. Hell, take Adrienne, who I genuinely grew to love, because I can handle anything you throw at me and bounce back. I'm Nicolas-fucking-Deschanel."

"You should consider putting that on your epitaph."

"I'll put Oz on the task. What I'm saying, Mercy..." He lifted his head. Her stony gaze disheartened him, but if he didn't get the words out, they would die in his throat. "What I'm saying is, I love you, and I need you to know it. I've never said those words to any of the women before you, and I'd like to never say them to anyone else but you."

"You don't love me," Mercy retorted, not missing a beat. "You think you do, but you're like the child who had their favorite toy taken away. I'm the first woman who has ever looked your bullshit in the face and decided *not* to let it in. I knew all along what you could do. I guessed you were a sensual influencer from the moment I knew you were a mystic. You yourself bore the confidence of a man who has never, not once, been rejected in any meaningful way. Yes, you've had loss. Terrible losses, and I wouldn't seek to diminish them, Nicolas, because no one deserves the cross you've carried. But guess what? You *haven't* dealt with it! You pretend to be a cold-hearted motherfucker, but the truth is, your repressed grief is going to eat you up and kill you one day. It will be the end of you."

Nicolas stared at her in disbelief. He'd only begun to digest her barrage of insults, but the foundation of them, the core of the words, was loud and clear. "Jesus, Clementyn. You don't have to take my feelings seriously, but none of that shit was necessary to reject me."

"Reject you?" She laughed so loud it startled him. "Solid gold! You are something, Nicolas Deschanel, something else all right! Blowjobs aside, when have you given me the time of day? So no, I don't believe you love me. *You're not capable of it*!"

What the hell was this feeling, a tingling in his chest, and behind his eyes? "Rage at me for fucking around on you, Mercy, but don't tell me what I am and am not capable of!"

"Words are words. If you wanted me to believe this confession of love, you should have showed me. Want to know the story your actions told? That you were slower to tire of me in the bedroom than most of your conquests. When you were done, you couldn't just get rid of me, or stop calling, or whatever it is you usually do when you discard women. Because you asked me to move in with you, you ridiculous man!"

Mercy stood, ripping her towel off the chair. "Love... damn you, Nicolas. Because I do love you, a real love, not this sulking rejection you're feeling when you think of me. I won't stay here and watch your feelings snap back and forth with your moods. I'm not mad at you for fucking Eydis, I'm mad at myself for not valuing my short remaining life enough to leave when I knew your thoughts were straying."

Nicolas rose, spreading his arms. "Leave? Why would you leave, when this entire thing was your idea?"

"I wanted to help my people," she replied, dropping her voice. "I thought I could do it here. But I'm restless. I want to fight by their side." Wrapping her towel around her, she looked toward the open doors. "I thought I wanted to fight by yours."

This conversation was ending, regardless of how many words were left to be said between them. Nicolas swallowed down the lump comprising his fears. "I want to fight by your side, Mercy," he whispered. His voice broke. With it, the tears he didn't think himself capable of. "Please stay."

Mercy's softened. Her breath caught. She rested her palm against his cheek, catching a tear that he should have been ashamed of, but wasn't. "I can't."

Back in the bedroom, Nicolas spotted his laptop lying open on the bed. He moved to close it and set it on the nightstand, when he noticed the screen was on and unlocked.

Satisfied she wasn't behind him after a quick glance over his shoulder, he couldn't resist a peek at what she'd been working on. What had kept her squirreled away from the world even before Nicolas betrayed her.

Our Father of Light, Our Father of Fire. I am yours in the flames.

Our Father of Light, Our Father of Fire. I am yours in the flames.

Our Father of Light, Our Father of Fire. I am yours in the flames.

Our Father of Light, Our Father of Fire. I am yours in the flames.

Our Father of Light, Our Father of Fire. I am yours in the flames.

Our Father of Light, Our Father of Fire. I am yours in the flames.

Our Father of Light, Our Father of Fire. I am yours in the flames.

And on, and on.

A cursor blinked defiantly at the end of page fifty-seven, daring Nicolas to continue the chant on her behalf. His reflection stared back at him from the glowing screen, the shock and sinking despair written across his tired expression.

I'm writing my memoirs, she had said. So, where the hell were they? This surely wasn't it, this manifesto of blind faith and rambling prayers.

Or was it? Three thousand years she'd devoted her life to the teachings of Emyr. To the belief she was chosen for something great, and that her Ascension was her reward for that piety. Her words to Nicolas were of how foolish she'd been, and how she'd seen her version of the light when resurrected, but how do you turn off who you were for three millennia?

Nicolas saw his hand shake as he moved to close the laptop again. Then his eyes caught something else. *Page 57 of 58.*

He scrolled to page fifty-eight.

At last. A sign. Not like the phoenix in Rome, or Anders' false Ascension. Our Father has at last come to me! I am not forsaken after all. Not abandoned. I need only be patient.

Then:

He came to me in my dream again. My purpose is not here, with these rebels. The Brotherhood will only get in the way of the truer meaning I am meant for. I don't need Our Father to tell me Nicolas also stands as a wall between me and my cause. I've been foolish to love him, but what is life if not a series of lessons and tests? I will pass every one Emyr sets before me. I am His in the flames.

One final entry:

He's given me a glimpse of my purpose. Finally! Soon, all will be revealed. Earlier interpretations were misguided, but it isn't too late. What a glorious day it will be when I can stand for Emyr, as I have always wanted to, and declare myself his most willing vessel! Any day now... any day...

Bile sat in the back of Nicolas' throat, as he began to understand what he was reading: the ramblings of a madwoman. While he'd been downstairs toying with young girls or lazing around complaining about a lack of direction, Mercy had lain upstairs with her delusions, bathing in them like baptismal waters.

Her light steps rang in the hall. Nicolas gently closed the lid of her laptop and slid into the suite's bathroom, closing the door behind him.

He released the terrified breath he'd been holding.

60
JACOB

Jacob's mind had been so singularly focused on getting Amelia to safety, that it wasn't until she *was* safe that the weight of almost losing her hit him.

This wasn't like before, when she was imperiled. She'd let her empathic guard down long enough for the grief of others to consume her, causing her mind to hold her captive against her will. She wanted out, but couldn't find her way. Jacob had never once doubted she would fight 'til the very last to bring herself back.

Baldur had broken more than her body in that cabin. He'd stripped away her dignity, peeling back every layer of her resolve until she had nothing left but base instincts. There was a moment, when her refusal to submit turned to animalistic cries of terror and submission, and Jacob knew she'd fallen over the precipice. It was the catalyst that set Jacob to action, unearthing an ability he couldn't have guessed he had in a million years.

But she didn't come back, not because she was unable, but because she couldn't bear to.

The old woman, whom Jacob learned they called Freya, visited several times to fuss over Amelia, but there was nothing of use she could do. Amelia's physical wounds were healed or healing. Her heart carried vital blood throughout her body, pumping oxygen to her brain.

The baby? Jacob asked Freya hopefully, knowing the answer, praying for a better outcome than the one he knew to be true.

If your wife carried a child, she does so no longer.

Jacob was fully aware Amelia took her birth control like clockwork. In ten years, they'd never so much as had a pregnancy scare. Her conception felt like the work of divine intervention, but if that were true, why would they have this gift ripped from them in the cruelest, most vicious way possible?

The look in her eyes when Baldur revealed her pregnancy wasn't the same fear of the unknown she'd expressed whenever it came up between her and Jacob. A fierce, maternal flash passed over her eyes. She wasn't merely his wife in that moment, she was a mother, determined to protect her child at any cost.

Baldur's theft of her child was the last and final assault, the one that exceeded the sum of all those before. Now she was somewhere he couldn't reassure her of how utterly brave she'd been in the face of her attacker. They were alive now because of her refusal to submit. He couldn't have been half as strong, if he'd been dangling, beaten, and raped.

The recollection had a sudden, violent impact on Jacob. An immediate rage swept through him and he felt again, as he had in the cabin, his soul attempting to emerge forward.

With a start, he pulled it back. He reached for the water on the bedside stool, the mug he'd been dutifully feeding to Amelia every twenty minutes or so, and took a generous gulp.

His chest ached. *Padraig... you never mentioned anything about this!*

Where would he have drifted, if he'd let himself go?

"*Blanca,* if I could take everything he did to you, and make it mine to carry, I would. I would do anything, anything in all the world, to heal this, and strike it from your memory." Jacob curled into the side of her, nestling his head atop her shoulder, laying a kiss against her neck. Her skin was warm, her heartbeat strong, despite her decline. "The goddess told us it would be hard, but I never imagined... never thought she meant..."

He wrapped his arm around her, squeezing, breathing in the scent of her. Winter and clean linens. And love. "You're my heart, Amelia. Not a part of it, all of it. Every last beating inch.

"I thought when we came here that I'd lost my way, and could no longer see true to who I was. But I'm your Cianán, Amelia, the yin to your yang. You counted on me to be the roots of our tree over so many lifetimes... and I *remember*! I remember each lifetime now, the same way I remember the long plane ride from Dublin when I was sent to live in the orphanage, and as clear as the day you stood staring at me in the college pub. I don't know how it's possible, but I think I understand now that we aren't meant to have all the answers. Only the ones that matter. Our truths, Cerridwen. You're my truth, and I'm yours. And this isn't the end of our journey."

A flush rose to her alabaster cheeks. She stirred, but didn't wake. "I love you," he whispered. "And I'll do anything. Stay here and face the future the Quinlans insist on for us, or go home and forget all of it. We'll run away to the tropics and start a tiki bar for rich, bored celebrities. You can even take a pool boy as a lover, and I'll turn the other way and pretend I don't know. Whatever you want, I'll do. Just please, *Blanca,* come back to me."

The door opened to the sound of bickering. Two men pushed through, ignoring Freya's protestations.

Padraig had one hand on his hip, the other shaking at the taller, broader creature. Another Empyrean. *Great. I'm tired of guessing whether they're here to help us or kill us.*

"You are *not,* absolutely not, taking them on some sight-seeing journey!" Padraig exclaimed. "Seara thanks you for coming to their aid, but now they need to return back home with us."

The Empyrean smiled patiently down at the Quinlan. Then turned to Jacob. "I'm Holger. Birger and Astrid regret they can't be here, but they're off on official Brotherhood business, so they sent me, their emissary."

Padraig's whole body shuddered in a massive sigh. "Jacob, thank goddess, when Seara told us what happened—"

"Emissary for what?" Jacob asked Holger. "I don't even know who Birger and Astrid *are,* and no one's bothered explaining any Brotherhood, either." He smiled sheepishly at his trainer. "Sorry, Padraig. Thanks for coming."

Padraig nodded. "There was never any question. I left as soon we received word."

"It isn't my place to tell you about Birger and Astrid, or the Brotherhood," Holger said pleasantly. "But I've been asked to bring you to them, and I know they'll be more than happy to explain everything themselves."

"You've lost your mind! They're not going with you!" Padraig stepped forward, in front of Holger. He resembled a dwarf compared to the broad creature. "Jacob, we've barely started your training. I have so much more to show you, and Seara has much planned for Amelia."

Jacob gestured toward his wife. He rested a hand on her forehead. "Does it look like Amelia is traveling anywhere anytime soon?"

"She isn't safe in your tribe," Holger countered, but his eyes rested solely on Jacob. "I can protect her, Jacob. The Brotherhood can offer a protection to you that you'll find nowhere else."

"One of your own tried to murder them!" Padraig shrieked. "You're a bloodthirsty race, who betrayed us when it was too inconvenient to help."

"Baldur was not one of us," Holger replied. His unlined face was firm and set, but his eyes were bright. He watched Jacob with a soft look of a being who was somehow both warrior and caretaker. "I'd kill him myself, had Jacob not taken care of it."

Padraig snorted, looking away. "Violence and death, always your first recourse. Not that the scum didn't deserve it, but... wait... Jacob, how exactly *did* you get away from Baldur?"

A grin played at the edges of Holger's mouth. He gave Jacob a private wink.

"Long story," Jacob muttered. "Let's say I might be further along in your training than you think."

Padraig's jaw dropped as he moved forward toward the bed. "Did you time dance?"

"Time dance?"

"Amelia needs her rest!" Freya exclaimed, shooing Padraig and Holger back toward the door. "You can take your senseless feuding to the next room. Or the next house, even better!"

"Jacob, let's discuss this outside," Padraig implored. The young man looked worn from travel, but there was another weight on him. It seemed to Jacob he felt responsible for the situation at hand. "We don't have to leave today, we can wait until Amelia is ready to travel."

"I'm not leaving her side," Jacob answered. "I can't think when she's like this."

"Your place is with us," Padraig insisted. "With the goddess."

"The goddess is everywhere," Holger countered. "And you can't promise them safety from what's coming."

"Is that true?" Jacob asked Padraig.

Padraig said nothing.

THE DEBATE RAGED ON OUTSIDE THE ROOM OVER THE NEXT HOUR. Jacob stopped trying to listen about ten minutes in, because it was the same argument, over and over. Padraig insisting they needed the Quinlan guidance, Holger hinting something terrible was coming and Jacob and Amelia needed protection.

Jacob couldn't imagine anything worse than what had already happened.

Every second that ticked by brought renewed guilt. Jacob attempted to take his mind back to the exact moment he'd disconnected... not only the first time, but also later, here in the safety of the cozy house, when the memories started to come back.

Rage. Trembling, feverish rage. A fury boiling from deep within that had to escape somewhere. The overwhelming urge to destroy, to take. To reap what another has sown.

The first time Jacob felt this, he'd awoken in a hospital bed, recovering from the gunshot his father put in him. The nurse informed him offhandedly that his mother, brother, and sister died on the scene. Father, too. Then she went back to her rounds, smacking her gums, humming a song off-key.

He'd learned to channel this rage through his fists, but what Jacob thought were his greatest weapons had been nullified, pinned behind and above him as the horror unfolded. The fury boiled over, and had to go somewhere. So it went out.

If I could join with the bear... what else could I join with? He was tempted to find Padraig and ask him, but he didn't think he could handle the young man's inevitable barrage of questions.

Besides, Padraig would be scandalized if he knew why Jacob was asking... what he was thinking of doing. Jacob might be shocked, too, if the shock hadn't already been forever pulled out of him.

Amelia was dying. Doing nothing would allow her to slip away, where she was completely unreachable, until there was nothing left.

Jacob needed to show her how to fight. Show her *why* to fight.

The rage came immediately when he conjured the memories forth. The knife at his wife's neck, her nude figure drenched in her own blood. He could find enough fury for the rest of his life here, never running out of fuel.

Pushing, pulling from inside, as if he'd swallowed something unthinkably large and his body sought to expel it.

But he wasn't seeking to hurt. His aim was to heal.

Jacob's body fell back against the bed in a fugue. This extension of him—his soul? He didn't know... there was so much he didn't know—gazed down at the resting figure of his heart, and plunged.

CIANÁN PEERED ACROSS THE MOORS, SHIELDING HIMSELF FROM THE stifling winds rolling through the flat land. The sky was an even shade of grey. Muted. No color graced the blades of grass or the scattered yew trees bending with the gusts.

Cerridwen stood at the end of this greyscale world. Her feet played with the cliff's edge, as she seemed to test her bravery. Cianán knew without looking there was nothing beyond. If Cerridwen leapt, she would disappear and never return. Not in this life, or the next.

He could call to her, but he feared startling her, sending her over the edge by accident.

Time slipped away. Cianán broke into a low sprint, striding through the long grass and choking winds. The lack of pigment pulled at his soul, but his soul wouldn't answer this call. It was on another mission.

Cloudless rain poured from the heavens as Cianán strode across the plain, the journey lengthening with every footfall, making his goal feel less attainable the longer he ran. But Cianán had voyaged across the centuries for his heart, so what was a few acres of land?

Cerridwen's arms spread wide. She hung her head low, and even from the building distance, he could see the soft shaking of her shoulders as the sorrow beat through her.

He reached her, and didn't pause to give her time to adjust. He wrapped his arms around her and gently wrested her from the edge of the world, pulling her through the graying lands. "Síoraíocht, Mo mhíle stór," *he whispered as she cried against his chest, mourning what she believed was the loss of her own self. "Cerridwen, I need you."*

"I don't know how to erase the scars," she cried, squeezing a tuft of his hair in her fist. Her other hand wrapped around his neck, gripping tight. "I don't know if I should."

"They aren't only yours," he assured her, running his hands through her hair. A blush in her cheeks, the first color of this landscape, appeared. "I look into a mirror and I see your eyes behind mine. I'll spend the rest of our days helping you find a way to put this behind you. Behind us."

"Jacob, I didn't know about the baby. I swear to you, I would never keep a secret like that."

"I know, Blanca*."*

"I was throwing a fit, when you told me to leave. I wanted you to worry, the way I worried. It was revenge that caused me to run into those woods." Her mouth dropped, eyes widened. "My fault."

Jacob crushed her into him, the agony reflecting back too painful to look upon. "You've never said anything more foolish in your life," he insisted. "We've stumbled through this together. Neither of us has a clue what we're doing, and I'm tired of listening to everyone else. This is our life, Amelia. Ours to live, or ours to die. And dammit, I want to live, with you."

Amelia pulled away, and dropped her hands into his. "I don't want to go back to the Quinlans."

"Then we won't."

"They've told us what we need to know. I can't do this with them breathing down our necks."

"I know, Blanca. *Want to go to Bora Bora? I hear it's nice this time of year."*

She dropped her eyes, smiling. "You heard that?"

"Or maybe I thought it would sound good on our Christmas cards." Jacob pulled her hands up, pressing his face to her soft palms. "I don't care where we go. Really. Close your eyes and point at the map."

Amelia shook her head. "We can't run. We can't let creatures like Baldur hurt anyone else we love."

Jacob cringed at the sound of the devil's name on his wife's lips. "Then we'll hunt every last one of the bastards down. Together."

"What if I can't do this?"

"You can. I'll carry you the rest of our lives if that's what it takes. But I won't take one more step without you by my side, Amelia."

Her face settled into a stony resolve. "He won't win."

"No. We will."

AMELIA FLEW INTO A FIT OF HYPERVENTILATION WHEN HOLGER CAME into the room, scrambling back into the bed, nearly climbing the walls. Jacob held tight to her, reassuring her the imposing Empyrean was on their side.

"I've come from Farjhem, only days ago. I saw your cousin, Anasofiya," Holger said. Respecting her panic, he made no move to cross the room.

"Ana?"

Holger nodded. "She's well. As are Finn and Aidrik. And their dog."

"They have a dog?" Amelia frowned.

"A wolf. A familiar of Finn, the halfling." Holger ventured forward a step, but only one. In a gesture clearly unnatural for a man of his bearing, he showed his palms forward, raised slightly. "There are plans underway as we speak, Amelia. Birger and Astrid have sent me to bring you two to safety. By the time we reach Norway, Ana, Finn, and Aidrik will be out of Farjhem, and we will join up with them."

Jacob's own confusion reflected in Amelia's face. "But... why? What do we have to do with any of that?"

Holger's voice dropped, and he stepped forward again. "You have everything to do with it."

Amelia looked at Jacob, her expression a mess of emotion. "Do you understand any of this?"

"No," he replied. "And he won't explain it, either."

"Birger and Astrid reserved the right for explanation," Holger clarified, clearing his throat. "I'm confident they will hold nothing back."

Amelia gazed across the room thoughtfully. "Norway?"

"Aye. Not to Farjhem, though. We'll head to a safe house. From there, I've not been privy to the plan."

"And if we don't go?"

Holger's stone face was impassive. "Once the Senetat discovers you exist, you'll be destroyed. Amelia as well." He stepped further forward, then knelt by the bed. "The only goal for me in this world, at this time, is to protect you. I will lay down my life if the demand presents itself, in order to prevent the taking of yours. Please don't be foolish. The Senetat *will* find you. Events are in motion that will shake up the entire world as we know it, and you do not want to be left vulnerable when that time comes. Let me protect you. Both of you."

Amelia nodded at his belt. "Give me your sword."

"Eh?"

"My last encounter with an Empyrean left me with trust issues. Let me have your sword, and we'll go with you."

"You know Empyreans require no weapons for assault?"

"I wasn't raped with magic. I wasn't sliced open with a spell."

With a reluctant nod, Holger removed his sword belt. But he handed it to Jacob, not Amelia. "If you won't put your trust in me, I insist you put it in him. I can't abide us journeying unarmed."

Amelia slipped her hand through Jacob's and squeezed, nodding.

61

TRISTAN

"You haven't told me where we're going," Tristan said as they sped down River Road, driven by a very guilty-looking Richard, who'd declared at least a dozen times that Nicolas would murder him if he knew he'd taken them when the master of the house had instituted a lock-down.

"You said you trusted me," Harriett reminded him with a grin. "Besides, you haven't told me what's been on *your* mind, either."

"Huh?"

"Huh?" she parroted. "The stuff with Anders?"

"Oh. That." Tristan looked out the window with a sheepish drop of his head. He'd wanted to tell her when the moment was right, because if she didn't embrace it... if she didn't jump right on board... well, he didn't know *what* he would do.

"Yes. That."

"How do you know about that?"

Harriett tapped her temple. "When you're in my head, I'm in yours, too. I didn't even have to go looking. It's all you've been thinking about."

"Yeah... I didn't even know how I felt about it, really."

"But now you do?"

Tristan twisted in his seat, reclining against the cushioned door so he could face her. "He thinks I have something to offer the Brotherhood. I guess my distance telepathy is pretty rare even for them, but he also showed me I can do something else I didn't know about."

Harriett watched him.

"If I focus hard enough, I can breach a telepathic block. Over distances. That seems pretty badass, huh? Well, he thinks so, too, Harriett. And he thinks some of the important dudes in the Brotherhood will think so as well. He says they don't have *anyone* on their side who can do this, but the Senetat does. Can you imagine?"

"That you're amazing and special and rare?" She smiled. "That doesn't seem like such a stretch to me."

Tristan blushed. "You have to say that. You're my girlfriend."

"Is that what I am?"

Tristan's heart skipped. Was that too presumptuous? "I mean... unless...."

Harriett reached over and took his hands in hers, squeezing. "Feels like a silly word for what we have. My sister, Estella, went through boyfriends like socks. She probably couldn't even tell you all their names. Not that she ever cared, either."

"Well, what do you want us to be?" Tristan asked, in a mix of nerves and hopeful anticipation.

"I don't need a fancy title to love you," she replied. Leaning forward to kiss him, she added, "Wherever you think you need to go, Tristan Sullivan, I'll follow."

• • •

As they passed the sign announcing their entrance to Donaldsonville, Tristan realized exactly where Harriett was taking them: *Vivra sa Vie.*

His Uncle Augustus' plantation was more opulent than *Ophélie*, built in the Colonial style more familiar to Virginia or the Carolinas. Spanish moss draped over the live oaks and cypress, the gardens sculpted to every last detail, framing one of the most well-manicured properties in the state of Louisiana.

It was also where his mother wrote her letters goodbye, and then plunged to her death in a misguided attempt to protect him.

"I'll be back in an hour!" Richard declared, through a gap in the window from the front seat. "If you're not here, I'm telling Nicolas you ran away."

"Richard, we wouldn't dare be even a moment late," Harriett pacified him.

"Why are we here?" Tristan asked when the car was a spot in the distance. He'd been here once, as a child. Uncle Augustus offered it to his sister Elizabeth, Tristan's mom, when she was in one of her depressive spirals. *The change in scenery would do you good, Lizzy. If not for you, for the kids.*

Tristan and Danielle had swung from the low cypress branches, and fished with bare hands in the swamps beyond. Meanwhile, Elizabeth had lain in the master suite, staring at the patterns in the wallpaper.

Tristan might never know why she'd chosen to return here to die, but her reasons didn't matter. She was gone. Danielle was gone. Gone, gone, gone.

"I can't bring her back. Either of them," Harriett said. Her warm breath heated the space between his shoulder blades, and this closeness, this very *realness* of her, brought tears to his eyes. "They haunt you, Tristan. We all have our ghosts, but yours eat you alive from the inside out."

Tristan's gaze traveled to the third floor gallery, noting the coat of fresh paint on the patio below where his mother's blood had stained the beautiful portico and furniture. Her last thoughts had been of him.

"Neither one of them had to die!" Tristan shouted, raising his face toward the oak before him, to the green leaves extending into the sky where a storm was swirling. "But they were both my fault. Dani was trying to make me feel better, and my mom was trying to save me. I didn't ask for either of them to do it. I didn't ask."

Harriett caught him as he sunk to his knees. The sobs were unstoppable as they rolled forth, rooting him to the grass. "You didn't kill them, and it's time for you to stop blaming yourself for things you had absolutely no control over."

He buried his face in his palms, ashamed of his tears. "I miss them both so damn much. It isn't just this family that's cursed, it's me."

Harriett's arms were around him in an envelope of protection. Her face rested in the fold of his neck as she rocked him. "You are *not* cursed! You saved my life! You traveled across the world to help bring your cousin happiness, not knowing if you'd return. You've given up your life to help others. You are the bravest man I know, Tristan Sullivan."

Her words offered a deeper comfort and validation than he'd ever known in either the arms of his mother, or the giggles of his sister. Harriett had no other motive than her pure truth, and her words were the simplest and truest form of sincerity.

Tristan was not the boy of a year ago, sadly lusting after a married woman because he didn't think life could be better.

Drinking himself through the city because he didn't think he *deserved* better. Punishing himself for being the one who lived.

"You have to forgive yourself. It's okay to grieve, and you will, for the rest of your life. But you can't hold on to this guilt. *I won't let you,*" she whispered. Her own tears tickled the back of his neck.

"I can't stay in New Orleans anymore. I thought helping Nic might be enough, but I have to go, far from here. I *need* to go, like Anders suggested. Please say you'll go with me. I don't want to take this adventure without you," Tristan sobbed, turning to bury his face against her chest.

"I already knew, silly. I've been mentally packing my bags for weeks," she teased, lifting his chin. "But we have one more thing to do here first. You still trust me?"

Tristan nodded, his eyes following her as she stood, and pulled a padded envelope from her bag.

He wanted to ask, *What's that,* but as she was pulling back the seal, and removing the contents, he was thinking of the day he opened a similar envelope, to find his mother's final words to him. Her final sacrifice as a parent.

Harriett handed him the letter, then reached into the envelope and pulled out one more thing: one of Danielle's ridiculous drawings. One of a million times she'd drawn the same thing, but the only one he'd saved, tucked down in a box of toys he once loved and no longer needed.

She reached into her bag once more, and removed a small gardening spade. "Colleen brought it for me," she explained. "When she came for her weekly meeting with Nic."

Tristan reached forward and took the hand spade from her, understanding finally why they'd come.

They walked to the base of the oldest live oak, the one with the deepest roots and longest branches. Tristan knelt down between two of these roots and dug the spade into the damp earth, removing small triangular wedges until he'd made a hole the depth of his forearm. Any deeper and he feared he'd hit the water table.

Harriett passed the mementos to him, then placed both hands on his shoulders. They were his to bury.

He folded his mother's letter inside the old drawing, then placed them both in the ground. Harriett helped him alternately push and pack the earth back over his memories, until there was nothing but freshly disturbed ground.

"I wish I could have saved you both," he said to the stately tree now shielding his guilt. Harriett sprinkled some small seeds out of a packet, then smoothed the ground over. "But she's right, I couldn't have. I don't know where we're going, but it's time for me to live my life now. Take care of Dad for me."

"Thank you, Elizabeth, for bringing this wonderful man into my world. And Danielle for being an amazing sister," Harriett added. "I promise to love him with all my heart, and take care of him for you."

Time passed, and the storm clouds rolled in. Tristan pulled Harriett into his arms and they curled up together under the protection of the mighty oak.

"Do you know where we're going?" Harriett asked.

Tristan shook his head. "I don't know if Anders is sending us ahead of him, or if we go when he goes. He doesn't seem to be leaving imminently."

Harriett sighed, snuggling closer. "It doesn't matter. I don't know how much longer we all have, so I want to spend whatever time God gives us, together."

"Until the very last," he promised, pressing his lips to the crown of her head.

"Wherever fate takes us," she added, as the first of the rain fell against the earth. Soft drops ran down wide leaves to gently patter disturbed dirt, coaxing the impatiens seeds Harriet had sown to life.

62
CYLER

"Great show, wouldn't you say?" Oriana remarked to him, swishing her ivory kimono across the packed chambers. Agripin sat at the head of the long table, the Senetat gathered around the room without bothering to sit. Firing questions, making demands. Cyler lost track of the specifics about a minute in.

"I don't find treason amusing," he muttered in response, distracted. He watched Agripin closely as he fielded the Senetat's rapid-fire commentary. His master's thin veneer had been close to cracking since they took his friend and empress away in chains. Cyler worried he was on the verge of losing it.

"For one who practices it on such a frequent basis, I would think otherwise, Vakkar," she smartly retorted.

He didn't protest. Better to say nothing, and further, he had no time for her games. Everything was sport with Oriana, and while in moderation this could be charming, she was wearing him down. Outside her usual backdrop, the magic of her delectable facade seemed the crude work of smoke and mirrors.

And now, he no longer had to put up with her, and dance around topics. Agripin was the leader of all Empyreans, now, all obstacles removed. Oriana would slink back to her cave, neutered and disempowered, and Cyler could get the hell out of Farjhem. Sooner was better.

But with or without Aggie? The night before, he thought they were in accord. Now, his master was exhibiting some very troubling behavior. Having second thoughts was the only conclusion Cyler could come to, since he hadn't been able to sneak even a second in private to ask what the hell was the matter.

"You didn't think Agripin would still dote on you once he took his crown, did you?" Oriana accused in a sing-song pitch. "Aww, Vakkar, you did. Poor dear."

"I'm his bodyguard," Cyler snapped back, eyes never leaving Agripin. "My job is here, where I can see the room. And the door."

"I hardly think the Senetat is going to drag him out and engage in fisticuffs!"

Cyler gestured behind him, toward the door leading back into Farsengel. "We were at the same coronation, right?"

She scoffed. "Criminals. They deserved it. Ever notice how all races, all cultures on this Earth, consistently view treason as an offense punishable by death?"

Cyler rolled his eyes toward the ceiling, praying to Emyr for the strength not to strangle the emperor's sister.

"Unless you're implying they might drag Agripin out because *he* himself has committed treason?" She blinked her eyes in insufferable innocence.

"Watch it. You're walking a fine line, Oriana."

"Duchess!" she exclaimed. Several of the eldres turned to her outburst with annoyed looks, then went back to the task at hand. “I don’t care who you bend over for, Vakkar, you will afford me my proper respects.”

Please, Aggie. Can’t we kill her? You wouldn’t miss her, and if someone was hell-bent on taking the reins of The Menagerie, it wouldn’t be a hard sell.

“Ahh, look! Pay close attention, Vakkar!”

Cyler looked forward, annoyed at his compliance. Agripin stood and faced the room. His smooth face had worry lines deeply embedded. The dark crescents under his eyes were harrowing. “We will move forward with the execution of Aidrik the Wise.”

Cyler’s heart flipped.

The Senetat was appeased.

They had the answer they wanted.

The second test was over.

63
ANASOFIYA

Ana paced the small cell, back and forth, back and forth. Stopping every few rounds to see if they'd dragged Aidrik to the scaffold yet. Her pupils dilated, struggling between the dingy light of her compartment and the glaring ones of the arena outside.

No one had been by again. Not the guards, or Agripin. A skin of water landed in her cell with a flop but when she went to see who tossed it, no one was around. She turned her head in disgust, the flask untouched on the dirty hay despite her thirst.

In the moments after Agripin walked away from her, Anasofiya Aleksandrovna Vasilyeva St. Andrews Deschanel ceased to be entirely in control. The dark swirl that formed within her heart when she was only a girl, and had increased in substance and awareness after the birth of her son, had shifted from a position of plaguing influence to a bold assertion of control. It found a voice, not one that sounded like Ana's own inner monologue, but a wholly unique and separate sound. The rasping lilt of something ancient and ominous.

The shift from a whispering sensation to a forceful entity demanding recognition meant Ana could no longer ignore it.

Who are you? Ana asked the darkness. Inside her, it swirled and re-formed into various shapes, poking at her ribs, creating a silhouette as it pressed against her. *What are you?*

I am you. You are me. We are I.

No, you are not me because I don't speak in enigmas. You're renting space in my body, and I have a right to know. I demand to know! Who are you? A demon?

I am what you are, Anasofiya. You created me.

I can't create something I can't even identify. You came from somewhere. Tell me!

You conceived me in your heart. I took form when you were born in heartbreak, to a mother who didn't love you. I grew as your sadness grew. Every retreat to the darkness, fed me. I came from nowhere but you.

That's impossible.

Finn is right. You are a silly girl.

Ana fell back against the wall, clutching her knees. Laughing. *I'm losing my mind. That's the only explanation, I'm having a goddamn conversation with myself before I die.*

Worry not, silly girl. You grew me from your darkness, and so darkness I am. Darkness like you've never seen, child. The world isn't ready, but you are. You've accelerated toward this moment your whole life.

My death at the hands of a bunch of evil, narrow-minded men?

I've always done what you cannot, Anasofiya. You are who you are. I am who I am. We are what we are, our natures fixed, functioning in perfect symbiosis. You've simplified me to a wraith and a voice because you've not seen what I can do. But you will.

Ana's laughter sounded strange and foreign to her, strained to the point of insanity. How did any of this matter when very soon she would be nothing but a memory, returned to the earth? *Is that a threat, Wraith? Death to the non-believer? Grab your pitchfork and stand in line behind the rest of the angry mob.*

Hurt you? I could never. Was it her imagination, or did her invisible passenger sound offended? *I am you. Safeguarded you for all your years, to the extent I might, in my restricted form.*

How are you talking to me now?

They're coming. Guards.

What? Why?

But her wraith had slipped back down under. Ana had no illusions of it going away for good, though. Something pivotal had happened in its development, something that made conversation possible. What it meant, other than her apparent complete descent to madness, she couldn't guess.

A shadow passed before the cell window. A face filled the bars. "Rise and be brave now, you treasonous whore. Your concubine is saying his final words," the guard taunted with an audible sneer. His footsteps faded down the hall.

Ana shot to her feet and rushed to the bars. Aidrik, her evigbond, stood proudly on the raised platform atop the scaffold, holding his head above the Senetat who gathered before him, declaring their pronouncements of his fate. They'd waited a long time to watch him suffer for free-thinking.

Behind them, Agripin watched. His expression had a purposeful poise to it, but he shifted from foot to foot, grimacing. *You disgusting creature. You weasel of a man. I'll haunt you 'til the end of your days, and then follow you to hell if I have to.*

"Aidrik the Wise. What do you say, in answer for your crimes?" Grand Eldre Servius boomed. His voice was absorbed into the throngs of Empyreans watching in silent fascination. Hundreds, maybe thousands. Watching one they'd once held as the best of them, and now doing nothing to speak for him.

"I answer to only one: Our Father, Emyr." Aidrik's voice was strong.

Ana was incredulous at the callousness of this mob mentality, this entire race eager for a retribution they didn't even understand! "Not one of you? Not even one of you bastards will speak for him?" she screamed through the metal bars, though her shouts were drowned in the vast space between her and the center of the arena.

Aidrik looked up. Their eyes locked, but before she could soak it in, that she was looking at her evigbond, most likely for the last time, a guard threw the door open, knocking her backward.

Ana bounced off the wall and rushed forward, plowing into the creature so hard he was knocked back a step. Frantic, she pummeled him, beating blindly with her fists, scrambling for the door.

"Anasofiya," the guard said. "Kjære."

This stopped her. The guard's hands were on her arms, gently, helping her up. One of those who had tormented her on the ride to prison. But his eyes...

Ana sagged in the guard's embrace. Her knees wobbled. "Aidrik?"

"Aye," he replied. An arm slid around her middle, pulling her up. "Don't ask how. There was much about my life as a mystic I never had time to share."

"You can't let them do this, you can't just let them kill you, Aidrik!" She pawed at his face, her heart skipping, then stopping, racing again. She glanced out the window to see Servius mounting the platform toward Aidrik's vessel.

"Anasofiya, this battle is lost." The weight of his pessimism hit her harder than any other moment leading up to it. He was her rock. Her solid mate who she'd drawn so much strength from, even when she was pushing him away.

He pressed his forehead to hers. Tears spilled down his borrowed cheeks. "I have loved thee well, Kjære."

His cracked lips kissed her roughly. She threw her arms around him, begging him to fight, to pull out some last stop as he always had. Always! He always had a way out, and never, ever gave up.

"Please, I'm begging you, I will do anything. Please, Aidrik, if you can do this temporarily, you can take this body forever, please," she sobbed, pressing her arms into his strong chest, pushing him away so she could wrap her arms around his chest and pull him closer. "*Please,* Aidrik! *I love you*!"

The guard went limp, drooping in her arms before sinking to the floor in a heap. She stepped over him, rushing toward the open door, in time to see Aidrik raise his arms to the sky, to the god he'd never stopped believing in despite his failed religion, as all nine members of the Senetat brought down a rain of joined lightning upon him.

As the electricity passed through him, his resolved grimace evidenced his unflinching strength, even now in the end, when there was no victory to be had.

Aidrik dropped to his knees. He wavered in the air and then fell face-first off the platform, into the center of the scaffold.

Anasofiya's heart stopped beating. The world spun into a blinding white wave as she threw her head back and howled.

64

ALEKSANDR

Aleksei awoke from the worst nightmare of his short life. His father stood trial for an unclear crime. His mora was forced to watch as his life was snuffed out. As he died, she fled to a place he could no longer detect her.

His teeth clattered as the room flowed into focus. *A dream, only a dream. I would know if something happened. I'd sense it.*

Aleksei waited for the clutching panic to pass. His dreams were often vivid and awful, but mercifully the feelings passed as soon as he regained all his senses.

Moonlight spilled through the wispy curtains, cutting a swash across his quilt. He breathed in, breathed out. Grabbed his head and shook it, squeezing his eyes shut, then opened them again.

The feeling wasn't passing. *It. Wasn't. Passing.*

His breaths turned to gulps, which quickly faded to whimpers. *No, no, no, no, no, no, no.*

Uncle Nicolas appeared in his doorway. His look was a mirror of Aleksei's troubled, disbelieving heart. When he saw

Aleksei's tears, he closed his eyes and bowed his head low, releasing a drawn, resigned sound that removed all doubt.

Aleksei leapt from the bed and rushed into his uncle's arms in one long, inelegant stride. The sobs left him in strangled, choking moans as Nicolas' hands pressed him close, comforting him, wordless.

THEY FOUND ANDERS OUTSIDE, STARING DOWN THE PATH LEADING TO the road. His head tilted to the side, frowning in pensive thought.

His eyes widened in close examination of both Aleksei and Nicolas' expressions. "Tell me."

"Aidrik is... gone," Nicolas said, giving a careful glance to Aleksei. Gone, dead, destroyed, executed. They were just words, and they couldn't hurt him. They couldn't cut like knowing he would never see his father again.

Anders nodded and looked toward the river. "I sensed the ward on the property break. I wasn't sure of the cause."

"Mora can bring him back," Aleksei realized, brightening. "She can bring him back, like she did Mercy! Right?"

Nicolas looked down. "Aleksei... I think... I think if she could have, she would have by now, son."

"Anasofiya is okay, then?" Anders clarified. "And the other, Finn?"

Nicolas nodded. "I'd know if Ana was hurt. And kid here would know about his dad. We both felt it when Aidrik..." He bowed his head. "I felt it from Ana."

"I wonder what happened. Do either of you know?" Anders asked, as if he were inquiring about why it had rained when the weather called for sun.

"They killed him!" Aleksei cried. "And they're going to kill Mora too, and Far, probably, if we don't stop them!"

"Stop them?" Anders repeated with a blank look. "How, Aleksei? Can either of you open a portail to Farjhem? No? And even if you could, what then?" He sighed. "I'm sorry about Aidrik. Grief can come only after we solve our very big problem."

"The ward..." Nicolas' eyes widened.

"Ward?" Aleksei asked.

"The reason you and your family were safe here. Why your mora sent you," Anders responded. "Aidrik's ward has been attached to this property for centuries. More than likely it is the singular reason the Senetat never learned of the Deschanels' existence. The center of it rests here, over *Ophélie*, where the strongest protection resides, but the magic has a radiating effect. Weaker as it spreads, so its tendrils have likely sheltered your relatives in New Orleans, too." He glanced toward the house. "His death released it."

Nicolas rubbed his eyes. "Fucking hell. How long do we have?"

"Not long enough," Anders replied. "Only a mystic can create a ward. By fate's sense of eternal humor, we happen to have *two,* but I'm going to go ahead and guess you haven't ever created one?"

Nicolas shook his head slowly. Aleksei looked down in shame. He'd spent his time at *Ophélie* pouting, angry at the world, and his parents, for not thinking him worthy of coming along. Aidrik could spin wards, so that meant he probably could, too. But he'd never bothered to learn.

Anders raised both brows. "Well, we will know pretty quick whether you can or not. A ward is as simple as imagining a blanket of protection. You stretch as far as your powers allow, and then envision it adhering."

"This isn't like the movies at all. Where's the training montage? The months of failure?" his uncle muttered, but there was no glint of mischief or smart-ass grin. He looked hollowed out.

"Have you been listening to me at all these weeks?" Anders blinked. "There's no great secret to magic. You have it or you don't. You use it or you don't. You can improve, but this isn't *Harry Potter,* where you have to attend a damn university for wizards. I made you train to develop focus, not train to *do* magic. We don't weave spells, we envision outcomes."

This gave Aleksei hope. Focus was no great task for him. He could focus for hours on end when he was deep in a book he loved.

"So try, both of you. Now," Anders prodded.

Nicolas stepped away from them, squishing through the wet grass. Aleksei looked after him a moment, then squeezed his eyes closed, focusing as hard as he'd ever focused.

He envisioned a thin membrane, invisible to all but him, stretching up from the ground. It started at the river and grew, expanding well over the top of the three-storied mansion, disappearing behind to cover the outbuildings, into the swamp, and further still, down the interstate, following the river as it bended toward the city. The sheath grew legs as it rooted, digging deep into the ground, further even, into the Earth's mantle.

When all the legs were plunged in, Aleksei opened his eyes with a hopeful smile. "I think... did I do it?"

Anders' eyes darted to the river, and back. "It's not rooting. You can create, but you can't adhere. Damn it!"

"What about Uncle?"

"Useless," Anders muttered, without apology. "I always wondered how Aidrik sealed his ward. Maybe he had help?"

Nicolas grabbed Aleksei by the arm, tugging him back toward the Big House. "We're getting out of here. I'm not sitting around waiting to be picked off like fish in a goddamn barrel."

"Stop," Anders commanded, but the sting was gone from his voice. "Keep trying."

"But you said—"

"Maybe it's different for halflings. Maybe you do need to practice. Hell, I don't know." Anders ran his hands through his rust-colored hair, tapping his foot. "Running will do nothing. If we stay, we have the advantage of knowing the landscape. Call your other halfling relatives, and we can make a stand here, together. That's worst-case scenario. Best case, one of you figures out how to make Aleksei's ward stick."

Aleksei looked to Nicolas for guidance. There was no other in the household he trusted like he did his uncle. His mother placed her faith in him, and so he did as well.

"He's right," Nicolas said finally.

"I could stop time," Aleksei said quickly. Heat rose to his face. "I did it before. If they come here for us, I can stop time."

"No," Anders said steadily. "You're a long way from being ready to use that ability on your own. And even if you could, it's too dangerous to stop time for more than a few moments, at most. You'd cause more harm than good, Aleksei. A ward is the best way. It's all we have."

"What about Mora and Far? What good would a ward do, when they're in danger now?"

Nicolas set a hand on his shoulder. "You don't know your mother as well as I do, Aleksei. I have a feeling that whoever hurt your father is about to know some pain of his own."

65
AMELIA

Floating somewhere in the North Sea. That's what Holger had said when Amelia asked exactly where they were. That they'd walked from somewhere in Ireland to somewhere near the Norwegian shores, in a matter of minutes, was less jarring than it should have been. A terrakinetic? A portail? Sure, why not?

As a counselor—a doctor now, actually. She kept forgetting this hard-earned designation in the face of the ongoing madness—she understood the distinction between a healthy suspension of disbelief and full-on delusional acceptance. But where was the line in their world, where anything seemed possible?

Her own world continued to close in on her, despite the promise to Jacob. He wanted so badly to save her, to be the hero this time, instead of sitting idly by while she suffered alone. Amelia wished she could give him this gift, more than anything. He deserved that and so much more. The best she could offer was to pretend, for now, until she no longer could.

They'd required clothing. The jeans and sweater Amelia had been wearing when she left the Quinlan village lay destroyed on the floor of the old cabin. Jacob's were thrashed also, a story she knew he'd tell her one day.

Here, Freya said before they departed with Holger. *It's not what you're used to, but fashion is of the least import at the moment.*

Amelia had been given a pair of women's riding capris and slender boots with laces to the knee. A peasant blouse accompanied the apparel, which was topped off with a man's waistcoat.

How very Steampunk, Jacob noted with a bemused grin, until he was handed his own Victorian-era breeches, hunting shirt, and travel cloak.

Hopefully when they found Birger and Astrid, clarity would follow.

THE BARGE THEY WAITED ON WAS FLAT, SO MUCH SO THAT SHE HAD TO squint to see where the ship ended and the sea began. Shoreline bobbed in and out of the fog blanket.

"Why aren't we moving in?" Jacob voiced her question.

"Waiting for a signal," Holger replied. He passed a skin of water their way. Amelia accepted with a grateful smile and took a generous sip. He nodded toward a small shelter, a tent basically, in the center of the vessel. "You can rest if you'd like. I'll wake you when the time comes."

"Where's Farjhem?" Amelia ventured, squinting toward the shore. "Can we see it from here?"

"No," Holger replied. He pulled an apple from his coat and tossed that at her as well. She caught it squarely. "You can't see it because those tall glaciers block the view. See over there?" Amelia and Jacob nodded. "Beyond that, though... ah, I can already smell the baking bread."

The nostalgia in Holger's words was a sad kind. He hadn't offered any better glimpse into what awaited them, but Amelia was quite confident they would not be breaking bread or singing songs around a hearth.

"We're meeting Birger and Astrid?" Jacob pushed, his innocent approach clearly designed to get Holger to share even one detail. His tactics were transparent to Amelia, and so she was certain they were to their host, too.

"Aye." Holger tossed Jacob an apple, then began to carve up his own.

"And then what?"

"You'll need to ask Birger. Don't worry yourself; Birger is one of the finest creatures I know. He'll give you his full protection, aye, but also his famous hospitality."

They'd get nothing more from him than that, she was confident. Sitting in awkward silence for untold time would be unbearable, though, and his barge afforded no real privacy or place to slip away.

"Open your mind to me again," she whispered to Jacob. He'd closed it back in the cabin to protect her.

I want to know what he's not telling us, Donnelly. I don't think he's hiding anything maliciously, but I don't like walking into things blindly.

Preaching at the choir, sweetheart. But the man's Stonewall Jackson. Or like those guards at Buckingham Palace... the Queen's Guard, with the funny red hats? We could try tickling him to death, or insulting his ma. Want me to teabag him?

Amelia suppressed a smile at Jacob employing his best defense. *I'm serious. I don't have a good feeling about this.* She glanced again at the shore, bobbing as they ebbed on the soft current. *He's cut himself three times on that knife. Things aren't going the way he expected.*

So, you don't want me to teabag him?

No, I do, absolutely. She did smile this time. Jacob squeezed her knee. Holger shot a curious glance their way, then went back to his apple. *My seer's sense is all out of whack, ever since...*

Jacob nodded. *Yeah.*

It's all over the charts. Maybe it's malfunctioning, I don't know.

You? Malfunctioning? Never!

I know, I know. Completely illogical in my vast and unending perfection. She shocked herself at how easily she played back. Bantering with Jacob was her favorite pastime, but she no longer felt like the same girl who had giggled at his jokes as he kissed his way down her body. She wished she could get that back, but her actions now were on autopilot, the result of her mind and body still being in a state of shock. Once it faded...

It's Ana. I sense something terrible has happened to her, and I can't get it out of my head.

"Jacob," Holger broke in. They both jumped at the unexpected intrusion, forgetting for a moment they weren't alone. "I've only met a handful of draoi in my wandering. All of them buzzed with the Earth's energy, as you do. But the others were constantly drawing. I haven't seen you do so once."

"I only draw when I need it," Jacob replied.

"It's a part of you. Don't guard yourself so closely. Let the goddess work through you always," Holger admonished. He tossed the apple core into the fog, where it disappeared in mid-air.

"Says the Empyrean," Jacob teased lightly.

"Our two kinds go way back," Holger replied. Sadness flashed in his eyes. "There are still some who would seek to protect that alliance."

"Like Birger and Astrid?"

"Aye."

Score! Jacob sang in her head. *Played him like a fiddle.*

A fortuitous accident, Donnelly. Don't add that one to your score sheet just yet.

"Have you time danced yet, then?" Holger asked.

Jacob wrapped his arms around Amelia as a cold breeze whipped over the current. "I don't know what that is."

"Time travel. Time spinning. All kinds of names for it, I suppose," their host responded. "I see from your blank look you've no idea what I'm on about."

"I'm still learning," Jacob defended with a sheepish half-smile.

"And I've taken you away from your teacher." Holger seemed to realize this now, when he didn't while arguing with Padraig. "I'll teach you myself, then, Emyr willing."

"You can time dance?"

Holger shook his head and laughed. "No! I know of no Empyrean who can time dance. Manipulate the strands, yes, if you can find yourself a powerful mystic. But ride through time? No. I did once meet a draoi in the middle of a time dance. He was disoriented but having the time of his life."

Jacob leaned forward. "How did he do it?"

"I can't say for certain. But all draoi power is culled from the same source. It's a matter only of learning to use it for your needs. Same as your warg skin."

Jacob's eyes glassed over in thought. "Fascinating."

"Fancying yourself a time jump?" Holger teased.

Jacob didn't reply, too enmeshed in the possibilities of this new revelation.

"It's no more than a whimsy," Holger went on. "Useless ability for anything beyond entertainment value. You can't change the past. A great help for impressing the ladies, I suppose, though you're not struggling in that area."

Thinking of going back to catch the aliens building the pyramids? Amelia teased.

Busted. I'm actually considering what you said earlier, about Ana.

Oh. Maybe it's nothing. She'd gone from earlier trying to convince him of her urgency, now to wanting to protect him from it, and she didn't know why.

It isn't nothing, Blanca. *Something feels rotten in the state of Norway to me too.*

Denmark. Not Norway. It's from Hamlet.

I know you like to pretend I'm your little uneducated proletarian Irish wharf rat to shock your Catholic school girlfriends, but I have read Dickens.

You know that isn't true! I never said I found you on the wharves.

Jacob's head dropped on her shoulder, and she felt his whole body shudder with a sigh. *God, I love you so much. So bloody much. You'll tell me when you need me, won't you? You wouldn't hide your suffering from me?*

So he'd noticed the act. Of course, he was always sensitive to her changing moods and needs. *Right now, I have to focus on what's ahead. I can't look back. As soon as I do, it's over. Even when my memory hits the edges, my heart stops altogether and the world goes black.*

I won't let it, he promised, with the errant foolishness of one who knows his words might not be true, but believes they could be if he says them enough. Oh, how she loved this man. *I'm sorry for what I did back in the clan. I did what my pa would've done, and I'm not proud of it. You can punish me any way you like.* At this, he winked. *But please, Amelia, don't push me away. Don't keep me from protecting you.*

I won't, Amelia promised. She closed her eyes to prevent the tears that threatened. *You can best protect me now by helping me look at the path ahead. Later we can look back. Maybe, I don't know.*

Okay. Anything you need.

You mentioned a tiki bar. And a pool boy. It was easier to banter on the surface, where she was still the same girl who could.

Jacob's eyes glinted. *Deal.*

66

ANASOFIYA

Ana's howls pierced through the disorder. The onlookers now diverted their gazes upward, where she hovered outside her cell, pulsing with the visceral darkness of her wraith, the latent energy of her evig-bond, and something altogether new. The third energy pierced her body, a flash that could not be contained and fought to escape, sending pins of light through every pore of her inflamed skin.

Many had come here with bloodlust, thirsty for a justice they didn't understand but craved anyway. Some still held on to that, reverting to behavior better suited for Neanderthals as they sounded their whoops and cries. Declaring the goodness and purity of their god through one side of their mouth, while their hunger for war and revenge spewed vilely from the other.

Most stood slack-jawed and pale-faced, staring into the horrifying results of what they believed they'd wanted. *Aidrik represented the best of us.*

Anasofiya could see no difference from one Empyrean to

the other. Every single one of their flaming heads and perfect ivory faces had sat by and *done nothing, said nothing,* as these overlords sent the sum of their magic through a being who had never inflicted harm on any of them. Not one.

Slowly, all eyes began traveling her direction. The empress, escaped from her prison, but that's not what drew their awe. It was the high-frequency quivering that started in her toes and radiated north, buzzing and humming as it traveled through her veins, her bones, her scorching flesh. In tandem, a wail that was neither human nor Empyrean nor anything else she could ever seek to define, escaped not only from her mouth but out every limb.

Aidrikaidrikaidrik.

I will avenge thee.

Ana extended her arm before her, gazing at it in brief astonishment. Then, on its own accord, the limb shot forward, and a blinding stretch of light, a thousand beams joining together in a power drawn from within her, arced across and downward, forming a ring that extended around the spectators.

"Guards!" Servius boomed, his flowing robe flapping as he pushed through the other eldres, searching in desperation for escape. Ana smiled and shot her other arm forward, sending a focused light that ripped down the center of the grand eldre and sent his body splitting into a thousand needles of exploding light.

The rest of the eldres gaped in horror. All except Maxima, who was nowhere to be found. They didn't bother yelling for the guards, because the guards were running the same direction as everyone else: the single door, which Ana focused on locking with her mind, melting the metal latch into one mess of steel. The panicked screams, the abject, raw terror coursing through every being in the building fed her. She grew taller, *fuller,* consuming their fear and turning it into more hatred, more of the same pulsing light.

With a great rush she expelled a breath. Dozens of voices pointed, screaming, *Look! Look!*

Eddying before her was her wraith. Its molecules swirled into a loose mass, then tightened into succinct spirals. In, out, with each unbreakable beat of her heart. *I am you. You are me.*

Say the word, Anasofiya.

You know my heart, Wraith. Or what remains of it.

So I do.

Her wraith shot forward, stretching its black skin to blanket the scaffold, where her evigbond lay slain. Empyreans attempted to scatter but the throng to the door was a thick, unbreakable chain of horror. The wraith fell upon them with a furious dive. Ana didn't wait to see the outcome.

Not that there was much left of *Ana* anymore.

All of her, her blinding rage, her heartbreaking losses, her incomparable love, had merged into one single entity, an energy that could no longer be contained within her.

The ferocious trembling at her feet caused spidery cracks to web out in all directions. The cement heaved under the weight of her unyielding rage. Somewhere, her wraith continued its own reign of terror, but that seemed so far away now, unimportant.

The quake fished through her calves, and up into her hips, igniting her belly. Pushing forth upward, outward, any direction it could find release. It burned every inch of her skin, scorching her soul with heat so consuming her vision vanished in a blaze of white light.

Let go, Anasofiya, her wraith sung from somewhere.

Ana obeyed the voice, as the last of her mind fled with the

rest of her human senses. The world went from white to black, with a sound so loud it could be felt deep in the marrow of anyone still unfortunate enough to be alive. So loud it would have taken her vision from her if was not already gone.

"AIDRIK!" she screamed with the last vestiges of her heart, before the entire world exploded.

67
NICOLAS

They couldn't do it. Maybe because they didn't have the skill, or maybe it was the lack of training, but after an hour of trying, Aleksei's tears put an end to their frustrated attempts.

"We'll figure something out," Nicolas said, the only words that came to mind, and ones he didn't really believe. Harriett's vision would come true after all. Everything they'd done since then to avoid their fate was pointless posturing... grasping at invisible straws.

Mercy appeared on the porch. She sprinted toward them, with Lucia and Livia in tow. "We need a Quinlan," she said. "To adhere your wards. That's how Aidrik did it."

Nicolas' stomach flipped to see her with purpose in her eyes once more. A purpose other than whatever he'd seen in her manuscript. "How do you know?"

"A mystic's ward is their most sacred ability," Mercy explained. She removed her reading glasses, tucking them into her cardigan. "And a product of the alliance between the Empyrean and Quinlan empires. The mystic created the ward, and the Quinlan would draw from the Earth's energies to seal it. This was always the way, until we broke our pact with them. Over time, the mystics who remained stopped trying, because they knew it was useless without a Quinlan's aid."

"Where did he get a Quinlan, Mercy, if we broke our alliance?" Aleksei asked, wide-eyed.

"I don't know," she replied, with a quick glance at him. "Aidrik kept a lot of his experiences close to his vest. He shared very little."

"Forget Aidrik, where the hell are *we* going to find a Quinlan, whatever the fuck that is?" Nicolas exclaimed. The sky over the river crackled with electricity. *Great. A fucking storm, on top of everything else.* "Could drive into Vacherie I suppose, ask around."

Mercy rolled her eyes. "You always have an answer for everything, don't you? *You're* the one who let your cousin's husband run off to Ireland. You know, the Quinlan?"

"What was I supposed to do, tie them down? They weren't indentured servants. Everyone was here because they volunteered, Mercy. You know that."

"Eydis said before they saw another one, with your cousin, Ana. But they're also on the other side of the damn world!" Lucia tugged at her flaxen hair. Her red roots were nearly an inch deep. *All you had to do was ask, chick. Condi could have picked you up some L'Oreal at the Piggly Wiggly.*

"Finn. Of course he's a Quinlan." Mercy shut her eyes. She pulled her hair back in a tight fist, looping her hands over her head. "An ocean separates us. And for all we know, he met the same fate as Aidrik."

"His son is standing right here!" Nicolas draped an arm around his nephew, gaping at her.

Mercy stared back, her gaze a test, as everything since she arrived had been. He couldn't keep up with her moods, as she vacillated from angry to reclusive, to passive aggressive and indirect.

"It's okay, Uncle, I know my far is okay," Aleksandr assured him.

"Can we take this conversation inside?" Lucia cut in, jutting her thumb toward the darkening sky. "I'd prefer not to be vulnerable *and* wet."

Nicolas snickered at the double entendre. Mercy stormed past him in a huff.

THE RAIN STARTED AS THEY WERE SITTING DOWN AT THE MAHOGANY dining table. Colleen and Luther showed up in haste, like clockwork, declaring they'd sensed a disturbance at *Ophélie,* asking why no one had called them. "That's putting it mildly," Nicolas replied. "What could you have done if we did call?"

"Never mind that. We're here now," Luther replied.

"Our family's strength has always been our ability to work together," Colleen added, rushing toward the kitchen to throw around orders for refreshments. "Evangeline will arrive on the next plane, and the other Council members are on their way now."

Markus showed up next, his first return since leaving to tend to his sister.

Tristan and Harriett joined them, though the latter resembled an apparition in her long white nightgown and blank expression. Tristan guided her to her a seat like an invalid, steering her as she bumped into the chair and table, apparently blind as a bat whose sonar was on the fritz.

The night before she'd been lucid and cheerful. Nicolas deduced this didn't portend well for the current state of affairs.

"We need to call the rest of the family!" Tristan looked

battle-worn as he struggled to keep Harriett from face-planting into her place setting. "Bring them here!"

"The important ones are here already," Anders said, straddling the head chair from behind as he joined them. "Unless you mean Jasper? He was relatively useless at anything except hiding the fine china from the visiting vagabonds."

"What are *you* still doing here, Anders? This isn't your fight. You could walk away unscathed, as you always do," Mercy snapped.

"You could stop being a reclusive, ungrateful bitch," Lucia retorted. She started forward in her chair, and Nicolas dropped a hand on Lucia's knee, cautioning. She shot him an annoyed glance, but he felt her muscles relax. "If you joined us every now and then, you might know we came to help."

"We're not calling anyone else." Nicolas shot a pointed glance at Colleen and Luther. "I mean it. We don't even know if anyone is coming for us, and I'm not sending this family into a panic. We Deschanels love that shit, but panic just breeds stupidity."

"This is not your decision to make alone," Luther rebutted, pouring himself some tea with the easy gestures of a man not on the verge of doom. "We'll wait until the rest of the Council arrives."

"You don't need a council to tell you you're doomed," Anders muttered.

"Luther," Colleen countered, motioning toward Nicolas, "as a council, we offered to help Nicolas. From the onset, this was his venture. His and Mercy's. It is their decision where we go next."

"It affects the whole family, Aunt C!" Tristan declared. His eyes shot wildly from chair to chair, looking for an ally. "He doesn't get to decide if we all live or die!"

"This time last year, we didn't know who Aidrik was, or

that a protection existed," Colleen reminded him. "*Ophélie* belongs to the heir. Nicolas is that heir, until the time he passes that honor to Aleksandr. The heir has always operated outside of the Magi Collective rules. The protection was meant to serve his line. Not ours."

This sobering thought sent an uncomfortable silence through the room. No one, not even Nicolas, had ever considered this.

"That isn't really true," Livia spoke up. Nicolas realized this was the first time he'd heard the girl speak since she showed up at their door with a small knapsack. "A mystic's wards are strongest at their center, but the power from them ripples beyond the source, and radiates for miles. Sometimes hundreds of miles, or more, depending on the strength of the caster and the adherer. The effect is diluted the further out you go, but I suspect Aidrik has protected this entire family with one ward. At least, those living in the region."

Lucia smiled proudly at the young girl, and gave her arm a light squeeze. "Livia is right. Thorvald taught her well."

"That would explain why only the residents of *Ophélie* had their abilities squelched all these years. They were closest to the source," Luther mused.

"See, this impacts us all!" Tristan professed.

Nicolas cleared his throat. "Everyone is assuming the Senetat's got scouts parked right on the fucking levee, waiting for Aidrik to drop and his ward to dissolve, but how would they even know to come here?"

"The Senetat has someone in their employ who knows how to breach a telepathic block. It's almost certain, at some point, Ana, Finn, or least-likely Aidrik, thought about *Ophélie* during their stay in Farjhem," Anders pointed out. He nodded his head at Aleksandr. "Probably quite often."

"Aidrik would have known that. He would have prepped Ana and Finn accordingly," Mercy defended.

Lucia fell back in her chair, arms crossed over her chest. Nicolas braced himself for whatever was about to come out of her mouth. "Why is it you have such a hard-on for Aidrik, but you think Anders is worse than the devil? They both abandoned you."

"Luc," Anders warned. His lips peeled back in a light snarl.

"Yes, but only one lied to me," Mercy returned, with a pointed glance at Anders.

Colleen perked, looking around the room. "Where is everyone? The children?"

"Oh, those. We lost them," Markus snickered.

"How do you lose children who have nowhere to go?" Luther boomed.

"And Anne? Is she napping?" Colleen added, with growing disconcertment.

"Nope, she ran off too," Markus returned, suppressing a smile.

"Is that funny to you?" their aunt demanded. "How did things come to this? Why, for the love of God, did you not reach out to someone if it was getting this bad?"

"Funny? No it isn't funny at all. It's damned pathetic that we ever thought we were even remotely qualified for this task." Markus stood. His chair tottered for balance. "We couldn't stop Anne, any more than we could have stopped those insolent brats who threw a fit when Nicolas wouldn't bang them, or allow them to burn the barns down!"

"To be fair, Nicolas did bang one of them," Tristan whispered. "And Sindre did burn a barn down."

"You keep saying the Curse is dormant, for now," Markus went on. His palms slammed down on the table, and he leaned toward Colleen. Everyone gaped at the bold disrespect. "Look around us! It never ends!"

Aleksandr's eyes widened. "What curse?"

Luther pushed his tea aside. "Where the hell are Pansy, Kitty, and Jasper anyway?"

Nicolas was gripped with an onset of a nested vision. In the background, the bickering continued across the table, but his mind was ripped crudely away, and dropped in the middle of complete mayhem.

Thousands of Empyreans were engulfed in flames as they piled before a door that was melted closed. A specter hovered above the carnage, swirling into various form. It seemed to be dancing.

Ana looked down at her charred hands. A match for her soul. Her terrible, horrible, exhausted soul. She was tired. So very tired, and there was nothing, not anything, holding her up any longer except the sheer luck of not falling.

With a rolling sway, Ana leaned forward, over the scaffold where Aidrik's remains were buried under the bodies of so many others, and pitched toward the ground.

Nicolas awoke on the floor, Mercy and Colleen kneeling on either side. The others peered over their shoulders in fearful curiosity.

Aleksei released a keening moan from the other side of the room.

"Ana," Nicolas croaked, clutching at his chest as if he could somehow stop his heart from breaking.

She's not dead. She's alive, sort of, there's that. But what's become of her?

Mercy held a cold compress to his forehead. She'd pulled a chair up next to the sofa in the study, where he lay, though he had no memory of how he'd gotten there.

"Your aunt and Luther took Tristan, Harriett, and Markus back to The Gardens. Emergency Magi Collective meeting they said. Livia, too. Not as though we can protect them better here anyway, with Aidrik's ward broken."

"Quiet, finally," Nicolas sighed.

"Anders and Lucia are still here. And Aleksei. He wouldn't leave you."

"Good." Nicolas struggled forward.

"Don't sit up," she said gently. She put the washcloth aside and instead laid her palm against his brow, brushing his hair back. "Ana's alive, but Aleksei's lost touch with her. I don't know what it means, but she's alive."

"She wasn't herself," Nicolas whispered, straining to find his voice. "I don't mean that in some metaphysical bullshit way. I mean, she wasn't her actual self. She's changed."

Mercy nodded. Once again she was the woman he'd fallen for, strong and solid. "I wish I had some insight for you. But I don't. When Aidrik gifted her with the Sveising, we all knew it would lead to something significant and potentially tragic. We just didn't know what."

"I didn't know that," Nicolas argued. "No one told me."

"What could you have done?" Mercy asked sadly. "The alternative was her death. Aidrik made a choice that saved her life."

"And now he's gone," Nicolas mused. He turned his head, resting his cheek against the coarse upholstered pillow. His head throbbed. "I'm sorry, Mercy. I know he was important to you."

Mercy bowed her head. "I mourned Aidrik many, many years ago. I don't know that I ever fully registered his return. I'm sorrier for Aleksei, that he'll never know the great man his father was."

Nicolas worried Aleksei wouldn't get to know any of his

parents if events continued down this dark path. "What should we do?" He'd never felt, or sounded, more vulnerable. "I'm asking you, specifically. I trust your judgment."

Mercy animated in surprise, but her expression quickly dimmed. "You won't like my answer."

"I still want to hear it."

"Anders is in there talking about making a stand with all the Deschanels. If you bring them here, Nicolas, they're going to die. But they're going to die if they remain where they are. Do you understand what I'm saying?"

Nicolas nodded. "Yeah. God bless Harriett and her twisted fucking visions of accuracy."

"I don't mean that you should give up," she added quickly. "If I know Aidrik... well, he didn't go to his death in surprise." She swallowed, blinking. "He was always so far ahead of his enemies. He would have prepared for this. I don't know how, so don't ask. I could *never* guess the content of that creature's mind. But I have faith an answer will present itself."

Nicolas couldn't help himself. "Isn't your faith what brought you to this shitty situation?"

Mercy didn't miss a beat. "*Misplaced* faith. My faith in Aidrik never steered me wrong, and I'll hold to that belief until the day I die."

A strong contrast to the dogmatic words she'd committed to page. He saw no signs of that madwoman before him, but she was there, somewhere. He wished desperately that this Mercy, the one sitting before him with the look that pierced his heart, was the only one within her.

Because the other one would be her undoing. He was sure of it.

. . .

When a visitor arrived, everyone in the house tensed. Anders pushed forward, declaring, "Do you really think the Senetat would bother to knock?"

A tall, dark-haired man stood in the open doorway, holding a duffel bag. At first Nicolas didn't recognize him. Though it had been less than a year, an eternity of events had transpired since he last saw him.

"Jon St. Andrews," Nicolas recollected, as the events of last winter in Maine flooded back in a slide-show. Finding Ana hostage to that psycho Alex, watching her nearly die, discovering her reason for running in the first place.

Then, her reason for fleeing back home. *My brother tried to rape her*, Finn explained one day, with a pained grimace. *He'd been messing with her head for weeks and then one day... if I hadn't walked in, he would have. And my brother would be a dead man.*

"I found the address in Ana's ledgers," Jon started, shifting uncomfortably.

Nicolas stared at the man standing in his doorway. The man who had hurt his Anasofiya and sent her down the path that led to one of her loves dying before her eyes, and her other to a fate maybe worse than death. He regarded him with the frustrated hatred of all these things and before conscious thought intervened, he was on top of Jon, sending them both to the ground as he pummeled him with closed fists.

"You... fucking... caused *all of this*!" Nicolas cried between blows, losing himself in the motion, unaware of Jon's surrender.

Mercy flew forward, pulling Nicolas away. "Nic, stop!"

In his rage, he shoved Mercy to the side. Then Anders was upon him, lifting him from the waist as Nicolas continued raining blows upon the air.

Jon nursed his bloody face. Anders suppressed Nicolas, waiting for him to grow weary the way a parent might let a child cry out a tantrum. "I know why you're angry at me. I'm angry at myself." Jon looked down at his duffel bag. "I wasn't always like this."

"Fuck you and your pointless self-reflection," Nicolas spat from Anders' limiting embrace.

"What's going on here?" Mercy stepped forward. "Nicolas, what is this?"

"This," Nicolas replied, pointing a fist at Jon, "is Finn's brother, and the man who hurt Ana before she came home to us."

He expected Mercy to attempt to reason with him, but instead she stepped forward and launched a fist at Jon's face, sending him flying back off the porch. When he looked up, his nose was pointing to the left.

"There," she said with a decisive sigh. "I broke his nose, and I'll break more if he can't give us an adequate explanation for why he's here. Now, let's invite him in before we draw attention from the road."

FOR THE NEXT TEN MINUTES, BETWEEN DABS OF A TOWEL Condoleezza supplied for his nose, Jon laid everything out. Primarily his regret at what he'd done to Ana, and subsequently losing his brother. Some more bullshit Nicolas rolled his eyes at. And finally, his desire to start anew and do something good with his life.

"Finn and Ana aren't here," Mercy said, when Nicolas struggled for something civil to say. "Even if they were, I'd guess they wouldn't want to see you."

"Finn wrote me a letter. It wasn't a very nice letter," Jon replied with a frown, "but I deserved his anger. In it, he said you were doing important things here. He didn't say more than that, but he sounded proud to be a part of it. He hinted at some trouble with Ana."

"Nope, no trouble," Nicolas said with satisfaction. "Married. Have a kid."

Jon's eyes widened, but his face settled into a smile. "I'm glad to hear it. They both deserve happiness."

Nicolas' anger rose all over again. At Jon's ignorance, and Nicolas' attempt to hurt him backfiring, both reminding him that Ana's well-being was far from secure.

Hell, none of their well-beings were secure. By this time next week, Nicolas and his family might be making good on their reserved spaces in Lafayette Cemetery No. 1.

"I thought maybe you could use someone with a medical background," Jon added weakly.

"Richard, find him a room. I can't deal with this right now," Nicolas declared as he started toward the stairs, and his suite, where he could be alone and think. About what, only Emyr knew.

But he wasn't alone. Mercy looped her hand through his.

68

AGRIPIN

It took nearly a day to voyage to Trondheim, as they took the necessary re-routes and detours to avoid easy detection. Agripin doubted anyone was on their trail after what Anasofiya had done at Farsengel, but they hadn't come this far to fall to carelessness.

The litter was less comfortable than he'd accustomed himself to over his years as duke, but inauspicious was the goal. In Trondheim, the Brotherhood could regroup, and reformulate the next stage of their plan.

Larger cities were not usually their choice for a gathering, but, for once, they needed the cover of crowds and the luxury of blending in. A significant thing had happened in Farjhem, one everyone would be buzzing about for years to come.

Agripin looked across the plain carriage at Anasofiya, who slept like the dead. Healing her body had been no great task, with the power traveling in this caravan, but who knew what her state of mind might be when she woke?

He knew all along what she was. Now, because of what she'd been forced to endure, so did she. The others, especially

Cyler, insisted they leave her behind to her fate, to die amongst the others. She was a liability, they said. Worse, a danger. When was the last time they'd seen an etheric summoner? Most in the traveling party could say never.

They'd found her lying as if dead on the landing outside her cell, her specter nowhere to be found. *Not strong enough yet to wander on its own,* Trygve had explained, lifting her limp frame with ease.

Ana's entire body was covered in burns, most of which seemed to have emanated from within, not from the fires scorching the ground below. Her pulse throbbed slow and ragged. Without healing, she would die there.

Once he'd healed her, Leif applied the magic bindings. *Will keep her familiar at bay. For now.*

Agripin couldn't bring himself to abandon her. If pressed to explain why, he might say he felt guilty for betraying her, but it was far more complicated than that. She was kin to him, not by blood, but by the disposition of her heart.

With any luck, she might not kill him when she woke.

THE LOFT IN TRONDHEIM WAS A SPARTAN FLAT WITH FEW furnishings, but spanned over four thousand square feet. Spectacular for any building in Europe, let alone a Norwegian apartment.

Birger worked to prepare a feast for all the voyagers, and the Brotherhood slowly assembling. Cyler muttered incessantly about the foolishness of collecting the resistance leaders in one place, but Agripin, for once, dismissed his counsel. Cyler understood plenty, but was too young to understand when you forwent strategy with experience.

Agripin sat at the end of the bed in the private room he'd requested for Ana. He watched her, in the morbid curiosity reserved for a creature who'd only just realized he was in love with the object of his inquisitiveness.

Regret soared inside him, but he had no choice. Right? He couldn't save them both. He had to choose, and he chose the one the Senetat most wanted gone. Agripin couldn't imagine a scenario where he'd have chosen otherwise, though there were many options that involved losing them both.

Her bright blue eyes startled him. She strained forward, but invisible hands held her back. "What have you done to me?" she cried.

"I'm sorry. It was for your own good," he explained calmly, though a storm raged inside, grasping at the best answer. "I'll have Leif release the bonds later. I promise."

Her eyes darted to and fro, like a cornered animal. "Where are we?"

"Trondheim." No reason to lie to her. "With the rest of the Brotherhood. Maxima is here also. She's one of us."

She didn't ask after Aidrik. She wasn't a foolish girl, holding on to false hopes. "Why am I here?"

This wasn't a question he was ready to answer. "I didn't betray you. Someone else betrayed *us*. Servius figured out our intentions and I reacted for the good of the cause." It sounded so noble spoken aloud. He didn't feel noble. "It came down to a sacrifice and I chose Aidrik."

Ana's beautiful face broke into a sinister grin. "Oh, Agripin. Your betrayal comes either in the form of your painful ignorance, or your brutal dishonesty."

He had no idea what she meant, but he was afraid of her. Terrified, truly, but wasn't that an aspect of her inexplicable appeal? "I knew what you were. I gambled on it coming forward and preventing the need to execute you, too."

"Thank you for your honesty. But I'm still going to destroy you."

Then Ana was out again, dead to the world.

Dagr peeked a tentative head in the door. Agripin nodded. "There are rumors that not all Senetat were destroyed. They'll be amassing an army."

Agripin closed his eyes and sighed. "Perhaps they're referring to Maxima, who sits in our kitchen, breaking bread with the Brotherhood?"

Dagr shook his head. "She's a known traitor. Others. Some are saying there was a secondary group of eldres, waiting in the wings. I don't know. But we should prepare ourselves, Emperor."

"Aye," Agripin concurred after a painful pause. "For now, eat. Sleep. We have much ahead of us."

Not the least of which would be justifying the survival of this volatile creature sleeping before him.

69
AMELIA

Holger's patience eventually ran out, and they found their way to shore.

When their contact wasn't at the rendezvous point, he pushed on, toward Farjhem, driven by what seemed less a concern for Amelia and Jacob and more a fear of something far larger.

They trekked across the dark fjords, cold and shivering, Holger fearful of using a portail for reasons he wouldn't explain.

Jacob at first tried to envelop her in his jacket, but eventually the gesture got in the way of convenience and she shrugged him off, venturing forth behind their leader.

Early into the morning, he stopped, looking toward the twin glaciers with something between fondness and fear. "Farjhem," he whispered, though Amelia could see nothing other than more icy landscape.

Holger took them to a safe house, as he called it. Turning to them with dread, he pleaded with them to wait there and hold still while he investigated.

"Is this where we meet Birger and Astrid?" Jacob asked, though he knew the answer, and so did Amelia.

Holger didn't respond. He turned toward the glaciers again, with trepidation. "I'll return as soon as I can. *Don't move!"*

The small home with the red roof and stucco siding was cold and dark. Jacob wrapped his arms around her, and a blanket he'd found around the two of them, and they sat in silence.

Something is very wrong, Amelia ventured first.

"I wish we could see what he sees," Jacob replied, out loud. Of course, they were alone. No need for their secret voice.

"We don't need to. Something awful happened in Farjhem."

"Your seer's voice still off the charts?"

Amelia nodded against his shoulder. "Forget my seer's voice, Holger wouldn't react this way if things weren't way off plan. Did you see the way he looked at Farjhem?"

"We can't stay here," Jacob concluded. He stood, stepping toward the window, toward the foreign land they couldn't see with their eyes. "Tell me what you sense, *Blanca.*"

Amelia closed her eyes, drawing on the visions that had come in waves since they entered the North Sea. "Ana in danger. Death, lots of death. Lots and lots of death." She looked at her husband. "I don't know how much of it's true, but something is very wrong."

"I don't need to be a seer to know that," he agreed. His gaze traveled outward, waiting for Holger to return. He turned to her. "Birger and Astrid aren't coming."

"No."

"Something terrible has happened, and we chose to follow this path."

"Yes."

"I'm not letting anything happen to you again, Amelia. I won't watch another person harm even a—"

"Jacob—"

"I didn't do enough. I was terrified he would kill you, and I let it go too far—"

"Jacob, stop! That's not true. Neither of us would be alive if not for you, and—"

"I want to try time dancing."

Amelia looked at the door, as if Holger might waltz through. "Holger will be back any minute."

Pressing his forehead to hers, he said, "I'm not okay with wondering what comes next. I can't risk losing you."

You won't, she wanted to promise, but stopped short of saying the words. It would take so little to crack the shell protecting her mind from *thinking* and *feeling.* And though she couldn't see where their host had ventured, she could very nearly hear the screams of the suffering resonating through her head.

"You don't know what you're doing."

"I don't need to," he told her. "The Earth responded to me when I needed it most, before. It will again."

"I don't know. Where will we end up? It could be worse than here, and what if we can't get back?"

"Amelia, I really don't have the answers. I wish I did. As long as I'm with you, I don't care. If we stay here..."

She buried her face against his chest in response. Jacob's arms tightened around her. His power, something known to her only in name before, pulsed in the air around them as he gathered the energies to him, seeking the Earth's help.

Amelia closed her eyes and put her trust in her husband.

70
FINNEGAN

Finn's mind wandered as he lost himself in the craftsmanship of Ulfberht. He'd been in thrall of this piece of steel since he first laid eyes on it but he never, not in a million years, expected to be in possession of the sword.

He didn't know what Thorvald and Nerys said or did to the oil tanker captain to hitch a ride down the Mississippi, but they were guaranteed a front door delivery to *Ophélie*. The river was quiet, other than the ingress and egress of other ships carrying their goods down the wide waterway. A lone pelican landed on the railing, watching him.

Thorvald perched on a cargo box, as useful as a stone gargoyle. He stared straight ahead, wordless, from the moment the ship left port. Nerys paced the deck, stopping from time-to-time to lay a comforting hand on Finn's shoulder. She disappeared into the galley at one point, and emerged with a bottle of water, offering it with a smile. He accepted, thanking her.

Forbia released a low, playful bark. Nerys tossed her a piece of meat, winking. "Didn't think I forgot about you, did you?"

Soon, Finn would see his son again. For as much as he'd longed for this moment, it would be a bittersweet reunion for he'd have to tell him his mother didn't make it out. His second father, dead.

The only consolation was that Ana was out there, somewhere. Nerys explained there were plans far greater than what Agripin was ever privy to. She stopped short of calling him a pawn, but it was evident the Brotherhood had used him, and only let him in when absolutely necessary. Finn couldn't keep track of loyalties anymore. *Emyr willing, your wife is with Birger and Astrid, and the other leaders now. If it was safe to glimpse, we would look in on them. We left before we had a good grasp of the results.*

What about Aidrik? But Finn knew. He knew, because Aidrik had told him the night before, when he pulled him away. His Sveising brother had known exactly what was coming, as he always did, even at the end.

"Finn, may I borrow you for a moment? I'd like your help with something."

Aidrik hadn't ever asked Finn for help with anything more complex than skinning a boar, and he immediately detected something in his brother's tone, something that made him wary of following him back into the chambers.

Ana nodded at him. "Go on," she urged, then went back to her thoughts, gazing down into the glittering night of Farjhem.

Aidrik led him beyond their shared chamber to a separate room, a sitting room rarely used because they weren't here to entertain guests. He closed the door, locking it behind Finn.

Finn raised an eyebrow, but took a seat when Aidrik asked him to.

"I don't expect to emerge from tomorrow's coronation alive," Aidrik started. Right to the point, as always, but no less shocking to Finn who nearly fell off the plush seat.

"Aidrik, what the hell!"

"Apologies, Finnegan. I have never been renowned for my words. I have a request of you."

Finn nodded and shook his head in one contiguous, flustered gesture. "Why... why would you attend, if you believe that? Of course, of course, I'll do whatever you need. But Aidrik, shit. Did you know this all along?"

"The risk was ever present," Aidrik replied. "Before we stepped foot in my land, tomorrow's outcome waited as one of many possible. Agripin plans to play us false. The hour is too late for escape. We are watched, day and night."

Finn's throat was scratchy and dry as he swallowed. "Are you sure about Agripin?"

"I hope I am wrong," Aidrik said, without conviction. It was evident to Finn they wouldn't be having this conversation if Aidrik had any doubts of what was coming. "If my suspicion is correct, I will sacrifice myself in order to create enough time for you and Anasofiya to escape. Your departure will be simpler than hers." What Aidrik didn't add, but Finn heard, was the fear she might not make it to safety either. Finn wouldn't cast aside that bit of hope, no matter what Aidrik implied.

Aidrik reached around his waist, untethering his ancient, beloved sword. He placed it in Finn's lap and his knees sagged with the weight of the epic weapon. "You will take this. Take it with you to Ophélie. *She is yours now."*

Finn gawked at the hulking mass in his lap. This, and not Aidrik's words, is what made his predictions real. His hand hovered over the hilt, frightened. "I'm not ready for this, Aidrik."

Aidrik's face tightened into his version of a grin. "You are ready, brother. For this and more." His expression evolved back to his usual, serious glare. "You are more than you know, Finnegan. To protect you and Anasofiya I've thus withheld knowledge. You're a draoi. That means nothing to you now, but it is the sum total explanation of who you are. Why you have been, and always will be, worthy of Anasofiya. My last hope in this world is that Birger and Astrid's emissaries can help you."

It seemed Aidrik was nonsensically rambling at this point, a phenomenon Finn hadn't experienced. He nodded, feeling the lump in his throat build, ready to be done with the conversation.

But Aidrik wasn't done. "When I perish of this world, my ward on Ophélie *will cease. A mystic can build a ward, but only a draoi can seal it."*

"What do you mean? You did it yourself, didn't you?"

Aidrik shook his head. "No. I employed the help of an old friend. He's long since departed this Earth. You, Finnegan, can seal the ward our son creates."

"Aleksei? He's a mystic? How do you know?"

"I've always known, and soon, he will know this, too. This is why you must depart immediately, even if Anasofiya does not follow. Especially *if Anasofiya does not follow. The entire clan will fall if the ward is not restored."*

Finn wanted to ask his brother a thousand questions, but Aidrik stood, ending the conversation. There wasn't time.

Before he turned to leave, Aidrik clapped a hand down on Finn's shoulder. Finn shook his head and pulled Aidrik tight into his arms, hugging him with a fierce and abiding respect.

"You are my brother, Finnegan. A most worthy companion on my final travels."

Finn wiped the forming tears away. "I love you, Aidrik. If this is truly the end, then I hope you go to your ever after knowing I was happy to share this time with you."

"Aye. The only true happiness I've ever known."

. . .

"We're here," Nerys announced as the ship eased into port. From the looks of it, they were half-a-mile from the plantation, upriver, near where Finn used to fish after Ana disappeared.

Minutes later, they were moving down the long driveway, past thick foliage that protected the Big House from prying eyes on the west bank of River Road. Thorvald lagged behind, keeping vigilant eyes on their back.

"The protection is gone," he muttered, joining them. "Aidrik is gone, then."

Finn lowered his head and belted Ulfberht properly at his waist. The weight there would take some getting used to, but he would adjust until the sword was an extension of him, as Aidrik had.

Aleksandr appeared on the broad porch, flying out from between the Ionic columns as he soared down the driveway toward his far.

Finn crushed his son to him as they dropped to their knees, embracing in tears on the soggy grass. "Oh, Aleksei. My baby boy."

"Mora?" the boy asked.

Finn shook his head.

"We'll find her, Far," Aleksandr cried into his chest, wiping his tears on Finn's shirt. "She's out there still."

"I promise you we will," Finn vowed. He held his son's face before him, examining it. He realized in that moment he'd never expected to see him again. "If it takes the rest of our lives, Aleksei. We *will* bring her home."

"Thank the fucking stars," Nicolas called from the doorway. Faces both unfamiliar and familiar appeared behind him, gazing down in wide-eyed wonder.

"Just in time," Mercy added. She rested her head against Nicolas' back, smiling.

EPILOGUE

Finnegan

Aleksei closed his eyes. He'd been practicing, he said, and Finn's heart swelled with powerful pride.

While *Ophélie's* residents, Thorvald, Stian, and Nerys, observed, Finn closed his own eyes, and saw what his son had created: the barrier spreading up and over the plantation, back beyond into the charged swamps. Further outward, stretching to nearby lands, past the petrochemical plants, into nearby Vacherie, and beyond, to New Orleans. The energy radiating from Aleksei was palpable. His hands and mind remained steady, never faltering.

At last, he breathed out a long breath. Finn could hear his son's proud smile. "Your turn, Far."

"Tough act to follow," Finn said lightly, but he did exactly as Anders guided him, picturing the edges of the barrier growing long fingers that stretched into the ground, running deep beyond the Earth's crust, plunging beyond where anyone could ever reach them. His mind traveled along the perimeter, feeling the trees react to his request with a pulsing vitality that he was sure would be green if he opened his eyes.

The Earth released a low tremble as the last finger settled. The ward was sealed.

Finn opened his eyes to see Aleksei grinning like a fool. Forbia sat contentedly at his side, her large head under his hand. "We make a great team, Far."

"Aye," Finn said, saying a silent word to his fallen brother, who he believed was watching, from somewhere, nodding in wordless pride. "The perfect team, once we bring your mother home."

INSIDE THE PLANTATION, EVERYONE HAD QUESTIONS. WHAT THE HELL happened? Where was Ana? What was going on across the sea? Is that Aidrik's sword? Is that a *wolf*?

Finn owed his son explanations first and before anyone else. And then, maybe a good long nap. He didn't have the heart for much else.

He politely told everyone exactly that, tugging Aleksei's hand up the stairs so they could retire quietly, Forbia padding softly behind.

Thorvald embraced Lucia, who pressed her face to his chest like a lost child. "*Mi bellezza,*" he whispered, proffering comfort.

Nerys ushered the others into the study, promising to fill them in on what they knew. She smiled and nodded at Finn to go on. *We've got this.*

"Finn," Jon, his brother, said from behind him. He'd registered his presence numbly upon arrival, but in the complete overload of information, hadn't processed the potential meaning. Even the sound of Jon's voice didn't incite him in the same way.

"I don't have the energy right now, Jon," he said, weariness weighing heavy upon his words.

"It's okay. Take whatever time you need. I'll be here, waiting."

Nicolas

NICOLAS WRAPPED A TOWEL AROUND HIS WAIST, DREADING THE evening ahead. Aunt Colleen and the rest of the Deschanel Magi Collective Council would be holding a meeting in the dining room at *Ophélie*, to discuss all the things no one had a clue about: how to find Ana, why no one had heard from Amelia or Jacob in over a week, where on Earth the children and Anne had gotten off to, what to do about the bickering Empyreans downstairs who all had vastly different ideas on how to proceed next. He suspected Anders and Thorvald would slip away soon to find the runaways, Collective consensus or no.

He couldn't avoid the meeting any more than he could continue to avoid the remaining distance between him and Mercy. Their relationship was civil after their last talk, barely, but it still lacked the easy warmth he missed.

He'd considered the things he would say to Mercy in the shower, but none of the words felt adequate. *I love you, dammit. I'll do anything to prove it. Want me to toss out my porn collection? Wear a chastity belt when you're not around? Hypnosis to cure me of my addiction to vaginas?*

And then he would need to approach the other, darker subject. He couldn't come out and confess he'd read her file because that would quickly shut the door on rational discussion. Maybe he could ask her instead what she'd been up to, or where her head was at. Never in his life had he asked a woman those questions wanting a real answer. But he wanted one now.

Mercy startled him when he opened the door to find her standing immediately on the other side. Her face was a radiant shade of fresh honey, and her smile the brightest he'd seen her wear since... maybe ever. Her hands clutched together under her chin like an excited child, and then she shot them out and gripped Nicolas' cheeks in her palms.

"It's finally happened," she breathed.

Nicolas eyed her carefully. "What's happened?"

Mercy peeled one of his hands off the towel and placed it against her smooth belly, her warm hand resting atop his. "Emyr has sent us the greatest gift, Nicolas."

He wanted to yank his hand away, though he couldn't say exactly why. "What are you talking about?"

"A baby!" Her smile spread from cheek to cheek. Her sigh was childlike and wistful, full of promise and dreams.

Nicolas shook his head, inadvertently backing away from her. "You can't get pregnant, Mercy. Aunt C covered this with you. When Ana brought you back—"

"No, you don't understand. His own son, Nicolas. A child of Emyr."

The color drained from Nicolas' face. He looked at her, then, the keeper of his heart. The only woman he'd ever genuinely loved, who was now battling something he could neither understand nor properly help her with. Defeated sadness rippled through his entire body, traveling from head to foot.

"Okay, Mercy. Okay, sweetheart," he repeated as he pulled her face toward his chest, resting his head on top of hers. Her mind was gone, off somewhere safe where she couldn't be affected by the tragedies surrounding her. Where she would forever be a disciple of Emyr, worthy of His love. Where He'd given her His own divine child as reward for her piety, choosing her as his version of the Virgin Mary.

Nicolas understood instinctively she could never find her way back from this on her own.

He had two choices, but only one would leave them both whole in the end.

He decided to follow his heart.

Amelia

OUTSIDE THE SAFE HOUSE, SCREAMS ESCALATED, FILLING THE AIR WITH terror. The smell of burning—bitter, not the comforting scent of a camp fire—traveled toward them, though their eyes couldn't see the source of the flames.

Farjhem is burning, Amelia realized, pressing her face into Jacob's chest as he focused on pulling them out of the danger. She prayed Holger would find his own escape, and forgive them for not keeping their promise and staying.

"Hold on," Jacob whispered, as his grip tightened and the air around them went from still and pungent to the sensation of being whirled through a vacuum canister. Her skin stretched tight against her bones, as if it might peel from her frame if the gust grew any stronger.

Amelia dared not open her eyes. What remained of her lucidity might float away with the swirling wind.

The gust stopped. The smell of fire faded to the pleasant scent of saffron and other exotic spices.

"Open your eyes. *Blanca.* Look!"

Amelia did as Jacob asked. She backed slowly away from his arms, taking in the sweeping view of *Ophélie* from Brigitte's Garden. The topiary and flora were low to the ground.

"I don't know how, but I got us home," Jacob said in awe as

he knelt down, taking a handful of earth in his hand. The dirt sifted through his fingers.

Amelia frowned, glancing toward the Big House, and the missing Belvedere. It was a feature added later, not built with the house. Turning left, she saw the fresh coat of ivory paint on the newly constructed *garçonierre*.

"Not... exactly," she replied, as she added together the visual cues. "Jacob, I think—"

"The birthday festivities are starting!" a young blonde woman in a low-necked, corseted evening dress declared, sashaying toward them. Her skirt rustled over the top of the cage underneath.

Standing before them, the young girl scrunched her browse in perplexed study. "Why, look at you. Are you a guest of my father's?"

Jacob gaped, speechless, his gaze traveling between both women.

"Ah... uh, yes," Amelia asserted, tucking her shaking hand behind her. "We—"

The woman's face lit up. She clasped her hands together. "Oh! You must be from London!" She artlessly fingered the stitching on Amelia's riding coat. "Tell me, is *this* the current fashion for ladies?" Not waiting for a response, her words continued to rush forth in an excited gale. "My brothers brought me the finest corsets from Paris when they went on their Grand Tour. They completely neglected London!"

"A shame," Amelia said with a polite smile, biting her tongue to hide her disorientation... and her decidedly different accent. She hadn't realized how much the dialect had changed over the last century-and-a-half.

"Come, gather inside! You can tell me all about London after the dance, when the men break for cigars and brandy."

"Yes, thank you," Amelia said pleasantly. Then the young

girl turned, with a practiced motion, lifting her skirts as she made her way back toward the Big House.

"Don't recognize her?" Amelia asked her husband, still staring down the path toward the house. "I thought you were an expert on the Deschanels."

"It can't be." His jaw went slowly slack.

"Oh, it is. That's Ophélie, and today is apparently her birthday. The place isn't crawling with Union soldiers so I'd guess this is before the war... which puts us around 1859 or 1860, judging from her age."

"Jesus," Jacob whispered, rubbing his face with the edge of his palms.

"Actually, I think it's the goddess you should be appealing to right about now," Amelia mumbled with a half-smile. Her face creased in concentration as her mind struggled to catch up with everything around them.

Jacob was too stunned to tease back. "What do we do?"

"When you closed your eyes and asked for the help getting us here, did you specifically wish to take us home?"

"Not really. What I asked was to get us out of danger." He scratched his head. "I didn't think that far ahead. I should have focused on somewhere specific. Should we try again?"

Amelia looked toward her family's plantation and beyond, toward the river, teeming with commerce. Brimming with life full of hope, before war would tear it apart.

With all her heart, she wished she could go back to her own moments of peace, before her world was torn in two.

But her scars were her own, as Ophelie's would be hers. All Amelia's family owned their hurts, bravely and with a resolve that defined them.

"No. We were sent here for a reason," she said after a considerate pause. *Everything that happened up to this point has been for a reason. From the moment we stepped on to the plane, to the child I refused to have but was given anyway, despite our precautions. Given, and then taken. Even Baldur's vicious attack has significance.*

"What could be the bloody reason for *this*?" Jacob's incredulous eyes scanned the garden and the slave cabins in the distance, still inhabited by those they were built for.

"Hell if I know, Donnelly," Amelia replied, her sigh as confused as her thoughts. "But I suppose we'll find out."

She held her arm out and Jacob took it, with a lazy, slow smile. "The situations we find ourselves in, *Blanca.*"

Indeed. Things great and terrible, Amelia thought. *But at least together.*

"*Síoraíocht, Mo mhíle stór,*" Jacob whispered, as they made their way toward the future past.

Anasofiya

He is safe. Nerys sent word. Both are safe.

What of the other two? Your scout should have returned by now.

Holger lost them. He searches for them, but fears the worst after what... happened.

Aye. We will need to return to Farjhem and assess what is left. What remains.

For another day. Our war will never end if we cannot right the wrongs done.

Voices familiar and unfamiliar carried from the other room, but Anasofiya had no interest in their words, or the meaning of them. There was no intention pure enough to sway the darkness inside her toward anything beyond the burning revenge keeping her heart beating.

Her chest moved with her breaths, but the rest of her was

bound, body and magic alike. *For your own protection,* Agripin had told her, but they both knew it was for his.

Until you can come to terms with things, he'd added, his voice soft and cloying like that of a confused lover searching for answers. The different masks he'd worn over the course of their fractured relationship were no longer a matter for her interpretation. She didn't care who he was, on the surface, or deep down.

There would be no *coming to terms* with a betrayal of this magnitude. Only a soul-deep patience, as she and her wraith waited in silence for Agripin's guard to slip. The smallest opportunity would be sufficient.

In the dark room, far from home, this aching, wrenching desire for revenge was the totality of all she understood. All the other things that made her who she was, were buried deep and packaged away.

They were of no use to her here.

MYTHS OF MIDWINTER EXCERPT

Quillan

Quillan Sullivan had, over the course of many years, developed the necessary skills to endure his father's lectures. He felt confident that he could successfully mask his complete lack of interest with an outward appearance of contrition. With twenty-six years of experience in this, he was damn near an expert.

"Right, sure," he said, nodding furiously, as Patrick Sullivan paced Quillan's small living room. His father's long, heavy steps nearly shook the cheap lamp from Quillan's equally cheap desk. Both accouterments his father disapproved of. The Sullivans did not work hard for all these years to live in such affront to good taste, after all. Quillan smirked.

"This is funny to you?" his father demanded, stopping.

Oops. "Not exactly. You see—"

"What I *see* is a child that I raised, who is ungrateful, immature, spoiled, and completely out of control! Do you know how hard it was to convince Colin to let you stay? Do you understand how absolutely outlandish it is that we even had to sit down to discuss whether or not a Sullivan would be allowed to continue practicing law at our *family* law firm?"

Yes, Quillan was quite aware. Sullivan and Associates was practically a birthright for any Sullivans choosing to go into law. Getting removed would be akin to the Prince of Wales being disowned. Which is why Quillan felt a strange sense of pride about the way things were currently going, though showing even a sliver of that to his father would not end well.

His father's red face matched his hair, and the veins in his thick neck protruded, as they often did, when dealing with his only son. A look of control settled over his face as he seemed ready to reign in the dialog that seemed to be going nowhere. "I'm tired of these discussions, Quillan. I have better things to do than lecture my grown son on how it's unacceptable to consistently drop the ball at work. I've decided to pass this babysitting job on to someone else."

Quillan looked up. His attention was piqued. "Sorry?"

"Lauren Weatherly." He studied Quillan's blank face. "You know her. Your cousin Cameron's sister-in-law. Been with the firm about five years now... seriously, Quillan? You work in the same office."

Well, it's not like I spend a lot of time there, is what Quillan wanted to say, but instead replied, "I'd probably know her if I saw her."

His father sighed in exasperation. "One would hope, Quillan. Well, you'll know her soon enough. I've asked her to keep an eye on you, and give you some direction. Maybe remedial lessons on how to actually do the things you were supposedly trained to do in law school."

Quillan shifted in his seat uncomfortably. He wanted this conversation to be over. "Sure, okay."

His father rolled his eyes to the ceiling and sighed again.

"Of course, tell me what I want to hear like you always do. It doesn't matter. You're going to succeed, whether you want to or not. You're going to because you're my son and I want to see you be successful. More importantly, you're going to pull your head out of your ass because it's not just your reputation on the line... it's mine. I *am* actually proud of where I come from. You could learn some personal pride yourself." His father laughed at the last part, as if pigs would fly before this happened.

"I said I would," Quillan insisted, already ushering his dad toward the door. Quillan was beyond tired of listening to people giving him passionate diatribes about what he *should* be doing. What he *should* have done was not listen to them in the first place, and pursue something that actually interested him. *First and foremost, I should have moved far away from these crazy, superstitious Irish kooks.*

But you don't like anything. What would you have done if not this? He could hear Riley's words in his head. *I would do anything to have your worries.*

There was no one else who could get through to Quillan, and appeal to his better nature, the way Riley could, yet his words didn't change anything.

"When you come in Monday, go straight to Lauren's office." His father was holding the door open as if he thought Quillan might close it in his face. "Woe betide you if she has to come looking for you!"

When his father was gone, Quillan went to the kitchen, opened the cupboard that contained all of their bar items, and started to pour a drink. He stopped halfway, looking at the clock to see it was only noon, shrugged and continued pouring.

"You weren't very nice," Riley interrupted his misery.

"And?"

"He just wants you to be okay. He loves you."

"Ah, things are so simple to a seven-year-old," Quillan said and brushed past Riley, walking out on to the small deck overlooking the shared garden area. Scents of jasmine and oleander filled his head, calming him.

"I'm not like other seven-year-olds," Riley insisted, following him.

"Be that as it may, you have absolutely no idea what you're talking about."

Riley wrinkled his nose, as he often did when trying to give Quillan advice on a topic that was foreign to him. "I wish I did," he said finally.

At this, Quillan softened. "I know, buddy. Anyway, it's no big deal, right? I just have to meet with this chick, and then Dad will cool off for a bit, and it will be all good. For a while anyway."

"Do you think so?"

Quillan nodded. "Do you really think they'd kick a Sullivan out of their own law firm? I mean, c'mon, there's like fifty of us there. It's a collection."

Riley giggled. "As long as you don't lose your job. It would make Mom sad."

Quillan thought his mother's sadness was often over-exaggerated, but Riley couldn't understand that, so he offered, "It's all good, buddy. Don't you worry about a thing. I've got this under control."

A large smile spread across Riley's face. "Can I watch you play video games?"

Quillan finished his drink and left the glass next to all the other empty ones that someone—probably Leander—would have to take care of later. "Sure."

Leander came home that evening in a foul mood. It was sometimes hard to tell the direction of Leander's disposition as the scowl on his face was nearly always present, but Quillan picked up on the thud of Leander's old backpack hitting the floor and the fact he was still wearing his shoes when he marched into the living room.

"Thy panties appear to be in a twist," Quillan remarked without looking up. He was finishing the last lap of his racing game. Riley had disappeared the moment Leander's key turned in the lock.

"Clearly," Leander snipped. He marched toward the balcony, saw Quillan's glasses spread out on the table and chairs, then snorted, and sat down in the old recliner instead. His hand moved instinctively to brush the bangs from his eyes, but stopped in mid-gesture. He had shaved his head the day before in a moment of particular frustration.

Quillan finished his game and tossed the controller carelessly into a cardboard box. "Want me to tell you about my shitty day? I had an awesome conversation with my father."

"Not especially."

"Ooookay. Want to talk about yours then? Are you getting tired of being the eternal student? Wishing you had enough *cajones* to ask that shark chick out?" Leander shot him a look. "Well, she studies sharks, does she not?"

"She's a marine biology major," Leander clarified evenly.

"Exactly, the shark chick. She shoot you down? Ooh, Lee, she shot you down, didn't she? What a bitch."

"No."

"Then what?"

"Not everyone's problems can be summed up into booty call complications," Leander said obtusely, and walked into his room without another word.

"Alas, there are other sharks in the sea!" Quillan called out after him.

He wasn't too worried about his friend. Leander's moods

were nothing new to him, nor were the glaring differences between the two of them. Riley had summed it up best when he said, *Leander is like the kids in class who keep their heads down when the teacher says good morning to everyone. You're the kid who screams good morning back as loud as he possibly can.*

Quillan and Leander had been best friends since the third grade when Leander had shown up to class after having been skipped ahead a grade. Years later, Quillan would realize what a horrible decision that had been. Leander was smart, there was no doubt, but he would always struggle socially.

Where Leander had problems making friends, Quillan had problems turning them away. He never understood what made him latch on to the quiet, odd boy who came into their class that day, but he never regretted it either. Not then, and not now, years later, when they lived as roommates in their crappy French Quarter flat.

Their differences did not stop there, though. Where Quillan had grown up in a relatively normal family, everything about Leander's home life was bizarre. His parents, Pandora and Jasper Broussard, were local celebrities, known for their pandering of occult artifacts, tours, books, and services. Their profession was horrifying to Leander, who was still in medical school pursuing a noble life of research science. His littlest sister, Harriett, went over a decade without speaking, and then only did when she fled home.

But his middle sister, Estella... ahh, now that was another matter entirely. Estella with the long blonde cornsilk hair that glimmered in the sun. Estella of the tiny nose and full, voluptuous apple-red mouth. Estella of the moonlight pale skin and blue eyes like a clear spring day.

Estella was the great love of Quillan's life, though he knew he was not the same to her. She had been away at college in

France studying the occult for the past four years, which had allowed Quillan's fascination for her to dull only somewhat.

The feelings had always been a bone of contention between Quillan and Leander. Leander did not like his sister. Quillan was not sure Leander even *loved* her. *She's an angel*, Quillan would say. *She's a disgusting bitch*, Leander would respond.

For Leander, Quillan was an escape from the prison of his own mind and the world he grew up in. For Quillan, Leander was a breath of fresh air, and a reminder that perhaps his problems were not nearly as dramatic as they seemed.

Though, for all their closeness, Quillan had never talked to Leander about Riley. Never discussed him directly, not even in the context of their childhood, before everything had gone to hell. If there was anyone Quillan could have told, it would have been Leander, the man who had grown up in a household of complete nuts and was more than a little nuts himself.

But Quillan could not bring himself to tell anyone. Not Leander, not his parents, and not anyone else he had ever known.

How exactly does one tell someone they have regular conversations with their dead little brother?

Pick up your copy of *Myths of Midwinter* now, and have it ready to curl up at your next reading session!

EMPYREAN & QUINLAN
ENCYCLOPEDIA

Aanya: A kind and beautiful Empyrean Agripin once loved, but was forbidden from claiming as his duchess her due to her lack of lineage.

Aidrik (Also: Aidrik the Wise): Once a well-respected member of the Eldre Senetat. After Aidrik discovered their true nature, he sliced the Mark of Emyr from his face, freeing him from the Senetat's tethers. He met and saved Anasofiya from death, becoming her evigbond. Lived in a triad with Anasofiya, and her husband Finn, until his death, at the hands of the Senetat.

Aleksandr: Empyrean son of Anasofiya, Finn, and Aidrik. Shy, introspective. Named heir of the Deschanels by Nicolas. A mystic, and time shaper, whose abilities are still surfacing.

Anders: An Empyrean Mercy co-habitated with for a short period of time. She believed him Ascended, but he was, actually, a scout for the Brotherhood, under the direction of Thorvald. His most recent assignment brought him to *Ophélie*, where he is tasked with training and protecting the Brotherhood children.

Arborkinetic: A form of telekinesis involving flora. A strong arborkinetic can command plant life to do their bidding, and some can communicate with plants. Anne Fontaine Deschanel and Duchess Nerys are both arborkinetics.

Ascension (Also: Grand Ascension): The ultimate death and rebirth all Empyreans are promised. It is tied to Emyr's Mark, which is said to come alive when their time is near. Once active, the mark is then supposed to usher them through death and rebirth, into the arms of Emyr. The truth is the mark is simply an infusion of dark magic administered by the Eldre Senetat, from which they control the activation and subsequent death of Empyreans.

Astrid: Brotherhood leader of Ireland and the British Isles, alongside her evigbond, Birger. Birger and Astrid are in the minority in their decision to make peace with Quinlans. They also co-exist peacefully with humans in the nearby villages where they live in a tribe of other similar-minded Empyreans. Many look to them as the moral compass of the Brotherhood. They have one child, Eydis.

Baldur: A sadistic scout for the Senetat who captures Amelia and Jacob, torturing them for information. Is killed by Jacob.

Bestiakinetic: One who can commune with animals. Finnegan becomes a bestiakinetic after being given the Sveising. Yiva and Jorun are also bestiakinetics.

Birger: Brotherhood leader of Ireland and the British Isles, alongside his evigbond, Astrid. Birger and Astrid are in the minority in their decision to make peace with Quinlans. They also co-exist peacefully with humans in the nearby villages where they live in a tribe of other like-minded Empyreans. Many look to them as the moral compass of the Brotherhood. They have one child, Eydis.

Blacksmith: Forger of Ulfberht, and creator of Empyrean Steel.

Bodhran: Goatskin drum used in Quinlan ceremonies.

Brotherhood: See "Dragon Brotherhood, The."

Brother of Emyr (Also: Sister of Emyr): Another way to reference a halfling (or, someone who has both human and Empyrean blood).

Brynja: One of the oldest, original Empyreans. Together with her partner, Einar, they are Brotherhood leaders, residing in Russia. Part of Runa's rebels who escaped after her execution, they are often called, by Runeans, "Adam and Eve."

Child of Man/Men: What Empyreans call humans.

Christiane de Laurent: Aidrik's original evigbond. Human. Lived at the end of the 16th century, as a courtesan of the French court. Wife of Marquise Deschanel, and mother of Claude.

Cianán (Also: Jacob Donnelly): One fourth of the prophecy, descended from the Tuathan tribe of Gorias. He has been reincarnated over thousands of years, with his lover, Cerridwen. Their journey evolves in each lifetime, with the ultimate test being their love bringing them together in their final lifetime, when they have no memory of former lives, thus fulfilling the prophecy. Their child is meant to join with the descendant of Falias and Murias. Jacob is the reincarnated soul of Cianán.

Cerridwen (Also: Amelia Donnelly): One fourth of the prophecy, descended from the Tuathan tribe of Findias. She has been reincarnated over thousands of years, with her lover, Cianán. Their journey evolves in each lifetime, with the ultimate test being their love bringing them together in their final lifetime, thus fulfilling the prophecy. Their child is meant to join with the descendant of Falias and Murias. Amelia is the reincarnated soul of Cerridwen.

Claude Deschanel (Also: Viscount Deschanel): The first halfling Deschanel, being both human and Empyrean. Child of Christiane and Aidrik.

***Crann bethadh*:** Also known as the "Tree of Life," and the center of the Quinlan tribe. It gives life to the tribe, by providing everything they need, from food to shelter. Also a portal between worlds, and the spiritual link to the goddesses.

Crimson Guard: The official guard of the Farjhem, under command of the Senetat. Their uniform consists of blood-red robes.

Cumdach: A lavishly ornamented shrine used in Quinlan ceremonies.

Cyler: Agripin's young, brash second-in-command, and lover. Often shirks orders and goes his own route, though he is known for being excellent with strategy. Is a frequent visitor to Oriana's Menagerie.

Dagr: 7,000 years old. Born without Senetat knowledge, and is one of the Brotherhood leaders, residing in Morocco.

Daughter of Emyr (Also: Son of Emyr): Referencing pure-blooded Empyrean women.

Deschanel Magi Collective: A secret, ancient society, created with the intention of cataloguing all the family's abilities, as well as protecting and preserving the family. Each generation has a Magistrate, the current one being Colleen Deschanel.

Dragon Brotherhood, The: Secret organization of Empyrean rebels. There is no central leader, but instead regional leaders across the world. Some leaders are ready for battle, others content to live in peace.

Dragon Empire, The (Also: Dragon Brotherhood, The): Another name for the wider Dragon Brotherhood.

Draoi: Male Quinlan. It is said these males are sacred, as their occurrence usually portends something important, and prophetic. Draoi are often quite powerful, able to spin wards and time dance. To birth a draoi is to be considered blessed. Male druids often come into their powers when they reach sexual maturity. Attempting to draw from them earlier can sometimes lead to disastrous results. Jacob, Finnegan, Padraig, and Father O'Connor are all draoi.

Drekar: A term of familiarity amongst the Brotherhood. Translates roughly to "dragon."

Duchess Nerys: Nomadic daughter of Grand Emperor Aeron, and sister to Agripin and Oriana. Known for her love of all creatures, and her call to traveling. A bestiakinetic, with loyalties to no one and nothing except peace. Joins forces with the Brotherhood, as she believes they are most likely to achieve that.

Duchess Oriana: Beautiful, wayward daughter of Grand Emperor Aeron, sister to Agripin and Nerys. Known for having a menagerie of human pets, and for her cruelty toward defectors. Is loyal to the Senetat.

Einar: One of the oldest, original Empyreans. Together with his partner, Brynja, they are Brotherhood leaders, residing in Russia. Part of Runa's rebels who escaped after her execution, they are often called, by Runeans, "Adam and Eve."

Eldre Aeslius: One of the nine members of the Eldre Senetat. Following the events at Aidrik's execution, his fate is currently unknown.

Eldre Brutus: Was originally a member of Emperor Elof's privy council, but when he discovered Elof was plotting with rebels, Brutus betrayed and exposed him. The Senetat "Ascended" Elof, giving the crown to his son Aeron. Following the events at Aidrik's execution, his fate is currently unknown.

Eldre Cassian: One of the nine members of the Eldre Senetat. Following the events at Aidrik's execution, his fate is currently unknown.

Eldre Felix: One of the nine members of the Eldre Senetat. Following the events at Aidrik's execution, his fate is currently unknown.

Eldre Lucrecia: One of the nine members of the Eldre Senetat. Following the events at Aidrik's execution, her fate is currently unknown.

Eldre Maxima: One of the nine members of the Eldre Senetat. Has been a secret sympathizer of the Brotherhood for many years, and officially joined their cause following the events at Aidrik's execution.

Eldre Tacita: One of the nine members of the Eldre Senetat. Following the events at Aidrik's execution, her fate is currently unknown.

Eldre Valerius: One of the nine members of the Eldre Senetat. Right hand of Grand Eldre Servius. Following the events at Aidrik's execution, his fate is currently unknown.

Eldre Senetat, The: The ruling government over the Empyrean race. Established many millennia ago, they claim to be blessed by Emyr, and charged with doing His will through enacting and protecting laws. The Senetat grew corrupt with this power, and unknown to most Empyreans, are controlling the fates of all citizens. The creation and installation of Emyr's Mark is the vehicle by which they exact their control.

Empath: The ability to sense feelings, emotions, or sensations in others. There are varying degrees of empaths. Amelia Deschanel is considered the strongest empath in the family. Lucia and Livia are also empaths.

Empyrean (Also: Farværdig): Also known as the Farværdig ("Father's Chosen"), Empyreans are as old as man, and similar genetically, but with several key differences. Where some DNA is dormant in humans, the entire strand is active in Empyreans, giving them special, paranormal abilities, including greater strength and speed, and immortality via perfect cell replication. Their home is Farjhem, in the northern expanses of Norway, but most Empyreans live scattered throughout the world, blending in with men. All Empyreans are born with red hair (which fades to a chromatic silver as they age), and are exceptionally tall. They are also primarily solitary, not subscribing to traditions such as a nuclear family, marriage, or commitment. The exception to this is evigbond. In their early days, they enjoyed a strategic alliance with Quinlans, but, once broken, both races were thrust into strife.

Empyrean Laws: Mandates set by the Eldre Senetat. include regulations around childbirth, mating with humans, and other fundamental freedoms.

Empyrean Steel (Also: Crucible Steel): A rare steel with high carbon content, smelted in a small furnace, and cooled slowly. In swords, it was both strong, and flexible. The technology was not used anywhere else in the world, and was considered better than Damascus Steel, which is the closest point of comparison.

Empyrean traits: Born of fire. Elevated body temperature. Red hair (the redder the strands, the more pure the blood) that takes on silver chromatic hues as they age. When emotions are heightened, they are said to emit an orange glow. Most have pale, smooth skin, and are very tall. All have special telepathic/telekinetic abilities, with some stronger than others. Average lifespan is two thousand years, though it is believed without the mark, an Empyrean could be functionally immortal.

Emyr (Also: Our Father): God, to Empyreans. He is represented by a phoenix, rising from the ashes.

Erikr: Brotherhood resistance leader who led one of the only semi-successful rebel revolutions after Runa's. Was executed in a block of ice. Leader of the Second Runean War, and considered the father of the Dragon Brotherhood, which was formed with the help of Ptolemy I.

Etheric Summoning (Also: Etheric Summoner): More rare than a mystic, an etheric summoner can draw from their greatest weakness and manifest it into a physical strength. Also known as a wraith. Anasofiya is an etheric summoner.

Evigbond: The physical and chemical bonding process that occurs when an Empyrean meets their permanent mate. It is irreversible, and only severed by death. An evigbond between Empyrean and humans is especially potent. Aidrik's first evigbond was Christiane, and his current is Anasofiya. Mercy experienced evigbond with Nicolas, until her "death." Evigbond can occur in two different ways. The first is an uncontrolled, chemical reaction. The second is through consummation.

Eydis: Fifty-year-old daughter of Brotherhood leaders Birger and Astrid. She is halfway to maturity, and emotionally equivalent to a young girl of around nineteen. Wide-eyed, rebellious, but kind-hearted. She sees how in love her parents are because of their evigbond, and is determined to find hers. Her birth accompanied a year of great prosperity for crops in Ireland. Is an illusionist with a specialty in influencing.

Falias: One of the four tribes of the Tuatha Dé Danann. All Quinlans descend from one of these four tribes. The tribe of Falias is mentioned in The Prophecy as such: *A male Quinlan, pure of heart, and a special affinity for animals.* It is not yet known who the subject of this reference is.

Far: Empyrean word for father. Can be used by a child speaking to a parent, or in reference to Our Father, Emyr.

Fardag (Also: Father's Day): Annual Farjhem celebration held in homage to Emyr.

Farjhem: The homeland of the Empyreans. Translated to "Father's Home." Located between two glaciers in northern

Norway, it is not accessible by anyone except Empyreans, or those with Empyrean blood.

Farsengel: The place of law and order in Farjhem, where suspected criminals are sentenced and detained awaiting further punishment. Many stories high, the outside edges contain hundreds of cells, and the inside of the arena has a large stage.

Farskilt: Deep in the bowels of Farjhem, beneath a volcano. "Separated from father." Empyreans are sentenced here for "rehabilitation" when they commit spiritual offenses. Citizens are told that offenders are "reunited with Emyr" and the end of their rehabilitation results in guaranteed Ascension. The reality is they are labor mines, and Empyreans work there until their inevitable starvation and death. The Empyrean equivalent of a prison camp.

Farvann River: (Also: River Farvann): The river flowing through the fjord and glaciers of Farjhem.

Farværdig (Also: Empyrean): See "Empyrean."

Father O'Connor: A draoi descended from the tribe of Gorias, and the man who saved Jacob from tragedy as a youth, sending him to New Orleans. Brother to the tribe elder, Seara. Great-uncle of Amelia.

Feast of Officium Maximus: Once every hundred years, the Scholars graduate their group of fledgling Empyreans into the world. This ceremony, for which many return home, is accompanied by a great celebration.

Findias: One of the four tribes of the Tuatha Dé Danann. All Quinlans descend from one of these four tribes. The tribe of Findias is mentioned in The Prophecy as such: *A female Quinlan, and halfling Empyrean, reincarnated over two-thousand years, originally Cerridwen. Lover of Cianán.* Amelia Jameson Donnelly is the subject of this reference.

First Father: When an Empyrean child has multiple

fathers (via Sveising), the initial father, at conception, is referred to as First Father.

First Runean War: Resistance to the creation of the Eldre Senetat, led by Runa, a warrior who represented the opinions of many Empyreans. Despite her strong supporters, the rebels were destroyed, and Runa publicly executed. Their stunning defeat weakened the resolve of many Empyreans who believed in her cause (henceforth dubbed Runeans by the Senetat), and most went into hiding.

Fledglings: What the Empyrean youth are referred to when they reach the age of spiritual maturity and are released into the wider world.

Forbia: An abandoned Hudson Bay wolf pup discovered and adopted by Finnegan. She becomes his familiar, and he names her Forbia, after his beloved ship he left in Maine.

Galon: A kinsman of Aidrik who was forced into Ascension by the Senetat after he angered them.

Goddess Danu: The goddess and leader of the Tuatha Dé Danann.

Goddess Morrigan: The goddess of divination, and one of the surviving Tuatha, foretold one day that four individuals—one descendant from each original clan—would unite the Empyreans and Quinlans once again. This prophecy was delivered to both a Quinlan and an Empyrean, and said that they would go through nearly two millennia of war and strife before finding peace.

Gorias: One of the four tribes of the Tuatha Dé Danann. All Quinlans descend from one of these four tribes. The tribe of Gorias is mentioned in The Prophecy as such: *A male Quinlan, known as Ciandán (little ancient one), reincarnated with Cerridwen.* Jacob Donnelly is the subject of this reference.

Grand Eldre Servius: The ruling grand eldre of the Senetat for several millennia. Was lesser-ranked at the time of Aidrik's service. Was known for his "scorched earth" policy and for taking the restrictive laws of the Empyrean race to the far extreme. Killed by Anasofiya at the execution of Aidrik.

Grand Emperor Aeron: The last ruling Grand Emperor of Farjhem, and the Empyrean race. Had a reputation for being kind, and benign, but showed no interest in meaningful involvement with his people. Was activated when Agripin spread false rumor of his treason. Agripin then succeeded him as grand emperor.

Grand Emperor Agripin: The current ruling Grand Emperor of Farjhem, and the Empyrean race. Previously Grand Duke Agripin. The only son and oldest child of Aeron and Theda, both deceased. Fought in the Second Runean War, where his distaste for the Senetat was born. Over the years, his love of easy living kept him from taking action, but his partnership with the Brotherhood grew over time. He used Aidrik and Anasofiya as part of his campaign, which results in the burning of Farjhem. Is currently in Trondheim with the rest of the Brotherhood, plotting their next move.

Grand Emperor Elof: Father of Aeron, who succeeded him when he was "activated" for suspected trafficking with the rebels. Betrayed by Eldre Brutus, who was his closest confidante.

Grand Emperor Seti: Ruling emperor of Farjhem at the time the Senetat was created. Supported the Senetat's inception, as he was not interested in being the upholder of laws.

Grand Empress Anasofiya: Born a halfling of the Deschanel clan in New Orleans. Aidrik gave her the Sveising to save her life, which gifted her with more potent versions of her existing abilities, as well as suspected immortality. Married to Finnegan, but evigbond to Aidrik, which created an unorthodox polyamorous triad between them. Mother to Aleksandr, who is the son of both men. Her skill as a resurrection shaman pales in comparison to her most potent ability of all, etheric summoning. She is currently magic-bound by Agripin following the execution of Aidrik, where she destroyed hundreds of Empyreans.

Grand Empress Theda: Mate of Aeron and mother of Agripin. Deceased.

Great Cleansing: Following the creation of the Senetat, Empyreans who refused the mark were sought out and executed. Those who survived were branded Runeans.

Great Commitment (Also: Officium Maximus): The graduation ceremony, once every hundred years, when Empyreans reach their age of maturity and are released from the Scholars' tutelage, out into the world. This ceremony includes the installation of Emyr's Mark, a magical brand in the shape of a phoenix that is said to include a part of Emyr Himself. In reality, it is a device of the Eldre Senetat, as a means to control the Empyreans once they leave Farjhem.

Hakon: Still a fledgling, son of Emperor Aeron through a tryst he had with Hakon's mother. The mother escaped from Farjhem, and she died after birthing Hakon. Trygve took him in, under his wing, in Mongolia. Is a bestiakinetic.

Halfling: Humans with some amount of Empyrean blood/ancestry. A human is considered a halfling even if their Empyrean blood is many generations back.

Holger: Kind and helpful scout of Birger and Astrid, sent to look after Jacob and Amelia.

Illusionist: One who can manipulate the reality of others. Some do this by changing the physical interpretation. Others do this through influence. Markus is an illusionist who can change his appearance. Eydis can influence people to do her bidding.

Inner Voice: Empyreans believe in the concept of an "Inner Voice" guiding them toward their destiny. For Mercy, the Inner

Voice was an illusion crafted by Aidrik, who was guiding her toward safety.

Jorun: The Brotherhood leader over South America. Quiet and reclusive, she relates better to creatures on four feet, as a bestiakinetic. Lives apart from the other Empyreans of the region, but looks after them from afar.

Killianshire: A small village in southern Ireland, where Jacob was born and raised. Father O'Connor presides over the cathedral here. The village is Quinlan-friendly.

Kjære: Aidrik's term of endearment for Ana. Translates roughly to "my dear" or "my dearest" in Empyrean.

Leif: The Brotherhood leader over the Caribbean region. Was once a member of the Senetat, but over time grew weary of their hypocrisy. He escaped and became a critical leader amongst the Brotherhood. Can bind the magic of others.

Livia: Born in Spain to an Empyrean mother and human father. Her father had dark olive skin, and her darker skin tone puts her in danger, as no purebred Empyrean has these tones. Is closely guarded under the wing of Thorvald, and has a special bond with Lucia. Empath.

Lucia: Escaped the Scholars when she was still a student, leaving Farjhem without a plan other than the idea of her freedom. Thorvald found her and took her under his wing in Spain, dubbing her *mi belleza*, and fostering her great loyalty. He makes her a scout, and pairs her with Anders. Her most recent assignment took her to *Ophélie* to help train and protect the children of the Brotherhood. Is an empath who can absorb the pain of others without impact to herself.

Mark of Emyr (Also: mark, Emyr's Mark): A magical infusion, in the shape of a phoenix, given to all Empyreans at their Great Commitment. The mark is about two inches in diameter, and can be placed anywhere on the body, a choice made by the Empyrean receiving the mark. Empyreans are told the mark includes a part of Emyr Himself, and that when it is time for their Grand Ascension, the mark will call them home to Emyr. In reality, the mark is a sinister plot by the Eldre Senetat, created as a means to control the Empyreans and destroy them.

Marquise Deschanel: Husband of Christiane de Laurent (Aidrik's first human evigbond). He was the First Father of Claude Deschanel, the first Deschanel born with Empyrean blood.

Mercy (Also: Clementyn): Lived three thousand years as an Empyrean who believed in the illusion of Grand Ascension. Piety drove all of her life decisions, often to the point of folly. In her youth, she spent many years with Aidrik, and they did not part on good terms. She found herself crossing paths with Nicolas Deschanel, and when her mark activated, she died but was resurrected by Anasofiya, then becoming human. She currently resides with Nicolas at *Ophélie*.

Mora: Empyrean word for mother.

Murias: One of the four tribes of the Tuatha Dé Danann. All Quinlans descend from one of these four tribes. The tribe of Murias is mentioned in The Prophecy as such: *A female Quinlan, born halfling Empyrean but given far more at maturity.* It is not yet known who the subject of this reference is.

Mystic: Most powerful of all magi, among Empyreans and halflings. Mystics manifest their abilities in different ways. Some are strong healers, others can engage in nested visions, dream suggestion, wards, and other unique traits. All are strong telepaths. Aidrik, Nicolas, Agripin, and Aleksandr are mystics.

Nested Vision: A nested vision is an ability only accessible by mystics, wherein the mystic can travel into the mind of another and observe the world through their eyes. The most powerful mystics not only observe, but also control the host.

Nicolas Deschanel has newly discovered he is a mystic who can engage in nested visions.

Old Aita: Believed to be the oldest living Empyrean, she is shamed for not having experienced her Grand Ascension. Scholars use her as an example of how not to end up, and as a means of driving fear amongst the fledglings. She is said to have pure white hair.

***Ophélie*:** A plantation on the west bank of the River Road in Louisiana, about an hour from New Orleans. *Ophélie* has been the family seat of the Deschanels for over 200 years, and is passed down through the oldest male in each generation. Nicolas Deschanel, the current heir, has lived there his whole life.

Our Father (Also: Emyr, Our Father of Light, Our Father of Fire): Additional names for Emyr.

Portail: A portal created by a terrakinetic that can send travelers to any point in space.

Quinlans: An ancient line of druidic women, descendants of the Tuatha Dé Danann, and more recently, the Goddess Morrigan. All Quinlans descend from one of the four Tuatha tribes: Findias, Gorias, Falias, and Murias. They believe nature is unconditionally sacred, and that everything is interconnected, and balanced. Their powers are all drawn from nature. They live in secrecy, in protected groves and simplistic structures, all centering around their *crann bethadh*. In their early days, they had a strong alliance with the Empyreans, but that alliance was broken and both races have suffered the consequences. While the Quinlan genetics are passed through the females, in rare cases the male will also manifest. These males are known as draoi, and are more power than the females of the tribe. Most Quinlans keep the Quinlan surname.

Quinlan, Deirdre: Daughter of Seara. Mother of Noah, Nora, Nevina, and Niamh. Grandmother of Amelia. Is the youngest, and so has never taken a strong position of leadership. More of a free spirit, even for a druid. Married Kellan Jameson, a human. Kellan did not know what she was, until after Noah (her youngest) was born. When he threatened to leave, she secreted her daughters away to the tribe. Upon return to fetch her son, she learned Kellan had taken him to New Orleans.

Quinlan, Fiona: Only daughter of Nora. Is young—25—as Nora did not have her until later in life.

Quinlan, Meara: Middle child of Seara, sister of Deirdre and Philomena. Always happy, joyous, but simple-minded. The rest of the tribe closely protects her. Childless, she is not capable of a mutual relationship.

Quinlan, Nevina: Middle daughter of Deirdre, sibling to Nora, Niamh, and Noah. Does not travel outside the tribe. Is worried Jacob and Amelia are too "modern" for the job, and that the goddess waited too long to manifest the prophecy,

Quinlan, Niamh: Youngest daughter of Deirdre, sibling to Nora, Nevina, and Noah. Kind-hearted, and powerful, but often quiet, and whimsical.

Quinlan, Nora: Oldest daughter of Deirdre, sibling to Nevina, Niamh, and Noah. Tapped to take over as leader when the current one passes. Her practical nature makes her a competent leader.

Quinlan, Padraig: A draoi, and husband to Regan. He descends from another tribe of Falias. Trains Jacob, who has newly come into his draoi nature.

Quinlan, Philomena: Oldest child of Seara, sibling to Meara and Deirdre. Bitter to not be her mother's choice as successor. Strong-willed and often quick-tempered, especially now in her old age, which is why Seara did not choose her. Had one son in her youth, and gave him away when he was not a draoi.

Quinlan, Regan: Daughter of Nevina, sister to Kieran. Married to Padraig.

Quinlan, Rosemary: Mother of Enid, and grandmother of Jacob. A member of a tribe of Gorias, she has traveled to Seara's tribe to help with the prophecy.

Quinlan, Seara: Current leader of her tribe. Mother to Philomena, Meara, and Deirdre. Great-grandmother to Amelia. Sister to Flynn. All three of her children were intentionally conceived by men she picked herself, and planned a one-night stand. Has the essence of an oracle, who sees all (the prophecy was passed to her by the last leader). Knows her time is near, and is training her granddaughter, Nora, to take over.

Resurrection Shaman: A healer who is able to resurrect the recently deceased. Resurrection shamans are incredibly rare, and the ability is often volatile. Rarely do subjects come back exactly as they were before death. Anasofiya Deschanel discovers she is a resurrection shaman after Aidrik infuses her with Sveising.

Royal Palace of Farjhem: Residence of the royal family of Farjhem.

Runa: Leader of the minority opposition who rose up when the Senetat was created. Her execution is a symbol of strength for her followers, Runeans. She is often deified amongst her most devout followers. Her uprising is known as the First Runean War.

Runeans: Rebels. Those who oppose the Eldre Senetat are generally lumped together as Runeans (followers of Runa). Secretly, they have organized as the Dragon Brotherhood. Some in the Brotherhood are bloodthirsty and feel a call to action. Others are content to live quietly, off the grid of Empyrean society.

Scholar Saxon: The philosophy Scholar who carried out

the execution of Mercy's parents after they were accused of heresy.

Scholars: A group of instructors selected by the Eldre Senetat to oversee the education of all Empyrean children. Their teachings often include propaganda-style support of the Senetat, and a fear-based deterrence of breaking rules. The Scholars spend a hundred years with Empyrean children.

Scholars' Temple: Place of instruction in Farjhem.

Second Runean War: Led by Erikr, the Runeans came together once more, in the spirit of Runa's beliefs, to overthrow the Senetat. As with the first uprising, they were squelched, and Erikr encased in a block of ice. This was the last large uprising of the rebels, who are now scattered and in hiding.

Senetat Sanctuary: Meeting place of the Senetat in Farjhem. Known for being sterile and devoid of any color excepting the crimson of their robes.

Shaman (Also: Healer): Another word for healer. There are varying degrees of shaman in the Deschanel family. Colleen Deschanel is said to be the strongest.

Sindre: Hails from the same Irish village as Birger, Astrid, and Eydis. A young elementalist who can conjure both fire and water, and often employs this skill to the hazard of others.

Skadi (Also: Skadi the Ruthless): The Brotherhood leader of Eastern Europe, residing in Bulgaria. She is known to be ruthless, cutthroat, and volatile to approach. She is remiss in her duties as a leader, in comparison to her peers, but is fiercely protective of her region.

St. Andrews, Finnegan: Husband of Anasofiya, father of Aleksandr. Born and raised in Maine to a normal, magic-free life. At his wedding, he accepted Aidrik's gift of Sveising, to grant him longer life and keener abilities. Recently learned he is descended from the Quinlans, and is a draoi, through this mother's side. Through his father, he is also descended from strong magic. Is a bestiakinetic.

St. Andrews, Ennis: Grandfather of Finnegan, father of Andrew, husband of Fiona. Lives in a protected, secluded clearing in the Scottish Highlands with his wife, who he keeps alive and young through potent magic.

St. Andrews, Fiona: Grandmother of Finnegan, mother of Andrew, wife of Ennis. Lives in a protected, secluded clearing in the Scottish Highlands with Ennis and is kept alive and young through his magic.

Stian: A Brotherhood leader who chose Africa as his region because of the strife. He never stays anywhere for long, and is always moving around, helping where he can. As a terrakinetic, he can create a rift in the Earth, allowing a man to leave one place and appear in another, called a portail.

Sveising: DNA fusion unique to Empyreans. It is the process that allows multiple fathers for offspring, as well as the means by which Aidrik is able to save Anasofiya. Sveising can occur through sexual consummation (in the case of creating multiple fathers), but a mystic can also do it without consummation.

Telepath: One who can read the thoughts of others. Rare telepaths can read thoughts over long distances. Very few telepaths can also break a telepathic block. Tristan is a telepath who can reach across long distances and breach blocks.

Telepathic Block: A block employed my magic users to keep telepaths out of their head.

Terrakinetic: The ability to manipulate the spatial elements of Earth to your advantage. Example: a portail. Stian is a terrakinetic.

Thorvald: Brotherhood leader of Spain. He resides in the *Costa del Sol*, where he trains warriors and scouts in preparation for the inevitable war against the Senetat. Also one of the ancients, or earliest Empyreans.

Time Dancing (Also: Time Dancer): A skill unique to draoi. The time dancer can "dance" through time, a form of time traveling, but cannot change the past. Jacob is a time dancer.

Time Shaping (Also Time Shaper): An Empyrean skill that allows the individual to stop time and "reshape" it. The effect can be catastrophic if the caster is untrained, or if time stops for too long. Aleksandr is a time shaper.

Tribe: A group of Quinlans, usually descended from the same Tuatha tribe. All tribes have an elder, and a scribe.

Trygve: A Brotherhood leader, over Mongolia. One of the oldest Empyreans, having also been from the time of Runa, Brynja, and Einar, and has the markings of the ancients: exceptional height, dark red hair. Has one of the larger followings of the leaders. Known to be fair and loyal, but also quick to action and swift to justice.

Tuatha Dé Danann: Descended from Goddess Danu, early deities in Gaelic history, originating in Norway and later settling in Erin (Ireland). Ruled Ireland from 1897-1700 B.C. Many of the tales of faeries stem from their legends. There are four major tribes of Tuatha, each with a unique talisman of power. They hid in *Tir Non Og*, the otherworld, after Milesians drove them out of their lands. They believe strongly in reincarnation. Tuatha were the original druids, though modern day druidism became its own unique thing. The Quinlans descend from the four tribes of the Tuatha.

Ulfberht: A Viking sword produced between 800 and 1000 AD, made from Empyrean Steel (known to Man as Crucible Steel), known for its unusual combination of strength and flexibility. Though man believes this sword was crafted for Vikings, it was, in fact, created by Blacksmith, an ancient

Empyrean metallurgist. The technology used to make Ulfberht baffles scientists to this day. Aidrik wielded one of the last of the originals, but gave it to Finnegan prior to his death.

Ward: A magical protection with unclear barriers, most potent at its center. The ability to create wards came as a result of the alliance between Empyrean and Quinlan, and it was set forth that only an Empyrean (mystic) may create a ward, and only a Quinlan (draoi) can adhere it. Aidrik's ward is one such example, the center of it cast over *Ophélie* where it is most potent, with effects radiating out to protect other relatives. The protection diminishes the further out you go.

Yiva: Brotherhood leader of Southeast Asia, specifically residing in Thailand. Yields a body-length spear and is a powerful bestiakinetic. Known as the "she wolf."

ALSO BY SARAH M. CRADIT

KINGDOM OF THE WHITE SEA

Kingdom of the White Sea Trilogy

The Kingless Crown

The Broken Realm

The Hidden Kingdom

The Book of All Things

The Raven and the Rush

The Sylvan and the Sand

The Altruist and the Assassin

The Melody and the Master

The Claw and the Crowned

THE SAGA OF CRIMSON & CLOVER

The House of Crimson and Clover Series

The Storm and the Darkness

Shattered

The Illusions of Eventide

Bound

Midnight Dynasty

Asunder

Empire of Shadows

Myths of Midwinter

The Hinterland Veil

The Secrets Amongst the Cypress

Within the Garden of Twilight

House of Dusk, House of Dawn

Midnight Dynasty Series

A Tempest of Discovery

A Storm of Revelations

A Torrent of Deceit

The Seven Series

1970

1972

1973

1974

1975

1976

1980

Vampires of the Merovingi Series

The Island

and more

The Dusk Trilogy

St. Charles at Dusk: The Story of Oz and Adrienne

Flourish: The Story of Anne Fontaine

Banshee: The Story of Giselle Deschanel

Crimson & Clover Stories

Surrender: The Story of Oz and Ana

Shame: The Story of Jonathan St. Andrews

Fire & Ice: The Story of Remy & Fleur

Dark Blessing: The Landry Triplets

Pandora's Box: The Story of Jasper & Pandora

The Menagerie: Oriana's Den of Iniquities

A Band of Heather: The Story of Colleen and Noah

The Ephemeral: The Story of Autumn & Gabriel

Bayou's Edge: The Landry Triplets

For more information, and exciting bonus material, visit www.sarahmcradit.com

ABOUT THE AUTHOR

Sarah is the USA Today and International Bestselling Author of over forty contemporary and epic fantasy stories, and the creator of the Kingdom of the White Sea and Saga of Crimson & Clover universes.

Born a geek, Sarah spends her time crafting rich and multi-layered worlds, obsessing over history, playing her retribution paladin (and sometimes destruction warlock), and settling provocative Tolkien debates, such as why the Great Eagles are not Gandalf's personal taxi service. Passionate about travel, she's been to over twenty countries collecting sparks of inspiration, and is always planning her next adventure.

Sarah and her husband live in a beautiful corner of SE Pennsylvania with their three tiny benevolent pug dictators.

www.sarahmcradit.com

ABOUT THE SONGWRITER

Raven Quinn is a Los Angeles based singer/songwriter, recording artist, and fantasy illustrator. Raven's albums seamlessly blend the genres of rock, pop, and alternative music, while her unique voice and emotive melodies and lyrics combine to create her signature ethereal sound. Currently, she has two full-length albums available: the self-titled debut "Raven Quinn," and her most recent offering, "Not in Vain." Although she is primarily recognized for her work in music, Raven is also a passionate visual artist with a whimsical style that is all her own. She is honored to contribute her art to a growing number of Becket's brilliant books for children.

FIND RAVEN AT:

www.ravenquinn.com
www.facebook.com/officialravenquinn

www.ingramcontent.com/pod-product-compliance
Lightning Source LLC
Chambersburg PA
CBHW020344310726
48979CB00015B/2500/J

* 9 7 8 1 9 5 8 7 4 4 0 6 2 *